Cyn
DENNY

BLACK POINT

A JAKE MONTOYA FBI CRIME THRILLER

Now listen you rich people, weep and wail because of the misery coming to you.
James 5:1

SAM CADE

Black Point
Copyright © 2020 by Sam Cade

All rights reserved under the International and Pan-American Copyright Conventions. No part of this book may be reproduced or transmitted in any form or by any means, electronic or mechanical, including photocopying, recording, or by any information storage and retrieval system, without permission in writing from the publisher.

This is a work of fiction. Names, places, characters and incidents are either the product of the author's imagination or are used fictitiously, and any resemblance to any actual persons, living or dead, organizations, events or locales is entirely coincidental.

Warning: the unauthorized reproduction or distribution of this copyrighted work is illegal. Criminal copyright infringement, including infringement without monetary gain, is investigated by the FBI and is punishable by up to 5 years in prison and a fine of $250,000.

Print ISBN:
Published by: Black Point Press
Edited by: Cathy Dee
Contact at Cathy.Dee@gmail.com
Interior formatting and cover art by: Rising Sign Books

Acknowledgments

There are some that can put a book together A to Z all by themselves. I'm not one of them. Thank you World Wide Web! Here are some wonderful folks I've met there.

Katie Salidas (Las Vegas). Katie is an author as well as a freelancer on all aspects of indie book publishing. She lives neck-deep in that world. She took my artwork and turned it into a nice cover as well as formatted the manuscript for this book. Check her out on katiesalidas.com. Find her book *Go Publish Yourself!* on Amazon.

Edited by Cathy Dee Contact at Cathy.Dee@gmail.com

Walton Jones (Asheville, NC). Walton is a cryptocurrency specialist (Bitcoin and Monero) and is well acquainted with the Tor browser, VPN, and encrypted verbal and written communication. I had a fun conversation with him. If you suddenly find yourself needing to go off the grid, call him. But, there's no telling what name he's going by now.

Laurie Kelly (Lone Tree, CO). Laurie is retired from decades as Director of Compliance for a large commercial bank. She's a Certified Anti Money Laundering Specialist.

Brian Pfeifer (Tallahassee, FL). Master's Mechanical Engineering. Ph.D. Civil Engineering. Quality Forensic Engineering, LLC. Brian was very generous with his time listening to my plan for a mechanical malfunction in a school bus crash.

Rae Owens (Medford, NY). Rae is a Squarespace specialist and created a website for me. Find her at raeowens.com.

BOOKS BY SAM CADE

Black Point

The Scheme

The Midnight Man (2023)

Mission Beach, San Diego, California
November 20, 2018

WE KILLED YOUR DADDY! I know How. I know Who. I know All of it.

Lucky's phone chimed behind him as he faded in and out on the couch, casually watching a Fox News story about an ISIS attack. He reached blindly over his shoulder, grabbed the phone off the lampstand, and read the text.

His jaw tightened as he studied the words. Reading the short text over and over, his respirations quickened. The phone exchange was local, but he didn't recognize it. And very few people had his number.

He punched in a question with his right pointer finger.

Who is this? Tapped SEND.

Immediate response. ***Message Blocked.***

He sat up. A hum of irritation sizzled through his nerves.

Someone was playing a very dangerous game.

IT WAS 9:45 on a lazy, cold Tuesday night at the beach, fifty-one degrees, when the text hit.

A tangy brine scent sifted through the small flat, floating off Lucky's damp wetsuit lying over his surfboard. Three hours ago, after a two-mile, open-ocean swim, he finished the afternoon surfing through a blazing California sunset until the night became too black to see.

Lucky's day had been exhausting, just like the previous day and the one before that. The morning started at six sharp with seventy-five minutes of exercise to defuse his aggression, then hours of phone calls, bank meetings, and emails. All for the goal of funding an elite security firm, Knight Force.

Eighteen months ago, Lucky's world went from exceptional to dismal in a single heartbeat. The family business had been decimated, forced into bankruptcy.

And now his father, the company CEO, had suffered a horrifying death.

For forty-three years, Lucky had led a charmed life, sure of everything. Now he was sure of nothing.

For twenty years in the US Navy he had been a badass. His mind and body were trained to do what they needed to do for survival. But now? Business-funding opportunities became dimmer by the day. Sleep was difficult, his thoughts racing endlessly through the deep night.

Now he was drifting, flailing against the tide.

Sitting on the edge of the couch, he tried to force the words of the text from his mind. His eyes glanced over the coffee table. Two empty beer bottles and a mostly eaten microwave lasagna sat on a stack of *Tactical Weapons* magazines. A bookmark from Warwick's in La Jolla poked out of the last chapter of *The Terminal List,* a thriller written by a buddy of his, former SEAL Jack Carr.

Gusts off the Pacific rattled the sliding door as he exhaled a sigh and stood. Time to ditch the dinner trash, hit the hay for real, and pray for sleep to come.

Then his phone rang.

HE GLANCED AT the screen. Same number as the text. No name. He answered.

"Yes." Tone sharp as an icepick.

"That get your attention?"

He didn't recognize the voice. A local-looking call, but was it? A spoof? If so, the caller could be sitting in the apartment next door, or two states away.

Screwing with me, you better be masquerading.

"Who is this?" said Lucky. Expected to hear, "Sorry, man, wrong number." But he didn't.

"For the sake of the matter, call me Zeus."

Zeus wasn't two states away—he was five states away, sitting in a twelve-year-old Subaru wagon in the parking lot of the Beau Rivage Casino in Biloxi, Mississippi. He was talking on a throwaway cell phone he bought thirty minutes earlier at Walmart.

"Zeus, the god of sky, lightning, and thunder." Lucky spoke through his irritation.

"You know mythology, commander. Smart guy, but I knew you would be."

Lucky snorted. "So, your text. What did happen? Think I missed it."

"Oh, no, you didn't miss it. I can assure you, your dad did nothing wrong, and yet forty-five years of his blood and sweat were wiped out by a lawyer. Now he's dead. And that practically makes us brothers."

"Brothers?" Lucky coughed out a short laugh. "And how's that?"

"My family was also destroyed by a lawyer."

"So what do you want to do? Start a therapy group? Meet in a circle in a church basement once a week, discuss our feelings?"

Zeus laughed. "Little more than that, my friend. I want to be made whole. And even more than that, I want to get even. And you're the perfect guy to bring into the scheme."

"The *scheme?*" Lucky took the last sip of his beer, the third bottle of the night, and lay back down to talk. "I like that. Diabolical. You almost sound like a scary guy, Zeus. And what is this scheme?"

"Well, before I get into that I would be remiss if I didn't mention a small, deep-background detail that should bring focus to the issue."

"And what's that?"

"Your dad's trial."

"Yeah?"

"It was rigged. Your old man got screwed."

Lucky's muscles tensed. "Rigged?" He shook his head. "Where'd you come up with that crap?" Words filled with ire.

"Sorry, jack, it's true. Here's the deal. I didn't just ... *come up with it.* I know who rigged it and exactly how it was rigged."

"Who?"

"Me ... I was hired to do it."

Lucky's heart began to thunder.

He'd been in the Middle East when the proceedings took place, but he'd studied every word of the trial transcript. *Who is this deluded fool?*

"Let's leave that and move forward to reparations, if you don't mind," said Zeus. "One hundred million dollars for me and you. You keep eighty percent. I keep twenty. I could make do on five, but giving you almost the whole enchilada sounds desperate on my end."

"Hold on a minute ... *Zeus.* I need to grab another beer. I had no idea a lunatic would be calling tonight or I'd have been ready."

Focus on the voice. Who is this?

Lucky, wearing sweatpants and a Padre's tee, padded sock-footed to the kitchen, grabbed two longnecks out of the fridge, a pretzel bag off the counter, returned, and picked up the phone.

"Okay, I'm back. Almost scared to ask. Why are you calling *me*?"

"Simple. I can do things you can't do and you can do things I can't do. And I believe we have a common goal. Symbiotic, you might say."

Lucky considered that, took a bite of pretzel, washed it down with a swig of beer. "Me and you, symbiotic." Lucky chuckled. "So, Mr. Zeus, god of gods, what can *you* do?"

"I'm telling you with absolute certainty. Millions and millions and millions of dollars are sitting at our fingertips."

"Uh huh." Another slug of beer.

"And I'm somewhat of a financial Houdini. I can shift money around the globe, quickly evading procedures put in place by agencies that track funds, all of which have become increasingly tightened since 9/11. I'm an expert in most global currencies and have been involved in cryptocurrency since its inception. I will use multiple identities, multiple countries, multiple banks, multiple anonymous shell corporations. But ultimately, I can provide clean funds for our individual uses."

"Are you reading that crap from a Patterson novel?" Lucky snorted another cynical laugh. "And, anyway, bigshot, what money are you talking about? Because I don't have any."

"I'll get to the money in a moment. Let's focus. I need you for one single reason. Just one."

"And what might that be?"

"I need a trained killer. A hungry, angry, broke, trained killer ... and that, sir, is who you are."

Lucky took a slug of beer, mulled over those words, didn't say anything.

Zeus let the silence hang a couple of beats. Smiled. Wished he could see Lucky's face.

"I've studied you thoroughly, Lucky. My skills with a computer and a phone line are way above average. I'm a database addict. I retrieve documentation no one is supposed to see. I love gobs of outlandish and seemingly unconnected information. I analyze data and unravel puzzles. Extremely complex puzzles."

"Well, Einstein, I'm pretty decent with a computer, too."

Zeus exhaled loudly. "Well, here's the thing about life. You just don't know what you don't know. And I guarantee you this, Lucky, there is a lot you don't know. It's not stupidity, I'm not saying that. You're calculating and intelligent, a Naval Academy grad. You just haven't been taught."

"Uh huh."

"When we hang up, I'm going to email some research I've dug up on you ... and your family. It'll blow your mind."

Lucky nursed his beer, quietly getting pissed.

Who is this guy?

"Okay, now to the money. Let's see if we can plump up your bank account a bit. Here's what I suggest," said Zeus. "Think about this. Fact: the top 100 litigators in America have a total net worth of $4 billion. We should be able to slide a measly $100 million out of them. Eighty million to you. I'm estimating now, okay, but *at least* eighty. Crumbs to me."

"And how does that plan work, money man?" Lucky snorted at the absurdity of this Zeus character.

"We rip every single dollar out of their cold, greedy fingers. That's how."

Lucky sighed deeply, tried to digest this insanity.

A thought knifed his mind. He let the call go silent. Traipsing through the Middle East, South America, Eastern Europe, that was business. A job. This nutjob was talking about his *family.* This was personal.

His fists clenched at the mention of his father.

"You still there?" said Zeus.

Lucky's mind stepped back in time twenty-three years, retracing words spoken to him by his dad. *Son, you and I will grow the family company together when you get home from the navy. That's been a lifelong dream for me.* It was spoken on a hot and humid May afternoon on the field of Navy–Marine Corps stadium in Annapolis.

Graduation day for the United States Naval Academy.

"Yep, I'm here," said Lucky, with a distracted tone.

"Out of the blue, this is a lot on you. Tomorrow, I will send you stone-cold documentation of how the trial went down. Every single detail. It will be hard to take, but you'll know what you have to do.

"Oh, oh, oh. One more thing, Lucky. Abbottabad. May second, 2011. Now, that was an interesting evening." Zeus let it hang for a few moments. Dead silence.

He continued. "If this thing works out between us ... I gotta know what it was like coming in hot on those choppers right into Bin Laden's compound. That's balls out, man!"

Lucky said nothing.

"You sit tight, partner. Focus on one thing. A lawyer paid me to help him kill your daddy. And it's time for payback ... that's all you need to know ... time for payback." Zeus rang off.

ZEUS SMILED TO himself when the phone went dead. He knew he had drilled under Lucky's skin. He stepped out of the Subaru, placed the new phone in front of the left front tire. He got back in the car, drove forward, heard the plastic crunch, and proceeded out of the parking lot. He drove across the bridge to Ocean Springs, then out to the interstate and headed east on I-10.

LUCKY STARED PAST the television, through the sliding glass doors into the windy, black night. He chugged a couple more beers after the phone call. Depressed after thinking about his father.

After getting a little drunk deliberately, he pulled on a fleece and stepped out into the cold, California night. A sea breeze blew into his collar. He crossed his arms to hug the chill away.

As he looked up, the beer melted his brain open. Stars sparkled in the sky like tiny diamonds on black velvet. Clouds raced across a three-quarter moon. It was gorgeous, the vastness of the universe.

Scanning the sky, he screamed out in anger. “How the hell did all this happen?”

He stood outside for thirty minutes while the cold and the heavens flushed the mellow buzz from his head. His white-hot desperation abated. A roadmap started to appear. His blood flow began to trickle again, battlefield cold, and determined.

Indecision time was over.

Damn right he’d look at what the man had. Lucky was ready to get back what he was owed. And then some.

They killed my father.

1

BLACK POINT, ALABAMA

DUDE CODGER WAS a thief.

Every single workday he stole exactly 3.1 percent of Vic Stapleton's money. He was meticulous about it, like a financial guru at Goldman Sachs. Three-point-one percent. Slow day. Big day. Didn't matter. Three-point-one, baby.

Vic Stapleton had no clue he was being robbed.

Yet.

But that would be the least of Dude's worries.

2

BLACK POINT

7:40 P.M. ON A DAY IN LATE JANUARY. The night was blustery, with lows expected to drop to thirty degrees.

"I'm sure gonna miss this food, I can tell you that," said the fellow sitting at the bar. A mostly eaten hamburger was in his hand. He was Broyle William, a tall, whipcord-thin man with sun-beaten skin stretched tightly across his face like a pale tarp.

Broyle and the rest of his crew had been eating at the Rusty Anchor bar three or four times a week for the last month. They were in from Texas, working a large painting job at a new beach high-rise.

Dude had his back turned, jerking a pitcher of beer from the tap, when he heard Broyle speak. He turned around slowly to look at him, a huge grin creasing his face.

"The finest restaurants in Dallas can't turn out a burger like this," continued Broyle. "Sure can't."

"I appreciate you saying that, sir."

Broyle stretched his right hand across the bar for a shake. Tendons stretched out like baling wire. "Been a pleasure, Dude. Me, Javy, and Luis"—Broyle poked his thumbs at the men sitting on either side of him—"are heading to Panama City for a few days to bid three jobs. We'll all be back in Texas this weekend."

He stood, put on a leather bomber jacket and a Cowboy's ball cap, and walked to the front door with a two-finger wave trailing over his shoulder. "Gimme Three Steps" pounded out of the jukebox. Broyle held the door for an attractive woman coming in.

Gina Swims walked straight to the bar and sat in the seat Broyle had just vacated. She was a dark-haired, dark-eyed real estate agent, eight years older than Dude.

Without a word, Dude poured her a glass of white and placed it on the bar in front of her.

"Thanks, Dude." She took a feminine sip, leaving a touch of lipstick on the glass. "It's so cold outside tonight." She mimicked a shiver. "And my poor husband is snowed in at O'Hare International. Might be days before he makes it home."

Dude placed his forearms on the bar, leaned forward into her space. "You know, Gina, you almost have the rosy glow of a woman looking for a warm man on an icy night."

She picked up her glass, tapped it gently on his nose. In a sultry drawl, she said, "Well ain't you a little mind reader."

AT 31, DUDE WAS living his best life. Thankfully, he had an understanding wife.

So he thought.

IT WAS 10:12 p.m. Gina had left the Anchor over an hour ago. Almost time for Dude to shut the joint down for the night, swing by Gina's house.

He was thinking about her trim figure as he sat at a desk in his office, a space heater warming his legs. The scent of fried potatoes and burger grease sifted in from the kitchen in the next room. Classic rock played on low from a clock radio.

Cash and coins covered the desktop. He'd just finished counting the day's receipts. He tapped 3.1 percent into his calculator and came up with his daily prize winnings. Feeling pleased with his jackpot, he started humming along to The Band as they sang about pulling into Nazareth.

The back door crashed open, followed by a frigid blast of moist air.

"Gimme that money, shithead." It was spoken angrily in Spanish-accented English.

Dude jumped, saw who it was, then laughed.

"Dammit, Squeaky, cut that Cheech and Chong crap out." Then he laughed. "Funny, though."

"Pony up, homes. I gotta get to bed." He stood before Dude wearing a down vest over a black tee. A sterling silver crucifix hung around his neck, resting on his chest.

Squeaky Perez ran a three-crew landscaping outfit in Black Point and two taco trucks at the beach. He was also the main supplier for Dude's sideline dope business that he ran out of the bar.

Dude counted out 740 bucks, placed it in a white envelope, and extended his hand to Squeaky.

"Hey, man. I'm playing guitar at the folk Mass on Sunday," said Squeaky. "Why don't you join us? Come for the music. Leave with eternal life."

"Hel-l-l no, jack. I'll be sleeping."

3

ANOTHER BLAST OF cold hit the room as Squeaky hit the road. Dude stood, pulled a fleece on. It was 10:23. He didn't want to keep Gina waiting.

He walked into the bar area, saw the same three people. Waddell Skipworth, a local painter and Dude's best customer, and two Hispanic women, five seats down from him. A forty-year-old jukebox pumped out "Margaritaville."

The two women, painters with Broyle William's crew, had arrived ninety minutes ago. Their usual paint-speckled sweatshirts were gone. They'd spruced up for a night out. Fresh flannel shirts and polished boots. Shiny dark hair and white teeth.

Immediately, they'd placed their order for dinner plus a couple of Coronas.

They'd finished their first beer by the time the food was served. Dude brought another round. By 10 p.m., the women had drunk four beers each.

Dude approached the women, placed their tab on the counter, and began wiping it down. The signal. Hit the road.

They didn't budge.

Dude glanced down at Waddell. The drunk stared into space, uttering to no one some alcohol-fueled nonsense about nuclear proliferation.

He stepped closer to the ladies. They took no notice.

"What're your names?"

The younger woman tapped her bottle on the counter. Held up two fingers. *Ah, hell.* Dude grabbed two bottles out of the ice, wiped them with a towel, popped the caps, stuck a lime wedge in the spout. "Final round, ladies."

"Isabel," said the older lady.

"Maribel," said the younger.

"Isabel and Maribel. Beautiful names." Dude made a show of glancing at his watch.

He stepped into the kitchen for a quick inventory, heard a car leave, and knew it wasn't Waddell. *Better be money on the counter.* Ten forty on the clock. Dude peeked back at the bar, walked in. Maribel was still there.

"Hey, where's Isabel?"

"She went home. Sleepy."

"How are you getting home?"

"Taxi." She stuck the bottle in the air, empty.

"That was last round."

Maribel tapped her pointer finger straight down on the counter. "One. More. Beer."

They waged a battle with their eyes. "Maribel, are you paying for both of you?"

She shook her head. "No money. We'll let you pay, Mister Dude." Maribel shot him a smug look.

"How'd you know my name?"

"Senor Broyle. He said you'd take care of us."

This ain't the Salvation Army, he thought. Give and take is how the universe works.

He grabbed a Corona from the ice, popped the top, carried it to his office, looked around for those pills a buddy had brought from his trip to Key West. Three tablets in a micro-size Baggie sitting next to an old cigar box holding bar payables. He removed one, pulverized it, stirred the powder in the beer with a straw. He raised the bottle up to the light. Didn't notice a thing. Smiled.

Dude figured he'd give Maribel's little taco a taxi ride. That ass all tight in those jeans. Melt-your-heart brown eyes. Making all these demands. Okay, sure, he'd cover dinner.

He'd make this quick. Pop Maribel, then head to Gina's. Make tonight a twofer.

Dude carried the beer out, placed it on the counter. She looked at it. Then twisted her head side to side, inspecting it. Suspicious. *Oh, hell. She knows.*

"Everything okay, Maribel?"

Shook her head. "Problem. A very big problem," she said, eyebrows raised.

"Yeah?"

Maribel pointed to the spout, tapped the glass with a finger. "Problem."

Dude leaned down, looked at the bottle. He didn't see jack. *How does she know?*

"No problem," he said.

"Problem," she said. She pointed again at the spout. She shot Dude a serious look. A look that said there were consequences for these kinds of shenanigans. Maribel waggled a finger at Dude to come closer. Her eyes were fixed on his. Dude leaned in. Her mouth was four inches away.

"I need a fat, juicy, tangy lime," she said slowly. "Right in this little teensy hole." She slid her index finger in and out of the spout several times. "Sounds good, no?" Her eyebrows arched.

He quickly obliged her on the lime. Next, he took a red Solo cup, filled it with ice, threw in a couple ounces of his best bourbon, filled it with real Coke, swizzled it, and approached Waddell.

"Waddell, my old pal, I've brought you a friend for the road."

"What? Got at least another two hours yet. What about that Mexican? Is she sleeping?" He cocked a thumb toward Maribelle. "She's got a whole beer to finish."

"Taxi."

"What taxi? They don't run after eight," said Waddell. "Ah, never mind."

"The drink is on the house." He pointed to the door. "Now, scram."

Dude locked the front door after Waddell left, shut down the TVs, and snapped off most of the lights.

In five minutes, Maribel's head rested on her forearms on the counter.

Dude tapped her on the arm. "Maribel." She muttered, "Mmmm." He put his hands on her elbows, shook her softly. Her brown eyes opened half-mast, sleepy.

"Got the money, Maribel? Last chance."

Almost a smile. With her hands on the bar she raised a single index finger, pointed at him. "You pay ... Mister Dude."

He walked around the bar, came up behind her, started massaging her shoulders. It was faint, but it was there, a soft moan. He stepped to her side, her face still resting on her hands. He lifted her dark hair, brought his mouth to her neck. Clean soapy scent, no perfume. He kissed her neck. Tasted like a fresh shower, he thought. Dude caressed her back, massaging her muscles with his right hand.

He stepped behind her and began massaging her shoulders. After three minutes he slid his hands around her sides, taking a bra-covered breast in each hand.

"I get it now. You want a piece of ol' Mister Dude. Well, you ain't the first."

He unbuttoned her flannel shirt slowly, untucked it from the jeans. Maribel jerked a little.

"No."

"I say yes," he whispered in her ear. "I'm gonna take you back to the Elvis Suite."

Dude picked her up like he was carrying a child from a fire. "I gotcha, baby. Big ol' piece of candy coming, little Miss Maribel."

He eased her down onto the single bed in his office. That's when he felt fire scrape across his face. Maribel's fingernails carved three tunnels of skin out of his cheek. He put his hand to his face, brought his fingers out in front of his eyes. Wet, hot blood.

"You little bitch!"

Dude roughly pulled off her cowboy boots, tossed them across the room. He reached in, unsnapped her jeans, slid down her zipper, and pulled. Maribel's ass popped up off the bed, her jeans flew to the floor. He ripped a black thong off her body and tossed it over his shoulder.

Dude put his hand to his cheek again, still bleeding. He wiped his face on the white sheet. Plenty of blood.

"Senorita, there ain't no free meals."

Maribel was splayed face down on the bed, naked except for socks, eyes closed, legs immodestly open.

"You're gonna thank ol' Dude, girl. 'Bout to spoil you rotten."

Dude unsnapped his pants. Slid his zipper down.

4

THE XANAX DID nothing.

Ella Codger's eyes were striped with spidery red vessels, while her white-hot rage held on like it had claws.

It was 4:37 in the afternoon. The sky was bleak, gray. Winter darkness racing in like a train. Ella and the kids were pulling in on the school bus she drove.

Storm winds had blasted Dude and Ella's trailer last night as bitter weather roared into coastal Alabama. Icy-cold drafts grabbed the rickety unit like pliers from all sides, then went to work prying through fissures to rip into the family's skin like cat teeth.

The electricity had been disconnected thirty hours ago.

Ella slid her phone from her pocket, tapped CALL on her husband's contact. It was the fifth attempt of the day. Five rings, then it hit voicemail. "It's Dude, you know the drill."

"Screw your drill, Dude," said Ella. "The trailer heat's out. No lights! We're freezing to death! Sick of this silent treatment. Where the hell are you?"

She slung the phone onto the couch.

Dude hadn't been around in two days. Playing games again. Crap like this had happened in the past. Always meeting some new cooze at the Rusty Anchor, then lying his ass off about it. Ella thought, *He's probably putting some skeezer up in the Holiday Inn Express right now, spending fifteen hours a day there with his pecker hanging out, eating a free continental breakfast, thinking he's Brad Pitt.*

Four days ago Ella, in a tantrum, woke Dude, screaming about the unpaid bills. Electricity and phone were overdue.

Dude said he would pay them.

He didn't.

Ella's mind raced day and night with one agonizing thought: *How did I marry that lowlife, lying bag of piss?*

The way she figured it, he had something coming. Oh, he sure did.

And she was bringing it.

5

BROYLE WILLIAM, JAVY, and Luis arrived back from Florida at 12:40 in the morning. “I’m whipped, fellows,” said Broyle. They were renting at the Oak Haven cottages on Great Bay Road, in Black Point. “Let’s see if we can get seven hours of sleep, grab breakfast, and roll back to Texas.”

Broyle had his own cottage next to Javy and Luis.

Luis and Javy’s cabin was dead silent, dim light on over the sink. Breakfast bacon scent still in the air.

Luis went straight to his bedroom. “I’m home, baby. Safe and sound.”

“Come to bed, Luis.” He could smell the beer as Isabel spoke.

A rap on the door. “Luis, tell Maribel to come to her bedroom,” said Javy.

“What?” Luis opened the door, naked belly hanging over his belt.

“Maribel’s in here, right?” said Javy. Luis turned on a bedside lamp. Just Isabel in the bed. Luis hustled to look at Javy’s room. His son-in-law was right with him.

Luis rushed to his room, rustled Isabel’s neck. “Isabel, where’s Maribel? Isabel, wake up.” Luis prodded her again. She sat up. “What? Come to bed, Luis.”

“Maribel’s gone. What happened?”

Isabel swallowed, closed her eyes, scrunched her face, then opened her bleary eyes. “Now, what did you say?”

“Maribel isn’t here. Where is she? What’s going on?” said Javy.

“We go to Rusty Anchor to eat, drink beer. I got sleepy, come home... ummm, maybe ten thirty.”

Luis looked at the clock on the dresser. Approaching one in the morning.

“We make Mister Dude pay. Maribel say she’s getting a taxi.”

“Javy, go get Broyle.” Sounding tense.

BROYLE TOOK A right at the red light next to the gas station taco joint. Destination two miles away. US 98 was straight, dark, empty.

Broyle jumped the truck up to ninety, high beams on. Quiet. Minds racing with bad thoughts.

He cut the headlights before he pulled off the road. Only a dim hint of light from the building. He pointed to the back of the lot at the Camry. “Probably Dude’s car.”

A decades-old, blue Chevy pickup sat in a dark part of the parking lot, out near the highway. Three ladders were cinched tight on a rack. A painter’s truck freezing in the night. Looked as if it hadn’t run in months.

Broyle peeked through the front-door glass and saw low-intensity spotlights that shone down on neat rows of liquor bottles on the backside of the bar. TVs off. No movement. Didn’t see anyone.

Javy and Luis circled one side of the building, Broyle the other.

They met each other at the back of the building, at a rear door. There was a ten-inch transom above it, light shining through.

Luis and Javy put their ears to the office door. They heard movement.

"Luis, cup your hands, lift me up for a look," whispered Javy. Luis nodded. He intertwined his hands into a locked vice grip, bent down so Javy could step on.

"Now," said Javy. He pushed off the ground with his left leg, Luis grunted, Javy propelled upward. He cinched his fingertips onto the ledge of the small window and pulled upward for a peek.

Javy spotted his wife. Maribel was face down on a bed.

Naked.

6

THE BAR'S BACKDOOR boomed with thundering knocks. Boom, boom, boom. Dude heard voices yelling in Spanish. Boom, boom, boom, boom.

Wood began to splinter. Somebody kicking.

The door exploded open.

Dude grabbed his pants from the floor but had no time to put them on. Luis bull-rushed him, tackling him hard. Spanish cursing was nonstop.

Javy went to Maribel. "Baby, baby, baby." She appeared unconscious. Her legs were slightly spread.

Luis began beating Dude on his face and trunk. Blood dripped off his knuckles from ripped skin. Luis beat him unconscious in thirty-five seconds. He jumped up to check on his daughter.

Luis pushed Javy away from Maribel. He hugged her, tears on his cheeks. Javy went to the floor, squatted, then bent with his hands cinched behind his neck. He bellowed a deep animal howl as he began slamming his fists on the floor.

Maribel spoke as Luis hugged her. "Papa, I'm sorry." Voice groggy.

"No, no, no, baby, will be okay. Papa here, Javy here, everything fine. Love you, little girl."

"Help her dress, Javy," Broyle said, thinking fast. "Wash your hands, Luis. Let's take this prick, make him pay."

It took three minutes to rip the bar apart to look like a burglary and vandalism.

Wearing gloves, Broyle pulled Dude's Camry to the back door and popped the trunk. Zeppelin's "Whole Lotta Love" blasted from a rock station. A heavy mist filtered through a bitterly cold morning.

Javy and Luis wrapped Dude in a bedspread and threw him in the trunk.

Broyle jumped into the Camry's driver's seat. "Y'all follow me at a distance. Gonna run this thing right down the boat ramp, way down Great Bay Road."

TWO BEADY EYES peeked through a steering wheel in an old, scuffed, Chevy painter's truck parked in the shadows on the front side of the Rusty Anchor. Even as drunk as Waddell Skipworth was, he could see that the pale-faced, balding white man driving the Camry wasn't Dude.

With his brain bobbing in a sea of alcohol, Waddell lit a smoke.

Crazy damn dream, he thought.

7

FERNANDINA BEACH, FLORIDA

CREDE HENDRICKSON STEPPED outside onto his balcony overlooking the Atlantic, steam rising from the coffee cup in his hand.

The blustery morning broke with a worrisome red, the eastern sky promising temperatures too cold for Florida. He was surprised at the intensity of the wind. Bunched blue-black clouds raced with the westerly wind over the white-capped ocean.

The air smelled like rain. Clean, but with a stern warning of caution.

Wanda stepped out. “Better get with it, Crede, if you’re driving almost to Mississippi.”

Crede watched the gusts rip up the ocean.

“Looking at these clouds, I don’t know. Heavier weather coming behind this from the Gulf. Pretty sure I’ve gotten soft sitting behind the desk over the years.”

“Oh, come on. You used to drive in snow across the Rockies at midnight.”

“Used to ain’t now.”

“Nonsense. You need to get it going, get a decision made. New trucks will turn some heads, might bring some interest from drivers who aren’t pill heads.”

"Well, I better get to the office. I need to put in a couple hours before hitting the highway."

He gave his wife a peck on the cheek. "See you tomorrow."

Crede Hendrickson had started his trucking outfit with just a high school diploma and a gut full of gumption. By age nineteen, he was a sturdy country boy smart enough to know he didn't need a boss to tell him how to throw stuff on a trailer and drive it someplace. All he needed was a few bucks to get his own truck.

Then his girlfriend's daddy stepped up. Dr. Jeryl Knight. He read Crede as a winner. So, he financed the first truck. And another, and another. Crede Hendrickson's outfit was firing on all cylinders within a year.

Forty-five years blew past like campfire smoke in a breeze. Today the dentist's only daughter lived in a four-million-dollar oceanfront home in Amelia Island Plantation, and Hendrickson Trucking was about to buy twenty-five million dollars' worth of state-of-the-art tractors.

To make his final choice, Crede would personally drive seven hours to deliver a heavy load of airplane parts to Black Point, Alabama.

Somehow, he knew it was a mistake.

8

BLACK POINT, ALABAMA

IT WAS ALMOST midnight when Crede rolled into the Highway 98 commercial corridor in Black Point. He drove past the usual suspects. Banks, fast food, drug stores, gas stations. He planned to sleep in the truck at the plant, five miles south of town.

Deep blackness met him after he passed the convenience store near the high school. He was past the median-lights zone, leaving town. It was like walking into a mountain cave at one in the morning. Four lanes edged into two. He felt hemmed in, almost claustrophobic after leaving the lit commercial sector.

Rain-soaked gusts buffeted the heavy Kenworth. Wind out of the southwest.

The GPS said he was close, so he backed his speed down to fifteen, trying to spot the Lycoming plant through the rain. Wipers were cranked on high but there was still limited visibility. He lowered his driver's window halfway. Had to see.

He'd been up eighteen hours, eyes fatigued from the drive. There it was. He was right on it, straight beside him on the left. A lit Lycoming sign hung on the building, muted by rainfall.

Dammit. It was a closed entrance with a chain link fence wrapped tight with a chain. He needed to turn around.

He reached a closed Shell station a mile down, at the US 98 intersection. He twisted the rig into the gas station entrance and snaked out the side exit, bringing him rolling back toward the plant.

Where to park, he thought. The highway was as straight and flat as a yardstick. Drainage ditches, flooded with rainwater, sloped steeply downward, two feet from the road. There was no way to edge to the side.

A half-mile up from the gas station, Crede came to a section of road that had a wide entrance to an open storage barn, thirty yards off the highway. It was jammed with farming equipment.

He babied the heavy truck off the road, just missing a small, unlit sign he didn't see.

Oak Hollow Farm.

He parked five feet off the highway.

After easing into his rain jacket, Crede launched out into the dreary night. Reflective cones were placed forty yards in both directions, waiting for headlights to fire them alive. Flashers stayed on overnight.

Back into the Kenworth's sleeper, Crede changed into some dry clothes, He stuck his hand into a plastic sack for a pack of cheese crackers and a Coca Cola and leaned back into soft pillows. He couldn't sleep without a snack and a book.

He pulled a tattered paperback from his small duffel, *The Deep Blue Good-By,* the first Travis McGee novel.

A soft cone of light from the reading lamp crossed Crede's shoulder. He opened to a rabbit-eared page, the start of chapter seven, placed the book on his lap, then opened the plastic-wrapped cheese crackers. He smiled. Cheese crackers always reminded him of his mother. She called them Nabs. That was fifty-five years ago.

SHE HAD TOLD HIM she was going to the doctor.

"What's wrong, Mama? Why do you need a suitcase?"

"Oh, baby, it's my silly old head, sometimes it don't think right. Might take a couple days to get it all better."

"Does it hurt?"

"No, baby, it don't hurt." She put her small suitcase on the vinyl backseat of the shabby, secondhand Ford, climbed in the driver's seat, rolled down the window.

"Crede, could you be a good boy and run back in and grab me a pack of Nabs and a Co'cola? Might not get lunch on the way."

He raced into the small cottage they called home. It was a sad, little, lap-sided house that fit into the financial spectrum two rungs below the papermill workers.

He was back in less than thirty seconds. "Brought two of each, Mama. I don't need my Coke and crackers today, don't want you hungry."

"Ahhh, baby, come here."

Crede leaned into the driver's window on his tiptoes, gave his mother a tight hug, a long one. He loved the smell of her. Ivory soap. She was his safe haven.

"You be a good boy, Crede. I love you, son."

"I love you, too, Mama."

Crede, wearing cut-off dungarees and no shirt, ran behind his mother, waving as she pulled out of the sandy dirt driveway onto the street. A burst of dark smoke shot through the car's rusty muffler as she punched down on the accelerator.

He stopped in the middle of the street, waved until the car left his sight.

It was the last time he saw her face.

CREDE EASED HIS mind back into the truck. He thought about his company and his wife. But mostly about the day his oldest son would join him in the family business.

That single thought kept him going.

Alone in this darkness was not a good place for him. He fought his ruminations about the inner bleakness he felt most days. Crede never spoke about it with anyone. He knew his life could only be viewed by others as remarkable, if not spectacular. But his even best moments could only be described as not unhappy. His insides were gray, dull, searching. He never saw life in bright colors and happy birthday parties, like he felt other people did. But he pretended.

Always pretended.

Like his mother, he knew his brain didn't think right.

Outside, nylon tiedown straps whistled in the angry wind.

One damn lonely piece of highway.

Travis McGee held his attention for five minutes. His thoughts circled back to his mama. Nothing new. Every night Crede saw his mama.

Still felt the pain of the news.

9

FORT WORTH, TEXAS

DUDE CODGER SCREAMED like an animal being eaten alive. Primal. Guttural. Javy Quintana had just poured two pints of rubbing alcohol into the nine deep gashes on Dude's back.

Dude was strapped facedown to the four corners of a metal bed-frame.

Maribel took the butt end of the whip, put it against Dude's head, and pushed hard against his skull. "Now you remember me, Mister Dude? We had one date."

She went at it again. Maribel released her fury until he no longer screamed. Despite the cold warehouse temperatures, sweat stains appeared on her shirt. Dude didn't move. There was no fight left in his body. He was gone.

Javy placed his boot on Codger, gave him a solid push. A lifeless body. "You got him, baby." Javy smiled. "Proud of you, baby. Let's wrap him in a blanket. I'm gonna come back with Papa and Broyle and take care of the body. Remember, Neiman Marcus tomorrow. Anything you want, baby."

Maribel took a long swig from a bottle of water, then rubbed her damp brow with her forearm. "This shit's work. Let's run by Whataburger."

DUDE'S MIND THOUGHT he was dead. He knew he couldn't have lived through what just happened.

Total blackness. No light in his eyes. Dead.

Then he heard a door slam.

10

DUDE COULDN'T MOVE his arms or legs. He needed some air. His raw wounds felt like fire.

He rocked left. Then pushed hard to the right. Then left. He went over onto his back. Pushed left, then right, then hard left. And over. The blanket was coming loose.

Five more turns. He was out of breath, but free.

It took everything he had to stand. He felt through the darkness, trying to touch something. Short steps, hands in front of him. He reached a wall. Slowly, he moved left. A door. Light switches beside the doorframe. Moved his fingers. A flash. Lights on.

Freezing cold, bleeding, and naked, he walked into the main warehouse. The space smelled of paint and mineral spirits. Industrial tools covered much of the room. There were two large trashcans holding dirty painter's pants and twill shirts monogrammed with *Lone Star Paint Works.*

He rummaged out a poor-fitting shirt and pants. They stunk, but they looked like heaven. He taped a towel around each foot.

Dude ravaged desk drawers in an office. No money. He grabbed a vehicle key off a rack. Labelled Ford 22X. He turned the lights off and walked out into a thirty-six-degree night straight to a lineup of pickups that looked like the second-string bench for a high school basketball team.

There it was, 22X. He popped the lock, hopped in, hit the ignition. Flicked the heater to high. Gas tank three-quarters full. Slammed it in drive, turned out of the lot, and poured some coal to the accelerator.

He drove two blocks. Then hit the headlights.

And wondered, *Where the living hell am I?*

11

DUDE DROVE HARD, looking for signs to an interstate. Any interstate. Think, dammit. Needed money. Needed a phone. Needed shoes. Spotted an all-night Exxon, swung in, parked at the back of the building next to a dumpster. It was 2:45 in the morning.

"What the hell happened?" said the cashier, a pained look on his own face at the sight before him.

"Car wreck, bad one. Is this Dallas?"

"Fort Worth."

Dude grabbed a Texas map from a rack, unfolded it, studied the roads. He picked a route and memorized it. Interstate 20, running on the south side of Fort Worth, touching the southern boundary of Dallas, and on to Shreveport.

He walked out, shivered as he hit the cold, and saw two vivid-orange Covenant Tree Service trucks at different pumps taking on fuel. Artificial light rained down from the pump canopy like a night game for the Rangers. Big, Jesus fish-decals were prominently displayed on the trucks. Christians. *We'll see.*

He approached one man. "Hate to bother you, brother, but I'm desperate—could you spare a few bucks?" Guy was maybe twenty-five, stocky, wore a mountain-man beard. He pointed over his shoulder toward the other truck. "Talk to the boss man."

Dude walked to an identical-looking vehicle, two men leaning on it while diesel fuel flowed like a river into the tank. One had just bought a bear-claw Danish and a Coke inside the store. Dude's mouth watered as he watched the man hold the Danish by the wrapper and eat it like Thanksgiving dinner. Both men eyed Dude warily, not speaking, knew they were about to be hit up.

"Excuse me, sirs, is one of you the boss man?"

"First thing I want to know is what happened?" It was the older man. He didn't move an inch, his arms were folded across his chest, leaning back on the truck. The younger fellow kept working the Danish and Coke.

"I got beat up by the cops in a tent city, all of us did. They took all our stuff, threw it in a garbage truck and told us to leave town. Trying to get in touch with my brother and get him to send money for me to get home."

Old guy pointed to the patch on the shirt. "What's Lone Star Paint Works?"

"Don't know. I got this at a shelter." They didn't see Dude's truck.

Boss man was maybe sixty, dressed in khakis, still had a headful of dark hair. "I want to know something, son. This is *the* most important question in your life."

Dude nodded. "Okay."

"Do you know the Lord?"

Why lie? "No, sir, I don't."

"Well, the Lord feeds his sheep. I'm talking about the Bread of Life and Living Water that saves each one of us from the lake of fire. Christ died for your sins and mine."

Dude nodded, "Yes, sir."

"Will ten dollars help you?"

"Yes, sir, greatly."

"What's your name, son?"

"Robert Carl."

"Robert Carl, I'll be praying for your journey home and into a local congregation of your earthly shepherds and saints."

Boss man opened the truck door, reached across the seat, and grabbed a small, red Bible from a stack. He took out his wallet, pulled out two fifties, flipped through the Bible to the first book of the New Testament, slid the cash in. "Start reading here. The book of Matthew."

"Thank you, sir, thank you." Dude hugged the boss, went in the store, bought four bear claws and a large Coke.

After the men left, Dude turned right out of the lot, headed east. On-ramped the interstate. Still dark, traffic light before rush hour kicks in in less than two hours.

Had to disappear forever. Otherwise he was a dead man.

Gotta warn Ella.

12

IT WAS THIRTY-ONE degrees inside Ella's trailer when they woke for the school day. The twins, Carly and Abigail, slept with Ella in a bed. Bobby Carl, Jr., slept in a sleeping bag under covers in his own room.

Wearing the same clothes they wore yesterday, they jumped out of bed, brushed their teeth, washed their faces, and dodged mud puddles as they ran to the Gemini school bus Ella drove. The kids carried Pop Tarts and juice boxes.

"Cold as stink, Mama," said Bobby Carl, Jr.

"Bout to put on the heat." Ella saw herself in the sun-visor mirror. Dark circles under puffy eyes left her looking drawn. And much older than twenty-nine.

Rain splattered across the windshield. Ella watched limbs on old live oaks twisting in the breeze. If anything, the bleak weather had intensified.

She pulled her cheap phone from her hoodie. 6:40 a.m. The phone would die at 7:00 a.m. That's what the overdue notice said. Twenty minutes. She tapped Dude's contact picture. Five rings. Voicemail.

"It's Dude. You know the drill."

You just wait, mother hugger.

She slid her hand under the driver's seat before leaving. Felt it. The pipe wrench her daddy used working the shipyards for forty-five years in Mobile, Alabama. It was fourteen inches long with a dinged, red-paint coating. The look was eighteenth-century industrial. Rudimentary. Powerful. A brutal tool.

Ella was five-eight, a sturdy-boned brunette, with a short-bobbed ponytail and a cheerleader smile. She had natural-born coordination and meaty forearms that could swing an aluminum bat like an explosion.

Ella was about to use a four-pound pipe wrench like it was the state championship softball game.

THE PLAN WAS SIMPLE. By 8 a.m., the kids would be dumped in school. She'd cruise back to Hardees, park in the back lot, saunter into the restaurant, say howdy to a few folks, order the sausage biscuit breakfast.

Then she'd go about it.

A heavy shipyard tool was about to crush the teeth and eyes out of a man's skull.

It's Ella. You know the drill.

13

LONGVIEW, TEXAS

DUDE WAS RUNNING eighty with everybody else. I-20 was wide open after passing the southern edge of Dallas. He needed more gas, but he wasn't parting with a nickel until he got some shoes.

He exited I-20 at Estes Boulevard in Longview, and the damn store was sitting right there, bigger than the moon. The Walmart Supercenter.

He parked as close as he could to the front door, walked into the building and saw a blue-vested old lady wearing enough red lipstick to repaint a firetruck. "Please tell me where to find shoes and aspirin, ma'am."

She glanced at his feet, gave him a look, and pointed.

He grabbed a bottle of ibuprofen first, opened it, and dry swallowed four tablets. Next, he found the shoes. Picked some black ones marked down on closeout. Grabbed a two-pack of cushioned white socks, put on a pair, then the shoes, wore them to the checkout. He placed the sock bag on the conveyor along with the tag for the shoes and the ibuprofen bottle.

"Where're the shoes?" asked the woman cashier. Late forties, rattlesnake skinny, teased blond hair, smoker's skin, and enough mascara to make any sane person think of a rabid raccoon.

“On my feet.” He lifted a leg. No hurry, nobody in line.

She looked at the foot, then his face, thinking. Dude could smell the cinnamon gum she smacked. The cashier pulled a smartphone out of her hip pocket, swiped the screen, tapped an app, pointed it at Dude’s face and snapped a pic.

“Why’d you do that?”

“Cause I know shit when I see it. And right now, I’m looking at some shit.” Her eyebrows shot up. “My husband’s a cop. He likes it when I report shit.”

“Ma’am, I was in a hit-and-run accident.” Dude’s ass clinched tight.

She rolled her eyes. “Know what that was, what you said?”

Dude shook his head, too scared to say the wrong thing.

“That was some lying shit, the worst kind of shit in my opinion.”

He wanted to pay, walk out the door, and haul ass in the truck. He knew if he laid a twenty down and walked, she’d likely hit buttons for security, maybe start screaming.

“Lemme show you something, Romeo.” She picked up her phone, popped up his picture, pointed at the screen. “If I didn’t know better, I’d say that looked like a dad-blame booking shot. All we need is a number for you to hold.”

Face like stone, he still didn’t say anything.

“Lemme show you one other thing.” She glanced at the phone a moment, found what she was looking for. “See that? That trash can whatchamacallit? I accidentally bump my finger right there and that booking shot disappears. Gone. I mean you have to be some kind of Leonardo by-God da Vinci to come up with this phone stuff.”

Dude nodded.

“Here’s the thing.” She calmed her tone, smiled all the way up into the lines of her eyes. “I bet if some man walked down my checkout aisle today and said something like, ‘Darlene, you look so friggin' hot and sexy this morning I wanna buy you a fresh pack of smokes.' Well, course I'd smile, and I'd say, 'Thank ya, darlin', Marlboro Reds would be just fine.' And I bet my little old pointer finger would accidentally scrape over that trashcan thingy and lose all this awful shit I seen today. Start the rest of the day with a fresh slate of sunshine and blue skies."

"Ma'am. When you're ringing up my shoes and socks, would you mind adding in a pack of Marlboro Reds? No, make that two packs."

"Well, sure thing, I can do that for you, baby."

14

DUDE DROVE TWO miles, parked behind a cheap highway hotel, and took a power nap. Thirty minutes helped calm his nerves after tangling with that Walmart witch. He stepped into the frosty air with five bucks in quarters in his pocket and walked into the rear entrance of the hotel. He spotted a cove with vending machines. There were two payphones.

He scattered the quarters on the narrow counter.

6:59 a.m. Time for brutal honesty. He knew Ella was gonna rip him a new one.

Dude fed the phone three bucks, tapped numbers on the keypad.

The phone rang one time.

Dude had no clue about Black Point weather. He didn't think about this being the time Ella was driving the bus to school. He forgot he was supposed to pay some bills. Not a thought that his wife might not answer the strange number.

The call was accepted.

"Yes," said Ella.

Dude exhaled. "Oh, God, baby, I just escaped. Those crazy-ass Mexicans kidnapped me. You gotta call—"

He heard a faint click. Then nothing. No dial tone, only dead air. He knew she'd be pissed, but ...

"Ella? ... Ella?"

He loaded the last two dollars in quarters into the phone. Dialed quickly.

Boop boop boop. "The number you have dialed is no longer in service."

The payphone refunded his quarters. Loaded the phone, tried again.

Boop boop boop. "The number you have dialed is no longer in service."

Walked to the truck, cranked it, bathed in the heat, and stared through the windshield. It struck him like a lightning bolt. Had to get back to Black Point. Fast.

The Mexicans would kill Ella trying to find him.

15

BLACK POINT, ALABAMA

ELLA GLANCED AT her watch. 6:56 a.m. She was late, late, late.

She pushed the bus up to sixty, thought she felt a floaty, dizzy sensation through the steering wheel on the wet road. She wrote that off as the Xanax soaping up her brain.

Both windshield wipers sloshed heavy rain off the glass. Temperature twenty-nine degrees.

Her thoughts were not on hazardous driving conditions. She thought more about a proper cemetery for a blood-soaked pipe wrench.

The bus ran fast by a cowboy-themed bar, a Dollar General outpost, and a block-wall bait shop with two ice coolers standing against the outside wall.

Her boot pressed down hard on the brake as she came into the business Highway 98 intersection with too much speed, readying for the yielding right turn. The brakes grabbed, the tires stopped rolling, launching the bus into a hydroplane slide. The tail end skated three feet into the other lane. Ella turned into the skid, let off the brake, and corrected.

"Whoa, Mom, cool," said Bobby Carl.

It scared the girls. "Slow down, Mama."

It didn't faze Ella. Her mind simmered on the blissful payback coming soon. She knew where to unearth her cockroach husband. Big-game butterflies floated in her belly. Coach always said if you weren't nervous, you weren't ready. She bumped the heavy wrench with her heel. Reassurance.

Oh, hell yeah. She was ready.

Making the turn at the Shell station, Ella faced a runway-straight open road for seven miles. She got on it. Sleety ice chips spit across the windshield. Limited visibility, but few cars. No concern. She could drive this section in her sleep.

6:59 a.m. Somewhere in America a computer was set to disable her phone in one minute.

A HALF-MILE north of the turn, on the same side of the road as Ella, a man had just closed the driver's door on a showroom-new thirty-eight-ton long-haul truck. It was hitched to a trailer bowed down with 22,000 pounds of steel aircraft-engine parts.

The flatbed rested five feet off the pavement.

Crede Hendrickson had just stowed the last of the safety cones that he'd placed the night before. Safety blinkers still on. He sat in the toasty warm cab, cell phone in hand, Lycoming plant number on the screen. KSJ Country radio was broadcasting storm reports every ten minutes.

He could already taste the buttered waffle with hash browns he'd eat at the Black Point Waffle House.

Crede used his right index finger to punch the saved number to the plant.

Two rings and a pleasantly playful female voice answered, "It's a cold morning at Lycoming, how may I help you?"

Crede pictured a spunky, twenty-seven-year-old blond who hadn't had to deal with kids this morning, and probably just had morning sex with her live-in boyfriend, well, because it's cold and, mostly, because it was a new day, and she was only twenty-seven.

EIGHTEEN SECONDS UNTIL 7 A.M. Ella was hitting sixty-three on slick asphalt, faster than her normal fifty-five. She blitzed past a closed produce stand.

Sleet smacked the windshield like buckshot.

Her flip phone nestled against her crotch, right up against the cold zipper of her jeans. A vibration buzzed into both thighs. She snatched it with her left hand. Looking down, she saw *Unknown.*

“Hello.”

“Oh, God, baby, I just escaped. Those crazy-ass Mexicans kidnapped me. You gotta call—”

A soft click. Silence.

“Dude?”

The time hit 7 a.m. The phone went dead. Nonpayment.

“Dude?”

Sixty-five on the speedometer. Ella squinted at the phone, then took her right hand off the wheel. She lifted her left knee to steady the wheel while her right index finger frantically punched redial.

Her right foot never let off the gas.

The bus drifted right, not much, but enough. Right side tires popped off the five-inch ledge of blacktop. Eighteen hours of rain had left the ground soggy. The ditch’s steep slope was only twenty inches from the pavement but was as full as a swimming pool.

The tires lost traction and began a slide down into the water. The bus canted thirty degrees to the right.

Abigail and Carly screamed.

“TRUCK, MAMA!” Bobby Carl’s eyes bulged.

Ella glanced up to a bright reflective strip running horizontal across the heavy steel trailer bumper.

She dropped the phone, grabbed the wheel, her right foot crushing the brake.

It seemed to be slow motion, something from a movie. It was anything but.

Ella jerked the wheel to the left. The right front tire was too deep in the ditch to respond. The school bus was out of control.

Crates of steel grew gigantic in the approach. The iron bumper looked ten feet tall.

Ninety-eight-thousand pounds of truck and cargo were parked stone-still in the bus's path. Two orange lights blinked in a duet on each side of the trailer.

Impact came at sixty miles an hour. Steel on steel.

The collision was heard two miles away. Half of the Gemini's diesel engine exploded into the bus cabin.

Four bodies, zero seatbelts. High speed.

Sleet danced over death and silence.

16

PIERCE DUNNIGAN BLASTED down Black Point Avenue, blew through the light at Colony Street, and slung his Wagoneer into an angled parking spot in front of a barbershop. The tires hit the curb and bounced back.

The barber, behind a large sheet of vulnerable plate glass, jumped as the truck hit the curb. Vern was putting the finishing touches on a cut that would make any monk smile. The top of the man's head shone like just-waxed linoleum.

"That damn Dunnigan," said the barber. "Thinks that crap's funny."

Pierce hopped out, cigarette dangling out of the corner of his mouth, eyeballed the barber with a don't-give-a-damn grin, popped his chin up in a redneck howdy. He hustled across the street wearing a rain slicker over his paramedic uniform. His ball cap said ProMed Ambulance Service.

Approaching the law office, he took a deep drag, flicked the cigarette onto the wet street, stepped on the sidewalk, spat, and then blasted into the front door of William Burnham's law office, dripping water.

It was one hour and twenty minutes after the bus crash. Dunnigan carried a piece of valuable cargo in his pocket. A cell phone that was found under the back of dead Carly Codger, one of the twins.

"What's bringing you out in a storm?" asked Liz Donovan, Burnham's longtime office manager.

"Legal business. Private. Tell Wild Bill it's important."

She picked up her cell and texted Bill, who was just one flight of stairs away.

Dunnigan's here. Says it's important.

Bill had a vertical electric space heater pulled up close. The old building had porous insulation, causing him to freeze in the winter. ***Tell him to come on.***

Dunnigan speed-stepped up the stairs, leaving wet footprints along the way. He walked into Bill's office with a funeral face. Earnest, distraught, but no tears.

Shaking his head. "I just left the worst damn scene I've ever been to. Loaded three kids on a Life Flight bird and their dead mama in an ambulance. Told my boss I had to call off cause my nerves are shot. I came right here."

Dunnigan was one of Wild Bill's most productive runners for his ambulance-chasing empire. He gave out no names, no business cards, no suggestions at the accident scene. But he would take your contact information. One of Bill's office reps would be in touch. Fast.

"Well, hell, Pierce, spit it out. What happened?"

He laid it out for Bill, exactly what he saw. Truck. Bus. Bodies.

"That ain't all." Dunnigan slid the broken flip phone from his pocket with two fingers, leaned forward and placed it on the desk right in front of Bill's face. "This is why I drove straight here."

Bill's left elbow rested on the desk. He massaged his chin as it rested in his left hand. His eyes flicked down. "What's this?"

"Well, if I'm right, it could be keys to a gold mine."

"How's that?"

"Found it under one of the kids. It was open. Somebody could have been talking, maybe texting while they drove. And drove their ass right into a truck."

"Huh." Bill was thinking. "That could be a problem."

"School bus crashed into a big rig. Dead kids. All I see is a money parade."

"Hmmm." Bill tried not to look excited.

Dunnigan leaned in, dropped his voice. "Ain't nobody but me and you know about this phone." Pierce pointed at the black plastic. "One thing I know about you, Bill. You're slicker than green diarrhea. Figure you know exactly what to do about something this important."

"Might belong to one of the kids. Driver may have had a phone in her pocket. Or a purse," said Bill, trying to lower expectations.

"Well, I bet you'll find out." Pierce stood up, started to make for the office door. "I'm headed to Greer's for a six of Bud. My nerves can't take all this wreckage at seven in the morning. I might go online, check out a new center-console boat, 'cause I want ten percent of your cut."

"Bullshit, Dunnigan. Five hundred bucks if I can land a case. Another five hundred if I rip something out of the insurance companies."

Dunnigan, at the threshold of the office door, walked back and grabbed the phone off the desk. "Sorry, champ. You ain't the only lawyer in town."

Bill stood up. "Okay, okay, ten percent." Dunnigan spun and walked out. Bill sat down, plopped his boots up on the small office refrigerator and unleashed the brilliance in his mind. He knew damn well the cops would be searching for cell phone records of the driver. Always do.

He grabbed the phone and raced down to Theo Fuller's office, his primary researcher. He heard booming drumbeats as he reached the door. He twisted the doorknob and pushed into the room. “Little Sister” by Queens of the Stone Age slammed against Bill’s eardrums. “Turn that crap down.”

The room was dark, lit only by colors bouncing off three 27-inch Dell gaming monitors. One monitor was loaded with technical specs for a cheap-ass Mississippi-made turkey fryer that had burned down the houses of several brain surgeons who didn’t read the instructions. Black sound-curtains covered the walls. If the devil had a den, Bill knew he was in it.

Theo killed the music. Bill placed the phone on the desk in the luminescence from a monitor. “What’s that?” said Theo.

“It’s a cell phone. Don’t know if they taught you this at your fancy college, but I need you to track phone records off this.”

“Okay.” Theo didn’t engage Bill. He placed his headphones on, looked away, and went back to his music.

Bill walked out, closed the door.

Theo picked up the phone. It split apart. No, they didn’t teach him how to do this in college. But he’d known how to do this since he was in about the ninth grade. The phone had juice, but no service. He popped out the SIM card, picked up his tool bag, and took out a SIM reader. He determined the phone number. ATT was the carrier. Twenty minutes later he was through their firewalls, a place he’d hacked before. He printed out the call history for the last thirty days.

He carried several sheets of paper upstairs, walked into Bill’s office, slid them onto the keyboard where Bill was typing.

“Damn. That was fast. Hold on a minute, let me look while you’re here.” Bill studied the sheet.

“Okay, so what’s happened with this phone since midnight?”

“This phone number is registered to someone named Ella Codger. Three call attempts were made after midnight to another phone number. That number is registered to Bobby Carl

Codger. May have gone to voicemail. No time for a real conversation. At almost 7 a.m. this morning, a call came in from the 430 area code to this phone. It's a payphone in Longview, Texas. The precise time was eighteen seconds before seven. The phone service died at seven on the dot for nonpayment."

"That's interesting, really interesting." Bill bit his lower lip, mulling the implications. "Good work, now beat it." He gave the air a swat.

Bill scrolled through contacts on his cell, found Dunnigan, hit call.

"Yo, Wild Bill, what's up?"

"Very important, Pierce. Very. What time did the ambulance call come in?"

"Just so happens I know that. I had a tasty ham biscuit in my hand from Lyrene's the second we got it. My iPhone was on the table. It said 7:04 when I took the 911 call. Dispatcher said it was called in from a truck driver at the scene."

"Thanks." Bill thought fast, fingers tapping on the desk. It's almost two hours after the crash. Have the cops run a phone search yet? Ha! They didn't find a phone, so probably not yet.

Bill flew through his office door, raced down the stairs like he was running from a fire, cut to the back of the building, walked into Theo's office, and pulled the headphones off his stepson's head.

"Do you have the brains to erase the history of the calls to and from the phone since midnight?"

Theo didn't answer as he took the phone. He lifted his right hand, waggled his fingers down with his palm facing Bill. *Buh-bye.* Bill felt it best to keep his mouth shut and leave, closing the office door with respect.

It took Theo seventeen minutes.

Ella Codger's phone now had no record of any phone activity since 9:37 last night.

17

THIRTY-FIVE MINUTES AFTER 10 p.m. the tires of the Lone Star Paint Works truck crunched over the oyster-shell parking lot of Giacotti's Seafood in Bon Secour, Alabama, twenty-three miles south of Black Point, close to the Gulf Shores beaches. Cold rain was still spitting through the night.

Dude parked and ran down the wooden dock to Delroy Vaughn's old shrimper. Since first grade, Delroy had been Dude's runnin' buddy.

"Delroy," Dude said loudly as he stepped on board. He opened the cabin door before Delroy could reach it and stepped inside. Smelled of cigarettes and beef stew. A small space-heater kept the place warm.

"Oh hell, Delroy, it's an emergency." Dude's words rushed out of his mouth. Sounded manic. "I'm in a life and death situation here. Now, listen to me. Listen."

"Dude." Delroy was subdued, not his usual angry self. He stared at Dude's swollen, bruised face.

"No, man, listen. I'm in trouble. Ella's in danger. The kids are in danger. I need to get home, but I can't. Need your help."

"Dude."

"Shut up will you, shut the hell up ... and listen. Delroy, you ain't gonna believe this shit. Never believe it."

Delroy's demeanor was withdrawn. Dude's voice calmed. "What, Delroy?" He saw Delroy's eyes welling up. "What's going on?"

"Just ain't no easy way to say it, so I'll just say it. Ella, Bobby Carl, and Carly are dead. Abigail's in a coma in the hospital."

Dude crashed into the fetal position. Groans came from deep in his gut.

The Mexicans.

18

DELROY VAUGHN ARRIVED at William Burnham's law office eight hours after Dude reached his shrimper. With all the billboards, everyone had heard of Wild Bill Burnham. Delroy wore pain on his face as he spoke to the receptionist. "Ma'am, I need one of those free consultations. Right now."

Liz read the urgency, escorted him upstairs to Bill's office.

Delroy didn't sit. "Mr. Burnham ... It's about a bad accident. A bus crash ..."

The meeting took seven minutes.

9:55 P.M. THAT NIGHT. Wild Bill, toddy in hand, watched through a window as the vehicle snaked down his curvy two-hundred-foot drive. Gravel crunched as the pickup made it to the roundabout in front of the home's entrance.

Bill opened the door before the visitors could knock. He saw a man with greenish-blue bruising over much of his face. Crusty deep scratches lined his left cheek.

"Well, dadgum, it is you. They did a number on you." Bill stuck out his hand. "Wild Bill Burnham."

"Dude Codger. Thanks for meeting me like this."

"Spent a lot of money with you down at the Anchor, Dude. Glad you tracked me down." Bill turned away, waved forward with a couple of fingers on his right hand. "Follow me."

Bill led Dude to a cozy den and pointed to a dark leather couch. "Make yourself comfortable. I'll grab you a beer." Burning oak popped in the fireplace. A full bookshelf covered one wall; the other three walls were pecky cypress holding wildfowl renderings lending the room a hunting camp feel.

They talked almost two hours. It was coming up on midnight. "You know, Dude, funny you should show up. I had my eyes on this situation, was about to reach out to the family. But, damn, man," Burnham took a sip of his drink, "I've been around the block a time or two, but I ain't ever heard anything like your story. Here's a critical first question. Are you sure nobody besides Delroy knows you're alive?"

"Yes, sir. A hundred percent sure. At least nobody who knows who I am."

Bill blew out a puff from a Cohiba, glanced at the sparks dancing in his fireplace, and took another hard slug of scotch. "I know exactly what we need to do." His head bobbed with a nod.

"First and foremost, you gotta stay dead. I mean forever."

Dude nodded in agreement.

Bill looked over at Delroy. "Mr. Vaughn, tomorrow you need to go to a payphone—wear a hat and sunglasses—and call the office number of the Black Point Police Department. Give 'em an anonymous tip. Tell them you heard that two guys from Florida robbed the Rusty Anchor and shot the bartender. Codger was buried in a field somewhere, dead. His car was run down a boat ramp into the bay. The killers were driving an old, red Jeep Cherokee. Don't let them ask questions. Don't give your name. Just hang up."

"Got it."

Bill pulled a wad from his trouser pocket, peeled off some bills. "Here's a grand for your trouble, Delroy. This step is critical to keep Dude alive. You got that, right?"

"Yep."

"Tomorrow morning I'm stopping by Walmart. Gonna buy a cheap pay-as-you-go burner phone so I can reach you, Dude. Only I will have the number. I want Delroy to pick it up at my office. I'll also have ten thousand in cash for you. And Delroy, don't come by the office after that. I have a feeling the Mexicans are gonna be snooping around town."

"What time?" said Delroy.

"Around ten is fine. Now, I'll get Theo, my data guy, on the research tomorrow. This guy can find out anything about anybody. I've been seeing Gemini school buses my whole life. I've seen Hendrickson's trucks on the road, but I don't know their background. It won't be long before we know every minute of their corporate life and how they're sitting financially. And, of course, what their insurance situation is. That's where we get the first payouts."

"For you, Dude, I need you to find a spot in the sticks, I mean away, maybe something over around Pensacola. Take a few thousand and let Delroy buy you a beater out of one of those little classified rags you see around. Stock up on food, and park yourself in front of a TV with the phone next to you."

Bill stared into the fireplace flames. Thinking a moment. Shook his head as he caught Dude's eyes. "I really hate to be the fly in the ointment at this point, Dude, but if you're dead, I need a client, and, unfortunately, that sweet, precious baby of yours in the hospital is incapable of making decisions."

A smarmy smile slid across Dude's swollen face, followed by a nod.

"Think I've got a solution for that, Wild Bill."

19

"HER NAME IS Doris Bell." That's what Dude had told Wild Bill. She was his wife's mother's sister, Ella's aunt. Ella's mother had been dead for five years, so she was not available to be a plaintiff in the lawsuit, nor offer information on Doris.

Doris had left the United States when Ella was two months old. Ella mentioned her existence to Dude on a couple of occasions, but the only information Dude had was barely a sentence worth. *Aunt Doris is a Christian medical missionary in Africa.*

Bill gave the name to his stepson, Theo, with one instruction. "Find her in twenty-four hours and I'll give you two grand."

Six hours later, Theo walked into Bill's office. Bill looked up with eyebrows raised. "Got something already? Damn, boy, you're good."

Theo recited the information. "Dr. Doris Bell received an RN degree from UAB, worked two years as an ICU nurse, then went to medical school in the Caribbean. Left for Africa after a three-year family practice residency in Savannah, Georgia. She receives some missionary sponsorship money from Pentecostal churches in Missouri and Oklahoma, but not much." Theo handed a slip of paper to Bill. "This is where she is."

Bill read the note out loud. "Chikudum village at the base of Didinga Hills in Sudan." He cut his eyes to Theo. "Where the living hell is this?"

EIGHT DAYS LATER, Bill was rolling out of Egypt in a ragged Range Rover wagon that looked weeks away from the scrap yard. Inside were three armed men who agreed to take him to the village for a ninety-minute visit for $25,000. Egypt was the safest entry into Sudan, they informed him. Prior to the trip, Bill found that other than a face-to-face visit, rapid communication to the area was all but impossible. Which was perfect.

Sudan was one of the poorest countries on earth. It was war torn and flush with crime, an extraordinarily volatile area. The three men all had AK-47s and a stash of ammo.

It took three days of rugged travel to reach the village and locate Dr. Bell. Bill knew her to be sixty or so, but life made her look older. She was an extremely thin woman who wore her silver-gray hair short, completely exposing her ears. Her skin was dry and weather beaten, but her eyes held a sparkle, a look of contentment in what looked to Bill to be a dismal existence. A black-and-white photo of her would remind someone of a woman living through the poverty of the Dust Bowl in the 1930s.

While he held no strong beliefs, Bill felt he was looking at a living angel of God. Certainly a woman who had made a hard turn down the road less traveled.

Bill introduced himself and was met with a skeptical eye from Dr. Bell. She said she met Ella as a newborn, and just that one time. Bill informed her of the awful accident and saw a flood of sadness come over her. She shook her head, said, "The storms we face, oh, the storms. I'm thankful my sister didn't have to bear that loss."

Bill explained that he had traveled to the African continent to seek her assistance in a lawsuit. It would be money that would provide the finest medical care for sweet Abigail. There would also be funding to upgrade medical facilities in the Didinga Hills and provide for Dr. Bell's ministry.

"Dr. Bell, we're going to drill a gusher. Everybody wins."

What came next hit Bill like a sledgehammer.

With a look of disgust, Dr. Doris Bell said, "Mr. Burnham, God provides, not the courts. Under no circumstances will I participate in a lawsuit. The news is sad, but this discussion is over. Have a safe trip back to the States."

Bill already had a Plan B.

"I'M BACK." Five days later Bill strolled into his Black Point office through the front door in the middle of a blazing afternoon.

Liz stood, surprised. Bill hadn't called. "So how'd it go? Did you find her?"

Full of smugness, Bill replied, "Sure did. Everything's signed and sealed with all the I's dotted and T's crossed. She welcomed me and said God delivered me to her as one of his great miracles. Said the lawsuit money will help upgrade the clinic into a much-needed small hospital. Everything's a go!"

20

BLACK POINT, ALABAMA

TWENTY MONTHS AFTER, the lawsuit was filed.

Wild Bill Burnham was dressed for war, wearing his cowboy power-suit, a black George Strait-style Stetson, a bolo string tie with a turquoise and silver slide. On his feet were new caiman-belly cowboy boots with three-inch risers he had custom-made at a boutique bootmaker in Austin.

He wanted to look Texas because Texas was big. Big land, big cattle, big oil, big business, and big, big, big money.

The courtroom was full, like a scrum of people rustling for cheap TVs on Black Friday. Harsh fluorescent lights turned everyone's faces a sickly shade of pale, fitting for the revelations to follow. Bill and the herd of defense lawyers had met with the judge yesterday, so no need for further discussion.

The judge took his seat at precisely 8 a.m., glanced around, observed that there wasn't an empty seat anywhere, and was ready to begin. He outlined to the jury the rules of the court and the order of events in which the trial would proceed.

"Mr. Burnham. You may begin."

Wild Bill rose from his seat wearing the face of a mortician, buttoned his suit coat, walked around the desk trailing a vapor of arrogant confidence, gave a perfunctory head bow to the judge, shot a glance at the table of four concerned defense attorneys, went right to the jury box, placed his left hand on the railing, and let his eyes run across the face of every juror. Each one locked his gaze, focused.

Bill liked what he saw. His people, every one of them.

He was silent for thirty seconds, pulled his right hand in a fist to his mouth, bumped his lips lightly with the thumb end, thinking mostly about everything his acting instructor had taught him. Memory-driven tears, the teacher said. Bill flashed a thought of his mother dying two years ago from painful brain cancer. And then it came, right here, right now. One tear from his right eye for every juror to see. He made a vivid show of pulling his handkerchief from his pocket, dabbing his eyes.

"Folks, I apologize." Bill stepped back four feet, centered himself for the jury, put the handkerchief in his coat pocket, assumed a casual stance, sniffled, and spoke to the jury.

"The needless death of this family has weighed upon me for many months now. It really has."

Fully recomposed, he continued. "My name is Bill Burnham, the attorney for the Codger family. People call me Wild Bill because I chase justice like a wild man. I don't stop, I mean I never stop, until the truth overtakes all the lies and propaganda you will hear thrown at you by a desperate legal team representing two different wealthy companies that, through both poor product design and equally poor decision-making, caused the deaths of two children and their mother. Needlessly, absolutely needlessly. And the third child, oh dear Lord ... in a coma. Paralyzed from the neck down."

Burnham paused, went to the railing in front of the jurors, and leaned on it with his left hand.

"Folks, I've handled over THREE THOUSAND vehicle accident cases. Out of those, forty-eight people have lost their lives. But listen to me here. Not one of those cases had the egregious negligence perpetrated by the defendants you will hear about in this trial. Not a one of 'em. Let me tell you what happened.

"A tractor-trailer driver decided to"—Bill shook his head like *who in his hot-damn right mind*—"park his flatbed for the night only a few feet from the edge of a busy US highway. Highway

98, you all know it, I'm sure. Now get this, the truck was carrying steel, the truck fully loaded. Steel, now. Twenty-two TONS! This is Hendrickson Trucking, one of the largest trucking outfits in the Southeast. Here's the real rub. The driver wasn't some new guy, some guy with no experience that made a horrible decision. Wasn't some greenhorn who went to some two-week fly-by-night trucking school. No, sir. The truck was parked there by Crede Hendrickson, the CEO. The head man, people. Mr. Hendrickson's lazy, foolish decision allowed his truck to wipe out a woman and her three kids. I mean, good gosh, people, at the edge of the road!"

Bill quieted for a moment, exhaled a deep breath, shook his head.

"Now let's talk about Gemini school buses, a seventy-five-year-old bus company. The company has received twenty-eight field reports of failed windshield wipers in wet weather over the last three years on the A390 model, the one Ella Codger was driving in that rain and sleet storm. What did Gemini do about the wipers?"

Bill shrugged his shoulders, arms in front bent at the elbow, palms facing the ceiling, face slack.

"Well, nothing, not that we can see. Did you hear that? They did *nothing.* No recall for repairs. A subpoena for bus maintenance records from our Bay County School System show they have received no information regarding this. Not so much as a phone call. And Bay County has sixty of these death traps."

"One final thing. I've got one thing for you that I have never had in any previous accident case. Three thousand cases, now remember that. In not one occurrence of a human fatality accident case have I ever had inside-the-vehicle, crystal-clear video footage showing *exactly* what I'm telling you. I have never had a case where the jury had it so easy to make the right decision for justice. But let me forewarn you."

Bill raised a finger, delivered a forlorn look to his face.

"After you see the video, you will be scarred for life. It's ugly, people. I'm telling you right now, it's brutal and bloody." Bill stopped speaking, took an exaggerated deep breath.

"So, let's do this, let's do our jobs, let's come quickly to justice. Then let us all thank God for each and every day we receive." Wild Bill went back to his seat.

The lead defense attorney for Gemini rose, maintained a neutral countenance, and approached the jury. He was from a large New York firm. Thick salt-and-pepper hair with a $200 dollar cut from a Manhattan salon, dark Armani suit. He spoke with a tone of upper-crust derision to the jury, as if he felt like they were a group of cornbread-chomping illiterates. His message carried the tone of castigation of one of their own, Ella Codger, for driving in the rain.

Doing her job.

The New York slickster had yet to realize he was standing neck-deep in quicksand.

21

WILD BILL THREW open the doors to his cash vault on this case. No expense spared on consultants. He had Georgia Tech engineers, Duke physicians, and a world-renowned audio-visual team producing a video using the buses' own cameras.

On the third day of the trial, after testimony had been heard from the consulting experts, it was time.

The video.

Bill stuck a hand in the air and swirled his finger. Vivid color appeared on the screens.

The driver's side camera displayed useless footage of the bus ceiling. It had been improperly installed, bungled, the focal plane shooting too high. It only captured a tiny portion of the hair on the top of Ella's head, missing her ears. There was not one frame from any camera that identified Ella's full face or lateral face.

An digital clock was visible in the lower right of the video, ticking forward on the day. The eyes of the courtroom were on the passengers, not the clock.

All except two people.

One was dressed up like an animated clown in a Roy Rogers get-up—Wild Bill. The other was a willowy man with dark chin scruff sitting in the end seat in the most distant row in the courtroom. He took in the show through faddish, retro, engineer glasses, the nerd style Malcolm X wore. Bill's researcher, Theo Fuller.

Only those two knew it was a stone-cold fact that Ella's phone had been answered only seconds before the crash. The film's digital clock read 6:59 a.m. Not a single camera captured Ella pulling her phone from between her legs, flipping it open with her thumb, and bringing it to her left ear.

Bobby Carl, Jr., stood behind his mother as she drove, blocking the view of her head from the rear cameras.

But in fact, Ella had heard Dude's frantic voice when she answered—something about kidnapping and Mexicans. The phone had died in mid-sentence, like someone pulled an electrical cord from the wall.

The courtroom didn't see Ella's right hand leave the wheel to try to redial Dude. They didn't see her left knee come up to attempt to steer a twelve-ton, yellow, steel box on a wet, icy road. They didn't see her foot remain on the gas pedal.

Then something happened with the weather. The audience saw the rains heavily increase. It took a moment, only a moment, and they realized why. They had been warned it would happen. Wild Bill made sure of it. The rain hadn't actually increased. The wipers had come to a dead stop, two inert strips of useless rubber, frozen to the glass. But it looked like fire hoses were trying to blast the windshield out of the frame.

The bus immediately leaned downward to the right. Wheels in the ditch.

At this point, the AV technicians sped up the video at a fast and harsh pace, racing toward a dead-stopped, forty-five-ton truck.

Spectators jerked in their seats as if they'd been hit themselves by the impact.

Shattered glass. Splashed blood. Fractured skulls. Ragged steel. Severed spines.

The courtroom was full of ashen faces and sniffling noses. Eyes shifted to the floor.

Crede Hendrickson, the owner of Hendrickson Trucking, sat bent over at the waist, crying hysterically. The previous day, Wild Bill had eviscerated the man on the stand for four hours.

Theo Fuller stood from his back-row seat, pulled up his hoodie, and hustled out of the courtroom. His face was flushed with anger.

Fuller fumed over one thought. Burnham had used him unwittingly in this farce.

It was the damn phone. It wasn't the wipers. It wasn't the truck. It was a woman driver jackin' around with her damn cell phone, losing control in an ice storm!

Fighting every bit of his DNA to keep a smug look off his face, Bill gave a side-eye glance to his right at his group of opponents, the defense lawyers. They were struck pale with fear.

Bill was positive he'd never felt better in his life.

22

MILTON, FLORIDA

"OKAY, I'M RICH. Now how do I get my hands on the cash?" Dude Codger sat in the front seat of Bill Burnham's Jaguar, windows down, engine off.

It was 11:17 on a steamy night in the parking lot of David's Catfish House in Milton, Florida. An hour and ten-minute drive from Black Point.

"Simple. I should receive $77 million into my trust account within sixty days. I cut my slice off, $25.4 million. Then I proceed into some very, very delicate financial surgery with the other $51 million. Remember, now, you're dead. But I've spent lots of time creating the solution."

"Right, right, let's hear it. I'm game for anything."

"You're in a pinch, Dude. Fifty million bucks and no way to touch it." Bill shook his head. "That's pain, man. This is likely over your head, but I've got a way for you to live with some big bucks in your hand. But, to the world, you're dead."

"Anything, man, you're the genius."

"Okay. I set up a philanthropic foundation with the fifty mil, your money. I go with a public announcement, say this is what the family wants. Call it something like Codger Family Foundation for Traumatic Brain Injury Research ... or something along those lines. Somewhere in the small print I'll bury Dr.

Doris Bell's name. Say something like as a physician she thinks this is a remarkable opportunity to make inroads into brain research with this money. We'll say that Dr. Bell will leave it up to the neuro specialists to suggest the appropriate locations for the money."

"Right, right."

"Let's say we commit to spend one to two million dollars a year on research. But listen closely here, Dude, this is the beauty part. I will set up several bogus research entities, got it? Those organizations will write checks to Joe Blow, MD, or a company name, or whatever. That's you, man! I can get you an ID that says anything. The bulk of the yearly donations end up in your hands. My office manager will oversee the main foundation. She will issue checks to the entities the board suggests, the legitimate research programs, and also the shell research firms. But I will be the only person writing checks to you, Dr. Joe Blow."

Dude slapped the dashboard like he was playing bongos. "Heck, yeah. Heck damn yeah!" "It's like the billboard, boy. Need a big kill, call Wild Bill."

"Yeah, buddy. Knew it was smart calling you."

"Now, Dude, there will naturally be a small administration fee for the service. Handling a foundation ain't as easy as it looks. I think $350,000 per year should cover our time."

"THREE HUNDRED!"

23

FERNANDINA BEACH, FLORIDA

SLEEP WOULDN'T COME. Not just last night but every night since the accident. And the enormous finding against Hendrickson Trucking? Right there Crede knew they were done. But it wasn't the money, it was the battered bodies he witnessed moments after the crash.

It was just as bad reliving it through the courtroom video.

Forty-two pounds of weight had melted off Hendrickson's body since the day the jury found against his company. He was down to 153 pounds on a six-foot-one frame, twelve pounds lighter than he had been as a tenth grader. His skin was pale and drawn, eyes sunken into his skull, and muscle was hanging off his arms and legs.

Twice every waking hour, for over 10,000 hours, Crede's mind screamed WHY WHY WHY? Why in the hell would anyone park where he did?

For over a year he didn't know the one thing he *needed* to know. The critical thing.

Ella Codger was driving the bus with her left knee, looking at her cell phone, distracted, with her right foot pushing down on the gas.

She drove the big yellow sumbitch right off the road!

HENDRICKSON TRUCKING'S INSURANCE didn't completely cover the jury award. His company assets didn't, either. Crede's lawyer quickly filed a Chapter 11 bankruptcy, attempting to reorganize, but was unable to obtain financing. A nationwide search couldn't find a buyer for the company, either. Competitors found it far too easy to just poach customers with horror stories of their shipments never making their destinations.

Chapter 11 went into a Chapter 7 liquidation. All assets sold. Crede's biggest mistake came when he personally guaranteed the loans of the $25 million purchase of new tractors. Now his personal banking and investment accounts were being seized.

The bankruptcy trustee had already been through his oceanfront home three times, interviewing real estate agents who might provide a quick sale.

Crede and Wanda Hendrickson were about to be homeless.

CREDE TOASTED A single slice of bread, lathered it with jelly, half-filled a glass with juice, and took it out to the table on their home's balcony. The mansion sat high on Amelia Island's tallest dune. It was 6:40 in the morning.

Crede didn't see the sunshine, sea oats, sandy beach, or the two-foot surf smacking the shoreline. The earth's tranquil seaside beauty. He was wrestling with thoughts that were strangling knots into his mind. He wasn't sad. Normal people get sad, then they get un-sad. Crede was trapped in a hellish twilight zone of blackness that never let up, a permanent state of exhaustion, but unable to get any sleep to stave it off.

Just like every morning for the past 500 days, he didn't know if he could make it through another twenty-four hours.

"Crede, what's with the suitcase?" His wife had just gotten out of bed, padding in barefoot wearing a nightgown, and spoke through the open balcony door.

"Ummm. Gonna run up to Atlanta today, see a regional vice-president at Suntrust. I might have a chance of getting some bridge loans with this guy. Quick trip. Probably come back late tonight. So, we'll see. Brought a change of clothes just in case."

Crede stood, gave his wife a hug, a longer one than usual.

His thin arm picked up the suitcase with ease. It was empty but for a clean T-shirt and a pair of socks. At the foyer he stopped, turned. "Hey, honey ..."

"Yes." She held his plate, not a single bite off the toast.

Crede's look said he forgot what he was going to say. "Guess it was nothing. Don't wait up."

He kept his eyes on her a few beats, a wan smile on his face and walked out the front door.

Crede Hendrickson had made his decision.

24

CREDE DROVE HIS pickup hard in the direction of Georgia. He planned to take the route his mother likely took almost sixty years ago.

He remembered the day he last saw her like yesterday. His daddy was sleeping off a drunk in baggy undershorts and a stained wifebeater when she pulled out from their little, dilapidated house. She wore one of her modest dresses, likely from Goodwill or a church bazaar donation, with Clorox-bleached Keds on her feet.

It was a hot day, just like today.

A quarter of a century passed before Crede started to understand something his mother told him that day. “Baby, my dumb old head ain’t thinking right.” She was headed to a mental health facility in Milledgeville, Georgia, for some experimental treatments for those without insurance. Something about a federal grant for poor people.

Crede drove through the lonely highways of south Georgia pine forests, ran past the Okefenokee Swamp, drove through Waycross, and hit I-75 at Tifton.

Seventy miles later, just past Perry, Crede spotted a sign advertising The Big House, the Allman Brothers Museum in Macon. His mind jumped back to the eight-track days, a long, long time ago. He had played his *Eat a Peach* album for months at a time until the player ripped the tape out in shreds. He bought another copy the same day.

The truck descended a gentle, miles-long swale in the road after Byron and was rolling slightly uphill toward the bridge, two miles out.

His foot began to push down on the gas pedal. He hit eighty-five, quickly. He veered the truck over to the far-left lane, began passing people. The accelerator was close to the floor-board.

He could feel the speed. Speedometer said ninety. Passing everybody.

Everything a blur.

Then he put the pedal all the way to the floor, practically stood on it. One hundred and seven. The big diesel shot the truck past the traffic.

Hartley Bridge was less than half a mile straight in front of him, the interstate traveling right under it. Clear road.

He was only seconds out. Speedometer said 122.

Crede carefully eased the truck off the highway and down into a concrete embankment in the median like a surgeon, careful not to slingshot across into oncoming traffic. He could almost feel other drivers hitting their brakes or stomping on the gas to get away from a madman.

Nobody wanted to watch what they knew was coming.

He controlled it, the truck. His forearms locked tight. He pushed back hard against the seat. His eyes ran wet with tears. Hot summer air stormed through the open windows.

Crede's body rocked with adrenaline. His pupils blew up, drinking in the green structural steel.

A skyscraper load of concrete was about to swallow him alive.

Mama.

25

MASSACHUSETTS INSTITUTE OF TECHNOLOGY
Cambridge, Massachusetts

ZEUS, THE MASTERMIND of the scheme he's pitching to Lucky, arrived on MIT's campus thirteen years ago and he could not have been more relieved. He was 1,400 miles away from a man he had despised throughout his childhood.

There had been no poignant goodbye dinner the day he'd left. There was no firm handshake and no wish of "good luck" from his stepfather. Stepdaddy had client phone calls to return, and clients were more important than his wife and stepson.

There was a long, lingering hug with his mother. Tears ran down her cheeks, sadness on her face. But there was something else. Zeus didn't realize it until years later as he thought about that moment. There was fear in her eyes.

ZEUS WAS STILL adjusting to dorm life when he received the call from his mother. She blubbered hysterically, barely intelligible. But she was more than sad, she was angry. Two times during the call she moved the phone away from her mouth to scream and curse. She informed her son that her husband, Zeus's stepfather, was dumping her to the curb after fifteen years of marriage.

And the man guaranteed her that she would see little in the way of money.

Eleven minutes after they hung up, Zeus's laptop chimed with the arrival of an email. It was from stepdaddy:

Sorry, champ. The money train is over. Time for the pizza delivery uniform.

This man was an imperious, controlling, arrogant bully.

He was a shitass lawyer.

Zeus was seventeen years and eleven months old when the news hit.

*I WILL NEVER FORGET THIS ... EVER***,** he thought.

FIVE YEARS LATER, Zeus graduated with masters' degrees in computer science and mathematics. And Wall Street wanted quants—basically, math geniuses.

Investment banks on the Street offered Zeus big money. But one man topped them all. Arkady Gerashov, a Russian oligarch with a hedge fund based out of London. Forbes pegged his fortune at $21 billion.

Zeus raced into the creation of algorithmic trading models from financial data. On his own time, he pursued an online MBA from Carnegie Mellon.

Over three years, Zeus was the fuel behind annual returns of 38 percent at the firm. Outrageous success. Gerashov told his bigshots to get out of the kid's way, he was a genius.

Then Zeus hooked into Anatomia Pharmaceuticals, a company whose stock was racing upward. Based in North America, they sold branded niche drugs worldwide and their own Anatomia brand of generics, about twenty extensively prescribed medications.

Anatomia's business plan was very simple. They acquired any and every other pharmaceutical company they were able to swallow. They slashed research and development funding.

There was wholesale firing of high-income scientists. Accounting and HR and advertising were consolidated.

Then they placed the cherry on top. They jacked up drug prices into the stratosphere.

It was outrageous, an outfit run by pirates without a soul. But it was profitable, exorbitantly so.

Zeus steered Gerashov like a pig at a feast. His first buy was $300 million. Then another at $700 million. On average, Anatomia was buying a company every three weeks. Zeus, feeling bulletproof with this outfit, shot in another $900 million of Gerashov's money, closing in on a two-billion-dollar investment in a single company.

Then the storm hit.

The public outcry over the price gouging was deafening. American congressmen were inundated with screaming constituents demanding: Please do something!

They did.

Medicare stopped covering Anatomia's products. The FTC launched a vicious investigation. Anatomia's share prices imploded. The company's valuation declined 80 percent.

Gerashov had $1.7 billion of his investment disappear in an instant. Zeus had blown himself up, too. He personally had thrown every dime he had into Anatomia. He maxed out a personal credit line to invest even more.

Zeus raced out of London stone-cold broke. He was on the hook personally for $3.8 million to the Bank of London.

He went to the last place he ever wanted to go. Back to his stepfather, the shitass lawyer.

But he had a plan.

One hell of a plan.

26

BLACK POINT, ALABAMA

ZEUS DIALED JUNG HAO the day after Lucky agreed to come on board. Jung, a partner in the venture capital fund Point Blue Capital, had been at his desk in Menlo Park, California, for fifty-five minutes when his cell rang. He spotted the caller, smiled, and answered. He knew Zeus from college in Boston.

"Are you harassing me again about DataCage, at what ... seven thirty in the morning?" It was spoken jovially.

"Sorry, Jung. It's just that I'm staring at a nice opportunity. So what's your latest prediction on my equity stake?"

"Well, looking at our time frame, we anticipate an IPO two years from now. Barring anything wacky in the markets, I think your shares should be conservatively worth $4 million, but more likely, six. You did some damn good work on that company. Right now you guys need to keep your foot on the gas to grab market share. Don't worry about profits, yet."

"Need a favor, Jung. Can Point Blue front me $500K on that? Use my equity as collateral?"

Jung exhaled. "Awww, man, that's bad business. Yeah, I can make it happen, but it will cost you eighteen percent per year. It's not cheap money."

"Not a problem. Email the contract. I'll shoot it back to you signed with the account information. And I appreciate it, I really do."

While in London, Zeus put in two years of afterhours time working as a long-distance coder and beta tester for a new venture named DataCage, an intricately encrypted cloud data storage site impervious to cyberattack.

His remuneration was 1 percent equity in the company.

27

NEW ORLEANS
Three Days Later

ZEUS DROVE HIS Subaru to the destination, spotted the house number, drove around the block, and came back to a stop sign at Magazine Street. The neighborhood had a voodoo feel to it. No telling what kind of creeps watching him out of their windows.

He parked on the street, walked past an antiques shop, a taqueria, and a vinyl record shop, jaywalked across Magazine, stepped up on a rumpled sidewalk, passed a vintage clothing shop with a scrum of eccentric women standing in front of it, chirping like they were plotting a flash demonstration of some sort.

New Orleans ... *Maybe they're not women.*

He cut down a side street, spotted the home, and traipsed up three weathered steps to reach the warped wooden front porch. It was a two-story faded blue Victorian.

The house served as residence and office of Meg Zimmerman.

Meg, early sixties and California slim, answered after the third knock wearing faded bell bottoms and circular, black-framed glasses. A smattering of colorful beads jangled on each wrist.

"You must be Harrison Holt, please come in. Okay, so I've got cold water, tea, Cokes, lemonade, beer, gin, rum, bourbon, and banana popsicles. What can I get you?" Her smile was bright and warm.

"A popsicle with a side of ice water sounds great, thanks." He wore a thick, dark beard, and his hair was tousled, hanging to mid-ear. In anticipation of a makeover, Zeus hadn't shaved or cut his hair for a month.

Meg extended her arm. "Have a seat in the den, Harrison, right around the corner."

Zeus admired the room, brightly lit with a wall of French windows looking out over a lush courtyard. The room had twelve-foot ceilings, white walls, and was filled with distressed-wood furnishings painted in an airy palette of pastels. Two deep-blue vases of tulips emitted a soft botanical fragrance.

Zeus squinted at a photo in a burnished silver frame. Brad Pitt in *The Curious Case of Benjamin Button.* He knew it was filmed in New Orleans. Did Meg handle makeup? *Damn.*

"Here you go, Harrison." Meg returned, sat on the opposite end of the couch, pushed a water glass in his direction. "Cheers, my new friend." Their glasses tinkled, each took a sip, then she slid her legs under her and sat back into a tea-stained cushion. Both peeled back the thin wrap covering their popsicles.

"Now, how may I be of service? I believe you said it was quite important and there was an urgency."

Zeus had found Meg on the web under searches for theatrical makeup artists. Thirty years in Hollywood had landed her three Emmys and two Academy Awards, and ample funds for retirement. She moved back home to aid in the care of her father, but still worked as an occasional consultant.

"It's delicate, Ms. Zimmerman. And embarrassing and heartbreaking at the same time. It's about my wife."

"Oh, dear. But, please, call me Meg." She reached into an antique silver bowl full of colorful gummies on the coffee table. "I think I need one of these, something a friend sends me from a little shop in Santa Monica." She plopped a red one in her mouth, chewed. "Mmm, sweet. I'm about to be infused with a delightful patina of THC coating my spirit." She held the bowl out to Zeus.

"Thanks." He took a green one, tossed it in his mouth.

After swallowing, Zeus said, "Meg, I don't want to go into it too deeply because I'll get emotional. I hate to cry in front of someone I've just met. Here's the deal."

Zeus leaned in with earnestness. "My wife is having an affair with a coworker. She denies it, but it's just one of those things you can feel, you know it in your gut. All closeness we had has vanished. I feel a disdain from her toward me, but I have no idea what I've done. The worst part is we have two kids, four and six." He looked down, shook his head.

"Oh my, I'm so sorry."

"I've confronted her about my thoughts, and she completely denies everything. I've suggested counseling. If there's anything I've done I want to correct it. I've even told her if she wants a divorce, I will make it quick and amicable. She comes back at me asking if I want a divorce. I tell her hell no; I want us to be a happy family. But all she says is nothing is going on, and she's happy. Well, something is going on, and I'm not happy."

Meg picked up the silver bowl again. "Please, Harrison, have another. This is a two-gummy story." She ate another herself.

"Thanks. These things are mellow. Feeling better already."

"Not sure a makeup artist is what you need."

"Meg, I'm not looking for marital advice. I have a plan I want to carry out. I just can't go on like this and I don't want to hire private detectives for thousands and go through all that crap.

I'm going to do the snooping myself. And I'm going to confront her."

"Okay."

"Here's what I need. I want you to transform me into a man in his fifties. I want a disguise so perfect that I could stand right next to her and have her not recognize me."

Meg nodded, focused on the ask.

"She's going on a business trip to Chicago for a week and I'm going to be there. My parents know all of this and they're going to keep the kids."

Meg took a sip of water, stuck her remnant popsicle stick in the wrapping, glanced out at the courtyard a moment, looked back at Zeus.

"Fairly simple task, really. Glad you don't want to be younger. That's difficult. I'll tell you what's easy. I can make you older, heavier, and taller. I'll turn you into a meek wallflower of a guy, layered into gray and browns, a nondescript nobody that people wouldn't take a second look at."

"That's it exactly, Meg. A nondescript nobody."

28

MANHATTAN, NEW YORK

THE 7 TRAIN, packed as tight as a cattle car, screeched to a halt at the Times Square-42nd Street subway stop, causing its captives to hold on, fight off the inertia forces. The doors slid open, signaling every man for himself. A funnel of humanity raced to the steps to reach street level.

Zeus emerged, checked his watch. It was 5:15 p.m. Fifteen minutes early.

His navy suitcoat ballooned outward, with the fat padding around his trunk providing a distinct middle-age paunch under a white dress shirt accessorized with a red tie. He was now six feet, two inches tall thanks to dark, three-inch elevator loafers. His forehead was carefully shaved and waxed into receding male-pattern baldness, while the rest of his dark hair had been thinned and infiltrated with strands of gray.

Zeus was now a tall, aging, distinguished businessman with a salt-and-pepper goatee.

He began walking with intent, not looking anyone in the eye, feeling a jittery anxiety settle in about the impending meeting.

Found this person on the darknet. This guy wouldn't be a Boy Scout.

He followed four women with rolling luggage into the lobby of the Sheraton Midtown Hotel, stopped, glanced around the lobby, thinking, *This could be a huge mistake.*

He had been instructed to wait in the lobby to receive instructions via text.

ZEUS WAS PAYING no attention to a mid-50s man in large glasses, wearing a brown-hued bowling shirt over gray slacks, reading the colorful *USA TODAY* newspaper. He sat in a chair in the far corner of the lobby. His cell phone had a text ready to send to the burner Zeus carried. The man pushed SEND.

Go to Room 3321.

The man saw Zeus glance at his phone, hesitate, then move toward the elevators. As the elevator door closed, the man texted another message to a different number.

In the elevator.

Then the man watched the lobby to see if anyone appeared to follow Zeus.

AS ZEUS EXITED the elevator onto the 33rd floor, he encountered a woman with a messenger bag over her shoulder. "We're not going to 3321. Follow me."

Jitters racked his stomach. They entered a cold, dank stairwell and walked down two stories to the 31st floor.

Walking down, he noticed she was wearing latex gloves. That was not reassuring. She took him to Room 3113, placed the keycard in the lock, and entered.

Zeus swallowed hard crossing the threshold.

Reaching the middle of the room, the woman pulled a metal-detecting wand from her bag. "Stand still for me, please. Let's make this quick. Do you have a cell phone?"

"No."

"A wallet with ID?"

"No."

"Any type of weapon or recording device?"

"No."

"Last chance to change that answer and remain friends. Anything?"

"No, nothing. Just the money."

She switched on the wand, then scanned over every inch of Zeus. Beeep. It went off over his left forearm. "Roll up your sleeve."

Zeus exposed his watch, one he'd bought in London.

"I'll take the watch." She looked at it. "Rolex. Excellent timepiece." She shook it, pulled the time-set wheel in and out, spun the hands. She dropped it to the tile floor in the bathroom, crushed it with her heel. Flushed eight thousand dollars of intricate watch parts down the commode. "We said nothing. A watch is something."

Zeus felt a knot in his stomach.

The woman squatted, started patting up each of his legs. Ran her hands up and down each arm, patted his trunk front and back, thoroughly inspected Zeus's crotch.

"Clean gloves. Open your mouth." She took her little finger and pulled open each cheek, looked around.

"Prosthetics. Smart. Cash stored in the fat pad?"

"Yes."

"Follow me." They left the room. She walked toward the stairwell.

Their steps echoed off the gray, musty concrete walls as they walked down an additional six floors, holding the metal-pipe handrail as they traveled.

Great place to get your ass kicked. Or killed. Bad idea. All of this.

They exited the stairwell and walked midway down a carpeted hallway that smelled of linen-scented carpet powder.

The prosthetics left Zeus's mouth feeling dry, or maybe it was cotton-mouth from nerves. He thought about the darknet ad that put him in a Manhattan stairwell with who knows what coming at him around the corner.

The website was NuYu.onion, a site to be opened only with the Tor browser.

NuYu.
The Finest Document Reproductions in The World
Your Face and Background on Anything Known to Man
EXPENSIVE-Guaranteed Satisfaction-EXPENSIVE
Tommy Xerox

They stopped at Room 2514. The woman knocked five times.

Zeus's gut ached. He thought, *Five thousand in hundreds on me and not one soul knows where the hell I am. Huge mistake.*

The door swung open. "Good evening, sir. Please come in. I'm Tommy Xerox." No handshake. Tommy swung his arm. "Come have a seat."

Tommy pulled up two chairs to a small table that held a manila envelope, one unopened water bottle, and a bottled tea. He closed the blinds, shutting off the view to the Manhattan buildings that were now coming alive with lights.

TOMMY WAS AN ordinary-sized man, maybe five-foot-ten, not more than 165 pounds, late sixties by the look of him. He wore a beard and glasses. An English driving cap matched his tweed sport coat.

An elaborate latex mask covered his face, but it was indiscernible. Tommy Xerox looked nothing like Wesley Gunterson, his real name.

Thirty-three years ago, Gunterson caught a help wanted ad in a Phoenix newspaper. *State Department Needs Artists. European Travel.* Sounded much more interesting than his job doing technical drawings for a defense contractor.

State Department? Common ploy. Over thirty years, Gunterson became the head of the Documents Department in the CIA's Technical Services Division. He also spent time as a case officer on the street, running spies in every corner of the world. He retired. His wife got cancer. Their savings went up in smoke trying to save her.

She died leaving him depressed, lonely, and largely broke.

So Tommy Xerox did what he knew how to do.

Tommy appraised Zeus, who sat across from him. "You've got some balls, you know that? Meeting someone in person from a darknet contact." Tommy shook his head. "Carrying cash, too. Likely seventy percent of those people would kill you and go on their merry way with your money."

"I have a crew tailing me."

Tommy harrumphed. "No, you don't. One thing I can guarantee. My boys and girls can spot a tail. Anywhere, anytime. You're alone, but no worries. I won't kill you." Tommy pointed to the envelope. "That's what you ordered. Take a peek."

Tommy grabbed the raspberry tea, wrenched off the cap, and took two huge swigs. "I swear I'm hooked on this stuff." He didn't offer any to Zeus, on purpose.

Tommy felt sure no cop would go undercover on a meet like this without backup. If the lobby lookout had a sniff of police, Zeus wouldn't be in the room. *So,* Tommy wondered, *who the hell was this guy?*

Zeus dumped the contents over the table. US Passport, Kentucky driver's license, social security card, birth certificate, utility bill from LG & E matching the Louisville address of the driver's license. The photograph on the documents matched the man sitting across from Tommy Xerox. The name was Edward Thomas Hurley.

Zeus fingered the documents, studied them closely. Same high-tech passport paper. Raised document seals. Holograms. "Wow. Looks real."

"Sir, those *are* real," said Tommy. "If you like them, I'll gladly take $5,000 from you tonight. But I do believe you mentioned multiple items."

Zeus pointed a finger at the unopened water. "You mind?"

"Please help yourself, sir." *Yes, my friend, get your grubby fingerprints on the bottle.*

"That's right, Tommy," said Zeus. "I need 125 different sets. Different information, same photo."

Tommy Xerox flung his head back, whistled at the ceiling. "Wow. $625,000."

"Nope. Dealing in volume now. Time for a price adjustment."

Tommy rubbed his chin, looked at Zeus. "Very curious about that, 125 copies, but I won't ask. How do I know you're not the FBI?"

"I don't think the FBI would be looking at a buy that outrageous, do you?" said Zeus. "Too many red flags."

"Wouldn't think so, no."

"So, here's the deal," said Zeus. "I'll give you $1,000 per set. And I want to see where you make the documents."

Tommy shook his head, looked at Zeus. Thought a moment. "That's quite amusing, sir. First, last, and only counteroffer. Two thousand dollars per set, total of a quarter million, and under no circumstances do you see where we make the sausage."

"Well, I don't know." said Zeus.

"Okay, sir. Close your eyes. Spark your imagination for a moment. My document room is pristine, like a pharmaceutical lab. Bright white enamel-painted floor, stainless-steel work counters, daylight wavelength LED lighting, magnifier lamps on the tables, Halo-Neutrodine air-filtering machinery to eliminate contaminants from the air."

"I use Gemalto security papers from Amsterdam, like most of the world governments. They're stored at a perfect temperature in a dark, airtight room. I use the world's finest printers, Leibinger, from Germany. I also employ Evolis holograph card printers, used worldwide and throughout the US."

Zeus held precision evidence in his hand. "Okay, Tommy, let's do it. Bitcoin work for you?"

"Preferred, actually."

Tommy stood, took his drink and Zeus's empty water bottle, threw them in the trash. Looking back, he said, "I know you'll be very pleased with the product. And I thank you for the business. Please wait here with my colleague for fifteen minutes before leaving." He dipped his chin. "Have a pleasant evening."

Tommy Xerox left the hotel through the kitchen to a waiting van in the back alley.

His female associate was reading the *Times* on her laptop when a timer sounded on her phone. "I guess we're done here. Good luck on your endeavors."

Ten minutes after Zeus left, she collected both plastic bottles from the lined trash container, placed them in a freezer bag and placed it in her messenger bag. She wiped down the table, chairs, and doorknobs, and was on her way.

Tommy Xerox would have a report on Zeus's fingerprints within three hours.

29

ATLANTA, GEORGIA

THE FEDEX BOX contained $250,000 dollars of cargo. Zeus picked it up at a shipping outlet located next to a Kroger in a northwest Atlanta shopping center.

It contained full ID packages for the 125 top-earning trial lawyers in America. Real people. Real addresses.

But they all used the photo of Zeus after his transformation by Meg Zimmerman in New Orleans.

DELTA FLIGHT 1466 departed from Hartsfield Jackson at 8:41 the following morning. The manifest had William Burnham, a lawyer from Black Point, Alabama, onboard the flight.

Zeus sat in his seat.

It was a one-way flight to Panama City, Panama.

From Panama, over the next three weeks, Zeus established accounts in multiple banks in Nevis, Singapore, Hong Kong, Georgia, in Eastern Europe, Isle of Mann, Lichtenstein, Denmark, Estonia, Netherlands, Thailand, and Luxembourg.

Zeus planned to control money distribution algorithms utilizing public Wi-Fi in coffee shops, fast-food outlets, and libraries, operating in locational secrecy via Tor and virtual private networks.

Extortion money from the trial lawyers would leave the receiving bank in multiple increments going to other banks. The funds would morph into Bitcoin. Bitcoin would be converted to Monero, a completely untraceable cryptocurrency, where the assets would hibernate in an opaque crypto cold wallet. A place where funds are locked from access via the web.

Depending on circumstances, it could take six months to years for the FBI and the IRS to locate and trace through the accounts before they realized the worst.

The money vanished.

30

MISSION BEACH, CALIFORNIA

"WE GOT NOTHING." That was the message Zeus passed to Lucky after sending a gentle, threat-free invitation to twenty-five lawyers. *Please send millions of dollars overseas. Thank you.*

"That was preposterous. Think I'm dealing with a deluded quack," said Lucky, snorting cynically.

"You're definitely not, I assure you. Tried to be a nice guy. But no more. Watch your mailbox. There's a package coming your way. It's time for hardball."

FIVE DAYS LATER, Lucky sat alone, sprawled on a chaise by the apartment's small pool. He wore a warm, fleece pullover while he read the last chapter of a James Lee Burke novel. He looked up when he heard the boxy, white mail truck rumbling into the complex.

He approached the driver with his driver's license in his hand. "I think you may have a package for me."

The mail carrier glanced at his only box. "I sure do."

Lucky took it by the corner with his thumb and pointer finger. The mail carrier noticed. "Whatcha expecting, anthrax?" He laughed as he fast-walked toward the complex's mailroom.

In his apartment, Lucky studied it. Fifteen dollars and fifty-eight cents postage, no insurance, no receipt to sign. Postmarked Hattiesburg, Mississippi.

He sliced the clear packaging tape at one end with a kitchen knife.

Out came a magazine, a burner phone, a laptop, and a sheet of white copy paper containing typed information.

He began to read.

YOU WILL NOW BE SWIMMING WITH SHARKS
REMEMBER—GHOST PROTOCOL—ANONYMITY—PRIVACY

The Laptop is setup with:

1-Tor Browser—The gold standard anonymity tool.
2-PROTON VPN—Virtual Private Network to mask IP address.
3-PGP—Encryption tool for text documents.
4-VERACRYPT—Computer encryption (please note your passwords to boot computer)

TO USE COMPUTER—

1-Go to *crowded* public Wi-Fi.
2-Assume you're on video
3-Boot up through Veracrypt
4-Activate Proton VPN
5-Utilize Tor browser
6-Log on to DataCage cloud site
7-Use Private PGP key to open the encrypted document.
8-POWER DOWN computer when done.

COMMUNICATION:

Use DataCage—the tightest encrypted cloud site on the planet.

ENCRYPT your docs with PGP prior to sending to DataCage.

DataCage—Login credentials:
USER: LoOpfRuiTt2jc!
PASSWORD: K$Vb*wWw@7%JmyZpqqA90#bDz!

PHONE

Use the phone to call the only preset number in contacts. LET IT RING ONE TIME ONLY THEN HANG UP. THAT IS THE SIGNAL TO CHECK DATACAGE—ONE RING ONLY!

NEVER ANSWER THE PHONE!!

NOW PROCEED

1-Make a hardball example of the shyster on the magazine cover, a lawyer in Charleston. I said HARDBALL!
2-Black Point, Alabama. Turn Attorney William Burnham's Rolls Royce into dust. Just the car, NOT him. Make it a SPECTACLE!

Lucky read and reread the instructions. It told him something. Zeus was organized.

And dangerous.

31

CHARLESTON, SOUTH CAROLINA

LUCKY ENTERED THE downtown Doubletree Hotel wearing stone-colored chinos with a color-matched sportscoat over an Indian madras shirt. Looking sharp. Could have been a tourist or a businessman.

He registered under the name of Dr. John Turner, a scientist with AmGreen Research. Presenting a Maryland driver's license, a Visa card, and a bogus laminated badge that said AmGreen, he made easy chitchat with the trim, early-twenties woman handling his registration. Offhandedly, he stated he was meeting with some scientists at the Medical University of South Carolina.

"Oh, cool, Dr. Turner. What's your specialty?"

"My doctorate is in plant pathology. I'm not a medical doctor."

"I didn't know the med school worked with plants, too."

"Well, it's confusing. AmGreen joint ventures with entities worldwide in efforts to genetically alter some plants to provide beneficial pharmaceutical applications."

Her cheeks scrunched; her eyes sparkled. "Wow. Makes me think of good weed." She blushed, flicking her eyes playfully left to right, then smiled. "Oops, I didn't say that."

Lucky smiled, too. With his key card, he walked toward the elevator.

Entering his room, it hit him. The legend I just presented was too memorable. Become a ghost. Shut your damn mouth!

He washed his face and brushed his teeth, readying for the first order of business. Pay respect to an old doctor.

LUCKY SPOTTED SECURITY cameras tracking every step as he ambled down the hall of the Live Oak Nursing Facility in North Charleston.

He located Room 152, gave a slight knock-knock on the doorframe. The door was partially opened in an effort to fight off the loneliness of the residents.

Dr. Mike Grantham, in his late seventies, looked Lucky's way, unfamiliarity in his eyes.

With sports balls and photos and trophies and pom-poms, the room was a shrine of love and respect. Grantham had been a high school team doctor for forty years.

Lucky knew he was in the presence of an honest-to-God legend.

Floating in the air was an unmistakable scent of piss, poo, and aging flesh preparing takeoff to eternity. On low in the background, a radio preacher was speaking on the Parable of the Sower.

He pulled a chair close to the bed. Looking into Dr. Grantham's defeated eyes, Lucky placed his hand on the doctor's right forearm. The skin was pale, withered, cool. Right-side stroke, the receptionist said. Doc's body was decaying to nothing.

"My name is not important, Dr. Grantham. You don't know me, but I know you. I've read about you and your career. What I read was the legacy of one of South Carolina's finest physicians."

Grantham's body didn't so much as twitch. Drool puddled at the right corner of his mouth. His right eye had a layer of ointment to keep it moist, but it skewed his vision.

"Dr. Grantham, I need to know if you can understand what I'm saying. Please blink your eyes twice if you hear and understand me."

The doctor's left eye blinked twice.

Lucky had stumbled onto Dr. Grantham's name while he was deep into his background intel on trial lawyer Braxton Green, the target. A Charleston weekly had published a magnificent tribute on Grantham's life, concluding with the sad news of the stroke.

Braxton Green had filed a finagled malpractice lawsuit against Dr. Grantham that was infused with lies and misrepresentations. Fifty-one years in medicine and the doc had never been sued. Not once.

Not until Braxton Green came calling.

Advertising to individuals with lung cancer, Green dug up a couple who were struggling to pay their oncology medical bills. Both had smoked since they were fifteen. Both had lung cancer. They were Dr. Grantham's patients for thirty years. He advised them to stop smoking at every visit. Said it in conversation, way too busy to write it down.

Green dangled the possibility of big money in front of these rubes. Grantham was at fault, he let them down. Their own doctor had handed them a death sentence.

Greedy, they lied on the stand. The jury was too ignorant to see through Green's fairytale.

When the verdict was read, Grantham suffered a stroke in his seat.

Lucky obtained the trial transcript. He thought of his father.

And he fumed.

"I know what Green did." Lucky's voice was soft, gentle, barely above a whisper. "I know all aspects of the legal case and the absurdity of it. Many, many, many people find it unconscionable." Lucky emphasized this point with his raised eyebrows. "I know it pains you beyond description to have felt his attack on your character and your life's work."

Dr. Grantham's eyes bored right into Lucky's skull. His left eye blinked twice.

"I know who you are, Dr. Grantham. You're a compassionate man filled with goodness, one of the finest doctors South Carolina has ever had. I also wanted you to know that Braxton Green won't be practicing law much longer."

With that, Lucky picked up Dr. Grantham's cold right hand, patted it a couple of times.

"I'm not cut from the same cloth as you, doctor. I'm not a compassionate man. I am an angry man, a vindictive man. I'm also a very dangerous man who will have no mercy on Green."

Grantham's left eye blinked three times.

Lucky stood, slid the chair back to its spot, readied to leave, then spotted a Bible peeking from under the blanket next to the doctor. He sat back down, slid it from underneath the bedclothes. It had a rugged black cover with a name engraved in gold in the lower right: Michael J. Grantham. Some of the delicate pages were loose, many passages were underlined, and notes were written willy-nilly in the margins.

"Dad read the Bible to me almost every night until I graduated high school. He liked to explain things, the meanings of parables and such. Dad was a good man, a church man, just like you."

Lucky started flipping pages, searching for a passage. "I want to read something short. Dad said a well-worn Bible was an extraordinarily valuable family heirloom. Okay, here we are.

The Old Testament, Book of Proverbs, chapter eleven, verse ten." Lucky glanced up and saw Grantham focused.

"When the wicked perish, there is jubilation."

He peeked over the text into Grantham's eyes. The doctor blinked five times.

Lucky tucked the Bible back in the covers as he had found it, squeezed Grantham on the shoulder and sashayed out of the room, leaving the door half open, as he found it.

THE DOCTOR DIDN'T know what to think about that unexpected visit. A dangerous man? The clean-cut fellow looked like he'd measure you for a suit at a local haberdashery, then pick out some matching ties. Maybe weighed a buck-seventy. Five-eleven, six feet? But dangerous? That couldn't be right.

Could it?

32

BATTERY PARK WATERFRONT
Charleston, South Carolina

STANDING AMONG THE oaks, palms, and azaleas in Battery Park, Lucky eyed an intricately detailed antebellum home with breathtaking views of Charleston harbor.

It was the mansion of Braxton Green, Esquire, a well-known Charleston litigator. And a successful one at that. Reports indicated that Green had pulled down over $250 million in settlements in the last decade.

Lucky strolled the waterfront dressed as a low country good ol' boy. T-shirt with the sleeves cut off, baggy dungarees, and an orange Clemson Tigers cap. His physique was wiry with some twisty cord muscle, like a runner or bicyclist, but intimidation was not part of thc package.

If people knew his story, they might reconsider.

Special Ops training in Coronado, California, had taught him skills to be everywhere and nowhere. He moved as quiet as blown smoke, cautiously slow, yet fast. Deployments in South America, Eastern Europe, and the Middle East introduced him to trouble. Some of it was the worst kind of trouble.

He was the smallest man in his operator's class at six feet, 178 pounds, but near the top on intelligence and physical stamina.

Lucky was a deeply calculating man.

This operation had no tight timeline like he had on special forces missions. This allowed tactical patience to reveal a pattern of life. He would develop the target, stack the odds in his favor.

Wealthy, soft, White people.

He liked the odds already.

33

HALLETT GREEN, BRAXTON'S wife, rolled out of bed, padded to her bathroom, peed, brushed her teeth, and washed her face. She smiled wide, leaned in toward the mirror, and wondered if she should try to squeeze in a teeth-whitening treatment today.

Coming back into her bedroom, she pulled a new tennis outfit out of her closet and dressed. It was the same style worn by one of the six-foot Russian blonds at the yearly Family Circle Tournament. In Hallett's mind that was how she looked on the court, only five inches shorter. Short skirt with a racerback top, sexily exposing toned arms and shoulders.

In the mirror she saw tight and trim. Couldn't restrain a smile.

She glanced at her watch, grabbed her phone from the dresser, tapped a contact. "Hey, girl, wanted to let you know I'll be five minutes late. See you at the club in twenty. Oh, oh, almost forgot. I'm leaving for Barcelona in the morning, so I'll miss the next match."

Lucky was listening in on Hallett's conversation from the attic on the fourth story of the home. He was lying on a yoga mat using his backpack as a pillow. Earbuds were in each ear.

Yesterday morning, after witnessing all the occupants leaving the house, Lucky had disabled the alarm, picked the lock of the garage door facing the rear alley, entered, and got the lay of the land. After studying the floor plan, he installed covert, wireless, radio-frequency bugs in the main living areas of the house. All bugs transmitted to a small receiver sitting next to him in the attic.

"Leaving for Barcelona tomorrow," she said.

Well, then. Today's the day.

34

KING STREET, DOWNTOWN CHARLESTON

7:03 A.M. "WHATCHA GOT, Jerrels? Let's crank this thing up," Braxton Green said into the phone. Jerrels was three minutes late. A junior partner, he was due precisely every morning at seven in Braxton's office to review cases.

After two hours of meetings, Braxton lost his focus, thinking. Eight days with Hallett in Europe would surely test his sanity. Once his wife started talking, it would be a week of exhaustive droning about listings, undervalued appraisals, and unqualified blowhards trying to purchase real estate outside of their price point.

He punched a call to his primary executive assistant, Gracie, one of the best hires he ever made. She was a hyper-efficient multitasker with an innate feel for productive workflow.

"Gracie, I've cleared your office schedule for the rest of the day. We have a table for a business lunch at Hall's at eleven forty-five. Why don't you run home to get ready ... and wear something appropriate." Braxton softened his tone. "Oh, and don't forget that red lipstick I love."

Gracie was thirty-four, sixteen years younger than Braxton, very natural with a trim figure, and a single mother of two beautiful boys, eight and ten. Her untalented, free-thinking, starving-artist husband divorced her three years ago, claiming he just didn't want to be chained down by an adventure-less wife.

So she would arrive ten minutes early to the steakhouse, freshly bathed, smelling of Chanel, wearing a sleeveless black dress, racy lingerie, and glossy black high heels. Her lunch would be a small piece of grilled fish with a salad and a half glass of wine. After Braxton finished his second martini, they'd rendezvous in an intimate pied-à-terre he owned, two blocks away.

She would leave with $500 dollars in tax-free cash that would help pay for her sons' activities.

Braxton would leave knowing he was living the American Dream.

8:30 A.M. HALLETT SPED AWAY from the mansion in a black Range Rover, heading to her tennis club.

Lucky left the home ten minutes later, with his surveillance gear.

9:30 A.M. LUCKY RODE the elevator down, donning a crisp suit while rolling his travel suitcase, with a laptop bag over his shoulder. He picked up a free *USA Today* off a table by the elevator and strolled to the front desk.

"Dr. Turner, you look as if you may have concluded your business. Are you leaving us?" The clerk had blemish-free dark skin and bright eyes. Her accent was from the islands, pleasant.

"Yes. And the work has been very productive." His tone exuded happy cheer.

"Headed to Maryland this morning?" she asked, looking at the address on his receipt.

"Yes, this afternoon, actually. In three weeks, I leave for Japan for a two-month project. Looking forward to Tokyo."

"Thank you again for selecting Doubletree. We hope your travels are safe."

Leaving the hotel, Lucky felt his first taste of adrenaline.

35

LUCKY STEPPED OUT of a clean, white Ford cargo van he had parked on Water Street, a short two blocks from the Green mansion.

He wore his tan suit accented by an ivory-colored Stetson straw fedora on his head. Except for the duffel in his right hand, he looked every bit the bon vivant strolling Calle Obispo in Havana.

Entering the home, he went straight to the second-floor den. The contents of the duffel were emptied onto the floor. He then undressed out of his slacks and sportscoat, placed them neatly in a chair, and slid into a black, body-hugging outfit.

With the balaclava mask covering his head, he now presented a sinister appearance.

The oddball stash of equipment on the floor included duct tape, plastic flex cuffs, a primeval tomahawk, a stainless-steel straight razor, and two Canon Mark IV high-definition cameras.

11:30 A.M. HALLETT WALKED into the club tennis shop. Armend Baehler, the thirty-three-year-old Danish tennis pro, was focused on the racket he was stringing.

"How'd you do?" he asked.

"Won big. What else could happen?"

"Excellent." Armend nodded, didn't look up, kept manipulating the strings.

"Going to be in Europe all the way through next week, and the stress is through the roof. Any ideas how to manage that?"

Armend didn't so much as move his head as he glanced with his eyes in her direction. Impish grin. "I just might. Thirty minutes?"

"Works perfectly. If you see steam coming from the bathroom, I just might be embarrassingly naked in a soothing hot shower. So be a gentleman and don't peek."

11:50. HALLETT WALKED INTO her bedroom suite, glanced at her watch as she slipped it off. She had a solid two hours of playtime. Her husband texted earlier that he had a long afternoon business meeting. Lovely.

She kicked off her tennis shoes, peeled up her top, dropped her skirt and panties to the floor.

Lucky was mostly hidden behind a chair in the corner, sitting with his knees pulled tight to his chest. He had a full vantage point to the room. Ops had trained him to be motionless and silent for hours awaiting an ambush.

Hallett opened the bottom drawer to her dresser. She pushed some folded flannel pajamas to the side and pulled out what she was looking for. Sex lube, four straps covered in black velvet, and a mask. She tossed them on the king-sized bed, walked out of the bedroom singing an old Sting tune, and moseyed across the hall to her oversize bathroom.

Ten minutes into her shower, Lucky heard her playful female voice. "Well, look who's here." *Good, Braxton's home.*

Armend dropped his tennis whites to the bathroom floor. Hallett opened the glass door. "Welcome, sir."

Ten minutes later, Hallett and Armend dried each other with two resort-grade towels. She grabbed his hand, walked him to the bedroom.

"Today, I'm the pro. You're the student," she said.

Major complication, Lucky thought. *Not Braxton.*

Hallett cinched Armend's wrists and ankles to the bed. She kissed him on the mouth, then slipped the mask on him. "I could barely sleep last night thinking about what I wanted to do with you." Her words floated with a sultry southern sway.

She squirted a little sex lube on her hand and applied it to herself. "Here, how about a little on you. Oh my, look at you ... is all of that for me?"

Armend was young. He needed no foreplay. Hallett took control. She came out of the gate like she was running a 100-meter dash.

Lucky was surprised at the naughty mouth on the woman. A live, cougar porno film was taking place right next to him. While he found the whole scene erotic, he was on a mission.

He stood from his position.

Hallett, hot, moist, and breathing hard, sensed movement in her left peripheral vision. She glanced to the side. What? Blackness.

Then she saw white around Lucky's pupils.

Her scream lasted six seconds. It was visceral, scorching. Her body shook. She flew off of Armend.

Lucky stepped up to the bed. Hallett screamed again as she swatted at him with both hands.

"What! What! What!" said Armend. "What's the matter, Hallett?"

She didn't answer. She hopped off the bed on the side away from Lucky, began grabbing at her clothes.

"Keep your clothes off." Lucky's tone was even and soft, without menace.

Hearing a man's voice, Armend began thrashing madly. He flung his head side to side, trying to release the mask. A waste of energy.

Lucky walked around the bed, straight toward Hallett's shrieking. Her face flushed deep red as she squatted into a fighter's crouch. Jugular veins bulged. Hands drew into fists. Her heart squeezed harder. Adrenaline seared through every cell.

She grabbed her phone off the dresser. Lucky snatched it from her hand and smashed it on the floor with his heel. He wore a pistol holstered low on his right thigh and a taser on his left waist.

He backed up several steps and slid the Sig P226 out of the holster. He extended his right arm, with the barrel three feet from Hallett's chest. She covered her breasts with her arms.

"I promise you I won't miss. So if you don't mind, I'd like to do this the easy way."

Hallett's body shuddered. Her chin bobbed up and down.

"Good. We're going to the den."

Lucky went to the bed, leaned down to whisper in Armend's ear. Armend sensed his proximity and became still as a statue. "Do exactly as I say and you will get through this. Stay still and do not say one word. Not one."

Armend figured Hallett's husband had found out about his wife's sexual proclivities and wanted to send a strong message to them.

The dreadful truth was far more dire.

36

AT 3:37 P.M., HALLETT'S SON, Brax, drove his Jeep into the back alley, parked close to the house, grabbed his backpack, and hustled into the back door.

He grabbed a Coke and a couple of cookies in the kitchen. "I'm home," he hollered. No response. He'd spotted his mother's car in the garage.

He bounded up the main staircase to the second floor, lost in thought of what he needed to pack. Three steps down the second-floor hallway he came to a dead stop.

There was a figure in front of him, dressed in black, totally silent.

"Whoa!" Brax froze. His face scrunched. "What the hell's going on?"

Standing eighteen feet away, the black silhouette tossed two pairs of high-tensile nylon flex cuffs at the teenager's feet.

"Sit down on the floor, please. Take your shoes off and place the first pair around your ankles and cinch them tight. Then put your arms behind your back and slide the other pair over your hands until they reach your wrists." It was a gentle instruction.

Brax was tall like his father, had four inches on this guy. Probably outweighed Lucky by twenty-five pounds. "Screw you, dude." Suddenly, he grew a set of balls. Brax dropped his Coke can and charged Lucky.

A nine-millimeter round shattered the boy's right knee before he could reach Lucky. Brax went down hard, howling like the wounded animal he was.

Lucky walked over to the flex cuffs and kicked them back to Brax. "Your right shoulder is next. So let's start over. Ankles first, then your wrists."

The teenager struggled to get the cuffs over his ankles.

"Now get in your bedroom."

Brax slid into the room on his left side, crying the whole way. Lucky duct-taped the kid's mouth. Then he squatted next to the boy. "Not a single word and you will be alright. If I hear a peep from you, I will be back to put bullets in both of your shoulders. You will be f-ed up for life. That's a promise. Do you understand?"

Brax nodded.

LUCKY WALKED OUT of the bedroom, closed the door. Needed to think. He sat on the floor in the hallway, leaned against the wall.

His thoughts raced back to his training days. Day after day after day of intensity. Everything geared to break him mentally and physically, only to make him stronger, focused on survival. Ambush techniques swirled through his mind. Then exfiltration. Lucky lived through many situations that evoked cold, stark fear.

Coming into this lily-white tableau, he didn't want to muff it up with absentminded carelessness.

Forty-eight minutes later, Lucky heard the electric garage-door opener fire into action. Not even fifteen seconds until he heard the rumble again, the door lowering. There was a slight bump as it hit the floor.

A door slammed on the first floor. It was the man of the hour.

Braxton Green ambled up the stairs with mail in one hand, his suit jacket in the other. He slowed as he started flipping through envelopes.

"Where is everybody?" He spoke loudly. "We have a big trip, people." He was still floating on a high of masculine superiority after a vigorous romp with Gracie.

Lucky had moved from the hallway to the den, with Hallett. He verified the positions on the two tripod-mounted Canons and started the video on both.

Braxton turned to walk down the hall to his bedroom. "Where is everybody?" Talking to air. Looking at mail.

It was a single moan at first. He stopped, listened. The sound was from the end of the hall. Dead silence, otherwise.

The sound came again, but it was louder. Braxton dropped the mail and jacket, made a quick dash down the length of the hall, stopped right outside the door of the den. He looked in.

Hallett was splayed out before him, naked, and trussed down on the couch with duct tape.

"Jesus dear God!" Braxton burst into the room. "What in the hell, Hallett?" He stepped to the couch to free his wife. Hallett's eyes were filled with anguish. Tears rolled down her cheeks. She nodded her head several times in the direction of Lucky, who was sitting in a chair with a pistol in his right hand and a taser in his left.

Braxton turned, saw the figure in black and the weapons in his hands. "What the hell!"

The lawyer's face turned pale.

Lucky tossed him two pairs of flex cuffs, exactly like the ones binding his son.

"Take your clothes off, counselor. Place the first pair on your ankles and cinch them. Then place your hands behind your back and slide the second pair to your wrists."

Braxton composed himself. "I will not. I absolutely will not. Do you know who the hell I am, mister?"

Lucky snorted. "Yes, I assure you I know exactly who you are. You are one very accomplished attorney." Lucky made a show of looking at the taser. Then he swiveled his neck so he could examine his pistol. "But your reluctance to follow simple directions, Braxton, places me into a decision-making mode. Which one of the tools I'm holding might best help you understand the serious nature of our meeting? In ten seconds, I will have my decision."

WELL, THERE IT is right there, Braxton thought. *It's about money. I'm successful and this guy isn't. How surprising.*

Lucky had reached the point of negotiation that Green preferred, settlement talks. The man had used his first name, Braxton. It was always preferable to have a dignified discussion among civil colleagues. Braxton wanted to tell the fellow that he always enjoyed concluding proceedings having made new friends, but he let Lucky talk. He knew to shut up, let the adversary make the first offer.

Braxton followed directions. He stripped, sat next to his wife, applied the cuffs to his wrists and ankles.

"PEOPLE HAVE A certain admiration for you, Braxton. Wrong choice of words. Not admiration, astonishment. I believe people are astounded by your boldness and tenacity. You display a complete lack of emotion and empathy as you damage hordes of people. I can tell you beyond any doubt that you astound me. I'm stupefied by the things I've read about you."

Lucky continued, "Reading the enlightening articles about you, evaluating some deeper research of your endeavors, I'm left with a somewhat more thorough description."

"Which is?"

"Calculating, treacherous, deceitful, and scheming. Do any of these words seem adequate?

"Oh, one more comes to mind, Braxton. Avariciousness. Avarice pressurizes your skull. Side to side, top to bottom, front to back. Aaaa-VA-risss. Do you know that word? Of course you do. Words are your ammunition."

"COMPLETELY INACCURATE, all of those descriptions," Braxton burst out. "Or at any rate, incomplete. I completely disagree with avarice. Completely."

Green knew this was about money because *everything is about money.* He wanted to get on with the process. He was ready to deal, take the short end of the stick, and let this pirate be on his way.

Braxton continued, "I think you are about to change your tune on me, mister. Once you just lay out your terms, I believe you will see me in an entirely different light. Perhaps open, honest, straightforward, gracious, and beneficent. I think a large sum of money would clear up this matter immediately."

"IF IT'S THAT simple, Braxton, I certainly think we should put you under another major category."

"That would be?"

"Chameleon. You're a lizard capable of changing colors to meet the needs of the social situation in which you find yourself."

Lucky walked over to the glass coffee table and glanced down at the hooligan tools. He picked up a stainless-steel, straight-edge barber's razor. It gleamed with evil.

GREEN'S EYES widened at the sight. He could feel his body switch gears. His mouth started to feel like cotton. Braxton could hear the thump deep in his left chest. He knew the oily fear showed on his face.

"Let's get to it, shall we?" said Lucky.

"Five million dollars. Let's go to the bank right now. Right damn now and get the cash."

Lucky made a show of glancing at a clock in the room. "The bank's closed."

"Okay, okay, not a problem. Let's sleep on it. At nine o'clock sharp, let's pick up seven-and-a-half million. Add two and a half. Better deal for you."

RIGHT THERE, Lucky knew. Zeus was right. There were millions to walk away with using his outlandish plan.

"Mr. Green, at first this was about money. But that point in time has passed."

"Well, what the hell else could it be about?"

"A sweet, gentle, caring soul. A man who provided immeasurable benefits to the world his whole life. You may have heard of him, Dr. Michael Grantham."

The blood left Braxton's face.

Lucky closed the door.

37

THREE HOURS AFTER leaving Charleston, Lucky exited off I-95 onto US 17 and stopped at the bridge over the Little Satilla River. He was just inland from Jekyll Island, Georgia. With no traffic in sight, he tossed the Sig into the water. With a slug in Brax's knee, the weapon needed to go.

Something else went into the water, destined for the riverbed. A female human head in a chicken-wire crab trap.

HE PULLED THE van into his Jacksonville beach rental at 1:30 in the morning. Lucky was grimy, covered with death, and exhausted. He took a long shower, water as hot as he could stand.

He killed the lights, hopped in bed. Sleep didn't come. His mind returned to everything he'd thought about on the ride home. In a few hours, a tornado of cops and press in Charleston would be chasing their tails. He'd matched wits with some of the deadliest vipers on earth. Now, what could US law enforcement throw at him?

Rather than lying in bed with his brain churning, he decided to upload the video to Zeus. First, he scrubbed it with editing software. No images of him whatsoever. He eliminated his voice responses. Braxton's responses remained.

An hour of raw film was quickly skimmed into fourteen minutes of footage. He drove across town to a 24-hour McDonalds, just off the interstate in Orange Park. He accessed their Wi-Fi and uploaded everything to DataCage, exactly as Zeus instructed.

Last thing. He pulled the burner phone out of his pocket, punched speed dial to Zeus, let it ring once, hung up.

At the counter he ordered the Big Breakfast and a large orange drink. Sitting at a table next to a window, he glanced through the early news on the net. Fifty-three minutes later his burner phone rang once. He signed on again to DataCage.

Spotted a message: ***Z Response.***

He clicked it open.

Holy Smokes, Man! Twenty guys like you at Bin Laden's house!! Bearded bastard had no chance!!---Hang tight. Watch the news. Chat in 7-10 days. Z.

ZEUS SPENT THE NEXT HOUR perfecting the video. It was now three minutes and forty-five seconds of devastating, true-crime violence.

He'd asked for hardball. He got hardball.

The plan was to wake up Charleston, get the ball rolling. Zeus siphoned two still photos from the video. Brutal stuff. He hit the SEND button to blast the first photo to Captain Rye Hewitt, one of Charleston's senior detectives.

He also created an insurance policy to pour a little gas on the fire. He fired an email to Dana Danson, one of Charleston's loud-mouthed, hot pants investigative reporters. Zeus was certain she would be maniacal about checking her inbox.

He sat back, waited. It took only ninety seconds for the reporter to open the email. A smile cracked his face. He knew she'd want to alert everybody in the Northern Hemisphere with her concerned face on a TV screen.

Detective Hewitt's email was read six minutes later.

Then Zeus popped off the second photo. Oh, he'd love to see their faces now.

LATER THAT DAY there was a bold headline in the online edition of the *Charleston Post and Courier.*

PROMINENT COUPLE MASSACRED
Son Shot, Tennis Pro Bound, Both Alive

38

ZEUS LOVED THE research. One by one, he was deep into data collection on the lives of the attorneys in his Top 100 list. Intimate knowledge of their lives. Big case details, partners and office staff names, photos of their homes, kids' names, ages, schools, pets, wives, ball teams, game scores, automobile models and colors, daily schedules, favorite restaurants, vacation photos, report card grades. Driver's license numbers. Medicine doses. Dental appointments.

Every. Damn. Thing.

All out there for the taking. Facebook, LinkedIn, Instagram, and Twitter. Google Earth Street View, PeekYou, and the Beat App.

Facebook was a goldmine. Even on privacy settings, it proved simple to hack. No work at all. Some genius had already helped him out. He used SamHacker.com, which gave him the UFD2 Decrypt Tool. Took only a few minutes, nobody knew they were hacked, and he left with a trainload of data.

And then, his black hat hacking. Tiptoeing around corners to view texts and emails.

Reliable financial information approximated a collective net worth of the Top 100 to be somewhere in the $4.2 billion range, give or take $200 million.

A hundred million dollars from these guys? Absolutely doable.

EMAIL INVITATIONS SHIPPED five days after the Charleston murders to the first twenty-five attorneys. The slaughter was prominent national news. Each lawyer also received a text on their cell phone sent from a burner in Memphis, Tennessee. It was the same group that rejected Zeus's earlier invitation.

Check Your Email. We're Coming For You!

Zeus was confident. There was no way this wouldn't work. The attached video to clarify things for the doubters.

Last Chance
CHARITABLE CONTRIBUTIONS REQUIRED IN
72 HOURS
OR
The Next Video is Your Family

39

ZEUS COULDN'T THINK straight, he was so amped. It was four days after the emails were sent, one day past the deadline.

He drove as fast as he could to a local chicken restaurant. Plenty of open parking, but eighteen cars jamming the drive-thru. He parked, grabbed his laptop and a legal pad, and went inside to order. Six kids behind the counter with big, white-toothed smiles. Cherubic-looking souls, they all had a cult-like wholesomeness to them. The same look in every Chick-fil-A. Always attentive and courteous, working with a full belly of the company Kool-Aid.

"How may I help you, sir?" The slightly built white boy looked about twelve, with close-cropped red hair. He was as clean-cut as an Eagle Scout except for a smattering of mild acne.

"Number one combo with an unsweet tea. Eating here." Zeus's mind was on his computer, not the order. In less than five minutes, he'd be signing on to overseas bank sites.

"My pleasure. Have a seat, sir, and I'll bring it right out."

Zeus ambled to a booth in the back corner near the restroom. He pulled the laptop out of his backpack, powered it on. Then it hit him. He wondered if Chick-fil-A would block a Tor sign-on. It was certainly possible. Probable, really. To many, Tor insinuated clandestine activity. Zeus went to connect, held his breath ... bang. He was on. And surprised.

His order was placed on the table. "Thanks."

He grabbed a waffle fry with a hand that was one moment from launching into a nervous tremor, scared out of his mind that he would see nothing.

Via the web, Zeus had followed the Charleston local news since the Green killings. There was little fruitful information coming from the cops. Early speculation was that it was a payback drug crime. The son's weed operation had been exposed, as well as his contact with a local gang member.

He sucked a swig of tea through the straw. After an exhale, he signed on to his first bank site. Panama. No change in the account. Logged out. Nevis, in the Caribbean. Signed on. Nothing. Lichtenstein. Signed on.

His eyes widened.

"YES!" Zeus screamed out loud, banged both palms on the table. Tables of diners turned to look at the commotion. The Boy Scout skidded around the corner, his manager right behind him.

"Sir, are you okay?" The manager had his hand on Zeus's shoulder. "How may we help?"

Zeus's face went red with embarrassment. Then it contorted into a goofy, oddball smile, like something you'd do if you were just saved from a hanging. He ran the back of his right hand across his lips. Was he drooling? Two hands rose palm outward in front of him in apology mode. "I am so sorry. No, no, nothing bad, everything is good. Great, actually."

The manager looked over at the patrons, held up a hand, nodded. "Everything's fine, folks."

Zeus thought fast. "Just an email. It's an old friend. Got lab reports today. His cancer is in remission."

Redhead looked at him with a sympathetic expression that was genuine, shook his head. "Wow. Praise God, sir."

"Absolutely." Zeus logged back on. Went to his Johannesburg bank. Signed in. Two deposits totaling $3.9 million dollars. Signed out. Went to his Singapore account. Same original balance. Signed out. Isle of Mann. Zeus kept his mouth shut this time. $4.9 million dollars.

He knew it. He damn well knew it! Plenty of oil in these wells.

Over the next two business days, more money flowed in. Time to inform Lucky.

He created a document, encrypted it, shot it up to the cloud, blasted a single ring on Lucky's phone.

BAD NEWS—Only 40% response rate.

GOOD NEWS—We Still Drilled a Gusher!! $14.3 Million rolled in. $11.44 Million will go into an account for YOU within the next week.

Will contact soon. You will be provided usernames and passwords for your new accounts.

40

JACKSONVILLE, FLORIDA

LUCKY WAS SURFING in an uncrowded spot off Atlantic Beach when his burner phone received a text. The phone was wrapped in a washcloth, stuffed under the passenger seat in his rental that was parked on the edge of a beach access road.

It was 9:10 in the morning, low tide, and waves were four feet with a little wind chop. Not California, but still fun. Facing east over the Atlantic, sunshine warmed his face as he straddled his board. He stared out to sea watching for the next wave set to flow in.

After two and a half hours, he paddled to shore, slid the spring wetsuit off, slipped on some dry shorts and a long-sleeve tee, and laid his board on some towels in the bed of the pickup.

He steered onto Hwy A1A and headed south to his apartment. Little traffic, he leaned down and snatched the phone from under the seat. He had been waiting on a Zeus update. The radio belted out sports talk about the Marlins' and Rays' prospects. Quick peek at the phone. A missed call. *Yes.*

Lucky leaned down on the accelerator, made it to his apartment in ten minutes, grabbed his computer, and walked straight back to the truck, excited.

He sped down to Starbucks on Third, a short drive. Morning rush gone, several places to sit. He ordered a coffee and two almond croissants.

He logged onto DataCage. The document was right there. He decrypted PGP and read it. Leaned back in his chair, brought a hand to his mouth, thought *holy crap!*

He downed both croissants in a hurry, went to the counter and bought a cheese Danish. Suddenly he wasn't in a hurry. He purchased the *Florida Times-Union,* went back to his seat. First thing he saw was something on the front page about the Iranian nuclear agreement. The worst nuclear deal ever struck by the United States. By the third paragraph, his mind was a roller coaster out of control. No energy to worry about nuclear attacks.

Because he was a multimillionaire.

He zipped out of the building to the sound of flip-flops snapping his feet. Needed to drive. And think. Too excited to even calculate possibilities in his head.

Lucky pointed the truck south on A1A, headed to St. Augustine. Popped on an oldies station. Brewer and Shipley. "One Toke Over the Line." Started singing along.

It took him thirty-eight minutes to reach the Surf Station, the old surf shop in a converted gas station on St. Augustine Beach. He thought, *Hell yeah, I'll buy another surfboard.*

Walked in the shop. Tons of boards. Spotted a blond guy with pink sunburn on his nose and cheeks. His hair, not quite to his shoulders, was damp. The Atlantic was only a block away. The guy had just pulled out of the water.

"Hey, man, I'm riding a six-two Channel Islands right now," said Lucky. "Kinda thinking about adding a longboard. You guys got anything interesting?"

"Jack, we got everything interesting. Look, man, I can make this painless unless you're one of those study-the-internet-reviews-for-three-years kind of guy."

"Okay, whatcha think?"

"The Walden Magic Model. Period. I just got off an eight-footer ten minutes before you walked in. I can ride that stick in two-foot mush or heavy ten-foot storm surf. We have nine-footers and ten-footers, too."

"Sold. I'll take it, the one you ride." He picked a red one.

Blondie stepped over to the checkout counter, slammed his hand down onto a flat, red button on a device purchased at Staples. Electronically, it blurted "THAT WAS EASY." Surf boy said, "As you might surmise, that button gets used a lot in this place." Lucky snickered inside ... *surmise.*

He paid with a credit card. "Thanks, man. But hey, I need to grab a bite and check some email. Any decent spots with Wi-Fi around here?"

"Heck, yeah. The food truck over by the marina looks like you, man. Shaded tables. Incredible views of the boats. Everything's chill. Tell 'em Jock sent you."

Eight minutes later, Lucky pulled up to the food truck, parked in the shade, and went up to order. A lean twenty-something girl with shoulder-length dark hair and a bright smile was at the window. Made Lucky think of a yoga instructor.

He glanced at the chalk-written menu on a blackboard. No one else in line. The attendant took the pencil from her ear, ready to write.

"Okay. Thinking here. I know I'll take a Corona. Okay, here it is. I'll take a grilled shrimp bowl over seasoned rice and spinach, add cilantro and almonds."

"Great choice. Eleven seventy-five, please."

Lucky handed her a ten and a five. "Keep the change."

"Thanks."

He watched her put three bucks and a quarter in her mesmerizingly short, cut-off jeans.

"A guy named Jock told me to stop by for a bowl."

She turned around slowly, rolled her eyes. "Not that friggin' douche. For crying out loud, dude, you had to ruin my beautiful day."

"Oh, sorry. Old boyfriend?"

"Puh-leeze. He's my idiot stepbrother. Were you at the shop? Wait a minute." She held up a hand, let her eyelids close slightly. "Please tell me he didn't sell you one of those lame Waldens."

Lucky went silent. Still as a statue. *What did she say?*

"Those A-holes in California pay outrageous commissions for that dick to dump that cheap crap on East Coast imbeciles." She had a serious look on her face. Like she was gonna file a complaint with the Federal Trade Commission over subpar surfboards.

Lucky averted his eyes.

"You didn't, did you?" She pushed the subject.

He looked at her, stone-faced. She looked him dead in the eye. Neither said a thing. Lucky felt two feet tall.

Then a smile broke across her face followed by a raucous laugh that made her next-door real. "Ahhh, man, I'm screwing with you, just jerking your chain. Walden's are awesome!"

"Well, I was starting to get a little pissed about your idiot stepbrother."

She laughed again. Louder.

"Oh, this is hilarious. Kidding about the stepbrother crap, too. That's my husband! He doesn't even work there, he's sitting in for his buddy, the manager, who snuck out to grab forty-five minutes in the water."

Lucky was smiling now. “Well, tell your jackass husband to get a job!”

Both enjoying the moment. “Yeah, he called as soon as you walked out. Said to screw with you, thought you seemed cool.”

“Ahhh, man, ya’ll got me, sure did.” Lucky laughed again. Made him think of some of the pranks in special forces.

“Oh, Jock is just kicking back right now. He starts med school at the University of Miami August fifteenth. He’s gonna be a surgeon.”

Medical school? A surfer?

Lucky was sitting at a picnic table with his computer up when she brought the food. His Corona, 80 percent gone.

“Bringing you another beer, on the house. Good sport special.”

“Great, thanks, you guys are awesome.” His eyes followed her tan legs all the way back to the food truck.

A doctor’s wife.

41

BLACK POINT, ALABAMA

WILLIAM BURNHAM'S WHITE '68 Rolls Royce exploded into a blizzard of steel, glass, and rubber at 5:37 a.m. in the morning darkness.

Nothing about it slow. Not a thing like a cartoon. The doors didn't slowly bulge. The roof didn't swell. No. It was quick. BOOM. Then it was gone.

The vintage automobile had been parked twenty-five feet from the front door of Wild Bill Burnham's law office, smack dab downtown Black Point, Alabama.

THREE HOURS BEFORE the blast, at 1:28 a.m., a mid-size Chevy rental had drifted to a slow stop on the side of Great Bay Road, nine hundred yards south of the landmark Magnolia Hotel, three miles south of downtown Black Point.

The driver doused the headlights a quarter-mile earlier, dropped it in neutral, and began a slow coast. The early morning was moonless, black, as the Chevy slithered to a stop. When the driver's door opened the interior remained dark, its dome light disengaged.

Lucky, lithe and nimble, was dressed head to toe in black. Camo paint was smeared on his face, a small polymer-framed

.380 was in a right-ankle holster, and a black fanny pack was strapped at his right hip.

He eased the door closed.

He gathered his bearings before moving, letting his pupils dilate. The air was thick with wet, nighttime heat. A smell of water weeds drifted from the roadside ditch. Mosquitos lit around his eyes. He blew them away with a puff of air.

Not a hint of traffic. Dead still. Tree frogs and crickets serenaded the night.

Tranquility.

Ambient outside light from Burnham's bayfront mansion sifted through a thick stand of oaks, pines, and magnolias. Surrounding ground-cover near the road grew untouched, lush, and wild. This was estate territory. Nothing sitting on the Point Clear bayfront went for less than $2 million.

Lucky glided through seventy-five yards of dense foliage, hugging tight to shadows, until he reached the Rolls Royce. Intel said no dogs. He dropped flat on his back on the white Bahamian rock drive, slid under the rear of the car, removed the compact mass of C4 from his fanny pack, attached the plastic explosive to the gas tank, placed the detonator, and slid out from under the car.

He blended into blackness as he speed-walked south to his car. Thought it a shame about that British classic.

TWO MINUTES BEFORE the explosion, an incoming email pinged on Burnham's Dell laptop as it sat lopsided in his lap. He was comfortable on the second floor of his two-story building, leaning back in his executive chair facing parallel to his desk, his polished crocodile-belly cowboy boots resting on a three-foot-tall black mini-fridge next to a Trump bobblehead, his hero. Within a hands' reach on his desk were six slices of microwave bacon and a cinnamon-raisin bagel, overloaded with cream cheese.

He was sifting for internet dirt on a shifty, backroom dealmaker, the CEO of a New Orleans paving contractor, who Bill understood to be bid-rigging state highway contracts. Bill loved the dear folks of Louisiana. Corruption came hardboiled in their DNA, leaving honesty just out of reach of their twiddling fingers.

Bill glanced at the sender, thought nothing of it, at first.

Panic@protonmail.com.

Spam nonsense.

It was titled: **U GOT 90 SECONDS**

Burnham wasn't aware the email had been sent encrypted through the sophisticated Tor data transmission process, seven thousand relays concealing the location and identity of the sender. The final layer decrypted the initial email so he could read it.

Panic? Ninety seconds? Well, dang, he couldn't resist. Bill clicked the message open.

Please Insert Ear Protection Devices at This Moment. Time for Lift-off.

Then the whole building rocked.

Burnham hopped in the chair as his ass muscles seized. His computer hit the floor. His heart jolted into a racing rhythm, deep and hard. His eyes suspiciously glanced across the walls.

What the hell—!

Running his mug on 126 billboards and counting, from Houston to Tallahassee, Wild Bill Burnham was the biggest billboard bottom-feeder on the upper Gulf Coast. His fleshy bourbon-flushed head was stuffed up into an oversized black Stetson with his leech-bait tagline on monster highway signs:

Go For The Kill
Call Wild Bill!
1-800-ALL-CASH

His phone rang more than the New York Police Department.

MORNING LIGHT EMERGED by 6:05. Downtown Black Point swarmed with fire, police, and paramedics; no one sure what happened with Bill Burnham's car.

Early June, the temps hinted of the blast furnace heat that would smother the town by noon. Each end of the block was cordoned off with yellow tape, a passel of police cruisers, and cops complaining about missing breakfast.

A mangled half-frame of an automobile sat in the middle of the road in front of Burnham's law office. Black smoke snaked skyward through the acrid stench of burned rubber.

Bomb-sniffing dogs were en route from Pensacola and Mobile. Nobody was too anxious to go strolling around until the K-9s gave the okay.

Within twenty minutes of the blast, Wild Bill was lying back forty-five degrees on a stretcher in the back of an ambulance with a silver pocket-flask of Old Grand Dad in his left hand. Both ears buzzed with the hum of what sounded like an industrial generator he couldn't shake out just yet. Sweat beaded on his forehead while his pulse jackhammered. The lawyer's body trembled.

But he didn't have a single scratch on him. That was the plan. The bomber was a pro.

Most days Wild Bill packed an attitude that was brash, overbearing, loud, and argumentative, all blaring from a five-feet, seven-inch fire-hydrant frame that came with a strut that screamed *you don't screw with The Man.*

The world-class Napoleon carried no swagger today.

42

FORTY-THREE MINUTES after the blast, a roaming television news truck hit the scene, parked, and quickly shot its transmission antenna into the sky. Kate Dallas, thirty-one, brunette, dark eyes, finished applying her lipstick, then hopped out to see if anyone had the slightest clue as to what was happening.

She ignored the yellow police tape, ducked under it, and strolled up to a tall guy outfitted in military-style cop fatigues.

"Whatcha got, chief?"

Pike Tatum turned, let his eyes take a slow walk over Kate. Tanned runner's legs. Skirt painted on. His first thought was, *How can a woman pull off late-night allure at six in the morning?* Well, that may have been his second thought.

"Got a dead Rolls Royce and twenty-four donuts on death row. Wanna interview one?"

"Got chocolate glazed?"

"Course we do."

"Then, hell yeah, I want one."

"Sounds good, Kate. I like a woman who can enjoy a donut and not rage into a dang panic attack about inflammation and sugar regulation."

Pike hadn't seen any dead bodies. He knew Burnham was still breathing. But one thing he knew for sure. Any nut job who can make one bomb can make two. No need to crowd the scene just yet.

Pike was rangy, six-four with broad shoulders. Twenty years ago, he was a hot-handed shooting guard on a mediocre Ole Miss basketball team. Having never married, he was still scoring.

A thought came to him as Kate stood a hint into his personal space after touching his forearm with her fingertips. Close enough for him to pick up a delicate scent. It was fresh and clean, with a tinge of jasmine and orange. In his peripheral vision, Pike saw the beginning cleavage in a blouse skewed open just below a jade necklace. It took every bit of his strength to keep looking her in the eye, a look that Kate held more than a moment.

Pike relied on first instincts, and Kate's cleavage was all the instinct he needed. He decided to kick things around here for twenty minutes, bark some orders, ask some people if they saw anything, and tell his officers and the firemen to stay well away until the dogs cleared the scene.

But first he needed to check on Bill. He made his way over to the ambulance, hopped in the back door.

"What the hell's going on here, Bill? Who'd you jerk around?" Pike spotted the liquor flask. Wild Bill put his hand up, shook his head. Voice weak. "Not now, Pike. Gotta settle my nerves."

Pike scampered out of the ambulance and thought this was a good time to answer his instinct. He'd slip over to Greer's two blocks away, grab a couple thick filets and a fifteen-buck bottle of red. Run it down to his condo overlooking the bay.

In an hour or so, after kicking a little more dirt and discussing some crime rationale, he might just slip a mention to Kate that he had a couple steaks that were gonna hit the grill while he watched the sunset over the bay on a fine summer evening.

Tonight, he'd come up with some little newsy tidbit for her even if it was mostly made-up. He'd wink, insist she list her sources as anonymous.

SITTING UP FORTY-FIVE DEGREES on a stretcher in the boxy ambulance, a chemical tranquility began to massage Wild Bill's brain. He wrestled his phone out of his tight pants and forced his fat fingers onto the keypad.

He needed to call a guy. He found the number, tapped CALL.

An alpha dog answered in the nation's capital.

43

GEORGETOWN, WASHINGTON, D.C.

JAKE MONTOYA WAS laughing out loud when his phone rang. He was deep into an article in the *Washington Post's* DC politics section while he ate a lazy breakfast on his porch.

A lean-muscled Belgian Malinois named Rowdy slept next to him. A lemon-yellow cast was on his dog's rear-left leg, covered with a good dozen swirls of Sharpie signatures.

The morning broke crisp and cool, and low humidity gave it an extra snap. With a little imagination, he could still catch a sniff of the sweet lawn-mower gasoline the yard men had burned eighteen hours ago.

The *Post* rested folded open to an article recounting some testimony in the Clinton-Lewinsky scandal from years back. The headline read *Midnight Pizza.* He broke the laugh when he got to the part where Clinton's secretary tells him late one night, "Sir, the girl with the pizza's here."

Jake had heard that Clinton joked that the pizza wars in DC were so cut-throat you now got a free blow job with the large vegetarian. He laughed as he thought he'd ask the president about that. They jogged together occasionally when Clinton was back in Washington.

"Hello, this is Jake." He leaned forward, spoke fast, concern in his voice. *Something with my mother?*

"Jake, the hot-damn maniacs found me. Blew my car apart, a damn collector's Rolls Royce." Jake had first heard that voice almost forty years ago in kindergarten. Billy Burnham.

"Billy, slow down. What guys?"

"Those crazy-ass lawyer killers. Gotta be those sumbitches that killed Green in Charleston. They're trying to bleed me. Jake, I'm just a small-town, redneck hack, but somehow, they found me. They're here. I'm a dead man, Jake. Ya gotta come home. Bring some feds, anybody.

Bill's call was perfect timing. Jake was serving a ninety-day paid suspension after an unexpected confrontation in a Virginia Beach suburb. Three men were dead, thanks to Jake and his dog. All bad guys.

A *New York Times* reporter cited unnamed sources in reporting the fact that Jake Montoya was the most dangerous agent in the FBI. Even speculated he brought a particularly violent psyche to the job stemming from "aggregational NFL head damage." Some suggested he submit to undergo psychiatric evaluation, brain scans, the works.

Jake didn't care. He didn't need a job. He didn't need money. Years ago, he had invested most of his NFL salary into Grade A commercial real estate and hot biotech companies.

He lived rent free in a Georgetown carriage house keeping his eye out for Ms. Sarah Bradley, who lived in the estate's mansion. She was a rich old lady who filled her days donating her money to needy animal causes and throwing hot piss and shade on every liberal Democrat she could find.

She also owned 7.5 percent of the Washington Redskins.

9:30 A.M. JAKE SLIPPED into a tight pedestrian alley off M Street, heading to a martial arts dojo. You had to know the place was there. Interesting clientele. International. Different languages. Different skin tones. The business had no sign, no hours on the door, no website, no Facebook page. But it was a spot known by the serious gladiators.

The smell hit him as soon as he walked through the door. It was the scent of energy production and aggression, and it smelled that way twenty-four hours a day.

Jake spotted Ben Staggers deep into the back of the room, warming up with a speed rope like a mad man. The skinny rope whirred like an airline propeller, Staggers breathing hard to stay alive. He was five years retired out of the Army's Delta Force, and well known in DC for his skills in Muay Thai, a brutal form of martial arts.

Jake met Staggers at Ms. Sarah's two years ago when she gave him a check for $100,000 for his animal cause. Stagger's organization provided service animals for vets with severe PTSD.

They worked on Muay Thai technique for thirty minutes. The next thirty minutes was pure MMA. And it got rough. Jake put Staggers on the ground five times.

After the last takedown, Staggers said, "Never fought a big guy as fast as you, Jake. I'm not sure I'm still having fun." They laughed.

Jake was six-three, 220 pounds, with a flat-plated chest.

"Give me ten minutes on the speed bag, then I'm buying lunch at Stachowski's," said Jake.

2:45 P.M. JAKE HAD time to think about the call. Billy Burnham. Now morphed into the audacious Wild Bill Burnham. They weren't close but there's something about a person you've known almost every day of your life. The childhood connection was undefinable and hard to ignore. But, still, out of a trillion lawyers, what made him special to somebody?

The decision came quickly. He was headed to Black Point. A Rolls Royce bombing in his hometown was way too interesting to ignore.

44

MISSION BEACH, CALIFORNIA

LUCKY PICKED UP the report Zeus left on DataCage at 12:40 a.m., six hours after he arrived from Black Point. It referenced an article from a Sunday edition of the *Los Angeles Times:*

Billionaire Lawyer Reports Extortion Demand

A notorious, disbarred Los Angeles attorney reveals he's the victim of an extortion attempt. Peter John Clemmons, known to America's corporations as the King of Pain, and also one of the wealthiest men in California, reports an unknown source has tried to extort $25 million from him. One of his bodyguards, a former Los Angeles police detective, filed a report on this matter with the FBI.

Get a load of this comment from the counselor I dug up on the *Drudge Report.*

"... no two bit **ssy ***holes will get a nickel out of me. I made my living being the King of Pain. They're f***ing with the wrong damn guy. I say come on, you motherf***ers!"

Here's the deal on this guy. Oh, the irony. This prick has operated as a mega-extortionist himself for three decades against American businesses. He was convicted of conspiracy to commit obstruction of justice and lost his license. Why? He paid upward of $15 million in kickbacks to buy plaintiffs over the years so he could start filing lawsuits against any and every corporation in America. He has destroyed countless companies and wiped-out thousands of jobs.

Reportedly a vile, vitriolic, vindictive creep (wow, shocker). Sentenced to three years in prison. Disbarred.

His law firm pulled in over $30 billion. Personally, he's sitting on $1.5 billion. That's B. BILLION! This prick thinks he's cock of the walk.

I tried to play nice with the man. Suggested $25 million, nothing outrageous. Trivial lunch money. Now he's calling you names.

And it looks like he wants to play rough.

I've sent links to background stories on this guy. I think you might especially like what he did to little Jeannie Marie Baughn and the pharmaceutical company that was poised to save her life.

WORK OR SURF? It was 5:15 a.m., still dark. A bowl of granola sat in front of Lucky with a banana sliced on top, and two pieces of wheat toast covered with peanut butter next to it on a paper towel. He had returned to California from Florida, and the surf has been head high and clean for eight days.

He worked out his dilemma. He grabbed two and a half hours in the water with the dawn patrol at Windansea, La Jolla. Afterward, he dried off, changed into a pullover fleece and hiking shorts, drove to his favorite downtown San Diego building, the iconic glass, steel, and metal central library. He arrived at 9:35 a.m.

He took his shades off as he grabbed a seat at an empty table in the happy, colorful children's section. Relative privacy.

The room had several large murals in ode to the legendary La Jolla children's author, Dr. Seuss. Staring Lucky in the face in dazzling color was the cover of the good doctor's last book, *Oh the Places You'll Go,* a raging bestseller.

He ruminated on that, the blatant truth of that title. In smaller text was an excerpt:

"With your head full of brains and
Your shoes full of feet
You're too smart to go down any not-so-good street."

He pondered Seuss's wisdom, then changed tables to face a window, and reject that advice.

He blasted through articles in *Forbes, Fortune, Business Week,* the *New York Times,* and the *Wall Street Journal.* All about Clemmons. By the time he hit the *Journal* and *Times,* he was skimming repetitive information.

The Jeannie Marie Vaughn story was recounted in a scathing *New Yorker* expose.

At age six, Jeannie Marie began experiencing vision loss, seizures, and involuntary movements. A year later, a deepening cognitive decline was recognized by most who knew the child. Her pediatrician sent her to Emory, which then referred her to Texas Children's Hospital. The diagnosis was a rare genetic illness, Batten disease.

Fulcrum Pharmaceuticals was close to bringing to market a medication that could halt the spread of the disease, and possibly reverse some of the negative symptoms. Then the Phase III trials hit a stumbling block. The FDA wanted some additional testing. The stock price dropped precipitously after the Phase III news was made public. That signaled blood in the water for the shark, Clemmons. He filed a class-action lawsuit alleging company fraud related to statements in the prospectus.

Total malarkey, said Fulcrum. The prospectus noted how few drugs made it to market. It sought only seasoned investors, and only then to invest with caution.

The King of Pain walked away with $200 million for the class, sliced off $66 million for his effort, and purchased a tiny island in the Caribbean.

Jeannie Marie died blind, unable to move, completely devoid of all cognitive function, in a small, hot, cramped, used camper that her father had bought after the family home was foreclosed on. They had no ability to pay $2.8 million in medical bills.

Here's all you need to know, Zeus had told him.

Peter John Clemmons spent spring through early fall at his secluded ranch in Placerville, Colorado, near Telluride. He employed four bodyguards, all former cops, who worked in teams of two, with one week on, one week off.

Zeus included information from the initial real estate listing with dazzling photos that captured the home and its surroundings. The home was constructed at the base of a mountain.

Lucky liked the high-to-low vantage-point possibilities. Immediately, his thoughts bounced back to the desolate and rocky mountain ranges of northern Afghanistan. Nothing better than manning the MK11 sniper rifle fifteen-hundred feet up, overlooking a small band of Taliban terrorists.

And now we have a lawyer stashed in an out-of-the-way box canyon, under the eyes of two city-slicker cowboys.

A crooked smile crossed Lucky's face.

45

ZEUS WAS NINETEEN hundred miles away from Lucky, sitting in his stepfather's law office, scouring LexisNexis for any information on faulty sensors in a sophisticated line of BMWs that were causing engine fires.

He took a break, walked upstairs with a detailed report. "I need ten days off. I've got five interviews lined up."

"Knock yourself out. Might not mention that Russian thing in your resume if they don't know about it." Stepdad snorted, walked away with the BMW file in his hands.

Breathe, just breathe, thought Zeus. This prick's time is coming.

ZEUS FLEW TURKISH Airlines out of Atlanta to Heathrow, arriving late in the day. He would take a former neighbor, a seventy-two-year-old astrophysics professor at University College London, out to dinner to drink wine, talk mathematics, and argue soccer.

The next morning he flew to Luxembourg to get about the business at hand.

1. Open an account for Lucky to use as a business. It was named Knight Force, an elite security firm, a real company.

Two million in a Luxembourg bank. Nine million in a cryptocurrency cold wallet.

2. For himself. One million in a Luxembourg bank that would split in half in two days, going to Tbilisi and Singapore. One million in a Mycelium Bitcoin wallet. Leave town with $1 million USD for Amsterdam.

3. Amsterdam. Buy $300,000 in investment-grade diamonds. Then $700,000 in one-kilogram gold bars. Divide into six separate shipments. Ship to three separate unbranded shipping stores in in the United Staes.

KNIGHT FORCE. The name for his new outfit came easy to Lucky. He felt the name meant business. Aggressive business. And Knight was his middle name, his mother's maiden name.

Zeus established an offshore investment trust based in Ireland, funded with cryptocurrency. The trust funded an aged limited liability company named Cascade Business Capital, LLC. It was set up by privacy attorneys in Cheyenne, Wyoming.

Knight Force was granted $7 million as a private placement from Cascade for a fictional 20 percent ownership in the company.

Lucky established a two-room office in California, installed a phone and fax line, outfitted the office with two computers, contracted with an answering service, and had Zeus build a professional website for the company.

Lastly, he leased a lightly used, rugged, single-engine turboprop airplane. A Cessna Caravan, with an option to buy.

To those looking, it would appear Lucky sought a legitimate venture-funding source and found one. But Lucky controlled the Irish trust. And Cascade Business Capital. And Knight Force.

Everything was his.

46

9:15 A.M. JAKE'S TAHOE was packed for the trip south. A Glock 21 with three extra magazines rested on the front seat alongside a fresh box of .45 caliber hollow points. A short-barreled pump-action scattergun in the tactical pistol grip configuration was packed in a thin, long, rectangular carrying case that he slid under one side of Rowdy's dog bed.

Two bicycles, an old red beach cruiser bought cheap on Hatteras, and a beat-to-hell mountain bike, were latched onto a rear bike-rack. Jake was double-checking the tiedowns on a roof-mounted kayak when he heard a voice.

"What's going on here?" It was Ms. Sarah Bradley walking over, just passing her rose garden, with a brown-paper lunch sack in her hand. Three hyped-up rescue dogs flanked her like a guard detail, taunted by the scent of the bag. Newton, Einstein, and Galileo. She had taught junior high science decades ago when her husband was in naval flight training.

"Taking a trip down to Black Point, Ms. Sarah."

Sarah, almost eighty-one, with cheerful eyes and cottony white hair, wore a crisp, white apron around her gingham dress.

She held up the bag and wiggled it. "I was bringing a few Virginia ham biscuits over for Rowdy. You'll have to ask him if you can have one."

"Oh, man, we love those things. Thanks."

"Well, you boys be careful on that trip. You know I love you. Now give me a big hug—oh, hold it." Ms. Sarah slipped a pen from a pocket in her apron, clicked it, took Jake's hand, and scribbled her phone number in his palm. "Never know when a cell phone will go on the fritz, and I don't like a man losing my number. I learned that when I was twenty, at a little oyster shack in Pensacola called the Pussy Cat Raw Bar. How do you think I met the admiral?"

Jake chuckled. "Well, don't you go pussycattin' around here. The world ain't like it used to be. I'll call you every day. I promise you that."

Right out of the driveway, Jake hit the radio. Baseball scores on a sports station. Forget it. Game was too slow. He popped it over to FM, zeroed in on a classic rock station.

Hummed an Allman Brothers tune. He made a couple of turns, came out onto M Street. Atlantic blue sky, not a cloud. Sixty-seven degrees edging to high seventies by lunchtime. People on the streets of Georgetown looked intent, stressed, hanging by their fingernails to the pace of Washington life.

Except for one guy.

Jake felt eyes on him as he sat first in line at a stoplight on M Street at Potomac, just outside of Dean & Deluca. Over to his left, starting to cross the street, was a sport walking a jet-black Labrador on a bright red leash. Lanky guy, early twenties, maybe six feet, bushy beard, and dark curls coming out from under a beanie.

The guy teed up a lollygag stroll coming off the curb, made it mid-street to the Tahoe, looked right at the front bumper, stared at Jake through the windshield, gave the hood two pops with his palm and hollered, "Allman Brothers! I like it!"

Jake, shades on, couldn't help it. With his face creased into a Hollywood smile, he shot him the thumbs-up sign. The hipster beamed some white teeth back at him, fired Jake a peace sign and moseyed on as a free thinker who'd never met a schedule.

Jake pegged him for a neo-millennial, urban mountain-man hippie headed to a kiln to fire some pottery, stream down some bootlegged Phish, and ramble on most of the day about his microscopic carbon footprint. The fellow probably called his mom twice a week to make sure she didn't lose the address to send his monthly subsistence check before she and her husband went to counseling to deal with their failures in parenting.

Light turned green, Jake eased on down M, and sang out loud to "Blue Sky." Right palm keeping time on the steering wheel.

Damn fine day to be alive.

47

LUCKY'S RIG WAS a custom .338 Magnum rifle with a Vortex Optics Viper scope, all finished in desert tan. The military-style optics looked substantial enough to study astronomy. It fired a round that was effective up to 1,900 yards and could pierce body armor from ten football fields out.

Many regarded it as the finest sniper weapon on earth.

He spent three days on the gun at the High-Power Shooting Club at the Pala Indian Reservation in north San Diego County. He fired hundreds of rounds at targets up to eight football fields away, carefully focusing on his breathing, squeezing the trigger on the exhaled respiratory pause, and purposeful follow-through on the trigger pull. It was everything he was taught and put into actual practice in the Middle East.

He was close to combat ready. And that was good enough. Because he wouldn't be in combat, he'd be in a rich man's backyard.

LUCKY'S PLANE TOUCHED down in Albuquerque at 10:40 a.m.

At the Enterprise desk he presented a Texas driver's license in the name of Jerry Trask and a prepaid credit card. He was on the road to Telluride by 11:45, driving a deep-green, four-door Jeep Wrangler, practically the Colorado state vehicle. He'd folded down the rear seat, tossed in a large duffel, a sleeping bag, a large cooler, and a camouflage backpack.

A hard Pelican Vault rifle case was in the cargo area, reaching almost to the back of the driver's seat. Lucky loosely fluffed a drop cloth over it, hiding it from view.

With the plane stashed well out of Colorado, Lucky began the six-hour trip toward Telluride. He reached Durango in four hours, where he picked up three days of camp food and refueled. Next stop, a river sports outfitter. He left the outfitter's parking lot with a touring kayak snugged tightly onto a roof rack.

Threading the Jeep through the San Juan Mountains on US 550, Lucky was two miles north of the Purgatory Resort when a flash caught his eye in the rearview mirror. He backed off the gas a moment, turned his head to look out the back window. Blue lights approaching fast.

He kept his foot off the gas, coasted to the side of the road to let the cruiser past. It didn't pass. The cop pulled in behind him. In the rearview, Lucky spotted the dash-mounted camera in the squad car. *Keep your face off the video.*

Lucky wore a long-sleeve tee, dark aviator sunglasses, and a Patagonia ball cap.

After a three-minute lull that felt like an hour, the officer exited his vehicle and walked toward Lucky on the driver's side of the vehicle.

The cop took off his shades at the back of the Jeep, stopped, glanced at the kayak, folded the glasses, and hooked the temple bar over the top of his exposed crew-neck tee. He eased up to the driver's window, standing slightly behind Lucky.

Lucky twisted his head while keeping his hands in sight on the steering wheel. "Officer." He nodded, smiled, casual demeanor. "Hope I haven't damaged my perfect driving record." Smiled again.

"Could I see your license, sir?"

Lucky was looking at a beefy cop, maybe five-eight, 215, a ring of black hair circling a bald head, dark mustache, a concrete block of a guy brimming with testosterone. Name badge said Sgt. John Lozano, La Plata County Sheriff's Department.

Lozano looked at the license. "Texas. Huh, long ways. Be right back." He went back to his cruiser, left the door open. Lucky saw him speaking into a mic. Four minutes later, Lozano was at the Jeep.

"Here's the deal, Mr. Trask. You drove past Purgatory doing fifty-three miles an hour. Speed limit is forty-five."

Lucky looked at the cop's clipboard. A ticket coming his way. *Abort the mission. Record of his presence.*

Lozano zipped off the perforated ticket, handed it to Lucky. "Ninety-five bucks. Mail us a check or call the toll-free number and pay by credit card."

"Well, shoot. You're right, I was hitting that speed when I went by. Had cruise control on." Lucky shook his head. "I just flat missed the signs, officer. Enjoying the mountain views."

Lozano looked at the kayak again. "How long you been kayaking?"

"About ten years. And, man, I love it. I've been planning this Colorado vacation for two years. Get out on the water and stress just evaporates. I can stare at computer screens in an office only so long."

Lozano nodded. "Roger that, partner." Lozano backed up and studied the kayak, then looked back at Lucky. "Yeah, my wife wants us to buy two of them. Says if we get out in nature together our relationship will improve. What I want to tell her is if you just stop talking to your divorced bitch girlfriends our relationship will improve. Most of her friends are angry, bitter women. Bunch of damn nutcases, really."

"Well, I'm no counselor, but I think her nature plan sounds pretty good."

"Lemme see that ticket a minute, Mr. Trask." Lozano diddled his fingers. Lucky handed it to him.

"I think I'm gonna change my demeanor for the rest of the day, not go home pissed off tonight. None of that's good for your heart, I hear." Lozano wiggled the ticket in the air. "This crap right here? This bureaucratic paper bullshit? I say screw it." Lozano crumpled the paper, put it in his pocket. "Ain't got time for this."

"Thanks officer. Promise, I'll keep the speed down."

"I'm gonna go home tonight with a pizza and a six pack, grab the wife, look at some kayaks online, tell her we're getting out in nature." The cop nodded. "Enjoy beautiful Colorado, sir."

Lucky eased the Jeep onto the highway, a weight off his shoulders. He set the cruise control for 43.

OFFICER LOZANO SAT in the driver's seat of his cruiser, watched the Jeep take off. Knew he hadn't done a thing all day. He pulled the ticket from his pocket and ironed it with his hand across his clipboard. Checked the box for *Warning.* He would update it on the computer at the station. No need for Trask to pay ninety-five bucks.

LUCKY WAS FOURTEEN miles out of Telluride when his GPS told him to pull the Jeep off the pavement onto a gravel road. The road would turn to hard-packed dirt, then loose sand.

He drove to the point where the oversized tires were spitting loose rocks backward like machine-gun fire as he willed the vehicle up the side of the mountain. The sandy fire-road was initially navigable, but tricky, and it narrowed tightly a few minutes in, and all but disappeared at a thick stand of Ponderosa pines. He killed the engine.

Dark was coming in forty minutes. He opened the back hatch, placed his cooler on the ground, and unfurled his sleeping bag inside the Jeep.

He placed a halogen headlamp on his head for use after dark. Grabbed his tablet off the passenger seat, pulled up Kindle. He was about a third of the way in on a Vince Flynn thriller. Sometimes he pictured himself as Flynn's CIA assassin, Mitch Rapp, an unstoppable badass.

6:05 A.M. SOFT LIGHT filtered into the woods. Lucky slid out of the sleeping bag, crawled through the hatch, and peed in the grass. He popped open a lightweight camp chair, then rummaged through three granola bars and a banana from the cooler, along with a chilled Diet Coke. He sat down, pulled up *American Assassin* on his tablet. He liked to read while he tanked up on fuel.

At 6:50, Lucky had three chapters left, but the mission came first. Time to go to work.

The woods were dead quiet save for the birds. The clear mountain air was a brisk fifty-one degrees with an aroma of summer flowers in the distance. He grabbed his backpack and camera from the truck. He wore a black fleece, hiking shorts, lightweight trail runners, and dark Costas. A ball cap was pulled low on his forehead.

Time to trudge up the mountain.

Lucky marked the position of the Jeep on his GPS, took a big gulp of air, and began the ascent through the pines and firs to get over the incline to his preset destination. It was up, then over the apex and down, to the areas he wanted to scout. A half-mile.

As he crested the peak, he spotted Clemmons' home nestled at the bottom of the box canyon. His digital rangefinder told him he was 1,112 yards out.

For the next two hours he combed around the mountainside, gradually descending, digitally marking three areas that would make a strong sniper perch, each at a distance he felt comfortable firing from, 450–700 yards. Each hide had a magnificent high-to-low view of the swimming pool area.

He went back to a perch protected by heavy brush, got comfortable, and watched the home with his spotting scope. Clemmons and his bodyguards grabbed lunch by the pool. Lucky hoped it was a daily habit. After eating, the bodyguards played cards under an umbrella. He made out handguns holstered on their hips.

After eating, Clemmons sat in a turquoise-colored chaise, reading a hardcover book. He was a soft, fleshy seventy-year-old with a frizz of graying hair that looked like a spent Brillo pad. He wore bulky glasses over a red-potato nose.

The spotting scope identified *Presumed Innocent* on the book cover. Lucky thought Harrison Ford was in the movie but wasn't sure.

The weather forecast was perfect for the week. Highs mid-seventies, lows upper forties. All sunshine, not a hint of moisture. Any day would conceivably work.

Lucky was ready for the moment.

48

HEAT WAVES BILLOWED off the asphalt. It was ninety-two degrees in South Carolina when Jake Montoya pulled up at the Sombrero Tower. The place was a slice of highway Americana, South of the Border, a highway oasis.

The Pedro empire was a convoluted mishmash of garishly colored wacky architecture, screwball souvenir shops, fireworks, gasoline, burritos, and a reptile lagoon.

Rowdy popped up wide-eyed and wary as the Tahoe came to a halt.

Jake parked, stepped out of the truck, took in the crowd, and pushed his hair back behind his ears. It hadn't been cut in three months and was now well over his back collar. He wore hiking shorts and a black T-shirt that advertised Big Jake's Game Day Grills.

As he placed Rowdy on the ground, the dog's ears went up. He looked past Jake, caught movement, and went steely-eyed. A twitch jiggled his lip, about to bare teeth. Jake turned. A man and his son approached.

"Hey, that's a great-looking German shepherd. What happened to his leg?" said the dad.

"Whoa, hold up." Jake put up his hand. "He's skittish with people getting near me. That's a Belgian Malinois, a service dog, but he looks like a shepherd. Rowdy saved my life and got shot for his trouble. He's a little high-strung right now."

The kid, fourteen, maybe fifteen years old, said, "Holy hell, Dad, they shot the damn dog."

"Hey, watch the language, son."

The kid looked up at Jake. "You a cop?"

"Yep."

"You don't look like a cop," said the boy as he eyed Jake's physique. "You do look like you could kick the living hell outta somebody's ass, though."

"Jeremy! Stop the language," said dad.

The kid noticed Jake's T-shirt. "Hey, my dad's got a Big Jake Grill at home." The boy cocked a thumb toward his old man.

"Sure do, how 'bout you, man?" said dad.

"Yeah, I've got one up in Washington. A friend gave me one for Christmas. Shirt came with it." Jake pinched out the tee.

"Don't mean to brag, but I played ball at Virginia Tech, you know, in Blacksburg. Started my senior year, placekicker," said dad. "I tailgate every home game. Hands down the best grill I've ever owned."

"College ball, cool." *Placekicker.* Jake grinned.

The kid stared Jake down. Had a look in his eye. "Know what's weird? You look like that guy."

"Who?"

"The TV commercial guy. My dad and I laugh our asses off at the one where that dumbass dude burns his house down using that cheap-ass grill sitting on the wobbly picnic table. You know, the house catches fire, burns completely down, the fire truck pumps water all over the ashes. Then the firemen and the dumbass go next door and eat burgers with the guy wearing an apron cooking on the Big Jake." The teenager pointed. "And he looks just like you."

“Last time for that language, son.” Guy popped his boy with a love smack on the back of the head, pointed to the car. “Go.” He gave Jake a wink. “Kids.”

In the oversized gift shop, Jake took a quick whizz, washed up, and bought a drink and trail mix. Just before paying, he grabbed an audiobook. Grisham’s original hit on audio, *The Firm.*

The kid approached the truck when Jake was filling the tank. “Hey, we wanna hear the story.”

“The grill story?”

“Hell no, man. The shootout. Where that asshole popped your dog.”

“Here’s what you do. Pull up YouTube, punch in ‘FBI shooting Virginia Beach.’ That’ll tell you all you need to know.”

“Hell yeah, man. Freakin’ video.”

Wind scurries hit the truck as Jake twisted through the parking lot, heading out to relaunch on I-95. A handful of fat water-drops splattered the windshield like goose droppings. He glanced toward the southwest. Clouds were bunching up, going dark at the base. A few strings of jagged lightning shot through the sky. Too far away for thunder.

Jake jumped on the interstate, and quickly had the truck running eighty. He had a detective to meet in Charleston.

He slid *The Firm* into the CD player. It started with a new grad lawyer from Harvard taking a job in Memphis for a law firm fronting for the mob. Lawyers, a shady bunch.

Grisham had a great story rolling, but Jake’s mind drifted back to the kid.

And the shooting.

49

LUCKY REACHED THE ridgeline at 7:05 a.m. carrying his rifle. He glassed the house. No movement. The plan was dynamic. He might finish today. He might not.

He chose to set up at the highest elevation of his three hides. The sun rose behind him, so no reflection off his scope.

He opened the case and unloaded the rifle. A heavy twelve-inch-long suppressor was threaded into the barrel. He slid the gun barrel through a natural ten-inch diameter opening in the brush, resting the rifle into the V-slotted bean-bag rests under the fore-end and stock.

The sophisticated Kestrel wind meter with ballistic calculator was placed on a small tripod to the left of the gun. The camera was set up on a tripod slightly higher, and just to the rear of the wind meter. It was outfitted with a 300–800mm zoom he rented from a camera shop in San Diego. Maxed to 800mm, the camera had a tight view of the pool area. With the touch of a button, video would roll.

First movement. It was 9:17 a.m. One of the guards walked out onto the pool deck in running shorts and a sleeveless sweatshirt. After stretching, he jogged off with moderate pace around the house, and onto the gravel drive that went to the highway. Lucky watched him turn north at the highway. The man was quickly out of sight.

Lucky had an inkling this could be the day. He was prone, comfortable behind the gun, which became a natural extension of his body. He leaned to his right so he could watch the area with binoculars. The runner returned an hour later.

Clemmons showed at 11:20, stepping on the pool deck from a sliding glass door. He had his book in his hand, wore baggy golf shorts and a pink polo shirt. Five minutes later a bodyguard came outside, coffee cup in hand and laptop under his arm. He set up at the table with the umbrella, flipped the screen up.

Perfect except for one thing. Where was the second man?

The laser rangefinder indicated 647 yards. Six-and-one-half football fields. This info was synced into the Kestrel. Wind 2.7 miles per hour, almost still. The Kestrel held ballistic information for the rifle and the bullet characteristics for the .338 Magnum round. The angle of the shot was calculated. From Lucky's position, Peter John had the left posterior of his head facing the barrel of the rifle. His face canted downward as he read.

Commotion. That would bring the hidden guard out of the house. Lucky thought, *GREENLIGHT!*

Time slowed. The day was as tranquil as a botanical garden. No battle chaos. No havoc. No dust. No berserk militants firing thousands of rounds in his direction. No radio comms buzzing through his ears. No choppers. No jet engine roar.

Mountain serenity.

The rifle was secure over its supports, positioned in the natural point of aim. The scope reticle was precisely placed, just behind Clemmons' left ear. Lucky slowed his breathing. His trigger pressure was controlled, delicate, intimate. *Make love to that sexy trigger, baby.*

At two pounds pressure, the bullet spit from the gun, *pffft.* The scope bumped up, barely. Lucky continued light trigger follow-through. The scope repositioned.

Jeannie Marie Baughn sends her love, counselor.

The heavy Magnum round punctured the back of Clemmons' head and ripped the right side of his face apart as it exited, lodging itself in the concrete pad around the pool. The force knocked Clemmons out of his chair. He was facedown on the deck with bloody brain matter splashed all the way into the pool.

Lucky imperceptibly shifted the scope to Kimbrell's position on the ground.

He ejected the spent shell, jacked another round in the chamber. He focused the scope crosshairs onto Kimbrell's left back, just behind the heart. Another round blew out of the gun. Kimbrell's trunk bounced in the air like it was struck by lightning. The round shattered a posterior rib before it liquefied Kimbrell's left ventricle.

Lucky eased the scope toward the bodyguard at the table. He was squatting behind his flimsy chair, gun drawn, scanning the mountain. The suppressor disguised Lucky's location. The guard's head swiveled in panic, seeing nothing but harmless trees. Lucky knew he was thinking about making a run for the house. He knew adrenaline likely had the guy's heart pounding like a sledgehammer and his eyes were dilated.

Lucky worked the bolt ejecting the shell and loaded another round in the chamber. It was fast.

The guard's head stuck up just above the table for a peek. A tiny peek. Lucky centered the reticle on his midface. The third Magnum round left the rifle at 3,000 feet per second. The man's head exploded.

Come on, little Superman, come out of the house, save the day.

Lucky scanned the windows at the rear of the home. He caught a hint of movement at the sliding glass door that opened to the pool. *There you are.*

Rising sunlight from behind Lucky cast a glare on the door glass. Half of a face appeared at the edge of the reflection. Lucky made out just one squinting eye of the bodyguard, then it opened wide. Fear.

He had watched his boss and coworker blown apart on the pool deck.

Lucky placed the reticle at the edge of the finely demarcated glare. Central face of the guard. The heavy gun bucked. Glass shattered. The guard's head whiplashed backward with the force from the Magnum round. The glass was gone. Lucky knew the man was dead. Nobody walks away from a .338 round to the center of the skull. But still. Lucky saw the soles of the guard's shoes. He tiptoed the rifle up to where his abdomen should be. *Pffft.* Lucky saw the shoes move. Adjusted the muzzle again, hopefully center chest or neck. He tickled the trigger backward. The body jolted once again.

Lucky hoped the man hadn't fired off a 911 call prior to placing his face in front of a tactical sniper round.

He adjusted the sniper rifle back to the guard lying on the pool deck. He'd only received one bullet. Another round blasted his remaining skull bone to shards. Double tap was the name of the game.

Seven shots. Fifty-nine seconds. Boogie time.

Lucky packed the rifle in the case, snapped it closed. Twelve seconds. Eighteen seconds to throw two tripods holding the Kestrel and camera and the shooting supports into the duffel. He froze, studied the area for fifteen seconds. Missing anything? *Look! Look! Look!* Six brass shells. He stuffed them in his pocket. Seventh still in the gun.

Nothing else. Haul ass.

Lucky's thighs burned as he thrust his legs to get to the crest of the ridge while carrying a rifle and an awkward duffel. The downhill would be dangerous. He needed maximum speed without catching a limb in the face.

Running, sliding, dodging trees, case and duffel flopping aimlessly, he quickly felt off balance. Twenty-five yards from the Jeep, his right toe caught a root he didn't see. The rifle and duffle flew out of his hands. He braced for the fall. His hands were late to the ground, forcing him to face-plant, leaving a skin-ripping abrasion on his forehead and nose.

He bounced up, flicked dust from his eyes, grabbed the gun case and duffel, and raced over to the Jeep, stepping on the front bumper, then up onto the hood. He hopped on the roof with the rifle case, stuffed it into the leg well of the kayak.

He jumped down to the ground, opened the driver's door, and threw the duffel onto the floorboard. He fired up the Jeep, glanced into the rearview mirror, saw blood running down to his chin. No bandages, no towel. He reached back over his seat, grabbed the drop cloth, wiped off blood and sweat. Looked back in the mirror. *The hat! Where's my hat?*

He jumped out, ran uphill hyper-focused, pupils racing over the ground. There, there, there. Upside down in the dirt, the Patagonia cap. He grabbed it, raced back, jumped in the Jeep, hammered it.

THE CESSNA CARAVAN was stashed in its hangar at the McClellan-Palomar airport in Carlsbad, California at 11:36 that night.

50

JAKE EASED THE Tahoe onto I-95, pushed it to seventy-five, then quickly hit eighty, hit cruise control. Settled on the highway, he slid *The Firm* into the CD player, ready for a good tale.

Fifty minutes later, he thought about the boy at the gas station. And the Virginia Beach incident.

He drifted into his memory. That was no easy day.

It was early March, a couple months ago, when the call came into Jake's DC office. Still cold, not a hint of spring. A Virginia Beach PD detective on the line.

The detective said he had a lead in the White Dragons Motorcycle Gang case. A phone number and possible address to Linda Chastang, former wife of Billy Chastang, the leader of the Dragons. Billy had been underground for a couple years.

Jake had driven down from DC the day after the call. On the road, Jake called one of his old football teammates who was a head ball coach at a large high school in the area. They set up an early dinner at a steakhouse.

Linda Chastang might have something interesting to share, but unlikely, Jake thought. Biker chicks knew to keep their mouths shut.

The Tahoe's GPS had brought Jake and Rowdy straight to the location, a subdivision called Brook Run on the edge of the Virginia Beach city limits. Easing through the entrance, he quickly found 533 Maple Tree Lane.

It was a cold, gray afternoon feeling the remnants of the mild nor'easter that blew in on the coast just after lunch yesterday. Light was fading. It would be dark in thirty minutes.

Jake pulled his SUV into the driveway of a nondescript tract home in the middle-class, working-man subdivision. Two thousand square feet or so, probably three-bedroom, two baths.

A late model Honda Civic was parked in front of the garage door. An economy model that fit the neighborhood price point.

Twenty-four months earlier, the FBI had begun an investigative effort into the workings of a motorcycle gang that had a strong presence from Georgia to northern New Jersey, the White Dragons. The crew had an appetite for violence and murder while they executed their primary mission, drug distribution. As a sideline, they strong-armed into large shipping warehouses at night and made off with tractor-trailer loads of merchandise for the black market.

He parked right beside the car, sat in the truck, and stared. Nothing fit. No way was anybody associated with the White Dragons living in this tidy place.

The Honda was shiny, with no counterculture propaganda of any sort stuck to the car. The rear window had a decal that said UVA Wahoos. Motorcycle gangs didn't send their kids to the University of Virginia, did they?

His stomach was growling. Steak and bloomin' onion thoughts. Meeting at Outback.

He popped the electronic lock for the rear window in the truck, the dog's exit. The glass hatch glided up and open. Rowdy, trained in Europe, was a vicious menace with a hair trigger. He went most places with Jake.

Rowdy stood and scanned as the window opened. Dog-on-duty, Jack.

Jake slipped out of the Tahoe, stood there for a moment, and looked down at both ends of the street. A few more cars coming home, done for the day. He walked all the way around the Civic. Rowdy's eyes were fixed to the path Jake walked.

Jake wore a winter-weight sport coat over a crisp, white oxford. A Glock .45 sat on his left hip under the jacket, holstered in a cross-draw configuration.

He took a long look in the passenger side window of the Civic. A curtain in the house parted an inch as he scoured the car. He didn't notice it.

Rowdy's eyes caught the brief movement. The dog's hackles raised, aggression right behind it. Jake had vested him just before entering the neighborhood. The Kevlar shielded most of his trunk and blended with his coat.

Jake bounded up the two steps onto the eight-by-ten-foot concrete stoop. He readied for what would most likely be a short conversation. He figured out a retired bookkeeper or dental hygienist or high school librarian, but maybe a nurse. The Civic was pristine. That was how those professions liked their lives, neat and orderly. Biker chick? Couldn't picture it.

Steak thoughts bore down on him. He made his decision right there. Large filet.

His finger blipped the doorbell. Didn't hear a ring, maybe broken. The entry had an aluminum-framed screen door in front of a solid wood door with a horseshoe knocker.

It was forty-two degrees and damp. A chilled breeze tossed his hair.

He pulled the screen door open, had his hand in the air ready to deliver a light tap. Before he touched the knocker, the door opened. There stood a wiry female, shoulder-length dark hair, early forties, with a hard face and suspicious eyes. She smelled of cigarette smoke. Her presence was softened by a conservative dress.

"Are you Ms. Chastang?"

"Who cares? What do you want?" She stepped out of the house.

Chastang pushed into Jake's space and caused him to step back down off the porch. Not a timid lady.

Jake spotted the tails of dragon tattoos on both of her upper arms. They peeked from under the sleeves of her dress. Hard to miss the heavy green ink. Around her right ankle he caught a glimpse of a Confederate flag tattoo. The woman also had a mouth on her.

He was in the right place.

"Ma'am, I'm Jake Montoya from the FBI. I'd like to come in and ask you a few questions, and then be on my way." He held his badge up as he spoke.

"Well, why don't you call for an appointment, for Christ sakes? Another time when I'm not busy."

"Ms. Chastang, this will only take a moment." Jake glanced at his watch. "I've got another important meeting to make in half an hour."

The aluminum door exploded open.

Two very large, menacing men moved into Jake's personal space. Hostility filled their eyes.

Jake's heart thundered.

51

"GET THE HELL in the house, Linda." Ice in his voice. One of the men jerked her out of the way.

Jake quickly backed up three feet. He didn't want to be in arm's reach of two men this size.

He knew exactly who they were. Bobby and Ricky Talton, probably fifty, from the mountains near Lexington, Virginia, General Robert E. Lee's resting place. Identical twins were an unexpected finding in biker gang circles, made it hard to forget.

Both were beefy, with graying long hair woven into a braid down their back. Each wore beards six inches long dangling from their chin, pulled into tight, thin ponytails bound with two skinny rubber bands, two inches apart. Ham-hock arms hung down, heavy with ink.

The psychology of twins raced through Jake's brain. Wearing the exact same clothes in middle age, same distinct haircuts, identical beards. Motorcycle gang. Made him think of a Tarantino movie, wacko, kind of funny, but dangerous. *Need more research on this phenomenon,* he thought.

At six-three, Jake had three inches on them. It was a different story on weight. The twins easily hit 280, sixty pounds more than Jake.

"Why don't you hit the road, cop. Or maybe you got some kinda warrant."

“Fellas, I just needed a few minutes to chat with Ms. Chastang. But I’m glad you’re both here. Makes it more convenient for all of us,” said Jake, wearing a friendly smile.

Bobby spat on Jake’s shoe, casual-like, almost like he was in a conversation about fishing. A heavy green glob landed on the top of his right foot.

Jake’s jaw muscles tensed.

“We ain’t talking today. We ain’t talking tomorrow. So why don’t you head on down the highway.”

Jake spotted movement in his peripheral vision. It was a smaller man coming around the side of the house, moving in silence, slow with caution, listening to the conversation. Jake turned. The guy was maybe five-eight with a gaunt face and hollow eyes, unhealthy. Had a yellowish skin tint. Hep C likely.

This runt was the deal, though. He wore colors of the Dragons on a black, sleeveless leather vest. His dark hair was buzzed into whitewalls on the sides with an inch of growth across the top, a prison cut. Four drops of tattoo tears on his face below his right eye. Proud ink of a killer.

It was Billy Chastang. The man the Bureau had hunted for two years.

“We’re kind of sick of this horse-shit harassment,” said Billy. “Bobby, you and Ricky want to leave a message for those Washington pricks?”

Chastang slid something small out of his jean’s right-front pocket. It was a hammerless, snub-nose .38, all black. Easy to conceal. He held it slack, next to his right leg. One of the big boys bent, slipped his hand down to his boot, never taking his eyes off Jake’s face.

He rose with a bone-handled Bowie knife.

Jake’s heart rate kicked up. Over five minutes, the day took a bad wrong turn. Thought maybe he should have brought some back-up. He maintained his cool.

Silent, Rowdy watched it all unfold.

The dog glided gracefully over the rear gate of the Tahoe once he saw the man come around the house. His paws landed softly. Harsh voices cranked his nervous system into raw anxiety. His lips quivered.

As Billy inched toward Jake with the pistol in his hand, Rowdy crept to the man's outer flank. The dog was twenty feet away from Jake, ten feet from yellow-eyed Billy.

No sun, temps dropping. The smell of fireplace smoke drifted by. It was 6:10. Almost dark.

The Talton brothers and Billy suddenly felt the aura of the dark shadow slinking over.

Rowdy stopped.

Jake knew exactly what his dog was thinking—*Got my eye on you, motherfuckers.*

"Ahhh, what's this crap? The copper brought Rin Tin Tin." Billy snorted a laugh. "He even went to a cop store, bought him a little costume, dressed him like Deputy Dawg." He sneered again. "Dog's gotta be a bitch. That thing's on the puny side for a cop dog. Need to get him in the gym, Mr. Po-leece-man."

Jake piped up. "Let's just talk this through." He didn't like the direction of this scene. His heartbeat began to thunder.

The three men snickered. One of the Taltons said, "Billy, take a pop at Lassie. See if that cardboard vest works."

"Hell yeah." Billy turned his hollow eyes back to Rowdy, raising the pistol. "Think I will."

It happened fast. Jake took two brisk steps to his left, away from Rowdy, shielding himself behind one of the Taltons from Billy's line of fire.

He hollered, "Billy!" Followed it with a shrill whistle through his teeth, Rowdy's signal.

"*AANVAL!*" Jake hollered. Dutch for attack.

Billy caught Jake's move with the call of his name. He took his eyes off a dog trained in handgun recognition. It was a split second. And it was the biggest mistake of Billy's life. Two seconds, that's all the dog needed.

Rowdy bared his teeth. Showtime.

After two broad strides, Rowdy launched into a pile-drive flight toward Chastang. A fierce growl pierced the air, then Rowdy's muscular jaws latched on to Billy's neck. Billy's windpipe and left carotid ripped free as he spun to release the psychotic animal. A quick shot flew out of the barrel of the snub nose into the sky as he attempted to pop a slug in the dog. Billy fired a second wild shot. He clipped Rowdy in the left hindquarters, but the dog hung tough through a three-quarter turn. At this point, a heavy slab of Billy's neck tore away from his body.

Rowdy hit the ground hard six feet away, spit out the flesh, popped up and trounced back to finish his attack on Billy, who was flat on his back.

The Mali latched onto Billy's face, ripped it savagely side to side like a hungry machine, while Billy's arms and legs floundered like he was being electrocuted. Rowdy shredded the nose and both ears right off Billy's head, leaving him unrecognizable. Blood gushed from his ravaged neck.

The dog left him dead in only moments.

Bobby lunged at Jake with the knife. Ricky dashed into the house.

Jake dodged the knife, locked his right hand onto Bobby's wrist, his knife hand, then placed his left on the big man's right elbow, twisted upward and forward in a brisk, violent motion. Tendons ripped in the rotator cuff as the shoulder dislocated from the socket. Jake launched his right leg into an explosive side kick, ramming his shin into Bobby's left ribcage. Three ribs snapped.

The big man hollered, dropped to his knees with his face next to the sharp edge of brick steps.

Jake bent, snatched a fistful of ponytail, pulled the man's head upward, then slammed his face into the edge of the steps. Fractured bone splintered into the brain.

He looked up for Ricky.

The big hoss screamed before he even opened the aluminum door. "You're a dead man!" He carried three feet of cold, black death, a cut-down AR-15.

Jake was still in a crouch. The cross-draw was faster than a snake. He drew the Glock from under his coat. Three rounds burst into Ricky's center chest as he crashed open the aluminum door. Ricky dropped onto his brother, face down. The assault rifle flew into the boxwoods.

The mid portion of Ricky's back was blown open by .45 caliber hollow-points.

Jake ran over to Rowdy, who was lying on his side, eyes open, low moans coming from his mouth. The dog's face and hind parts were soaked in blood. Bullet wound. Jake wiped blood from the dog's face with his sport coat, then looked in his mouth. Two teeth were broken, one a lower canine. A three-quarter-inch laceration was on his tongue, gushing blood. Rowdy had bitten it in his hysteria.

Jake heard sirens. Neighbors crowded onto the scene. Three Virginia Beach cop cars swerved up simultaneously. Jake held his FBI shield out as they approached. The police approached with caution, flashlights out, pistols drawn.

Total darkness now.

"FBI! Man down. Man down, officers." Jake went on, "Need an ambulance now! Move those cars out of the way. Make room."

An ambulance pulled up twenty seconds later.

Paramedics with flashlights ran a gurney up to the Dragon with the crushed face. Guttural sounds could be heard behind the bubbling blood in his mouth.

"This guy's alive," said one of the medics. They began to load him as the police attempted interrogation of Jake.

Jake pushed the officers aside, rushed to the gurney, dumped the biker to the ground. "Come on, dammit, the patient's over here." Jake pulled the gurney to Rowdy. He picked his dog up with the gentleness a parent gives their child.

A flashlight beam hit the dog. Looking closer, the cops spotted the Kevlar vest. They knew. Member of the force.

Two cops ran toward their cars. "Load the dog! Let's go!" Rowdy went into the back of the boxy ambulance, covered with the sport coat. Jake climbed in at his side. Doors slammed.

Two black and whites scorched out of the neighborhood, running hot. Ambulance tires screeched as they reversed, hit the brakes, spun around to follow the cops. Red lights, blue lights, sirens, horns, everything firing. Look the hell out.

Forty-five minutes later, after X-rays, a veterinarian was examining Rowdy at his emergency clinic. Dr. Bud Smith reassuringly nodded at Jake.

"We should be fine."

52

ZEUS SENT A short, intimidating video of a shooting exhibition to thirty-five lawyers. He included one simple question.

How would a .338 Magnum feel in your head?

$21.9 million arrived in nineteen separate bank accounts, all overseas.

Zeus smiled as he playfully typed his encrypted message for Lucky: *Seven shots. $17.52 million moving into your account. Nice return!*

53

AFTER SIXTY-FIVE MILES on I-95, Jake ran into hard rain dropping out of a summer squall. He popped on the headlights and wipers.

After a couple more miles, Jake reached back to stroke Rowdy's head. "You're a helluva dog, boy. Glad you're here."

The Grisham book was at the scene where the FBI agent warns the newbie lawyer about the devious snakes at the law firm.

Jake listened, drove head-on into the storm.

54

CHARLESTON, SOUTH CAROLINA

"I'M AGENT JAKE MONTOYA, here to see Detective Hewitt."

An early-sixties woman behind a desk looked him over, then stood, looked down at the dog with a cast on his leg, a badge on his collar, and a muzzle on his snout. Jake could see her thinking, *What's up with this guy?* Longish hair, three-day scruff, chiseled face, built, looking kind of shabby. From the way she looked at Jake, maybe as a younger woman she'd have been into him.

She pointed. "End of this hall on the right. Waiting on you."

Jake found Rye Hewitt behind his desk, tapping the keyboard on his computer.

"Good afternoon, detective, I'm Jake Montoya, and this is Rowdy." They shook hands.

"Have a seat, Agent Montoya." Hewitt gestured to an empty chair. "Good-looking service dog. The news filtered down that he'll have a full recovery."

"Please, call me Jake. And, yes, he'll be back full steam in about six weeks."

"Glad to hear it."

Jake eased into a chair, placed his right ankle across his left knee. "So, as you know, since the attorneys were taken down here in Charleston and in Colorado, the Bureau has been called in. We can bring a lot of resources in to help the local departments."

Hewitt nodded. "Like the sound of that."

"Officially, I'm on suspension after the Virginia Beach deal. Unofficially, I'm here to get an overview of what you guys know. I'm headed to Alabama to look into the car bombing of a local attorney to see if there may be any connection. But, anyway, whatcha got on this Green murder?"

"Jake, we've got a tiger by the tail, a calamity. Green, as you know, was a high-income trial lawyer, good looking guy, generally popular, all over the place in TV ads and billboards, also a major presence socially around town. His wife, Hallett, was also very well known. Their son, Brax, was weeks away from graduating from a local prep school. And the crime scene?" Hewitt shook his head. "Oh, dear God. Nobody in this department has seen anything quite like it."

"Okay. Break it down for me."

Rye exhaled. "Horrendous. Braxton and Hallett were both naked. The husband had his penis sliced off and stuffed in his mouth. And if that wasn't bad enough, he had a thin fluorescent tube rammed ten inches into his rectum. It was one of the skinny bulbs from a bathroom vanity light. The autopsy report said it ripped through the colon, caused massive bleeding."

Jake's jaw tightened. "Good God."

"The wife had her head severed from her body. It's gone. Not recovered."

"For God's sake, Rye." Jake readjusted in his seat.

Rye frowned. "Hell, I know."

"Their son was shot in the knee, tied up, and dumped into his bedroom. Thank God he didn't see his parents. We think a tomahawk was used to take the wife's head off."

"A tomahawk? Wait. How would you know? Was it on the scene?"

Hewitt shook his head. "Uh-uh. We received a photo by email. Hallett had a blindfold on. The tomahawk was photographed as it was held next to her neck. We received a second photo a few minutes after that. There was no head on the woman's shoulders. The weapon's not some little Indian souvenir, either. It's a wicked design with a spike on the other side of the blade. A damn evil weapon."

"Huh, a tomahawk. Yeah, I want copies of those photos."

"Gets even stranger. In Hallett's bedroom, a young guy, thirty-three, was found tied up on the bed with velvet-covered restraints, completely naked, with duct tape over his mouth, and a mask covering his eyes. He's a local country-club tennis pro, a guy from Denmark. Hallett was an avid tennis player and the chatter on the street was that she was into sleeping around with club pros."

"You serious? The day of the murders?"

"Yep, same day. And surprise. He don't know shit. We've also identified two other tennis pros, neither over thirty-five, who have admitted sleeping with her. They've been cleared at this point from any involvement in the murders. The pro in the house said Hallett put the mask on him and tied him up prior to the intruder or intruders arriving."

Jake screwed up his face. "Surprised they didn't kill him. Okay, so at this point where are you headed?"

"Here's where we are, Jake. Our main motive here is the drug trade."

"Drugs? What drugs?"

"Here's what we know. On the morning of the murders, a twenty-eight-year-old Black man went to Braxton Green's law firm. He gave no name and no ID. He wanted to deliver a package to a sixty-three-year-old female lawyer who had worked with Green since he started his firm. Back when he was nobody."

"Dope?"

"Uh-uh, no. A brand-new Porsche Boxster."

Jake whistled. "Interesting."

"Come to find out the car was purchased by the son, Green's seventeen-year-old kid. There was no financing. It was purchased with straight-out cash the week before. The Black guy who delivered the car was caught on video from both inside and outside Green's office."

"ID him?"

"Oh, yeah. Demarious Campbell, the leader of Charleston's top dope gang."

Rye continued. "The female lawyer at the office has no clue about the reason for the car's arrival, but admits she was very close to the boy since he was about ten years old. She said she assumes the money came from the boy's parents. The young man is ambitious. He's going to be an environmental lawyer and wants to establish an outdoor clothing company and an adventure travel outfit."

"Huh." Montoya rubbed his hand across his mouth. "Bizarre. The whole thing."

"We've torn the Green mansion apart. The boy's prosperous. Found $125,000 cash in a clever hiding place in the wall of his bedroom. Another $50K at the bottom of a deep freezer that he kept his fishing bait in. His phone has a lot of calls to California and other spots. And a lot to Demarious Campbell. Word out at the kid's private school is he is supposed to be a weed-only dope dealer for the upper crust set."

"So, the son's alive. What'd he have to say?"

"The kid's distraught, naturally. His doc has him on meds. He says he saw only one guy, dressed in black, like a ninja. Six feet or so, slim. Brax denies any drug involvement. Says he doesn't touch the stuff. He told us the lawyer, Allison Trotter, was more like a mother to him than his own mother, and he wanted to give *her* a present since he was going off to school. Says his old man gave him the money."

"You believe him?"

Rye shook his head. "Shit no. Lying brat. And there's no evidence we could find of $71,000 dollars coming from any of Green's accounts to pay for the car. The kid has an attorney, who has informed us his client has nothing more to say. We mentioned dope and the lawyer laughed in my face. Said the kid was headed to Duke."

"Okay, so what does Demarious Campbell have to say?"

"With a little less polish, he said, 'Suck my dick and then talk to my fucking lawyer,'" said Rye. "And that's an exact quote."

Jake laughed. "Good one. But what I really want to know is, did you find any extortion demand information aimed at the lawyer, or any large sums leaving his bank accounts going overseas?"

"Extortion?" A puzzled look creased the detective's face. "This is a straight-out dope case, agent."

"Huh." Jake's face showed no emotion.

Not quite.

55

BLACK POINT, ALABAMA

JAKE AND HIS lean-muscled, four-legged partner ghosted into town like night shadows. Streets empty. Everything quiet. Passing through the stoplight at Colony Street, the town clock read 4:14 a.m.

Black Point was a semitropical, leafy village situated on tall bluffs overlooking the waters of Mobile Bay, an enclave where trees were revered and a splash of happy flowers anchor every corner of the downtown.

Driving down Black Point Avenue, in the heart of the town, Jake glanced over at Billy Burnham's law office. Plywood covered the blown-out windows.

A quarter mile west of downtown, Jake cut left on Great Bay Road. Three hundred feet later, he turned left onto Fels Avenue. His mother's home was on the left. He slowed to look.

The cozy bungalow had been built in '36. It had exposed rafter tails, jonquil-yellow shiplap siding, and was covered with a rain-loving tin roof. A dim, yellow bug light shone over the front door. Though dark, Jake knew day lilies or salvia likely circled the mailbox.

The neighborhood was silent, no dogs barking, no cars poking around, just a few unseen Boo Radleys lurking in the dark. Night dwellers. By ten that morning the word would be out that he was in town.

He circled the block. Through rosy moonglow, he edged his Tahoe up over the sidewalk and right down to the edge of the forty-foot bayfront bluff. Locals were proud of this vista, with ample reason. Just before twilight, the western skyline would uncork wild palettes of corals and pinks and purples that drifted into a starlit indigo night. Sunsets every bit the caliber of anything in Malibu.

Jake stepped out of the truck, stretched, glanced toward the water at the lights, dull yellow from the Black Point pier below. Other lights danced like diamonds on the black water's distant surface. The lights of Mobile, Alabama, could be seen fifteen miles northwest across the bay. The scents of jasmine and algae drifted past his nose on salty bay air.

A vibe raked over Jake in the darkness.

This was a real good place for a murder.

56

GRAY DAYLIGHT, the earliest dawn before the sunrise. His watch said 5:35. Jake could finally make out the human movement he expected to see on the bluff, forty yards south of him. He quietly slipped out of the Tahoe and moved from tree to tree, drifting as silently as he could, in the direction of the motion.

Twenty yards from his target he heard the familiar voice. The small man faced away from him, with his arms and legs moving in slow motion tai chi as he spoke.

"Jake Montoya. I'm surprised you and your animal didn't notice me when I peeked in the truck. Your eyes were closed."

Woo Chow could be as silent as dew forming on grass. He was mid-seventies, five-six, 133 pounds. Soft gray hair complemented his wise face. At this very spot thirty-two years earlier, Woo had introduced Jake to martial arts, first Jeet Kune Do, then Brazilian jiu jitsu.

Jake laughed at his teacher. "You're too much, Woo. Never miss a thing."

Woo stopped his motion, turned toward Jake, walked over, and placed both arms around him. "I've missed you, Jake. I think of you almost daily." He released the hug and looked up at the much taller man. "I worry about your safety in this corrupt world. Always remember—"

Jake smiled, completed his sentence. "Empty your mind, become formless, shapeless. Be like water, drown your adversary."

"Yes, yes, Jake ... that's it. Water." Woo smiled. "See you five-thirty tomorrow morning?"

"Count on it."

JAKE TURNED THE Tahoe into his mother's short driveway, hopped out. He pulled the porch screen door open, stretching out the spring with a screech. The door closed with a slap of wood. His knuckles rapped the front door.

Footfalls approached from inside. Bonnie's green eyes peeked through a small window in the solid door. Wisps of gray in her strawberry blond hair fell over her forehead. The deadbolt rattled as she unlocked it.

"What in the world, What ... in ... the ... world! Ohhh, come here, boy."

Jake grabbed his mother in a hug, lifting her feet off the ground. "Anybody here want a cathead biscuit at Lyrene's?"

Bonnie popped a sudden tear of happiness at the surprise, wiped it with the back of her hand. "Ohhh, my goodness. You didn't call."

"Let's talk about it over breakfast. I'm starving."

"Give me fifteen minutes."

Walking into the cottage, the smell of his childhood washed over him in a cloud. The scent never changed. Ed's chair was in the same spot where he last sat in it. Jake pictured him reading the *Mobile Press Register* every day after work, maybe a beer or bourbon to relax. The same pictures were on the wall, the same knickknacks, and curios in the same crannies they were in when he moved in the home at age nine.

He inhaled, calming the poignancy of reminiscence.

Glanced into his old bedroom from the doorway. Before the accident, it was Chuck's bedroom, Bonnie and Ed's son. Jake changed nothing over the years. Chuck's model cars and fishing rod were right where he'd left them. A picture of Chuck and his parents at the Magic Kingdom rested on the dresser. The bed was made, everything clean and dusted. The closet still held some of Chuck's clothes.

The memory fought through his mind's barriers.

IT WAS 3:25 P.M. The Friday before Memorial Day. Last day of school. Thirty-four years ago. A sweatbox hot, crystal-clear afternoon. Bonnie and Ed had presented Chuck with a new mountain bike after breakfast. It had eight speeds and handbrakes, a new level of sophistication for the boy.

After school, Chuck was riding his bike downhill on Fels, showing off his speed. Jake and Kimbo were behind him on their bikes, intentionally letting Chuck win the race.

Bonnie was on her knees at the mailbox, trowel in hand, planting gladiolus. She looked up and smiled when she heard her son yell, "I'm winning, Mama."

Chuck flew past his mother. Bonnie jumped up. "Chuck, STOP!"

The boy ran the stop sign eighty feet from the cottage, his legs spinning madly in reverse as he attempted to brake, his fingers forgetting the hand breaks. The four-door Chevy Biscayne was running thirty, driven by an eighty-three-year-old retired preacher looking the other way at pelicans sailing over the bay water.

Bonnie saw her son's head explode on the windshield.

So did Jake and Kimbo.

BONNIE AND JAKE took a leisurely sixty minutes to chat with some folks at Lyrene's. Everybody in town felt they knew Jake or told people they did. He made people feel small-town proud. Nobody gave a rip about him being a federal cop.

In Alabama what they liked were champions. Football champions. Grown men and young boys could live their dreams through him. Jake held a state title from high school, a national title at Bama, and a Super Bowl title with the Redskins. That was the Jake story. Period.

57

JAKE BREEZED INTO Bill Burnham's law office with a clean shave and a fresh shower. "Like what y'all have done with the windows. Think I might get some plywood treatments for my cottage in Georgetown."

Liz Donovan, the office manager, laughed and rushed around her desk to hug Jake. She didn't hesitate to let her bosom rub across his chest while she planted a kiss on his cheek. Liz was dark haired and bright-eyed, still trim in her early fifties, and always the happiest person in the room.

"Good gosh, Jake. You're like hugging a sheet of steel, not like that powdered donut upstairs." She flicked her chin and eyes up, spoke in a whisper. "Bill's about to have a breakdown." She grabbed her phone, sent a quick text.

You have a visitor.
Who?
Some guy from Washington.

THE OFFICE SOUNDED with heavy footsteps clomping over pine floors from above. Then tat-tat-tat-tat-tat-tat-tat-tat-tat down the stairs like a machine gun.

"What the hell took you so long?" said Bill. "Upstairs, now." He slung his head toward the steps.

Jake glanced at Liz, rolled his eyes. "Still a prick."

In his office, Bill said, “Have a seat, Jake. Gotta show you something. My new advertising campaign.”

Bill picked up a foam posterboard leaning against the wall, held it by both ends, flashed it in Jake’s face. “This is going up soon on my billboards.” It was a vivid color photograph of Bill in a black tux leaning against the now-destroyed white Rolls Royce. Black Stetson. Fat cigar. Champagne flute in his hand. A marina full of yachts was in the background.

Million Dollar Bill
1-800-All Cash

“We took this shot in Orange Beach. Whatcha think? I mean who wouldn’t hire me, right?”

“You called me down here for that?”

“Okay, look, Jake. I got a little hysterical on the phone with you. But it was my damn Rolls. Look, we’ve *got* to keep this confidential, this extortion stuff. I paid those pricks. Whoever sent that crazy shit invitation out, I paid ’em after I saw that snuff video from Charleston. Cut that guy’s wacker off. That was over five weeks ago.”

“How much?”

Burnham swallowed. “Keep this quiet ... $5.1 million.”

“Damn, Bill ... five *million?”* Jake squirmed in his seat at the number.

“Yeah. Just between us. But I’ve been thinking since we spoke. I don’t think it’s those bastards blowing up the car. It’s a gut feeling. I think it’s somebody else.” Bill took a sip of his Mountain Dew. “Somebody local.”

“Stop jerking me around. Who?”

“Johnny Earl Shedd.”

“Shedd? Jimmy Shedd’s daddy?” Jake’s eyes narrowed. “Seriously?”

"The one and only. He was in the army for six years, a demolition expert." Bill leaned back in his chair, placed his boots on his mini-fridge, edging a sack of French rolls to the side.

"In high school I remember he had a goat farm in Point Clear," said Jake.

"Still has some goats. But his main gig is raising Labrador retrievers for hunting. Trains them, everything. Sells them around the country for top dollar. Famous for it. But the damn dogs bark and howl all times of the day and night. His place is about a hundred yards back in the woods from Great Bay Road, right close to my mansion on the bay. And those hot-damn mutts have a three-hundred-yard barking range."

"Okay, so what? Why would he blow up your car?"

"I've called the cops and animal control on him eight times for all the racket. A month ago, I filed a lawsuit against him and his hound-dog business. I wanna shut him down for good. At least in that location."

"Okay. But blow up your car?"

"There was one other thing, Jake." Bill's voice dropped to almost a whisper. "Four days ago, eight of his dogs died from poisoned hamburger meat."

Jake fired a hard look at Bill.

Bill didn't respond.

Jake stood. "I wish I hadn't heard that." He walked out of Bill's office.

At the bottom of the steps he saw a young guy in a black T-shirt with scattered whiskers on his face. He was talking to Liz.

As the office door was closing, he heard Liz say, "That's Jake Montoya."

Jake didn't notice the intensity in Theo Fuller's eyes.

58

JAKE WALKED TO the corner, turned left at the drugstore, made his way past a hot sushi spot, the Hampton Inn, and a haberdashery. A half-block away he entered the Black Point Police Department and approached the clerk, who was behind glass.

"May I help you?"

"Jake Montoya, FBI. Is the chief in? I don't have an appointment." The woman glanced at the badge he displayed. She knew Jake from years back but didn't mention it.

Three minutes later a steel door was opened by a trim man with thick, dark hair with gray slipping in around the temples. He was an inch taller than Jake and a few years older.

"Jake Montoya, huh? You're famous around here. I'm Pike Tatum." They shook hands. "Come on back," said Pike, doing a circle wave with his arm.

"Take a seat, Jake. Bet I know why you're here," said Pike. "Wild Bill called you."

"Well, yeah. He sounded a little panicked. I'm here unofficially."

"That damn Burnham."

Jake laughed, placed his right ankle on top of his left knee. "At least you didn't have to grow up with him. So anything on the bombing?"

"Too early. The ABI Bomb Squad was on the scene six hours after the blast. They scooped up everything they could and took it to Montgomery. They'll get back to me next week on the vapor signature. One guy said 99 percent chance it was plastic, either C4 or Semtex."

The chief didn't mention anything about the extortion on Burnham. Jake figured that had remained under wraps.

"Sounds good. I was just over at Bill's office. He said it could be Johnny Earl Shedd. Something about dogs."

Pike took a deep breath. "Ahhh, Jesus H — yeah. Small-town BS is about to wear me out. Lucky you don't have to deal with that. Bill's been jacked up about the dogs barking. He's called me ten times over the last six months. I've spoken to Johnny Earl after each complaint. He said it's his land and he can do what he wants."

"Bill said Shedd's an explosives expert."

Pike perked up. "Really? I didn't know that. I just thought he was a dog purveyor. Shedd did call us about the incident the other day. Somebody poisoned them, he said. I knew that would stir the pot. But Shedd mostly sticks to himself. He has a reputation of not getting along with people. He does better with his animals."

"Pike, would you mind if I spoke to him? I'm not in town to step on any toes. The Bureau's looking into the death of two lawyers at this point, looking for connections. A guy in Charleston and a guy in Colorado. There's a lot of work to be done. And, again, I'm not in it officially."

"Wait a minute. You think *those* guys are coming after *Bill*?"

Jake threw his hands up. "Don't know."

"Help yourself on Shedd. But I'd like for you to keep me posted. Listen, don't expect the welcome mat to come out from him. He hates cops."

"I'll get back to you."

PIKE WAS surprised after Jake left. Montoya hadn't gone all big-shot fed on him.

Thought, *Maybe he's alright.*

59

JAKE RAN BY Page and Palette, the local indie bookstore. He browsed for about twenty minutes and didn't leave until he bought two books written by a guy named Rick Bragg. Bonnie had told Jake that Bragg had a house in Black Point and knew the South like the devil knew evil.

Back in the bungalow, Jake punched up Google. Typed in "Johnny Earl Shedd dogs Black Point, Alabama."

The first result was an article from the *Mobile Press Register* four days ago: "Prize Gundogs Poisoned in Point Clear." The article reported a four-week-old litter of puppies as well as the mother were found dead in their kennel. The owner, Johnny Earl Shedd, refused to comment other than to say that he had lost over $15,000 worth of dogs.

Another result was a short video from Fox 10 television in Pensacola. A reporter was on-site the day after the poisonings and interviewed Johnny Earl on camera. Shedd had to be six-three, two-fifty, with an earthy, country-rough look to him. He was late sixties, red drinker's nose, and balding, with his remaining gray hair pulled back in a short ponytail. Both eyes glowed with fire as he spoke into the camera.

"The man or the people who did this better pray to God they end up in jail before I get 'em. YOU HEAR ME? YOU bleep bleep HEAR ME!"

Johnny Earl turned and walked away. Around his waist was a heavy, saddle-tan leather gun belt ringed with thick, brass ammo. Jake figured the bullets for .44 Magnums.

Definitely a guy that would blow a Rolls into next year.

60

JAKE WAS HITTING thirty-five rolling south to Point Clear, on Great Bay Road. Rowdy rode shotgun, head out the window.

At two-and-a-half miles they passed the Magnolia Hotel, a deep-South, bayfront landmark. The property was heavily landscaped, lush with oaks and magnolias. A snug marina was at the northern edge of the property.

Jake spotted the drive a half-mile down from the hotel. Johnny Earl had one of the huge rural-type mailboxes mounted on a thick piece of timber. A placard was screwed into the post below the mailbox. Southern Gundog Institute. It was painted in patriotic red, white, and blue. These days, that could mean there was a good ole U-S-of-A gun radical be waiting in the bushes with a M-16 and thirty thousand rounds of ammo. A smaller sign said, "No Trespassing."

It made Jake think, but only for a moment.

A red clay drive wound through a thick stand of pines looming over ground cover of briars and palmetto. Twenty yards in, he stopped, put the truck in park, leaned to his right, and slid a semiautomatic out from under his seat. He inserted a magazine of .45 caliber rounds into the pistol, chambered a shell, placed the gun on the seat, then crept forward at five miles an hour.

Rowdy's eyes scanned the scene.

After fifty more yards, Jake reached a pea gravel drive that would have been at home at an English country manor. A two-story white farmhouse was nestled in a copse of live oaks, pignut hickories, and black gums. Two huge southern magnolias stood like sentries at the beginning of the old brick walkway leading from the drive to the home. *Place could be in a magazine.*

He couldn't imagine the grizzled old coot he saw on the TV footage living here.

Jake stepped out, left the driver's door open, leaned in, and tapped the horn a couple of blasts. He waited. Nothing. He walked away from the truck to look behind the home. An expansive pasture contained goats and burros.

Two separate kennel buildings sat a hundred feet from the home. Their design matched the architecture of the house. Classy.

A younger man drove a green Gator utility vehicle into Jake's view from behind one of the kennels. It wasn't Johnny Earl. He killed the engine, reached behind him, brought up a long gun with a scope, laid it across his lap, put his right foot up on the dash, leaned back in his seat, and kept a steely eye on Jake.

Well, damn. Jake knew this guy could probably shoot his ear off if he wanted. He stuck his hand up in a wave. "Hey, how you doing?" The fellow didn't reply.

"Stop dead in your tracks, boy."

Jake looked in the direction of the voice, didn't see anybody. A gray bearded face slowly came into view, edging around a 150-year-old landmark oak. Johnny Earl was dressed exactly like he was in the news video. Only today he held a flat-black, pump shotgun.

He walked slowly toward Jake, right index finger in the trigger guard, flush on the trigger, left hand clutching a firm grip on the forestock, ready to ratchet another round in the chamber if his first shot didn't cut somebody in half.

"Mr. Shedd, I'm Jake Montoya, FBI. Mind if we chat a moment?"

Shedd spat to the ground. "Don't mean shit to me. You're trespassing. Take off your shirt."

"What?"

"Take off your shirt right damn now, 'less you want me to blow your right shoulder off."

"Why?"

"Ain't no damn why. Take your shirt off." Shedd was now eight feet from Jake. He'd raised the scatter gun toward Jake's chest. "Even I might not miss at this distance."

Jake started at the top, unbuttoned six buttons, slowly opened the shirt, and dropped it to the ground.

"Turn around, boy."

Jake turned a slow circle with his arms out to his side.

"Take off your pants, toss 'em to me."

Jake kept his eyes on Johnny Earl, shimmied down his pants, slowly stepped out, held them with his right hand, tossed them. Shedd took three large steps back, knelt, pulled Jake's wallet as well as his FBI badge out of a pocket. Studied the driver's license. Felt the heft of the badge.

"Jacob Montoya. Washington, DC." Shedd tossed the badge, wallet, and pants back to Jake. "What the hell are you doing on my property?"

"I wanted to talk to you about the dogs."

Shedd wagged a finger at Jake while a suspicious yet goofy grin creased his face. "No, no, no. Nooo. The FBI ain't sending somebody down here to talk about dogs. That's rat shit."

"Mr. Shedd, I grew up here."

"Hold it, hold it right there." Shedd looked over Jake's shoulder at the Tahoe. "Let's see the dog."

Shedd walked over to the truck. Jake dressed quickly and followed. Shedd looked through the open window at the dog. Rowdy's eyes bored into the old man, hard.

I'll chew the gristle off your bones, you old hillbilly.

"Belgian Mali. Aggressive, agile. Fine dogs." Shedd glanced back toward the house. The younger man was standing there watching, long gun still in his hands.

"Landry, get a bowl of water for the dog." Shedd looked at Jake. "Now, what are you doing here?"

"Why'd you make me undress?"

"You drove right past my no trespassing sign. Mistake one. Then you stopped the truck to load a pistol. Mistakes two through ten."

"You've got surveillance?"

"The question is, what the hell are you doing here from Washington? Looking into my dogs? That's nonsense."

"I'm from Black Point. I was a year ahead of Jimmy in high school."

Shedd started nodding slowly. He began tapping his index finger to his head. "It's coming back. Montoya. Montoya. You the football guy?"

Jake nodded. "Yep."

"You're Bonnie's boy, right?"

"That's right. She adopted me after her son was killed. I was about to go into the foster system."

"Sounds like something Bonnie would do. Awful about her son. I sure do remember that. She's a very nice person. We went to high school together. Now. Why the hell are you out here looking to talk to old Johnny Earl?"

"I'm in town because somebody blew up Bill Burnham's Rolls Royce. First, your dogs are poisoned. Second, a few days later his car blows apart. Third, you're a trained demolitions expert. And you're on television telling America you're gonna get the guy."

Jake and Shedd were roasting in the hot sun. Jake's shirt stuck to his back. Landry was back with the water. Jake held the bowl for Rowdy.

"The army taught me everything about demolition, and I ain't forgot none of it. So add ol' Johnny Earl Shedd to any list you want. You need to know one thing. If I wanted to blow Burnham to shreds, there wouldn't be a piece left."

"I'd like to see the video from the day the dogs died."

Shedd pointed at the drive.

"How 'bout you head on down the road. Tell Bonnie I asked about her. Tell the pricks in Washington to kiss my ass."

THE TAHOE TURNED off the clay drive onto Great Bay Road. "Rowdy, that's one dangerous man. Glad we made the drive."

He looked back at the dog in the rearview mirror. "Did I just see you smile? You did, boy. You just smiled."

61

"LIKE THE OLD days, tighten up my form." It was 5:40 in the morning. Jake was on the bluff with Woo Chow, moving through light stretching exercises.

Woo's voice was gentle, mesmerizing. "No talk. Just thought and movement through morning serenity. Mindfulness, Jake. Smoothness. Like sun warming the air. Let's get loose."

JAKE MADE IT back to the kitchen at 6:35 to eat a quick breakfast with his mother. "Taking the kayak from the pier down to Point Clear and back in a few minutes. Oh, we're eating at Woo's restaurant tonight."

The six-mile round trip over the bay's morning glass was tranquil, nothing like frantic DC traffic. Only gliding pelicans, happy gulls, and a haze hiding the mid-bay lighthouse. A great place to think about Shedd.

NINETY MINUTES LATER Jake was buzzed through the steel door into the business operations of the police department.

The receptionist said, "Pike's in his office looking at ESPN porn. He's addicted."

Jake slipped a smile. "Think he needs an intervention?"

"Without a doubt." Her eyes sparkled.

Jake cut down the hall to Tatum's office, walked in. "I want to tell you about my visit with Johnny Earl."

Pike held up his pointer finger, picked up the phone, hit one button. "Kaitlyn, you mind bringing a cold water and a peach tea back here? Thanks."

Jake launched into the visit in detail. Explained that Shedd saw him on video from the street, rolling onto the property, saw him load his pistol. "Old buzzard had me strip, too."

"Strip?"

"Yep. He was careful. He didn't give a crap about me being an agent. Literally said f-off."

"So, what's your read?"

"No doubt in my mind he could have done it. There was a younger guy out there doing some work. Went by Landry, maybe thirty or so. Know him?"

Pike leaned back in his chair, placed his shoes on the desk. "Oh, yeah, we know him. Landry Parnell. Likes to fight. Keeps a job, but he's a small time pissant. Nothing serious. Glad you mentioned him, though."

"Why's that?"

"He works for Mayfield Engineering, an outfit based in Mobile that does road work and bridge building across half the country. Pretty big-time company. And they do a lot of demolition."

"Huh. So, Landry Parnell has explosives at his fingertips?" said Jake.

"I would think so." Pike nodded.

Kaitlyn interrupted with the drinks. "Here you go, guys."

Jake read her name tag, looking for a last name. "Thanks, Kaitlyn." Their eyes locked again for a moment. Wondered if he knew her. There was something ... something about her voice. A little deep, sexy.

"You don't remember me, do you, Jake?"

He thought, *Oh no.* He didn't remember. Still, a glint of light through the cobwebs.

She rescued him. "P.E. class when you were a senior. I was a year behind you."

Jake stood. "That's right, absolutely. We played basketball and war ball." His face lit up. "I had a blast in that class. That was right after Christmas till the end of the year."

"Yep, the good ole days. Well, it's good to see you. You look great by the way, like you could still play ball."

"Yeah, yeah, you too, Kaitlyn. Thanks for speaking."

As Kaitlyn left the room, Jake stepped to the door to watch her stroll down the hall. Maybe five-five, 130, shapely calves in a conservative office skirt.

"Pike, you won't believe this. She weighed at least fifty pounds more in high school. She was a tomboy, but really cute, you know? Country cute. But now ... yeah." Jake shook his head. "Whoa. She's blossomed."

"She's terrific, I agree with you there."

Jake sat. "One other thing about Johnny Earl's video setup. When I asked if he had anything from the night his dogs were killed, he said yes. Was smug about it, wouldn't share anything. He did say Bill wouldn't have the balls to come on his land. I agree with that."

"No, the little general wouldn't have the guts," said Pike. "But, hiring somebody? I'd go with that. I think we're getting somewhere. He admits he has something on video. He's got motive to retaliate. He's got documented expert training in explosives. His buddy Landry probably has TNT, dynamite, C4, or what have you, at his fingertips in some warehouse at work. I'm no Sherlock Holmes, but I'd say we oughta talk to a judge about a search warrant."

Jake nodded, took his last sip of water from the bottle. "Sounds good. I'd love to go out with you on a search if you need somebody."

"Absolutely."

JAKE REACHED THE door to the lobby. He glanced to his left. Kaitlyn was speaking on a telephone headset. She had a prim nose, good posture, and dirty blond hair dropping just below her ears. And a smoky voice. But skin too healthy for a smoker.

She felt Jake's eyes on her, slipped off her headset, shook her hair loose, and looked his way.

"Good to see you back in town, Jake. And, oh, for what it's worth, I run down to Wildfire every Friday around six thirty for a couple of beers and some outstanding brisket. If you get bored, stop on by. I'll catch you up on everybody."

"If I get a break I just might. Great seeing you, too, Kaitlyn."

Jake went outside and hopped on his fat-tired beach cruiser to head two blocks over to Burnham's office. He started thinking. Certainly he couldn't go wrong with beer and brisket in the company of a confident and courteously assertive woman.

A couple beers would likely bring the kind of allure to her voice you could listen to all night. He knew he'd sworn off those cheap, pickup, short-term romance girls. But this wasn't the same thing. He'd known her since she was in the eleventh grade. Sure had. She had a smile in her eye when she asked, too. *No, no, nothing cheap about this.*

Things were starting to gel in Black Point.

62

JAKE WAS STILL thinking about Kaitlyn as he took a seat in Bill's office.

"Okay, Pike's digging down on Shedd. But I'm in town for something bigger. First thing I need, Bill, is all the banking information on the money you sent overseas. Date, bank name, account number, country, exact dollar amount. And I need everything you have that coerced you to give up five million."

"Oh, no. Oh, hell no. Whoever that was, they're gone. I'm sure of it."

Jake smirked. "Somebody blew up your car four days ago. Remember that?"

"Yeah. That redneck, Shedd."

"I need the email. I'm asking nicely. Otherwise we're gonna subpoena every scrap of banking data and every email from the date you opened business. We wouldn't even know you were involved if you wouldn't have called, sounding like a mad man. Secondly, Bill. I need access to all your legal cases going back three years. Everything."

Bill shook his head vigorously. "Not a chance. That's very, very confidential."

"You don't need to worry about some bunch of cockroaches you represent, you need to worry about whoever took five mil from you. Shedd *might* kill you. These guys *will* kill you. They know you're sitting on some big money. If I was them, I'd come back to the suckers who gave up some cash, which is you." Jake pointed at him. "I need the video they sent, too. Look, we're getting all the same stuff from the firms of the dead guys."

"Did the dead men pony up cash?"

"Don't know yet. Another thing. I need your CPA firm. I need five years of financials on you."

Bill sat upright in his chair. "What?" Indignant.

"Five years, Bill."

Bill's tongue pushed out his cheek. "This ain't right ... Okay, let's go see Theo."

"That your accountant?"

"Nope. My stepson. He handles IT and research. Come on."

Jake followed Bill down the steps, around the corner, and down the hall almost to the rear exit door.

Bill knocked on a closed office door. Nothing. He banged a little harder with his knuckles. Nothing. He twisted the knob and walked in. Jake followed. The room was dark except for three oversize Dell monitors blowing back blue light on the man Jake had seen two days ago in the office.

Theo Fuller felt their presence, turned around, slid his headphones off. He was listening to some ambient beats on Soma FM, totally relaxed. Jake noticed his eyes, couldn't tell if they were red, but both upper lids had a sleepy droop. *Stoned?*

The office was spartan, no windows, walls painted black. Theo worked off three folding tables with a faux-wood vinyl finish. There were two keyboards and a large fax/copier. No folders or loose papers anywhere. Theo was all digital, everything filed with strokes on a keyboard.

Jake spotted two Mac laptops on a table attached to charging cords, thought they might be for Theo's personal use.

A framed poster hung on the wall from the show *Mister Robot.* It was an eerie black and white shot of the unstable, oddball cyber-hacker character peering out of a dark hoodie. His two big, bug eyes conveyed a natural creepiness. The tagline was "Control is an Illusion."

Jake was indifferent to an old computer resting on a table under the poster. It was enclosed in plexiglass.

Nefarious looking hidey-hole, he thought.

"Theo, this is Jake Montoya. We went through school together."

Theo stood, extended his right hand after Jake presented his. Jake couldn't remember when he'd seen pastier looking skin. His black T-shirt and jeans looked like they were on a ghost. "Yes, I've heard of you, Mr. Montoya. You played football with Bill."

"Please call me Jake, Theo. That's right. You ever play?"

"No, never. I'm not much of an athlete."

"Here's the deal, Theo. I'm in the FBI now, down from Washington. I'm here looking into cases of extortion and murder related to two attorneys out of state, as well as Bill's run-in with extortion. I'm sure you know he's been a victim here."

Theo looked to Bill. Bill nodded.

"Yes, I know a little about it. It's insane. Who could do something like this?"

"We don't have much yet. Whoever it is, they are smart and dangerous. When they kill, it's ugly. Here's what I need. And Bill agreed to it, so we're speaking to you. I need files on every case y'all have handled over the last three years. Put them on a disk, thumb drives, whatever. I need to get this info to DC. Plus the video you received from the extortionists. We're looking for connections, if any, between Bill and these other lawyers."

Theo sat down, leaned back in his office chair. He gazed into space a moment, then looked at Jake. "Want to make it easy?"

"Well, sure. What're you thinking?"

Theo reached back, grabbed a can of Monster, took a swig, and wiped his hand across his mouth. "I can have this stuff ready for viewing in less than an hour. They can see it in DC immediately."

"Great. How?"

"I'll create an account on Microsoft's OneDrive cloud storage. I'll pay for a year of storage. Aunt Liz can call you in a little while with the username and password. You guys can download anything you want and save it to your servers. Sound okay?"

"Sounds awesome." Jake clapped him on the shoulder. "Thanks."

Walking toward the lobby, Jake reminded Bill he needed the information where he had sent the money. Bill frowned, said, "Upstairs."

Bill printed the neat invitation from his email, including instructions.

"The money was wired the day after that invitation, straight to Panama," Bill said.

Jake studied the page. "Jot down your accountant's name and number for me."

Bill scribbled something on a quarter-sized legal pad, then looked up.

"You're gonna get me killed, Jake."

"Well, yeah, probably. I'm curious. How's that work having your ex-wife's sister run your office?"

"Works way better than my marriage did, but I'm not sure why."

Something off about that, thought Jake.

63

FORTY MINUTES LATER. Killing time, Jake sat in the Black Point public library, a gorgeous stucco, brick, and glass structure, glancing at the *New York Times,* opened to obituaries.

He was reading about an orthodontist from Buffalo who'd been quoted saying he'd only lived as long as he did because he got out of the tooth business and built a tennis resort in Florida. "Hated dentistry," the guy said. *I'll bet,* Jake thought, when a text chimed from his phone.

It was Liz from Bill's office.

onedrive.com
USER: lawyer/burnham/cloud
PW: MontoyaFBI

Jake replied: **Thanks**

He scrolled through his phone contacts until he found Randy Garrison, FBI.

Texted: **Have movement here. When can we talk?**

The reply was almost immediate: **60 minutes.**

Jake dictated his response: **I'll call you.**

He read for fifteen more minutes, finishing with the Jason Gay column. He put the paper back on the shelf, neatened up the stack, left quickly through the front door, running into a blanket of wet heat.

AT THE COTTAGE, Jake fed Rowdy two Buddy Biscuits, grabbed several Fig Newtons and a sweet tea for himself. He took a seat at the kitchen table.

He chewed a bite of cookie as he flipped open the laptop, signed on. Pulled up One Drive, signed in. Bam, Burnham's files. Scrolling around, it only took a moment to know this would take a while to review.

Jake tapped a speed dial number. An answer after two rings. "Garrison."

"Randy, Jake here."

"Jake, you're on speaker. John Simmons and Emmett Cater are in here with me. John's a forensic accountant. And as you know, Emmett's in the Behavior Analysis Unit."

"Good afternoon, gentlemen," said Jake.

The men said, "Hello, Jake," almost in unison.

Garrison continued. "The heat's building since we spoke a few days ago. The director called me yesterday. And you know that's all we need. Oh! One very positive thing. I told him you're in Alabama and that you know the lawyer there. First words out of Blanton's mouth were 'Tell Montoya he's reinstated.'"

"Fantastic, Randy, thanks."

"It's all you, man. So, what's cooking?"

"First of all, I got a guy who has a great reason to go after Wild Bill Burnham. He thinks Burnham killed a litter of newborn hunting dogs. Poisoned."

"Damn. What kind of bastard would do that?"

"It wouldn't be Burnham himself, but he could have orchestrated it. The dog guy is an ex-military ordnance guy. Strong credentials. He's in his late sixties now, no recent run-ins with the law, but he's dangerous. The locals say he's the kind of guy that could kill somebody if provoked. His daddy and brothers were rough, Dixie mafia kind of guys, but they're all dead now. So what I'm saying is this car thing might not be the killers."

"What's the dog guy's name? Let us run background up here."

"Johnny Earl Shedd." Jake spelled it for Garrison.

Jake heard laughter on the other end. "Jake, this is Emmett. Let me get this straight. You got a lawyer named Wild Bill Burnham who is a billboard showboat wearing a big Stetson. And you got some redneck old man named Johnnie Earl Shedd who blew up a Rolls Royce because somebody killed his dogs? Hell, I'm almost sure I saw this episode on Dukes of Hazzard back in the eighties."

Montoya heard more wild laughter back in DC.

Jake was laughing when he started to talk. "I was wondering if y'all would notice that. John, this is for you and your team. Wild Bill sent a tad over five million overseas to Panama."

Whistles came through the phone line. Jake grabbed a quick sip of tea. "I've got all the banking contacts. I'll text that to you when we hang up."

"Jake, let me catch you up to speed on Green in Charleston and Clemmons in Colorado." It was Agent Garrison. "John's team has dug through the financials for both guys. Green has no money whatsoever going out of the country. And no other large, unexplained banking transactions. But we did find an email asking for money, an investment. It had crystal-clear overseas banking information and implications of a threat. Couldn't find any money going to that account. And Green is dead. So, there you go."

"Let me interject here." It was John. "As Randy said, we found the investment emails sent to the lawyers. Both of the accounts and destinations were different. Banks were in Cape Town and Nevis in the Caribbean. Clemmons was supposed to send money to Nevis. They're stonewalling us on bank info. Green's bank was Capetown. Took us weeks to find out it was opened with $250 bucks, and no further money has come into the accounts, or left. But here's where it gets interesting. The name of the person opening the Capetown account is the name of the attorney being scammed."

"Wait a minute. You mean for the Charleston guy, Braxton Green, the guy opening the Capetown account was also Braxton Green?"

"Exactly what I'm saying. But it wasn't him. We have copies of opening documents including ID photos. Photos and signatures don't match Green."

"I'll be damned. Last week when I stopped in to speak to the Charleston detective, they were following a drug angle."

Garrison answered. "You're right. They glossed over that email, thought it was spam, like the Nigerians send. Right now, we're letting CPD run with the dope play."

"That's good stuff, Randy. When I text the bank information, I'll include the username and password that will get you on a cloud site to look at Wild Bill's files from the last three years. Bill has an oddball stepson who does research for him. He put it together. Guy wears all black, sits in a dark room looking at three huge monitors, and looks like he hasn't seen the sun since he was twelve."

"Everybody's stepsons are oddballs. But, anyway, you're on duty now, Jake. See if you can get some of this material in a hard report for us and give daily updates."

"You bet."

Jake stood after hanging up, chewed the last Fig Newton, and swished it down with tea.

"Back on duty, Rowdy. Let's get a walk in."

64

A LIGHT, WISPY breeze cooled Jake and Rowdy as they sat on the pier at Billy Rigdon's boathouse, three hundred yards from Bonnie's place. Jake couldn't think of anything else to do on a lazy Friday afternoon, so he Googled "Mayfield Engineering," the company Landry Parnell worked for.

The company home page was clean, sharp, professional. He clicked on *About*.

There was a black-and-white photo of a man in jeans, a white T-shirt with the sleeves cut off, work boots, leaning on a shovel, staring at the camera. Nothing but a pile of dirt behind him and a sweat-stained Bama ball cap on his head. His arms indicated he was no stranger to a shovel.

The narrative started.

In the spring of 1971, Harvey Mayfield started his company with a shovel, a used dump truck, a rented twenty-year-old bulldozer, and $78 dollars cash.

Jake liked the sound of that from the first sentence. He downed two swigs of water and plowed on.

His cell rang at 4:21. It was the chief.

"Hey, Pike."

"Good news. The judge granted a search warrant for Shedd's place. We're gonna hit it about six tomorrow morning, about ten minutes after sunrise. I'd like you at the station at five fifteen so we can go over everything with the team."

"Sure."

Tatum continued. "We got some interesting facts on Shedd from the military. We tracked down Shedd's last commanding officer in an assisted living home in Colorado, a guy named Roper. He was career army, then sold used cars for twenty years. He remembered Shedd after almost forty years and you won't believe why."

"Think I'll like this. Why?"

"A woman reported to the base that Shedd was stalking her. She was a waitress at one of the bars the army boys frequented. Roper got into Shedd's face about it. Threatened to have charges brought up over the matter if it happened again. Roper said Shedd threatened to kick his ass, was hauled in, and ultimately discharged."

"Huh."

"But here's the beauty part, something that happened the day after the discharge became official. Roper's wife came home from the grocery store with their two kids in the car. It was winter, got dark early, and it was about six fifteen. Ten minutes after the wife unpacked the groceries, the family Impala blew to shreds, right in their driveway. She was on Valium for a year and wouldn't leave home without her husband."

"Damn!"

"Roper says he's absolutely sure it was Shedd. Had to be. Shedd had been in Nam and used C4 every day. Anyway, see you at five fifteen."

Jake did some time arithmetic in his head. He was planning for a long evening over beer and brisket with a hometown girl ... and then ... who knows.

Chances were slim and none an assertive, smoky-voiced woman would leave much time for sleep.

65

JAKE PARKED A block away from Wildfire, checked his teeth in the rearview mirror before stepping out of the Tahoe. He couldn't smell himself unless he took a good sniff of his forearm. Perfect. Fresh but not overpowering. He wore an untucked, light blue linen shirt over stone-colored shorts.

The place was packed. He let his eyes adjust just inside the door and glanced around. He didn't see Kaitlyn. Something grabbed his eye immediately. Four football jerseys on the wall with a small cone of light focused on each of them.

Bo Jackson and Pat Sullivan from Auburn. Kenny Stabler and Jake Montoya from Bama.

He felt someone touch his arm, glanced down. Kaitlyn. "Well hello, big guy, you here alone?"

"Um, temporarily, I hope."

Kaitlyn slid her arm into the crook of his elbow. "I've got a table, come on." She wore a pair of trim black slacks, heels, and a white sleeveless top. Jake thought, *Game on.*

Barely made it into the seat when a waitress laid two menus in front of them.

"How 'bout a drink, guys?"

"Bud Lite, please," said Kaitlyn.

"Same here."

"Jake, what's the story on that shootout in Virginia Beach? Everybody saw it on the news." A few smile lines formed at her eyes as she said, "Still doing that hero stuff, aren't you?"

"It's Friday night. Why don't you catch me up on some folks in town, first?"

The beer arrived in forty-five seconds. Kaitlyn picked up her bottle and extended toward Jake. "Cheers."

"Cheers, Kaitlyn."

She took a long pull. "Oh, man. That's good, super cold. I've got all night to tell you about high school buddies, but that story there is the kind that gets my juices flowing."

All night?

"Yeah, okay. But I'm not the hero, not even close, my dog Rowdy is."

Juices flowing?

The noise level was picking up. You could barely hear George Strait singing "Write This Down," a fine song to sing along to once lubed with a couple beers.

Kaitlyn leaned forward, looked him in the eye. "Can't go wrong with the brisket." She was halfway through her first drink, voice getting smokier. "But tonight's kind of special. I'm getting the Big Dick. And I've got a surprise for you, too." She winked.

Jake froze like a statue, gave nothing away. What ever happened to the chase, the romance?

"Folks are happy to see you, Jake. I know I am." Kaitlyn leaned forward. "Starting to get a little crazy in here. I'm so glad I told Bonnie I couldn't make it tonight. It's a rare event getting together with you after all these years."

"Bonnie? My mother, Bonnie?"

"Of course your mother. We've been in the same Sunday school class for the last ten years over at First Presbyterian."

My mother's Sunday school classmate?

The waitress was back with her order pad open. "Let's do it, folks." The waitress looked at Kaitlyn.

"Tonight's a great night for the Big Dick," said Kaitlyn.

A little smile crept across the waitress's mouth. "When's it not?" She cocked her eyebrows and slowly swiveled her head to look Jake in the eye. "Well, mister tall, dark, and handsome, what do you have to say about that?"

"I'll take another beer is what I have to say. You can bring me a little brisket, slaw, and mac and cheese."

Jake started to feel some pressure to be on his game tonight when a woman approached the table. She was yoga-class slim, maybe five-eleven, probably one-fifty-five, dark hair, wearing glasses like a creative-type.

"Surprise, Jake! I hope you remember Ann Chambers. She was Annie in high school. You guys were in the photography club."

"Sure, I do."

Kaitlyn stood, hugged Ann, gave her a light kiss on the lips. Ann leaned over and hugged Jake as he tried to stand, kissed his cheek. "Twenty-five years later, you're still the best-looking guy in the building. Great to see you."

Ann skootched in next to Kaitlyn and leaned in to sniff Kaitlyn's neck. "Oh, you smell good tonight. Girly girl smell."

"Guess what, Ann?" Kaitlyn leaned in, whispered something in Ann's ear.

Ann looked over to Jake while a wry smile spread across her face. "The Big Dick? I'm definitely in for that. Been awhile for me. I've been shooting in South America for the last month."

Damn! In little ole Black Point?

Right then, a guy bumped the table holding a tray above his head, a T-shirt slung over his shoulder and a smile that could light a dark alley. "Jake Montoya, how's it hanging!"

"Dick Ray! How you doin', man?" Jake surely recognized this guy, the most popular kid in high school. "Ah, hell, Dick, damn good to see you!"

Dick set the tray on the table. Jake stood up and gave him a bro hug.

"I didn't know this was your place. It's awesome."

"I learned everything in Austin, Jake. I quit the government, told 'em to shove it. But no more talking, time to eat some hot chow. Oh, your waitress said you were too cheap to order the Big Dick. So, I brought it anyway. It's the super platter, all-you-can-eat brisket, pork, and ribs. Enjoy! My treat, brother."

Jake eyed the food as Dick unloaded the tray. "Awesome! Looks awesome!"

He handed the T-shirt to Jake. "Wear it everywhere and make me famous."

"Thanks, Dicky." Jake unfolded it as Dick moseyed toward the kitchen.

Dick's WildFire. Smokin' Q and Sippin' Bru.

"I want to brag on Ann a moment," said Kaitlyn. "You probably didn't know, but she studied photography on scholarship at Parsons School of Design in New York and has worked for some of the hottest graphics firms in New York and Los Angeles. Now she freelances for high-end magazines, publications with artsy photography and incredible stories."

"Like what?" Jake forked a piece of brisket into his mouth.

Kaitlyn looked toward Ann. "You tell him, babe."

"*National Geographic, Another Escape, Surfer's Journal, Outside, Architectural Digest, Travel +Leisure.*"

"Big time! Way to go, Ann."

"But here's the best thing, Jake. I'm marrying Kaitlyn on Labor Day weekend, and we're creating our new lives together in Santa Barbara." She leaned over and gave Kaitlyn's neck a long, slow kiss.

A mouthful of brisket hit Jake's stomach like a pile of rocks.

66

JAKE LEFT WILDFIRE in a state of minor depression. He would have been just fine watching those two frolicking in a Jell-O-filled hot tub, but nooo ...

Rowdy greeted him with a wag at the bungalow. "Everything went sideways, boy. Almost stumbled into a buy one, get one free."

Fifteen minutes until nine. Needed to be up by 4:30 to grab a bite and freshen up with a quick shower.

The splash of Bonnie's headlights brush stroked the living room walls as she pulled in the drive. He walked outside. "Need any help, Mama?"

"Not a bit. They ate every one of those ham biscuits like vultures."

Walking into the house she said, "Jake, how many bay sunsets have we seen, maybe thirty thousand? Well, this one was the best ever, without question. It felt like Jesus himself was in the background painting a palette of a thousand colors. And the drifting clouds? Oh, my goodness! What a great night. Now, I'm going to take a bath, read my devotional, then ease out reading the new Nicholas Sparks book."

He hugged her and felt a firmer squeeze from her tonight. For as long as he could remember, the bayside sunsets always made Bonnie emotional, grateful. He gave her a kiss on the forehead.

"So glad you're here, Jake, so glad. As long as you're in this house I want that little kiss every night. Even if I'm asleep, in my subconscious, I'll know."

"You know I will, Mama."

He grabbed a Rolling Rock out of the refrigerator and took his first sip in the kitchen, broke out in a smile thinking about the scenario at Wildfire. His buddy Kimbo would get a laugh out of that.

He walked into the living room, signed on to his computer, and sat in the easy chair. A small lamp glowed on a credenza, leaving the room dim and peaceful.

He typed in Ann Chambers Photography on Google. A page of hits flashed on the screen. Placing a wireless headset on his ears, he clicked on a streaming jazz site. Hoping for some Diana Krall or old Billie Holiday, he was happily surprised with Norah Jones singing "Don't Know Why." Her voice was sweet smoke layered over caramel. Made him want to walk around naked.

Bumped on to Ann's website and was gobsmacked with her talent. He remembered a gangly girl in high school with a mouth full of braces that looked like they could chew apart a truck bumper. Tonight, she was a chic, trim, incredibly talented woman with a premarital glow. He made a mental note to get with her on this trip and pick up some photography pointers.

Still hungry, he popped a bag of microwave popcorn and grabbed another beer.

Maybe he'd go to bed after the drink, maybe think about what Kaitlyn and Ann were doing to each other right this moment. But just for the hell of it, he went to a used truck site to look at Toyota FJ40 Land Cruisers for sale. He'd casually looked for one for a few years with little to show for his efforts.

On the third page of results, he spotted a 1976 dune-beige model located in Point Clear, Alabama. *Three miles away!* The side-on picture looked decent. Stock appearance, no he-man jacked-up crap. The way he liked it.

Could this be a little luck blowing in on a digital breeze? The ad was placed yesterday.

"Widow Sale. Nice Truck. Original." No name, just a phone number with an 804 area code. Virginia. But no price. *Worrisome.* A distraught widow was parting with her husband's beloved toy at an outlandishly inflated price. Had to be.

He eyed the time on the computer. Ten thirty-five. Screw it. He grabbed his phone, punched the phone number as fast as he could or, otherwise, he wouldn't sleep. Four rings and no machine picking up. *Come on!*

Six rings—and BANG! Answered.

"Hello. This is Hope."

She sounded drowsy and younger than he would expect, not like some aging lady who would suck his bank account dry. Must be the daughter, he thought. The widow was in bed, probably sedated on Valium.

"Hope? My name's Jake, and I'm trying to reach the widow selling the Land Cruiser. Is that your mom?"

"Kind of late, isn't it? Almost eleven. I'm the widow. I'll sum it up. It's in great shape, forty-two thousand miles, and meticulously maintained ... just a nice truck. How 'bout we talk tomorrow, I'm in bed."

"Talk? Sure. Give me your address, I'll come by your place at eight a.m." *Shedd's place was likely only minutes from this Land Cruiser.*

"No chance on that. I'm playing a tennis mixer at Lakewood Tennis Club in the morning. Folks are coming from out of town and there could be some interesting guys there, so I'm not really sure."

Jake's lips moved silently, speaking to air. *Interesting guys?*

Husband barely in the dirt, dumping the old man's toy, and she's already looking for *interesting guys.* No concern for even meeting a serious buyer. Means she doesn't need the money.

Thinking fast, he said, "Look, here's some good news, some guaranteed news, I'm from out of town ... and I'm interesting ... and you can set your watch by me."

"I'm not quite sure you sound that interesting."

"What do I sound like?"

"Desperate."

Jake smiled at her description. "Okay, look, Hope, here's the deal. The world is full of tire-kickers and lonely men who drive around on the weekend test-driving vintage vehicles, pretending they're buyers. It's a hoax. Just tell me what time to show up and where."

"Oh, hey, one question. What's the asking price?"

"Negotiable. I've got to do some jockeying on a final price."

"Jockeying? Why?"

"'Cause you're the ninth caller. This thing might be worth more than I thought."

Jake's fists balled tight. "Okay, please let me see it *first.* Just tell me when and where."

"Lakewood Tennis Club. Twelve noon on the dot. Next guy's coming at twelve thirty. Oh, where'd you say you're from?"

"Georgetown, in DC."

"Okay, Jack from Georgetown. I gotta run, get some rest."

The phone went dead in his hand. *It's Jake.* Her nonchalance was not reassuring.

THE FIRST CALL *on her truck,* she thought.

Smiled. Jake from Georgetown.

67

JAKE STEPPED OUT of the Tahoe wearing body armor, FBI badge on his belt. A .45 was holstered on his left hip. He opened the rear passenger door in case he needed quick access to his shotgun lying across the seat.

The sun just hit the sky. It was Saturday, 6:07 a.m., and sticky. A dead-still summer morning.

Chief Tatum's fist pounded the front door three times as he hollered, "Johnny Earl Shedd! Black Point police. We have a—"

The door popped open before Pike could finish speaking. He jumped back. There was no one there, just an open door. The smell of bacon frying floated out. Black Point's version of a SWAT team stood behind the chief. Two guys with full-auto M4s, two guys with scatterguns, four guys with pistols drawn.

Jake had his back up against the wall, just to the left side of the door, facing the officers. His right hand held his Glock at his right shoulder, ready to swing around and open fire.

It was five seconds of terror. A door creaking open. Complete silence from inside. Not a hint of movement. Jake was ready to run. His brain screamed explosives. He pictured a grenade rolling across the threshold ready to blow some people's limbs off.

"Don't shoot, hot-dammit! I'm unarmed, in my pajamas," said Johnny Earl.

"Johnny Earl Shedd, we have a search warrant. Put your hands behind your head, let us see you."

Shedd slowly stepped into view. He wore a white tee over green plaid pajama bottoms, bare feet, sleep matter in his eyes, looking buck wild with his long hair out of the ponytail.

"Step on the porch, Mr. Shedd. Keep your hands up," said the chief. "Pat him down, Mike." A baby-faced cop ran his hands over Shedd's trunk, front and back. Lifted his shirt. Ran his hands up and down each leg, ankle to groin. "Clear."

Pike handed the warrant to Shedd. "We're checking out the house first, then every building on the property. And all vehicles."

AT 6:40 A.M. JAKE was checking out an equipment shed at the far end of the property. Mostly rusting farm implements and a decades-old Ford pickup.

He pulled out his phone. Knew he shouldn't but dialed anyway. Voicemail.

"Hi, this is Hope. Please leave your name and number."

Dang. "Ummm, good morning, Hope, this is Jake, we spoke last night. Still interested. Extremely interested. Please don't sell the Land Cruiser out from under me. Oh, hey. I'm in Point Clear right now. Could I run by? I can make it super quick." Hung up.

Three minutes later his phone chirped a text.

WHAT!?!? NOT EVEN 7! On Saturday morning!! YOU WOKE ME!! I said 12 NOON!! At Lakewood!

Why did I call? Why, why, why?

At midmorning Jake was standing around with the boys in Shedd's basement looking at ten AR-15s and $250K in cash hidden behind a concealed panel when his phone shivered with an incoming text. Hope, the truck seller.

Time Change. Make it 1:00. Lots of nice-looking men playing. And, sorry ... kind of having cold feet about the sale ... I'm iffy. Stop by, though. Take it for a spin.

Jake made his way over to Pike. "I think you guys have this squared away. I'm going to hit it. I've got an errand to run."

JAKE CHANGED AT his mother's cottage and was now pedaling his beach cruiser down Great Bay Road. His phone rang as he passed Two Sisters Bakery. Pike.

Jake pulled the phone to his ear, sat upright, and pedaled with no hands on the handlebars. "Tell me you got something."

"Well," Pike chuckled, "A colorful Fruit Loops box happens to have a nice quarter-pound cake of putty stashed at the bottom with a plastic wrapper that says Semtex-H. We found it in a living space above the kennels. That's where Landry Parnell lives."

"Good work," said Jake. "I'll put in a call to quality control at Kellogg's as soon as we get off the phone. That might not be safe for kids." He heard Pike laughing.

"Got another little bonus, too. After four hours of diligent search by six guys, we found DVDs holding footage from the night the dogs were killed."

"That a boy. Where'd Shedd stash it?"

"Sitting inside the DVD player ready to view."

Jake howled. "Shedd say anything about it?"

"Said he was sorry it wasn't in color. As for the ARs and cash, it all looks legit with bank straps and registrations for each gun."

"Good work, chief."

68

JAKE TWISTED HIS beach cruiser into the Lakewood Club after passing a collection of southern cottage homes nestled under a grove of live oaks. It was 12:35 in the afternoon. He was early.

The club was pristine, with a monied look about the place. A bolt of concern hit him immediately. No Land Cruiser in the parking areas.

He hopped off the bike in the parking lot and walked it to the tennis shop. He passed a classic Porsche 911, probably mid-'80s. It was a glossy black cabriolet, top down. Vanity plate said RESQ. *Had to be a doctor.*

He leaned the bike against the tennis-shop wall and walked through an alcove to glance down over the courts. A manicured green-clay stadium court was just below him. A small crowd, snacking from a table holding munchies, was watching a mixed doubles match. Three games and it was over. The players milled around, talking.

Jake walked in the shop and was greeted by a fellow stringing gut through a racket frame. He flicked his chin and kept stringing. "I'm Butch. What's up?"

"Looking for a lady named Hope."

Butch, five-eleven, tan, with a thatch of blond hair that said tennis pro, glanced backward and caught the eye of a trim honey-blond pro behind the counter. He smiled. She smiled. "Jennifer, could you help this gentleman?"

Jennifer walked Jake to the window. She looked out and pointed. "There she is. In the white top."

"Thanks, Jennifer."

"Are you the guy who called her about the Land Cruiser at midnight?" she asked.

Jake grimaced. "Well, it was more like ten thirty."

"Right. But called again at five this morning?"

"You know, it was easily six forty-five. Why, what did she say?"

Butch and Jennifer glanced at each other, laughed.

Butch held up the palms of his hands. "No comment. Heading to the beach in thirty minutes. I don't need any drama monkeying with my weekend mojo."

Jake's mind focused on reversing the phone damage he'd created. Had to think. He walked outside and stood next to his bike. Hope was walking up the steps from the stadium court, carrying two rackets.

The first thing he noticed were long legs carved with feminine muscle. Had to be five-eight. Short, dark hair cut just below her ears.

"Are you Hope?"

"Yes." She wore dark aviator sunglasses. "And you must be the night stalker."

He nervously laughed off the comment and put on his best chipper personality. He watched her glance toward to the bicycle. "Yeah, sorry about the calls. I got a little excited."

Hope slipped off her sunglasses. "Boys and trucks, I get it. Let me stash these rackets."

He eyed her. Aquiline nose, deep brown eyes. Her white racerback top hugged her smallish breasts and looked at home against her tennis tan.

As she came out of the shop, Jake thought, *Fit.* Her arms and shoulders proved she knew her way around light weight-training. Defined but not overly sculpted.

She glanced at the bike again. “Okay, wait a moment. Are you sure you’re not one of those tire-kicker, hoax guys? I mean, you’re here on a bicycle, right?” She shook her head. “Nothing about this makes me confident you have the means to purchase a like-new, vintage vehicle.”

“Definitely not a tire kicker.”

He followed her to the parking lot, pushing his bike. She stopped next to the 911. “As you can see, the Land Cruiser isn’t here, it’s at my house.”

Jake pointed at the 911. “This yours?”

“Yep.” Nonchalant about it. “Pull up maps on your phone and put in my address. I bike it all the time, a smidge over two miles.” She gave him the address and he was off.

His brain was going swirly. He had expected a plump, matronly lady in a brown Taurus wearing a bulky tennis dress cut by tent makers. Certainly not one of the sportiest women he’d ever seen, in a black 911 no less. And toned. He was into athletic women.

HOPE WATCHED Jake pedal away and cut down Battles Road. She put on her shades, fired up the 911, and shook her head. Said to no one, “A bicycle.” Giggled about that.

JAKE WAS a quarter-mile down the road when he heard the deep growl of the flat-six Porsche engine building steam, like it was eating asphalt. He was pedaling down the far-right edge of the pavement. Hope blew by him at sixty in second, about to hit third. Adam Levine’s voice blasted out of the car singing “She Will Be Loved.”

Hope downshifted at the next curve, then opened it up on a straight patch.

69

HOPE WAS LEANING on the 911 sipping a water, as Jake pulled in the drive. Two golden retrievers were lying at her feet, grinning like they do. The scene looked like a photo for *Garden and Gun* magazine.

Jake spotted the Land Cruiser backed into the garage, facing out. He dropped his bike to the ground.

"How 'bout some water, cowboy?" She handed him a bottle, then pointed at the dogs. "Jeep and Arlo, my two rescued children. What's your name again?"

"Jake." Just told her ten minutes ago. And last night. Not good.

"Kids, this is Jake. Well, it's right there in the garage, key in the ignition. Leave the bike as collateral, because I might have to get the cops to dust your fingerprints."

"I'll drive it down to the VFW and back, if that's all right?"

"Sure. But don't wreck it. I don't want to have to call the next batch of guys who are coming later today and disappoint them with the news."

Jake took a quick lap around the Cruiser in the garage. *Gorgeous.* He hopped in and twisted the key. It fired up instantly. He eased it out of the garage onto the highway. The clutch and transmission were as smooth as butter.

Ramped it up to fifty-five on Great Bay Road, windows down and his left elbow resting on the door sill. Another day in paradise.

Three miles down he pulled into the VFW, killed the engine, jumped out, walked around the truck examining the body again. He went to his knees to peek at the undercarriage. No rust. Not even a hint of a mud stain. About to lift the hood when a hot-rodded 396 El Camino rumbled up alongside him.

Two guys, early seventies, thinning gray hair, and white scruff on their cheeks. Vietnam-era dudes here for a drink. They hopped out and walked around the Land Cruiser. "Nice machine, fellow. How much you want for it? I'll buy it off you today."

"Not for sale, but thanks for asking."

"Well, hell. I think I'll go in and have one or two or maybe a dozen beers to ease my disappointment."

The El Camino passenger, with a deep voice rising straight through his beer gut, said, "You know, that thing looks almost naked without an old Boston Whaler hooked on the ass end."

Stole the thought out of my head.

JAKE HONKED AS he pulled into Hope's driveway. He hopped out of the truck, tried to maintain a neutral look. She stepped out of the house with Jeep and Arlo on her heels.

Her eyes locked onto his face, with a big smile on hers.

He knew that she knew that he sure as heck loved the truck. Jeep and Arlo came up and bumped his hands with their muzzles. They knew he sure as heck loved the truck.

Have to play it cool here, he thought, *because it's about to get real, the negotiation.* Disarm her for a moment. "So, you from Virginia?"

Hope let out a little giggle. "Dana Point, California, originally. Played tennis for the University of Virginia. Got married to a successful guy who died early with a hefty life insurance policy. A friend of mine thought I was depressed. She suggested I move to Black Point, Alabama, and teach tennis and enjoy the slower pace. And here I am."

"Well, are you?"

"Am I what?

"Depressed."

"I just got rid of a dead-weight, cheating pig and picked up $4.5 million in life insurance. Would you be depressed?" She slipped off her Ray-Bans. Her smile eased all the way into her eyes.

Jake noticed a few smile lines, which made her real.

"Oh, hey. Before I go all Warren Buffett on you, what's that sign mean on your mailbox? Refuge of Hope?"

"I'm starting a nonprofit to care for displaced animals. Jeep and Arlo are the first ones in, but they're keepers. I made them both co-vice presidents."

How bad can the witch be? Animal lover.

"I've got two acres here, but I'll need more land soon. And I'll be raising funds."

"It just so happens my landlady in Washington is a contributor to animal-related organizations. And I mean contributor with a capital C." He raised his eyebrows.

"Landlady? So, ah, Jake. You don't own a home?"

"Well, no, not currently." He saw her smirk of concern and started talking fast, like a seven-year-old lying to his mother. "Hope, okay, look, I've been searching for three years for a decent Land Cruiser. I have found nothing, all rusted junk, and I don't have the time, energy, or skills to restore some heap. You know you can't even buy a one new anymore. So, I can't play games here, I love this truck. The sooner you tell me a price, the faster I can write the check ... and heal from this unnecessary trauma."

Hope's arms were crossed across her chest, listening to this diatribe. "Seriously? You can't buy new ones now? That's gotta make this one quite a bit more valuable than I first thought."

He didn't smile. Wished she didn't have such white teeth and that stupid outdoorsy glow. Make it easy not to like her.

SOMEHOW, HOPE THOUGHT, something's off in the real story. He didn't act like a guy who rented beach umbrellas for a living. As nice as his legs were, though, Hope was intrigued by his arms. No cannonball weightlifter bulk. They were lithe, firm with ropey muscle. There was no space between the cotton tee and his skin.

He reminded her of some of the Spaniards she'd met playing tennis, only Jake was physically taller and stronger. Dark eyes under long eyelashes. Dark hair, a little long, appeared silky soft. Skin light olive. Chiseled facial bones.

"One question, completely off the subject of a rapidly appreciating Land Cruiser. What's your heritage?"

"Mixed bag, I'm told. Spanish Mediterranean, Italian, maybe a hint of Cuban."

"That's interesting." She was sure about one thing. Getting a date probably wasn't one of his problems.

JAKE FOUGHT HIS nerves and got to it. "So, what'll you take for it?"

"Still struggling with a number."

"What about this?" said Jake. "The Magnolia Hotel has a nice little steakhouse in it. I'm thinking that over grilled Angus, a couple of crabcakes, maybe a few oysters, and a nice bottle of wine, we could put our heads together and hash out a reasonable win-win for everybody, like business moguls do."

"You know, I hadn't thought about that."

He watched her think.

"Well, sometimes I get a little old fashioned on myself, but every once and again I like to know a guy's last name. Your first name is Jack. What's your last name?"

Jack?

"First name Jake. Last name Montoya."

She glanced at the sky for a moment. "Jake Montoya. Why does that sound so familiar?"

"Well. You ever eaten barbecue at Dreamland in Tuscaloosa?"

"Never."

Jake sighed. "Well, you should. Ever been arrested by the FBI?"

"Not yet."

"You ever watch a Redskins game earlier than ten years ago when you were in Virginia?"

"YES!" Hope jabbed her right pointer finger straight at him, coming to a stop two inches from his face.

"Bingo, buddy! I knew I knew it. Saw you on the *Sports Illustrated* cover in that great pic where you slam-dunked the football over the goalpost after a pick six. I still get that magazine."

"That's another lifetime. So, what about hammering out the fine print on this thing?"

"Hold it, hold it." She waggled her hands at him, shook her head. "Wait a minute on the truck. That picture was the flippin' Super Bowl!"

Jake stuck his tongue in his cheek, looked at the ground. "Um, yeah, think it was, you're right."

"May I make a suggestion?" she said.

"Sure."

"In the summer I'm not really a black dress, high heels kind of girl. I'm more tank top, short pants, and flip-flops. There's a cool spot in Orange Beach made of old shipping containers called the Gulf, right at Perdido Pass. Great water views. I'm kinda thinking fish tacos, oysters on the half-shell, cold beers, a sea breeze, and a setting sun. We can zip down in the 911, you drive. Whatcha think?"

He bit his lower lip, nodded slowly. "Think that might work."

70

BLACK POINT ANIMAL CLINIC

JAKE STROLLED Rowdy back to Kimbo Gage's office, tapped on the doorframe. Kimbo and his dad, Dr. John David Gage, were looking down at a set of plans on a drafting table. Around them was a mishmash of world maps, surf magazines, acoustic guitars, cookbooks, carpentry tools, and tennis rackets. A place like your retired uncle's old garage.

Ray Wylie Hubbard was singing whiskey-soaked outlaw country off a Spotify playlist. Jake felt that was too much hard truth for seven-whatever in the morning.

Both men looked up. John David, looking like a six-foot, four-inch white god, with a shock of thick, white hair and a tan, shuffled around the table. Jake held a hand outstretched for a shake. "Forget that, son, I'll take a hug." After the hug, he clasped Jake's shoulders. "You're looking fine, Jake, just fine."

"And you as well, JD. Basically like a beachcombing billionaire."

JD wore a linen shirt with the top two buttons open over dark, loose-fitting, drawstring pants. And JD did have money. Trained as a surgeon, he part-timed himself into developing beach condos from Panama City to Gulf Shores. He had thrown some early profits into emerging biotech stocks in the early 1990s and became magnificently wealthy.

JD put his hand on Kimbo's shoulder. "Son, I've got to bug off. I have three surgeries this morning. How about dinner this weekend, Jake? Out on the dock."

"Sounds great."

KIMBO, A TALL blond like his father, cut the cast off of Rowdy's leg, shot an X-ray. They studied the black-and-white image on a digital screen while Kimbo pointed out a couple of things.

"All this looks good. Now you have to slowly rehab him back into the full use of the leg."

"Hear that, boy? Getting you back in the game."

"Jake, let's go back to the office for a minute."

In the office, Jake took a seat, looked around. "You've got a full plate, don't you? Vet medicine, Big Jake Grills, music, design."

Kimbo, looking like anything but a vet, wore corduroy board shorts and a T-shirt advertising Yater Surfboards. He sat on the edge of his desk, looked down at Jake. "Well, that's why I have to surf an exotic location a week every month. I need some time for my imagination, otherwise my creativity steers into a rut. But there's a couple things concerning for us as manufacturing titans."

Jake laughed. *Titans.* "Shoot."

Kimbo shot his thumb over his shoulder. "That gorgeous beauty back there is the 250,000th grill we've made. Polling says 43 percent of America knows what a Big Jake is. That's crazy stupid. And you're funny as hell in the commercials. Like it or not, you're the face of the business, like we designed it. In about a month, we're putting four spice recipes I created on the market. Lined up at all the major grocers."

"Cool."

"Here's what I'd like to do. Come in big on the pro season. Maybe line up some NFL guys to get in some commercials with you. I'd like you to pitch it to Peyton Manning, first. Everybody knows him and he's funny as hell."

Jake sat listening, with his chin resting on steepled hands. "I've met Peyton. Let me see what I can do."

"One more thing," said Kimbo. "And I'm serious, this is close to my heart." Kimbo's smile disappeared as a look of concern swept his face. His eyes glanced away then back to Jake. His voice softened.

"Why don't you give it up, man? The FBI. That shootout in Virginia scared the hell out of everybody. I drove over to the plant when I heard. I wanted to see if your mother was okay. I knew people would call her. She was shaking, Jake, cried on my shoulder. You know, after Chuck got killed ... and Ed's gone. If something happened to you ..." Kimbo let it trail off, looked at the floor.

He turned back. "Life's good here. Black Point is growing. Interesting people are moving in. We've got a great business going ... just think about it, okay?"

Too much heavy talk this early in the morning, thought Jake. "I'll leave it at this for now. It feels good to have you thinking about me. I mean that." Jake ended the conversation, looked down at Rowdy. "Ready to go, boy?"

He reached the doorframe, turned back. "You know, Kimbo, there are two very deep scars from Black Point that I haven't been able to shake for decades—Chuck's bike crash and Sunshine's murder. I see their faces all over this town."

A glum look crossed Kimbo's face.

"Same here. And that will never change. Never."

71

JAKE WALKED INTO Pike Tatum's office as the chief was speaking on the phone. Pike pointed at a chair.

"Okay, so Tuesday you think ... uh huh ... okay, great, thanks, Tommy. Talk next week."

Pike hung up. "That was Tommy Markham from the ABI lab. Said he should have the signature on Shedd's Semtex next week. Hell, it's gotta be the same stuff that blew the Rolls. How could it not be?"

Jake shrugged his shoulders. "Let's hope so, it'd sure clear some things up. I've run through all of Bill's cases, but nothing in-depth. Washington has the info, they'll put a team on it. But nothing raised any flags."

"What'd you think about that bus crash? Burnham got his biggest payday yet, and the rest of the town was torn apart in grief over the whole thing. The bus crash, I mean."

"What crash? I didn't see it."

"Couple years ago. February, ice on the road, woman driving a school bus with her three kids on board, no other students. Skidded off 98 down by Oak Hollow Farm and ran straight into a tractor trailer parked on the side of the road. Killed the woman and two kids. One kid was in a vegetative state for months before dying. The saddest damn thing."

Jake pointed at the chief. "Yep, my mother mentioned it back when it happened, but I'd forgotten. I had no clue Bill was in on that. I didn't see it in the records."

"Good old Bill sued the bus company and the company that owned the truck parked on the side of the road. The final dollar amount was sealed, but whispers on the street say seventy-something million. That'd likely cut Bill a check for twenty-plus mil or so."

Jake scrunched his eyebrows, blew out through pursed lips. "Holy smokes."

"The trucking company went belly-up after that, but here's something else interesting. The woman's husband, I'm talking about the woman driving the bus, her husband, a guy named Dude Codger, has not been seen since three days prior to the accident. Completely different set of circumstances. Codger was the manager at the Rusty Anchor, the little roadhouse a few miles south of the high school, across from the polo fields. We got a call about it from Alonzo Bacon, the assistant manager.

"I know Alonzo. We played ball in high school."

"Anyway, a few days before the crash, there was a break-in at the Anchor. Could have been early morning. Back door smashed in, place ransacked, money missing."

"So where's Codger?"

"Don't know. But get this. A few days after the crash we got an anonymous call from a man. He said somebody killed Codger, ran his car down the boat ramp near Mullet Point. We got a diver on it. It was Codger's Camry, windows down, trunk open, but no Codger. We've run down everything and we've got nothing, no body, no workable evidence."

"Interesting."

"The owner of the Anchor, a guy who lives over in Grayton Beach, says he thinks it's an inside job by Codger himself. Vic

Stapleton, that's the owner, had suspicions that Codger was skimming, and that Codger knew the end was near. Twelve big flat-screen TVs were smashed, as well as every bottle of liquor. Stapleton thinks that Codger was being vindictive. He could have just taken the money and split. Stapleton has accounting evidence of theft. So, there's a pending warrant out on Codger."

"Strange timing, huh?"

"Codger might pop up one day on a traffic stop in Peoria, you never know but, seriously, I doubt it."

"Why's that?"

"I think Stapleton's wrong. Well, he might be right about Codger ripping him off. You know as well as I do there ain't too many bartenders who deal in cash all night who don't slip a few bucks in their pocket. There just ain't."

"And?"

"Okay, here's what I think happened. Assholes watched the place. Well after closing, it's dark, figure nobody's there. But Codger *is* there. Reportedly, he slept there sometimes. He sees their faces, maybe knows them. They shoot him, tie him up, whatever, after he hands over the money. They smash the place apart, throw Codger in a vehicle, dump the body God knows where, then run Codger's Camry into the bay."

Jake nodded at the scenario, thinking. "Been a couple years, nobody's seen Codger. Definitely sounds plausible."

"But here's why I'd stake my life on that theory ... or something close to it, that Codger's dead. He would have been sitting on a gold mine in the lawsuit on the bus crash. He'd be a big-ass multi-multi-millionaire right this very minute. He could have squared anything with Vic Stapleton, paid him off a hundred times over. I asked Stapleton about that. This is his exact quote. 'I just want my money back. I got too much fishin' to do to get into some legal crap.'" Pike laughed. "Too much fishin'..."

Jake laughed. "That's hilarious. Well, gotta run."

"You bet. I'll let you know immediately after I hear about the plastics."

JAKE CLICKED HIS seatbelt, started the Land Cruiser, stared through the windshield, thinking.

Bill's biggest case.

How could Theo leave that out?

72

TELLURIDE, COLORADO

MONTOYA AND SHERIFF Mitch Higgins loaded up in the county SUV for the drive to the Clemmons ranch. Higgins placed a large hot coffee in a cup holder. Jake had a diet soda in his hand. The sheriff turned west onto 145 and kicked it.

Eighteen miles away, Higgins punched four digits into a keypad and the ranch gate swung open. A gravel drive wound through a pasture blooming with vivid yellow mule's ears, blue columbines, and paintbrush. A half mile in they arrived at the home, situated below a mountain covered with ponderosas.

"Nice setup, here," Jake said.

"Yep. Suing folks is good money. I got a key."

The sheriff took him straight to the sliding glass door overlooking the pool.

"This glass is new. When we got here, one of Clemmons' guards was on the floor where you're standing, the whole sliding door shattered. One slug through the head, two in the chest. We speculate he may have been looking out at the pool when he was shot, probably eyeing Clemmons and the other guard."

Higgins slid open the door, walked out by the pool. Crime-scene markings were still evident, identifying the body locations.

"Clemmons was sunning, reading a novel ... written by? Yes, another damn lawyer. The bodyguard's laptop was on the table. Last website he looked at was something about an Alaskan cruise. He wasn't married, had a girlfriend. She told us the cruise was in the makings."

"So where do you think the shots came from?"

"The mountain. Had to. M.E.'s report on all three men says the head-shot trajectory is high to low."

Jake studied the vista of the mountain rising just past the pool. "Did you isolate the shooter's location?"

"Feel like we narrowed it down to about a seventy-yard by two-hundred-yard patch of land."

"That's a pretty big area, Mitch." Jake chuckled.

"You're right. So the answer is, we don't know exactly where the shots came from."

"Let's take a walk up and look around," said Jake.

"Too steep. That incline drops fast from the peak. Gotta approach it from the other side. Come on, let's drive around, ten minutes to get there."

UNAWARE, HIGGINS DROVE the SUV up the same fire road that Lucky had used and came to a stop within seventy feet of where Lucky parked.

"Check the soil, Jake. Sandy, rocky. We couldn't find any tracks. It's all sand and gravel back to the highway, as you just saw."

Jake looked up at the incline, saw yellow flags on some trees.

"Start marching, son. Just follow the flags, the best way to make the summit. I've done it five times already, just slow. You certified in CPR?"

"My card expired last month. But I think it's something about pushing on the chest. We'll figure it out."

Higgins laughed. "Yeah, something like that."

Jake hung tight by the sheriff, didn't want to march ahead like some fit jerk. Scaled it in twenty minutes.

"Great view, but this is a hell of a long ways out."

"Sure is." Higgins was breathing hard, sweat running down his face. "This is 850 yards, right here. We've checked everything with rangefinders."

Higgins sat on a large rock. "Need a break." He took a big breath. "We had fifteen guys combing this area inch-by-inch over three days. Nothing. No brass, no gum wrappers, nothing."

Jake folded his arms and scanned the area. "Anybody hear anything?"

"Nope."

"Y'all have a lot of big game hunters out here. Lot of them could make the shots."

"You hunt?" said the sheriff.

"Nope."

"Well, I do. And I wanted to go over this with you. Nothing in the reports about this. I didn't even discuss it with that officious FBI know-it-all agent in Denver. But you mentioned game hunters."

"Right."

"First, I wondered if anyone locally might have a grudge with Clemmons. But the guy kept a low profile, haven't heard of anyone he's pissed off. Then, of course, there's the whole extortion deal. Then him mouthing off in the papers like he's Rambo. I've got some basic thoughts. They might not get you anywhere, though."

"I would love to hear 'em." Jake took a seat on a decaying downed tree.

"Number one. Hunters rarely shoot over two-hundred yards. I mean two football fields is a long way. Especially since you want to hump out some large animal if you can even make the shot."

"Number two. The shell is a .338 Magnum. I don't know one single hunter who uses that. Many use the .300 Winchester Magnum. Some use the 7mm Remington, some the .270, some the .308, a few outliers firing the 6.5 Creedmoor."

"Okay, so who uses the .338?"

"Go online and look at the book cover of *American Sniper.* Chris Kyle's rifle is right there. He's that SEAL badass. That wicked gun he uses fires the .338. I understand that round is popular with all the special forces and marine snipers, probably some law enforcement, too."

"Interesting." Jake flared his eyebrows. "Keep going."

"Number three. Even if you did get down on this mountain to around two-hundred yards out, you're on a steep face. *Nothing* about that is conducive to accurate shooting."

"Sounds right."

"Number four. And pay attention here. We scanned this mountain and tried to find as many good shooting locations as possible, taking in natural cover and distance to the target. We couldn't find one we liked closer than five-hundred yards. Five football fields, now, got that?"

Jake whistled. "Yep."

"Now. Picture the scene. Clemmons reading a book. Guard checking out cruise whatnot on his laptop. Pow. Shot one goes right through Clemmons' skull. Guard probably jumps up like he was electrocuted, gun in hand, wondering what the hell? Pow. Shot two. But where? The guard's skull or Clemmons through the back? Don't know. Either way it was fast. Pow. Pow. Shots three and four. The guard's head has disintegrated. So, two in Clemmons, two in the guard. Now, here's a question. How much time elapsed before the second guard looked out the glass door?"

"Good question."

"Well, I think it was quick. I think he heard something, maybe heard the long gun, ran to the window. Pow. Right in the noggin. Pow. Pow. Two rounds through his body, lodging in the oak floor. We found his cell phone right next to him."

"Okay, it was quick. Why do you think so?"

"'Cause no 911 call. I think he rushed to the window, wasn't sure if it was anything. Saw his boss down, his buddy down, thought, hell no, I'm not running outside. Pulled out his phone. Bang. He's down. Couldn't get the call off."

"Interesting."

"Here's the summary. Three-thirty-eight Magnum, popular military round. Ultra-precise shooting from 500-plus yards. *But fast.* Who can do that? Hunters can't. Here's another fine point. People are living in two houses within 145 yards of this place. Somebody was at home all day for the days around the shooting. We checked. They heard nothing. Had to be a suppressed weapon. Who uses suppressed .338 rifles?"

"Military snipers."

"Bingo, agent. Now let's get out of here. I've got a date with a plate of chicken-fried steak at a Rotary luncheon. Re-election. Every vote counts. Gonna tell those folks I'm cyber-talented and my stock jumps fifty percent. I'll be a shoe-in."

73

9:10 A.M. DENVER INTERNATIONAL. Jake sat in a cushioned terminal chair with his back to the massive glass walls that overlooked the planes on the tarmac, a tablet in his hands, a Diet Coke on ice held between his legs, and an unopened energy bar in his shirt pocket.

He'd thought about it most of last night, Sheriff Higgins' shooting hypothesis. It sounded plausible. Damn plausible for a guy headed to a chicken-fried steak luncheon.

He signed on to his work email, spotted two replies he had been waiting on.

Opened the mail from Les Cox, FBI cybercrime department.

Jake. I hope leads are materializing. YES, you can purchase explosives on darknet. I didn't look extensively but I found products on two sites. ABRACADABRA99 and BLACKONBLACK. Saw C4, Semtex, dynamite, det cord, bomb plans. If you set up the Tor browser on your computer, you can look at these sites and others. Let me know if you need anything or help in setting up Tor. *Les*

He couldn't picture Shedd as a computer guy, especially something darknet.

Jake pulled out his cell phone, pulled up Pike Tatum's number and dictated a text.

Pike. Flying back from Colorado today. Want to discuss your search on Shedd's computer. One thing verified. Plastic explosive available online through darknet. Also, did you run the national database for theft of plastics?

The second email from the FBI source arrived titled **THEO FULLER BIO**. He clicked on it, found a two-page doc, read it slowly. MIT, mathematics, computers, MBA, startup on a cloud site. Russian hedge fund. Even solid poker winnings. It was an extremely impressive resume until he got to the part about the debacle in London. Theo owed the Bank of London almost $4 million.

And Theo Fuller was back working in a small-town law office.

Something ain't right.

74

BLACK POINT, ALABAMA

JAKE CUT THE Land Cruiser onto the shell drive that led to Kimbo's place on the bay. He lived four houses down from his parents. The first thing he saw was the black 911 Carrera, top down. *Ahhhh, gosh.* Jake hadn't spoken to Hope since they sealed the deal on the Cruiser.

"Well, look at you, ladies." Jake walked into the sun-soaked kitchen from the bayside screen porch. Heart-pine floors, a few small Persian rugs, commercial appliances, granite counters.

Three attractive, earth-friendly, natural women stood around the island chatting, each holding a glass of white wine.

Marin Gage, Kimbo's mother, wearing a bohemian paisley top over bleached bell-bottom jeans and Birkenstocks, raced around the corner of the island and grabbed a big hug from Jake. "About time you came down to see us. What took you so long?"

Before he could answer, Jan was next to him, on deck for a squeeze. Five-foot-two, busty, and short hair streaked sandy blond from the sun. Barefooted, she stood on her tiptoes. "Come here, you."

As Jan held on tight, Jake looked over her shoulder right into Hope's dark brown eyes.

Hope wore a casually loose chambray dress that dropped to her knees, leaving her graceful calves exposed. She offered Jake a gleaming smile, raised her hand, palm forward, and waggled just her fingers in a demure wave. At the same time that his brain was telling him how good Jan felt in his arms, he said, “Hey, Hope.”

Nothing better than the soft scent of women, he thought.

“Look at this, Jake.” Jan pointed to a colorful, oversize children’s book on the counter. “It’s the twelfth book in the series.”

He picked it up. “*Rufus and Cheeto Race to Yosemite*.”

“I love it.” The cover had the chimp, Cheeto, bouncing down the highway driving a VW bus with the donkey, Rufus, in the shotgun seat with his face out the window, wind flapping his lips.

Marin was a children’s book writer and illustrator. Her *Rufus and Cheeto* series explored America’s national parks.

“Last one in the series, Jake,” said Marin.

“Nonsense,” said Jan. “The last five made the *New York Times* bestseller list. There’re fifty more parks, so no stopping now.”

Jake flipped some pages, then glanced up at Marin with a closed-mouth smile. “I have every single book you’ve created on my bookshelves in Georgetown. I think twenty-four … or something like that. A daily reminder of you and JD and Kimbo.”

MARIN COULDN’T SPEAK for a moment. She knew he was thinking of Sunshine at this moment, just like she was. As a little girl, she came up with the names Cheeto and Rufus and asked her mom to make up a story about them.

Marin took the book over to the counter by the sink, blinked several times to dab out the tears welling in her eyes, pulled a

Sharpie out of the drawer, and wrote quickly with her splashy flair.

To one of the sweetest men on the planet. We all miss you and love you. Think about it. Think about coming home. Love, Marin

She handed the book to Jake. "Number twenty-five for the shelves. Open it when you are back in Washington." Jake hugged her again.

A SHIP'S BELL clanged in the distance. "Let's go eat, folks."

The dock setup could have been a photo spread from *Coastal Living.* A brightly painted picnic table held a feast. Grilled grouper and oysters. Boiled crabs and corn. A large bowl of summer seasonal salad. Three bottles of California wine on the table.

Candles ringed the railing around the end of the pier while gentle waves smacked the pilings.

The horizon was a strip of orangish pink under a violet haze. The day slipping into night left the water with a black hue.

After ninety minutes of tremendous food and conversation, Jake excused himself to make a bathroom run.

"Hang on, Jake, I gotta go, too. Want to ask you something," said Dr. J.D. Gage.

Walking slowly down the weathered dock, J.D. said, "How's your real estate going? Getting into anything new up there?"

"Nope. On cruise control. But I've been fortunate. I've invested with some good people. All lively commercial locations. It's been good."

"I want to share something with you. Good news but keep it under wraps, and whatever you do don't make any trades on it. Immu-Bioscience is about to be gobbled up for a 26 percent premium on the stock price. That values your shares at just over $8 million."

Reaching the house, J.D. grabbed Jake's elbow to stop him for a moment. "So, smart move listening to the old man on the stock." J.D. smiled. "But here's a bigger deal if you haven't heard it. We want you home. And you're set for money. So, hell, just think about it, would you?"

Jake had invested most of his NFL money into prime commercial real-estate projects over his ten-year playing time. Developers found him. Dr. John David Gage steered him into a few bio-science stocks. He was worth $25 million, give or take. A very rich cop.

And that didn't include Big Jake's Game Day Grill Company.

Jake returned from the restroom, remained standing next to Hope. "Folks, this has been the most amazing evening. Thank you so much for having me. But now I have to leave on official business." He looked at Hope.

"Hope, do you have any interest in running by a little roadhouse and watching a police interview?"

Hope glanced at Jan. Caught a wink.

"Well, sure, I guess."

TWO BEERS AND forty minutes later, Jake and Hope walked outside to the parking lot of the Rusty Anchor. Jake enjoyed talking to the manager, his old teammate, Alonzo Bacon, and digging into what he knew about the Anchor's burglary as well as Dude's background. There was no real reason to ask about that other than it was an unusual set of circumstances.

Jake left thinking Dude Codger was no Eagle Scout.

"That was fun. My first live police investigation. I kind of like the cop stories, love the action." She had an inviting look in her eyes.

"Well, I'm an action guy."

Hope glanced at her watch. “Only ten fifteen. Why don’t you stop by my place and put me under arrest, action guy?”

75

MONTOYA ANSWERED THE CALL at 10:42. "Jake, it's Rye Hewitt in Charleston."

"Good morning, detective."

"Might have something. You remember the tomahawk?"

"Sure."

"We tracked it down. It's called the Battle Hawk from One Strike Tactics."

"Good work. What's the story on the company?"

"Based out of California. Started by a retired Green Beret. They make tactical combat knives and hawks. Artisan quality, handmade. Sell a lot to military guys. Some to outdoorsmen."

"Did you say military?"

"Yep, special forces love the product. I spoke to the owner, a forthcoming guy, sounded like a good dude. Military guys view it as mystical, magical, and guaranteed effective since it was born, bred, and made by a spec ops soldier. They sell it to Rangers, Delta, and Navy SEALs. A lot of marines and regular army, too.

"Huh." Jake nodded. "Okay, the One Strike owner. You tell him what happened here?"

"Yes. He wanted to know."

"What did he say about that?"

"He said that if anybody called him to complain that the tomahawk didn't easily cut somebody's head off, he'd refund their money and call me to let me know who it was."

Jake laughed. "Well, there ain't no head on this lady's body, so they're meeting their quality standards. Let me get Justice working on a subpoena of company sales records, put some steam heat on the process. What's the owner's name, the guy you talked to?"

"Mayo Sexton, a southern guy like us, from Georgia originally. Check out One Strike on YouTube. That damn guy's throwing knives and tomahawks at oak trees. He sinks the blade in deep with every throw. Never misses. This Sexton guy, he's a big, no nonsense, tough-looking son of a bitch."

MILITARY CONNECTION. All Jake could put together from two separate murders, if anything, was a possible military connection. But still, anybody could buy a .338 rifle and a hatchet. Didn't have to be military.

And Wild Bill's Rolls?

Plastic explosive. Shedd was military ...

He fired a text to Ben Staggers: **Need to pick your brain. Call me if you get a minute.**

The phone rang twenty-two minutes later.

Jake filled Staggers in on what he'd found so far, then got to his question. "Could an ex-military guy do this?"

"Well, if I was of a mind to, I'd be great at doing that. So, yeah, a former military guy could do this. But why would he want to?"

"Same reason most people do things. Money."

"Well, I like money, but I'm not going to be doing anything like that," said Staggers, a retired Delta Force captain.

"I don't want to blow too much smoke here," said Jake, "but knowing a guy like you, I think of great character, impeccable ethics, strong moral code. In my mind, that's the level I view our military."

"Okay, I know where you're going. Could a military guy even *conceivably* stoop to doing this kind of violence?"

"Exactly." Jake tossed three almonds in his mouth, focused on what the former special ops guy has to say.

"Here's the deal. Military guys have all the same problems as anyone else walking the streets, and in all probability, even more pressures. To start, the money is crap. Hard to support a family. Marriage is tough. Lot of time away from your spouse. Affairs are common. Kids don't see their dads for long periods of time, which is not good in today's culture. And coming back in from a deployment? Oh boy. God forbid, you could always have a life-changing physical injury. But the epidemic issue is PTSD."

"I've heard that."

"It can keep you from sleeping, eating, loving. You'll drive away everyone you know. Guys walk around angry, half-cocked, or maybe in the other direction, hidden from life holed up crying in a bedroom closet. It can make you unemployable. Then zero money. That leads to desperation. The latest VA stat is twenty suicides committed daily by our soldiers."

"Ahhh, man. Glad you're doing well."

"Jake, I've been divorced twice. I'm okay, but most of that is bringing the war home. It has affected me, but I march on. Fortunately, I'm able to cope. Here's your answer. Yes, an ex-military guy could be involved in that craziness. Definitely."

Jake nodded, listening. "Okay."

"Here's the only place I find a problem in your story. I haven't heard of a single soul with solid combat experience who would know about any movement of significant money into overseas accounts. Almost a fact that if he was ex-military and has been on the ground in the Middle East, he already has kills under his belt. He knows how to do it and he's good at it. And one lawyer alone, that buffoon buddy of yours from Alabama, sent over $5 million, you said. Most military guys wouldn't know whether to spit, piss, or cry with $5 mil."

Jake barked out a laugh at that.

"Have you ever thought this might be some whacked-out NFL guy cut the second week of training camp who left school without a free degree?"

Jake laughed even louder. "Hadn't thought of that. Lotta suspects there." Chuckled again. "Thanks, man, good insight. Thursday at seven at the dojo?"

"Sure. I'll call Kreitzman. Always fun to kick his secret-agent ass."

FORTY MINUTES LATER Jake was sitting in his Tahoe outside a Five Guys eating a burger and fries, listening to Old Crow Medicine Show sing about poverty, cocaine, and wife beating. His phone rang with another important piece of info. Pike Tatum.

"Pike, whatcha got?"

"Got the plastics report. It's Semtex. But no match to anything found at Shedd's."

"What the hell? I thought we'd close the case."

"Me too. And we're kind of out of leads. But, you know, I kind of believed Shedd when he said he didn't do it. Might be he just hadn't thought of it yet. Or maybe he'd lay the pain straight on Burnham's ass."

"I thought he was shooting straight, too. Listen, you got any cameras focused down that block of Black Point Avenue?"

"Yep. And we've studied everything pretty good. Before, during, and after the blast. Saw Burnham pull in. About fifteen minutes later, boom. Could be the bomber mistimed his blast. Maybe Bill was supposed to disintegrate."

"I don't think so. Bill had that email come in that told him to hold on to his ass, just before the explosion. The killer may have been watching the street and set the blast off with a remote trigger."

"Yeah, maybe," said the chief.

"Hey, Pike, one question. Do you feel safe? I mean doing your job."

"In Black Point, yes. In Dallas, I was uncomfortable. Why?"

"Nothing, really. Some of my friends have just expressed concern for me while I was down there."

"Those are some good friends."

76

MONTOYA KILLED THE radio and thought back. He knew prior to getting drafted into the NFL he never had one single thought about law enforcement, ever.

Occasionally, he browsed an old memory that lived in the cobwebs of his mind.

JAKE WAS TWENTY-ONE years old, a rookie for the Redskins, when he was sideswiped by Buck Bradley. He had not seen Ms. Sarah's husband since he moved into their carriage house, four months earlier.

It was a pleasant spring evening, and Jake had the windows open. He heard a tap on his screen door, looked over his shoulder from the couch, and saw Buck Bradley, the former admiral and current director of the CIA. He was wearing paint-stained, cut-off khaki pants with an untucked navy golf shirt that had to be fifteen years old. He could have been a handyman at an apartment complex.

Jake hopped up. "Hello, admiral, come in, sir."

"No, no, but thanks, nice night, you come on out for some air." Jake stepped out on the porch. The screen door rattled the frame as the spring cracked it shut.

“Damn, I love the slap of a screen door. Makes me think of my childhood down in Beaufort, South Carolina,” said the admiral. “I’ll tell you I’ve had a fine life, but not one day of it was better than being a boy growing up in the Carolina low country.”

“I can imagine. Have a seat, sir.” Jake pointed to the Adirondacks.

“Look, Jake, I’ve been really busy so I wanted to catch up, set a few ground rules. First, cut the admiral and director crap, okay? You aren’t in the military or the CIA, we’re across-the-backyard neighbors now. The kind where you can come over and ask if they have any extra corn flakes or whatever and not be too concerned about bothering somebody in their pajamas.”

“Thanks, Mr. Bradley. That sounds good.”

“Hold it.” Buck raised his palm. “From now on, call me Buck, forget the mister.”

“Absolutely.”

“But listen,” Bradley leaned in, “I’m serious here about one thing, and I needed to talk to you about it. Sarah and I have a big investment in the Redskins, and I know you understand the gravity of this. Truthfully, it scares the hell out of me. So,” the director’s head lowered, eyebrows shot up, “listen to me now on this real close ... you miss a pick on an overthrown pass and you might get a visit from men with names I don’t even know. Black agents. So no bumfuzzles on the field, got it?”

Bradley bored his steely CIA gaze right through Jake’s skull.

“You need to understand something, Jake. The Washington Redskins ain’t south Alabama high school ball, and this ain’t Monopoly money. Am I clear on this?” Chin down, cheek scar in full view.

Jake's muscles tensed. "Yes, sir, Mr. Bradley ... uh, Buck. I'll always give you a hundred percent. Always." The admiral's tone was concerning. Bradley held the look a few beats to get the message across.

The director stood up, towered over Jake with a fierce look on his face. Then burst out laughing and slapped Jake on the back.

"Screwing with you, Jake. Man, it's just football, not a nuclear strike." Bradley was glowing. "We gotta have some fun with this. I mean, can you believe this crap? Pro football? Two boys from the south? You playing and me owning? America, son! How'd we get this lucky?"

Jake laughed because he thought he was supposed to, but it sounded uneasy.

"Now listen, son, changing the subject, I know some of the boys down at Quantico, you know, Marines and FBI—what say we ride down there and shoot the hell out of something this weekend, then grab a couple of beers and tasty pig at a little spot I know."

Come Saturday, Jake shot everything they put in his hands. Pistols, shotguns, full-auto M-16s, and loved it.

They pulled out from the range about 4:15, headed to a drive-in barbecue spot that opened in 1935. A dive called Fincher's. The director and Jake agreed on one thing for sure. They were barbecue nuts and there were not enough barbecue joints in metro Washington. Neither understood why.

Pulling in, Jake thought the ramshackle restaurant was ready for demolition. The neon was blown, the street sign tilted catawampus, paint was peeling off the rudimentary concrete block walls. The director pulled his car under a twisted metal awning that had rusting fifty-five-gallon drums every twenty feet, for trash.

In a snap, a Black man in a waist-length white coat was at Bradley's window.

"Yes, suh, what'll ya have?" A wisp of the pit-house smoke floated across the carhop's face. "Smell 'at? Tha's what heaven smells like when Jesus throws a bobby-Q. Yes, suh, sho' do."

They ordered a couple large pig sandwiches, fries, two longneck Buds, and ate in Buck's car.

"Maybe I'm wrong," said Buck, mouth half-full of barbecue, beer bottle resting between his legs. "but you seemed to enjoy the range."

"More than I thought I would. I've never fired a gun before." Jake pushed two fries into his mouth.

"Tell you what, son. You've got an eye for it and a steady hand. Wouldn't want you coming at me with a weapon." Both were hungry and ate fast.

Bradley tilted up the Budweiser, slurped the last of the suds from the bottle, and ran a small napkin across his lips. "Man, that's good. Pork barbecue and Budweiser. You could do worse."

"Right about that, Buck." Jake tossed back the rest of his beer.

Bradley took Jake's empty bottle with his, placed them on the tray hanging on the driver's door, and gave a quick toot of the horn. "Carhop will grab this in a minute, and we'll get rolling. You probably have three dates tonight."

Jake smiled, shook his head. "Not tonight. Finishing a good book."

"Read any of the Clancy books? Pretty good stuff. I mean, I made admiral, and I can't believe some of the info the guy has. If you haven't, start with *The Hunt for Red October.*"

"Already read it, Buck. I love Clancy, too. I'm re-reading some Steinbeck right now. Finished *East of Eden* two weeks ago. Now I'm into *The Grapes of Wrath.* I read Steinbeck slow, try to soak in everything. I want to insinuate myself into life in those times."

"Huh." Bradley had a puzzled look on his face. "Never would have never pictured a pro football player named Jake Montoya into classic American literature. Interesting, sure is. I like a man that reads." Buck thought a moment, twisted his head toward Jake, "Hold on. You do like girls, right?" Buck cocked up his right eyebrow, a wry grin of concern crossing his face.

"Oh, yeah, Buck, I definitely like girls." They both laughed. "Oh, hell yeah, I do."

Bradley went silent for a moment, gazing through the windshield at nothing. He took a breath.

"You're different, Jake. Can't put my finger on it. Sarah is crazy about you, and I can see why. I wanna share something. You're twenty-one, twenty-two, probably too young yet to grasp this, but America is America because we sweep the trash off the streets."

Bradley stuck a finger out the window, signaling to the carhop walking by.

The carhop, a skinny Black man about nineteen with chin fuzz and a single earring, could have been the grandson of the man who took their order, picked up the tray. Bradley handed him a folded ten for a tip.

"Y'all do a great job here, we thank you. Now, do the right thing. Open an outpost in Georgetown."

Bradley turned toward Jake as he twisted the car key. "The trash? That job ain't easy and it's not for pussies ..." The engine fired to life. "Now that you're out of college, time's gonna move fast, it's going to surprise you. You can't play a little boy's game forever. Something to think about."

Jake knew in his official CIA position Buck Bradley was a tough, mean, wily son of a bitch, but he found him damn easy to like.

For years, Jake had thought about that moment at an old barbecue drive-in, hanging on by its sheer memory to another era. Just a couple of thoughts from Buck Bradley. And chocked full of CIA sneakiness.

An invitation. Need more street sweepers.

77

WASHINGTON, D.C.

BACK AT THE OFFICE, Jake was digging himself out of the backlog of tasks he had to do on the White Dragons biker case. Now he was leading two large cases with a wide geographic focus.

Through all of this, thoughts of a pasty fellow sitting in a dark room kept tickling his brain. Theo Fuller, in Wild Bill's office.

Jake read *The Fall of the House of Zeus,* which Theo had suggested in conversation, and loved it. Theo said, "You'll love what happens to Scruggs. Swallowed in his own greed. God, it was beautiful." Jake had bought a similar book, *Circle of Greed,* read it, and planned to give it to Theo at the right moment. He wanted to gauge his reaction. Both books detailed the enormous crashes of two of the biggest dogs in the lawsuit game, which resulted in both men spending time in prison.

Theo's gut feelings were seeping to the surface. He was no fan of lawyers.

Jake picked up his phone, texted Bill Burnham:

Call me when you get a break. Jake.

His phone rang two minutes later. He leaned back in his chair, placed his feet on the desk. "Bill, thanks for the quick call. Wanna give you an update."

"Better tell me you caught those crazy fools. I'm scared to even ride in a car."

"Working on it, Bill. Pike might have told you, but that plastic explosive found out at Shedd's didn't match the bomb in the Rolls."

"I mean, are you serious? Pike told me that three days ago. The FB-damn-I ain't any farther along than that?"

"I told you. Working on it. We've got a lot of irons in the fire. Look, off the subject here, but hiring Theo into your office looks like a stroke of genius. He's an impressive kid. Probably takes a chunk to write his paycheck."

"What? Theo?" Bill barked a laugh.

"Yeah. I saw his resume. Figured he was giving you some great research on your cases."

"Okay, I'll give you this, he's sharp, okay. I'm sure you know he's not my biological child. But I don't know where you get this "chunk" stuff. I pay him nineteen bucks an hour, so he ain't getting rich. In case you don't know, that 'wizard' lost hundreds of millions for some sucker Russian in London. And, hell, *he* called *me*, Jake." Burnham snorted a chuckle. "Guess he wanted to come back to Black Point and get pointers on how the machinery in a successful operation works."

Jake's eyebrows scrunched toward the bridge of his nose. "Huh, okay." He didn't expect to hear that. "Well, anyway, I wanted you to know about the explosive. I'll be in touch."

Jake killed the connection, clasped his hands behind his head, closed his eyes, thought about that.

Two master's degrees from MIT. Calls Bill for a job. Nineteen bucks an hour.

Montoya nodded to himself. *Theo is a canny son of a bitch.*

78

PANAMA CITY, PANAMA

"ALL I WANT to know is this," said J.T. Newberry, a fixture at the American Embassy in Panama. "Will five hundred dollars American get me what I need?" It was lunchtime. Newberry and his guest were seated at Fonda La Especial, a reasonably priced Cantonese spot in the business district.

Ruben Acosta's eyes drifted down to the white business envelope lying on the table. As an eighteen-year officer of the National Police of Panama, he was very familiar with envelopes that were stuffed, yet unaddressed. Ruben slid his dinner plate to the side, let his fingers tickle across the table and slowly slide the envelope toward him.

"This is a very, very delicate issue, Mr. Newberry," said Acosta. "But you have come to the right man. I will look into this immediately. And, of course, I guarantee results."

Newberry smiled, stood up, extended his hand across the table for a shake. "I knew I could count on you, Ruben. Stay in touch."

Weeks ago, the Department of Justice made a formal inquiry with the Panamanian bank into which Bill Burnham wired his $5-million-plus. And they had received not a single morsel of information. This, despite phone calls and multiple follow-up written requests. Jake had put a guy on the case. At the Bureau, they called him “the grease.” He had his hands on discretionary funds hidden in secret drawers. He also just happened to know a gentleman in the American consulate in Panama, J.T. Newberry.

At 7:10 p.m. that night, Ruben Acosta pulled his car up to the home of Andrus Cuesto, his wife’s younger brother, his brother-in-law. Six children came to hug Ruben as he walked into the house. He asked Andrus to step outside. This would only take a moment, he’d said.

Andrus had been in management at Nuevo Banco for eight years. He was also a man with a constant fire in his loins and had produced three children more than he could comfortably pay for.

The banker proved quite pliable. For $250.00 USD, he agreed to hit a few keys on his computer to pull up a simple request.

79

SILICON VALLEY, CALIFORNIA

THE GLOBAL HEADQUARTERS of IntelliSurg Robotics was a stunning commercial design. Three stories of glass wrapped part of the building in a right angle that wowed the eye. The corporate-center architecture was an elaborate statement to excessive financial success in the digital era.

Jake was in a meeting with the CEO, the COO, the public relations/media officials, and two locally based FBI agents.

Two nights ago, one man had been killed, two men severely beaten, and a twenty-nine-year-old mother of two raped by three men. All victims were nighttime employees of IntelliSurg.

Another warehouse strike by the White Dragons biker gang, but this time two thousand miles from their normal territory. Ten Matisse surgical robots were stolen. Each worth $2 million a pop.

Jake's phone vibrated during a heated moment between the CEO and COO over company priorities. Chuck Blumberg calling. The FBI grease. "Gentleman, please excuse me for a moment." Jake stepped outside the office. He didn't want to miss a thing Blumberg had to say.

"Chuck, whatcha got?"

"I've sent you an email, Jake. But I know you hate email and would likely never see it. Got some news."

"Okay, shoot."

"Hope you're sitting down. Your lawyer buddy's money left Nuevo Banco in Panama two days after arrival. Over $5 million went to a bank in Hong Kong. Left a hundred dollars in Panama. Here's where it gets interesting. The account in Panama was set up by William Burnham, residence Black Point, Alabama."

"I'll be damn. Just like Braxton Green's account in Capetown."

"In your email you'll find photocopies of the Alabama driver's license, US passport, social security card, and a utility bill for Burnham's law office. Documentation required to set up an overseas account."

"Is it Burnham in the photos?"

"I don't know. I've never seen the man. Check your email."

"I will. Chuck, get this info to Justice so they can work on the Hong Kong bank. Need to follow the money."

"Will do."

By design, Jake didn't have an email app on his phone. He hustled out to his rental in the parking lot. He drove straight to The Domain Hotel, slung off his sport coat, and signed on to his laptop. Silicon Valley. Ultrafast internet speed.

He clicked on the email. He opened the driver's license and passport photos. Crystal-clear images. Same individual in both.

And it wasn't Wild Bill Burnham.

Jake rested his chin on his fist, elbow on the desktop. Smiled.

Crafty, these guys.

80

ATTORNEY JACK KIMBRELL ran his high-profile pirate operation out of Las Vegas, and he liked nothing more than flying his favorite people, who were essentially other lawyers mining the landscape for him, out to Vegas in his company jet.

Bright lights, all-night action, world-class food, incredible shows, and unlimited hoo-hoo for the boys. It reeked of debauchery and money. Truckloads of money. And the lawyers all went home transformed into big dogs stoked to vacuum their home turf for potential cases to fuel Jack's cash factory.

The best Kimbrell could figure, he was worth $190 million, give or take. He owned a ski chalet in Jackson Hole, an oceanfront home in Maui, an ultrafast McLaren 570S, a Bentley, and a business jet.

He also had a trophy wife twenty-five years younger than himself and two ex-wife bitches who he paid occasionally to just shut the living hell up.

Clandestinely, attorney Jack Kimbrell also owned one of the world's largest collections of pedophile porn, boys and girls. He spent over $400,000 dollars a year supporting two shelter homes for displaced children, making it easy for him to take a youngster or two out for an adventure weekend with Uncle Jack.

His most cherished property was in Kissimmee, Florida, a 10,000 square-foot home on forty-four acres with two large swimming pools, a go-kart track, four-wheelers, and three horses. It was a small equestrian estate only thirty minutes from Disney World, a pedophile paradise.

ZEUS LAUGHED THINKING about it. How much easier could it get? After only forty-five minutes on Kimbrell's Facebook page, a trend unfolded. For the last ten years the lawyer had hosted a two-week soiree. First week, lawyers and strippers, second week a hand-picked selection of boys. It took place at Kimbrell's Florida mini-ranch.

Hacking into office emails, Zeus spotted several that had been fired off to his lead personal assistant delineating some needs for the event. Employ a chef from Vegas, Michael Gaudet, a man who consulted on menus for restaurants nationwide. Provide five attractive ladies, twenty-five to thirty-five years old, a mixture of blonds and brunettes, not overly flashy, and preferably athletic. Women who would look natural riding a horse and, of course, would look even better riding an inebriated attorney.

Zeus pumped the data into the DataCage cloud site. He pinged a single ring to Lucky.

81

MISSION BEACH, CALIFORNIA

LUCKY WALKED INTO his apartment at 5:11 in the afternoon dripping a heavy sweat after a twelve-mile run. It was a spectacular, low humidity, Southern California day that was only missing one thing—decent surf. He strained to pull off his wet shirt, kicked off his shoes, tugged off his soaked socks, and jumped in the shower.

Twenty minutes later he was driving his red '66 Jeep northbound on the coast road toward Duke's in La Jolla.

He requested an outside table from the hostess. His waitress appeared in an instant. She was a sandy blond, tanned, tight-bodied, late twenties woman. The state bird of Southern California.

"I know I want the grilled tuna." Lucky scanned the craft beers on the menu. "Do you have a suggestion on a beer?"

"You look like a blond type of guy. I'd go with Duke's Blond." She cocked a spirited eye at him. "I don't think any of the blonds here would let you down."

He caught her gaze. "Bet they wouldn't. Sure, I'd love a blond."

He popped open what he came to call his *special op laptop.* Started the VPN, then search site DuckDuckGo. Typed in "Reviews Sig P 365." Liked what he read. He needed a micro-compact pistol.

Anything from Zeus? Pulled up DataCage, signed on. A message.

Jack Kimbrell, Esquire

This absentminded fool missed his payment of $8.7 million.

And just to make sure you know what kind of piece of garbage you're dealing with, check out this video. Found this after hacking through a double firewalled data site on an isolated single user server he maintains in the Netherlands. Clever, but not clever enough. I wonder if you might come up with a little surprise for him after you watch this.

Lucky backed the sound way down, looked around, made sure no one could see the screen, leaned in close, and hit "Play."

The video was short. Twenty-eight seconds of disgusting garbage.

Jack Kimbrell sat in a plush, cushioned chair in front of a magnificent twelve-foot-tall Christmas tree located just to the side of an oversized rock fireplace where six stockings hung. The tree was surrounded by no less than thirty presents, large and small, covered with shiny, happy Christmas wrapping. Kimbrell's ass sat on the edge of the cushion, naked except for a splayed-open Santa coat, and his head was covered with a lopsided Santa hat. Two boys, maybe ten or eleven, also buck naked, were with him. One stood between Kimbrell's legs with his hand on Kimbrell's penis. Kimbrell's left hand was on the back of the boy's head. The second boy stood at Kimbrell's right, sobbing, clearly frightened. The lawyer was coercing the boy.

"See. Nothing to be scared of. Let's let Michael rest. Now, Jase, you can get down on your knees and have your turn with Uncle Jack. Remember, that four-wheeler I bought you is the fastest one of them all." The boy shook and cried.

Lucky's face flushed red. There was not a shred of hope for Kimbrell at this point. If ever there was actionable intel, this was it. Just like Green in Charleston destroying a legendary family doctor in the golden years of the man's life.

His face hardened. Eyes furious.

Now it's my turn with Uncle Jack.

82

ORLANDO, FLORIDA

LUCKY PAID FOR a week at the Fairfield Inn with a prepaid debit card. It was only minutes from Disney World, a location he could pack in unnoticed among the masses.

He strolled to a snack bar by the pool, bought a sandwich and chips. Wore a hat and shades. A two-week beard covered his face. Cameras everywhere.

At an isolated table, he went online with his tablet and reviewed the photos from Kimbrell's ranch. Next, he studied the satellite images and Google Earth. He ate slowly as he constructed his mission. He marked a mental X on the Bermuda grass between the two swimming pools.

Finished with his sandwich, it was time for some reconnaissance.

KIMBRELL'S RANCH WAS off 192, almost to Kissimmee. Lucky wanted to make a quick run-by to make sure he knew how to get there. He turned his van off the highway onto an asphalt cul-de-sac.

He passed by the gates to four estates before he reached Kimbrell's place at the end of the road. Couldn't see the house from the road. Perfect. Ornate entrance with a metal gate mounted between two large, stucco columns, surrounded by blooming summer flowers. Video cameras focused on the gate from each column. Lucky made a smooth turn in the cul-de-sac, didn't stop, and drove back to the hotel.

7:43 A.M. TWO DAYS LATER. Lucky applied a vinyl pool company logo to the van and proceeded out to Kimbrell's dude ranch.

The Crystal Blue Pools truck came to a stop at the ranch gate. Zeus was remotely disarming the gate video from precisely 9:00 to 9:20. Lucky leaned out the driver's window, tapped in the code 358853 on the keypad. The gate swung open. The white van entered the property. In the rearview mirror, he watched the gate close as he eased his way toward the house.

At 9:10, Zeus, using Kimbrell's personal code, hacked into the computer at Orlando's PanVision Security to disable all the cameras at the home, both interior and exterior.

Lucky parked the van behind the house next to the pools. He grabbed a shovel, a folding chair, and a cooler from the back of the truck.

One pool was large and asymmetrical with slides and islands and a walk-through splashpad. The other pool was a rectangle with luxurious, weathered teak furniture.

Lucky threw his shovel on the grass and walked back to the van. He came back with his camera bag and pulled out a folded tripod and the Canon. Using video mode, he slowly panned the home, stable, and pools. Killed the video, switched to camera mode and focused on the single shovel on the golf-course-worthy lawn.

He grabbed a shovel and began chopping in the grass, outlining an area to dig, slightly larger than the coffin-sized box in the van. It would be a big hole, so he ate an energy bar and downed a couple of slugs of cold Gatorade before putting the shovel back to work.

In one hour and thirty-five minutes, Lucky created an elegantly simple hole in the ground.

83

JACK KIMBRELL'S JET touched down at 4:10 p.m. at the Orlando Corporate Airport, on the north side of town. He made a quick call to Hertz from the plane.

Kimbrell and his chef deplaned. Fifteen minutes later, two four-door Jeeps appeared by the plane. Kimbrell signed off on the paperwork.

THE LAWYER STUCK his arm through the open window of the Jeep and tapped in the code to the gate. It had taken them almost an hour to reach the ranch.

Lucky had moved the van onto the driveway and was sitting next to it in a folding camp chair, holding a water bottle in his hand. It was ninety-two degrees. Sweat soaked his shirt.

His cargo shorts held a taser in one pants pocket and nylon flex cuffs in the other. A nine-millimeter pistol was stashed in his waistband at his mid-back, under his shirt.

The Jeeps pulled to a stop next to each other, both drivers eyeing Lucky. He saw Kimbrell's eyes go to the van logo. Kimbrell and the chef hopped out.

"Mr. Kimbrell?"

"Yes?"

"I'm Jerry Tate from the pool company. Did Pete get you on the phone this morning?"

"No, who's Pete?"

"One of our managers." Lucky approached Kimbrell with a smile and his right hand extended.

Kimbrell took it and returned a hearty handshake. "Good to see you, Jerry. What did Pete have to tell me?"

"A pipe has broken underground between the pools. It shut down the filtration systems and now both pools have a huge bacteria count. Need your advice before I fix it."

"How long before you can get it right?"

"I can have your pipes replaced in three hours. I'll get the filtration running again, throw a shock treatment in the pool and you'll be swimming by morning. But before I can do anything, I need a decision on how far you want me to go on pipe replacement. You'll see what I mean."

"Well, hell, let's go take a look, get this job going. We've got a busy two weeks planned. Come on, Michael."

The men arrived at the edge of the hole. Lucky pointed down. "See that? That's the problem."

After a good look, Kimbrell's head swung back to Lucky, a puzzled look on his face. "It's a box. Looks like a damn coffin. Where're the pipes?"

It was quick. Lucky's right hand came out of his left pants pocket holding a squat little gun that looked like a beefed-up derringer. Two barbed darts blasted from the taser, lodging in the chef's chest. Fifty-thousand volts of electricity raced through the man's body, throwing him to the ground. His muscles rippled into spastic, pulsating waves while he screamed.

The nine-millimeter pistol was in Lucky's right hand, pointed at Kimbrell's chest.

"What the hell's going on here?" Kimbrell's face flushed in anger.

"Get on the ground, Kimbell, before I blow three rounds into your chest."

"Do you know who the hell you're messing with, you scrawny piece of shit?"

A nine-millimeter hollow-point round blasted through Kimbrell's right shoulder, sending him to the grass. Kimbrell wailed like he was gutshot.

Lucky leaned over Kimbrell with the pistol pointed at his nose. "Yes, I do know who you are. I know exactly who you are." He dropped two pairs of flex cuffs at Kimbrell's feet. Ankles first, then your hands."

The chef was flat on his back on the ground, regaining some composure. Lucky pointed the pistol at him. "Walk over to the pool deck and get on the ground."

He crawled over.

Lucky grabbed two more pairs of double flex-cuffs from the cooler and tossed them. "Ankles first, then put your hands behind you and pull them over your wrists." The chef did as he was told. Lucky cinched the high-tensile nylon.

Kimbrell was still moaning but he applied his cuffs. Lucky walked back, bent down and cinched them tight. Kimbrell's hands were on his frontside. "I need a hospital, you crazy son of a bitch."

"I'll get you there soon."

Lucky took the Canon off the tripod and began filming the men. He stepped to the edge of the hole, filmed the wooden box, which was lined with painter's plastic. He looked at Kimbrell. "Good thing we brought a pool liner for the new baby pool. Can't have that water leaking into the dirt."

He placed the camera back on the tripod, walked over to the chef on the pool deck, leaned down, and rolled the man to the edge of the pool.

"Nooo, nooo, please, nooo, I didn't do anything. PLEEEASE!"

"Bon voyage." Lucky gave a final nudge. The chef hit the water.

Lucky grabbed the Canon once again, went to the edge of the pool, and started filming. The man was frantic. Undulating like a porpoise, trying to keep his head above water. He turned to his side, began pulsing toward the steps.

Lucky was impressed. He'd done similar training as a SEAL. Fear of drowning is stark terror. He stopped filming, grabbed the skimmer, and pushed the chef to the center of the pool. Started filming again.

Water gurgling into the man's mouth, trying to breathe, coughing like he'd vomit.

Then he did vomit.

Lucky sat on a chaise lounge, video rolling. Wouldn't be long.

Lucky knew the chef's heart was pounding. Knew his stomach muscles were on fire. Water flowed down his throat. He fought to remain face up. A final vomit. The putrid contents spilled onto the water's surface, and also deep into his lungs.

The chef was cooked.

Kimbrell's eyes bulged with a look of terror. "Helllp! Helllp! Somebody helllp!" Too far away for anyone to hear.

Lucky walked over, looked down at Kimbrell. "Jack, what happens in a man's life to turn him into a piece of utter garbage like you? You're one of the sickest scumbags walking the earth."

He returned to the van to retrieve a wooden lid that would cover the makeshift coffin. Next, he retrieved a five-foot length of three-inch PVC pipe and a hammer and nails.

Kimbrell saw it, started blubbering. "Money's no object ... how much, name a figure, you can have it tomorrow. Just name it. We can forget this whole thing."

Lucky picked up the PVC pipe, swung it like a baseball bat. He squatted into a batter's stance. Swoosh. Another big cut. Kimbrell's eyes bulged. Squatted again. Swoosh.

"That would have been out of the park. I was a decent player back in the day. I had a good glove. Batting average was fair. Wonder how far I could whack your head? Ahhh, but don't worry about the plastic pipe. Too gentle, really. I wanna show you something super cool."

Lucky lifted his T-shirt, slid a knife out of a custom leather scabbard on his right waist. He held it in his palm, showed it to Kimbrell. “Now this baby is dangerous, I mean *dangerous* dangerous.”

Kimbrell cocked his head off the grass, studied the knife. Fear splintered his eyes.

“It’s a Karambit knife, a warrior’s weapon. This bad boy was custom-made by a soldier buddy of mine in California.” Lucky eyed the weapon. “This guy, man, well, Mayo Sexton’s a true artisan with steel, he really is.”

The knife was a beautifully sinister weapon with an exotic hardwood grip. The steel curved like a raptor’s claw. It had a ring at the base of the grip.

“Here’s how you use it. Put your thumb or pointer finger through the ring so you don’t lose the knife while slashing. And you slash with sort of a backhand movement, like this.”

Lucky whipped the blade through the air. “Across the neck, slicing the jugulars. Whoosh.” He squatted. “A guy comes at me, whoosh, I rip upward, taking the femoral apart in his thigh. And, man, that sucker bleeds.” He knelt with one knee on the ground. “I put my knee on the chest, then I start slashing the belly.” Lucky theatrically slung his right arm left and right. “Whoosh, whoosh, whoosh. Blood and belly guts going everywhere, Jack. And, man, the stink. Putrid.”

Lucky stood. “You’re a lawyer, you get what I’m talking about, decimating somebody.”

“Twenty million ... fifty million ... anything.” Kimbrell was almost unintelligible between sobs.

Lucky shook his head.

“What, dammit, anything, what?”

“The children. Remember them?” Said Lucky.

Kimbrell’s sobbing stopped. His face went pale.

“Yeah, the server in the Netherlands, Jack. We found it.” Lucky shook his head. “Lord, that was awful. That’s what brought me here today.”

He bent and placed his knee on Kimbrell’s sternum, reached down to unhook Kimbrell’s belt. The lawyer fought to breathe with the weight on him. He began to buck and fight and roll.

Lucky stood, pulled the pistol, and fired a round into the lawyer's ankle. "No fighting, Jack." Kimbrell's face became a mask of pain.

Lucky straddled Kimbrell at the level of his shins, bent and grabbed the man's pants and underwear, and tugged them down to just above the knees.

"This knife was good to me in the Middle East." Lucky picked up the Karambit blade. "I took three men down in close quarters combat. I felt like a freakin' monster, like I couldn't be stopped. I wonder if this is a first. Dick amputation."

"Nooo."

"A present from the kids, Uncle Jack." Lucky grabbed Kimbrell's penis and scrotum with his left hand, stretched them out, sliced the blade across the base. "Told you this blade was the bomb."

Blood gushed. Kimbrell vomited. Tried to twist into the fetal position. With his foot, Lucky pushed him flat on his back.

He dropped the bloody blade to the ground, bent, and started rolling Kimbrell to the hole. One final push and Kimbrell went into the box, landing hard on his back, face up, pants down to his knees, blood flushing from his groin. Lucky dropped Kimbrell's bloody penis on his chest. He picked up the Canon, shot some video.

"Ain't you a sight, counselor. Your colleagues are gonna get one hell of a kick at seeing this." Lucky snorted his derision. "Okay, let's put the top on, slam a few nails in. Don't worry, Uncle Jack, I've got a pipe for air. Safety first, buddy."

The wooden top slammed the box with a thud. Lucky stepped into the hole, hammered in four nails, and pushed the PVC pipe through the perfectly cut hole. Then he started shoveling, covering the box with dirt. "Don't worry, Uncle Jack, there's plenty of air coming through the pipe."

Kimbrell's voice echoed through the pipe, begging nonstop as the clay soil splattered the wood.

In twenty-two minutes, Lucky had a mound of dirt overlaying the coffin, rising up into a triangular mound around the PVC.

He unfurled a green garden hose, screwed it to a spicket at the house, turned on the water to a very slight flow. He walked it over the grass to the gravesite.

The hose was threaded down into the PVC pipe. He stuck his mouth up next to the mouth of the pipe and delivered a final message.

"The kids felt like it was their turn to throw the pool party, Jack. Enjoy your swim."

84

BLACK POINT, ALABAMA

4:55 A.M. BROYLE WILLIAM AND Clyde Boland wore ball caps, running shorts, and T-shirts as they cut off De La Mare into the alley that approached the back of Bill Burnham's office. They looked like other Black Point runners who hit the day early for a workout, except, with a closer look, these two carried an edge of danger.

They had arrived from Ft. Worth, Texas, four days ago with a need for information. They watched Dude Codger's trailer. Nothing. The Rusty Anchor. No sign of Dude.

They were aware of the Codger lawsuit. The plan was to get personal with Burnham's files.

A sodium vapor lamp provided orange-tinted light in the alley. Clyde removed his runner's backpack, tossed Broyle a tightly folded pair of coveralls and a black ski mask. He grabbed his next. Both men suited up, leaving off their masks. They pulled latex gloves on their hands.

"Let's get behind this dumpster and wait. Probably have twenty minutes before he gets here," said Clyde. They'd surveilled Bill's arrival for the last two mornings.

At 5:24 they heard footsteps. They slipped the masks over their heads.

Wild Bill reached the door, placed his briefcase on the ground, and fumbled with his keys. Broyle held the back of his hand up in front of Clyde's face. *Not yet.*

Burnham twisted the key in the deadbolt, stepped into the building, leaving his briefcase on the ground. He turned off the alarm.

Broyle saw the top of Bill's head as his hand reached back through the doorframe for the briefcase. He gave Clyde the signal. It only took a moment to race across eighteen feet of pavement to reach the door. Clyde bull-rushed Bill backward into the hall. Broyle grabbed the briefcase, closed the door, and twisted the deadbolt.

"Do exactly as we say, and you won't get hurt," said Broyle.

"Oh, shit, don't kill me, don't kill me, don't kill me." Bill was shaking. Clyde had a firm grip on the lawyer's shirt at the nape of his neck.

"Let's go to your office."

"Okay, okay, it's upstairs. Don't hurt me."

Reaching the office, Bill said, "What do you want? Anything you want, okay? Just tell me."

"What I want is for you to answer my questions. Got it?"

"Yes, okay. What?"

"Are your case files on paper or computer?"

"Computer. Everything. I swear."

"Question two. Business bank statements. Paper or computer?"

"Computer."

"Personal bank statements. Paper or computer."

"Computer. I don't do anything on paper." Sweat beaded on Burnham's forehead. He'd gone pale. Voice shaky.

"You aren't going to pass out, are you?"

Bill shook his head, eyes bulging.

"Do what I ask, and this will go quickly. Don't do what I ask, and we'll kill you. It's that simple. Got it?" said Clyde, voice deep, menacing.

"Yes, yes, yes. Tell me what to do." Bill dragged his right forearm across his brow, wiping off sweat.

"I want to see one case file. Just one. Sign on to your computer."

Bill moved to sit in his executive chair behind his desk. His fat fingers stumbled logging on. Clyde was right behind him looking over his shoulder, hand clenched on Bill's shirt collar.

The screen came alive. "Okay, what case?"

"The school bus crash."

"Wait. Why?" said Bill.

The smack was quick. Clyde took his latex-gloved right hand and bitch-slapped Bill hard across his right face. Bill screamed, touched his cheek.

"Get the file," said Broyle. Gravel in his tone.

Bill scrolled through documents, punched it up quickly. *Codger vs. Gemini Busing/Hendrickson Trucking.* "Here it is. Everything. All investigations. All court testimony. Video from courtroom consultants. Don't hurt me. Anything. I'll give you anything."

"Get up."

Clyde jerked Burnham out of the chair. Broyle sat down. He knew what he was doing around computers. He dropped two flash drives on the desk, then stuffed one in the computer's USB port. Clicked download. The single case's data fit easily on the one terabyte drive. It loaded in two minutes.

Broyle hopped out of the chair. "What banks do you use?"

"Why?"

Facing Bill, Clyde smacked the left side of his face. Bill bent down, holding his head, "Ahhh, gawwwd. Wells Fargo and BBVA. Business and personal accounts at both."

"Pull them up. I'm going to download all your banking data."

Clyde pushed Bill into the chair.

It took twenty-four minutes for the bank info to download onto a separate large-volume flash drive. Data was retrieved back to one year prior to the bus trial.

"Is that it? Every account? Last chance to be sure. If you're screwing with us, we'll be back," said Broyle. "And it will get ugly."

"Yes, that's all of it. I swear."

They left Bill trussed tight as a mummy, lying on the floor.

At the back door, both men shed the coveralls, folded them as tight as they could, and stuffed them in the backpack along with the masks and gloves.

At a brisk jog, they reached their car in just under a minute.

LIZ ARRIVED AT the law office at 7:51 a.m., made coffee, and started checking emails.

At the same moment, Clyde and Broyle were traveling at seventy-five miles an hour, just passing Waveland, Mississippi, on I-10 west, one hour out from New Orleans.

Eight hours later they'd hit Ft. Worth.

85

KISSIMMEE, FLORIDA

"**GUY'S A BIGTIME** pedophile. Good riddance to that friggin' pervert," said Kissimmee's chief detective. The man wore a face full of disgust and a dated summer-weight sport coat. Jake stood next to him looking into the reopened grave. He mused over the PVC pipe with a garden hose threaded into it, fascinated by the violent ingenuity of the killers.

The day was heading toward ninety-four degrees by 1:30. Jake wore shades and was sweating through his polo shirt.

"Agent, after thirty years in this business, I thought I'd seen it all. Last evening a sizable file of almost four thousand images of naked children, many involved in sex acts with an adult, hit my email. We believe whoever sent that was probably the killer. At least two hundred had Kimbrell in them."

Jake was digesting this unexpected information when his phone went off. Wild Bill. He thought about letting it go to voicemail. Changed his mind. Burnham would blow up his phone every five minutes.

"Hey, Bill. Can't talk, I'm at a crime scene. I'll call you back in an hour or so."

"Screw that, Jake! They're back, the killers. They jumped me when I arrived at the office this morning."

"Hold on one second." Jake put the phone against his chest. "Detectives, can you give me a few minutes for this call." Jake moseyed off twenty feet from the grave.

"Okay. Tell me exactly how it went down." Jake's brow furrowed. Another surprise.

Bill spoke fast, still running on fear-stoked adrenaline, relaying every detail. "They wanted the school bus case file."

"Did they ask for money?"

"No, but they will. They downloaded all my bank records. They wanna see what I've got, that's what I think. Then they're coming to bleed me dry ... or kill me. Pike's crew is dusting the office now. Poking around the alley and the streets. They don't have a clue. Hot damn, Jake, I might leave town. I won't be able to sleep."

"Probably a good idea. I'll get back to you."

Jake slowly walked around the swimming pool. Thinking. Kissimmee and Black Point. Connected? Jake couldn't see it, but still, two surprises coming his way within minutes.

At first Jake had been sure Kimbrell was a third lawyer killed for lack of payment. He was a big money guy. But now ... was it coincidence? Just about his sexual perversion? Payback?

Montoya had spoken to the FBI field office in Las Vegas thirty minutes before coming to Kimbrell's place. Told them to ransack Kimbrell's law office computers looking for digital evidence of an extortion attempt.

Maybe Bill was right, planning another run on his money. He paid once. Paid fast. Going back at him might be the smart play. The killers had to think that could be easy money.

The bus file.

There it is again.

86

10:05 A.M. ZEUS SAT in his office. Nerves buzzing. Door shut.

He'd spoken to the cops about the attack on Bill. He hadn't been there and didn't know what had happened, he told them.

But I might have a clue, he thought.

Lucky had done the Rolls. Zeus had asked him to, just to screw with Bill. Why would he be back for this? Had to be Lucky. Bill's description of the smaller of the two men fit Lucky's profile. Bill said he was "average size." Voice sounded American. Pike pushed Bill to define average. Six feet, maybe one-ninety. But he was in coveralls. Could have been lighter.

The bus trial. Dead giveaway.

Lucky's gaming me, Zeus thought.

Zeus grabbed his two laptops, drove his Subaru down Colony Street to Coffee Loft, a hip coffee spot repurposed out of the shell of a decades-old convenience store, squeezed a parking spot out of the small, crowded lot.

Inside, he ordered an iced coffee, took a seat, powered up the laptop he used for dirty work. There was a decal on the box, the logo from the TV show *Mr. Robot.* **Computer Repair With A Smile.**

He typed a short document, encrypted it, popped up to DataCage: **Need to know and no bullshit. Did you run**

through town after Orlando? Was that you in Bill Burnham's office this morning?

He pinged a single ring to Lucky's phone.

Zeus fought to simmer down, but the coffee drove him in the wrong direction. He didn't need Lucky going off the rails. Green's murder brought in $14.3 million. Clemmons' death added $21.9 million.

When the money came rolling in after the first murder went down, Zeus had begun buying crypto daily.

If Lucky would stay calm, they could finish this up in a few months.

Zeus expected Kimbrell's demise to bring in a landslide of cash. *Drowned in a box underground? Man!* Zeus edited Lucky's video into one minute forty-five seconds of life you'd never want to happen to you. The claustrophobia alone? Gave Zeus a shiver.

Zeus wanted another day of national media on the Kissimmee ambush to soak into the collective souls of American lawyers. Then, pow. Thirty-five lawyers would be receiving a highly personal digital demand, complete with video visuals of their ol' buddy Jack Kimbrell taking an airless swim in a wooden box.

And that included an email to Wild Bill Burnham.

Zeus's smile was like a razor.

87

A WEEK HAD passed. The man in front of Zeus at the coffee counter was late twenties wearing a frat-boy uniform, button-down oxford over khakis with a bow tie. He said to a buddy, “You watch. Saban’ll have Tua out by halftime with Bama up thirty-five points. Gonna screw the kid out of the Heisman.”

His buddy, a short, junior-sized frat boy, oxford button-down, khakis, bow tie, said, “Yep. It’s got me worried. Need that Heisman to go along with our national championship.”

Zeus rolled his eyes. He despised football. Ninety-nine percent chance those were two newbie lawyers or baby bankers. He paid for an iced coffee and a muffin, took a seat in a corner, and went online with his computer. There was Lucky’s response.

NO. I was not in Wild Bill’s office. Summary please. What happened?

Zeus left a description of the event. It concerned him. Lucky was lying to him. Why screw with success?

His mind suddenly hit on something interesting. A wry smile crossed his face. He began to type.

Check DataCage DAILY. Have your office look alive for a call from Burnham’s law office. I’m about to hit them

with something that might spur them to hire Knight Force for some protection.

Invite the devil into Wild Bill's kingdom.

Kimbrell's murder had caused a stir in the national media over the last seven days. Collection time had arrived. Zeus launched some invitations, complete with video.

Now, for William Burnham, a slightly different invitation. Zeus knew that Wild Bill had sliced $2 million off his cut and paid that jackleg ambulance jockey, Dunnigan. Then paid $11 million in taxes on the lawsuit windfall. Next, he'd pumped $12 million into buying a small collection of trailer parks in south Mississippi that inflated the value of his mobile-home portfolio up to $33 million.

He punched the SEND button on Proton mail. The digital message raced around the world on the Tor system only to land softly in Wild Bill's inbox, decrypted and poised to jump off the screen and strangle the breath out of him.

Zeus raced out of the coffee shop. He hoped to be in the office when Bill spotted the email.

THREE MINUTES TO reach the downtown parking deck. Zeus ran through the alley by the bank to Black Point Avenue, slowed for two cars, then sprinted to the front door of Burnham's office.

"Will summer please leave," Zeus wiped his brow as he walked into the cool office lobby, huffing. "Hot as living hell." Aunt Liz looked concerned.

"Something's happened, Theo." Liz had a subdued but conspiratorial smile on her face. "Hold it a moment."

"What?"

"Bill just screamed to lock all the doors. Hold all calls. Not sure what's going on."

Joy coursed through Zeus's body. He looked at Liz, let her see the beginnings of a smile with a chin nod.

Her eyebrows raised.

"I have work to do, Aunt Liz. I'll be in my office." Theo winked.

Walking down the hall he could taste the delicious pain Bill was feeling at this moment. Everything had gone perfectly ... but now ... Lucky trying to wrangle control ... *what the hell?*

MOMENTS AGO, Bill's computer had emitted a symphonic tone when Zeus's email hit. Bill's stomach rose into his throat when he spotted the sender.

Panic@protonmail.

The heading: **You've Been Selected**

He took a breath, opened the message, slid on his readers, leaned in to read it.

Congratulations!

You've Been Selected as a Rare Platinum Donor
You Have Thirty Days To Transfer the Deeds of ALL Your Trailer Parks Into The
Charity of Your Choosing
Thank You For Your Generosity
And, Please
Call A Press Conference, Take Some Credit
That Way We'll Know It's Done
And Then We're Gone Forever
Unless You'd Like to Star in Your Own Video

88

WASHINGTON, D.C.

"YOU'RE GONNA WANT to hear this," Agent John Simmons said.

Jake was holding a thin laptop, adjusting the contrast in some black-and-white photos when he answered the phone. "It's Monday night, man. Okay, whatcha got?" Simmons, a Bureau man only months away from retirement, was on the FBI's financial team tracking the overseas accounts.

"Burnham's money went to Panama. And you know the account holder's name in Panama is William Burnham."

"Right."

"Within days, the money left Panama and went to Hong Kong. Hong Kong got back to us. The Hong Kong account holder is one Braxton Green. American address is King Street, Charleston, South Carolina. Your first guy killed."

"You gotta be kidding." Jake took a strong pull of Rolling Rock.

"Nope. And it gets better. Over fourteen days every nickel minus one hundred dollars went into cryptocurrency, Bitcoin. The *alleged* Mr. Green was purchasing Bitcoin daily out of Hong Kong on six different crypto exchanges."

"So, we're screwed, right?"

"Oh, no, no, no. Many in the general public think Bitcoin is anonymous. It's not. Blockchain is a ledger system. Every transaction recorded."

"I don't have a clue what that means. I just want to know one thing, John. Can we track it?"

"Yes, but it will take a while. Coin can be spent in a thousand different ways, so don't expect any quick results. I also have my hands on copies of the account documents used to open the Hong Kong accounts. The ID photos. You'll love this."

"Oh, no. What?"

Simmons laughed. "Exact same photo that was on Burnham's ID in Panama, but this time with Braxton Green's name."

Jake exhaled. "So, we don't have much?"

"Got a lot, actually. It'll just take some time to run it down. Here's what concerns me. We have no idea how many accounts are out there from a bunch of different lawyers. It would be nice if some other guys stepped forward, let us know where they sent money."

"Yep." Jake shook his head. "But listen to this crap. Maybe it makes sense to you. Just got the info this morning from Burnham himself. He's received another financial demand. They included video of the Florida murder with it, so it's them."

"Really?"

"They've demanded Burnham *donate* his trailer parks to charity. Yes, I said donate to a *charity*."

"What the hell are you talking about? Wait a minute. An Alabama shyster named Wild Bill Burnham owns *trailer parks?"* Simmons laughed into the phone.

"Keep laughing. It's $33 million worth. Not a penny of debt. Throws off four million a year in profit."

"What! Thirty-three? Man, that's strong. But, yeah, I'm with you, doesn't make sense ... except for this. Somebody wants to seriously screw that guy, financially. Who'd Burnham piss off?"

"Pretty sure half the people in three states."

89

BLACK POINT, ALABAMA

THEO FULLER CLIMBED the stairs to the second floor, contemplating how this might play out. He tapped the closed door to Bill's office. "It's Theo."

"Come in."

The first thing Theo saw was Bill's right hand on the grip of a revolver resting on the desktop. After the trailer park demand, Burnham was off his game, looking anxious, eyes bloodshot like he hadn't slept. A man on his last nerve.

"Hey, don't shoot, Bill. I might have something to help you."

Bill carried the gun at all times. He also had an extra pistol in his car as well as one in his bedroom. He pointed the pistol toward a chair. "Sit." Bill placed the gun on the desk and rubbed both hands over his face.

"Can't sleep, Theo. Can't think straight. If you've got something to help let's hear it."

Theo handed Bill a postcard. "Maybe you've looked at it. We've gotten a couple of these things in the mail over the last few weeks."

Bill put some drugstore readers on, leaned back, and read the card out loud.

"Knight Force. Elite security. Global Protection." Flipped the card over, saw the website address. "I'll be damned." Punched it into the computer. Bang. It was up. Bill studied the home page for a moment. "Impressive. Have you seen this, the site?"

"Not yet."

"Come around here."

Theo came around the desk, looked at the website over Bill's shoulder. "Yeah, that's sharp graphics, pro quality." The background was black with crisp lettering and photos. At first glance the site left the right tone. *We're serious badasses.*

Theo pointed. "Click right here."

Bill clicked the "What" tab and read out loud. "Personal Security, Awareness Training, Anti-Piracy Training, Self-Protection Techniques, Phantom Surveillance."

"Nice." Bill clicked the "Who" tab. Theo read it. "Extreme Experience. Special Forces. Combat Veterans. Former FBI agents. Former CIA officers."

Bill coughed out a laugh and settled on a grin. "Whoa. Look at this shit." Bill scrolled his cursor over some small print.

"We've Killed A Lot of People. And They All Needed It." He slapped the desk, roared a laugh. "I just found my team. I mean, damn. This is a helluva site."

But Theo already knew that. He'd built it.

"Don't let the door hit you on the way out, Theo. I've got a call to make."

Theo's mouth twisted into a grin as he closed the door.

90

WASHINGTON, D.C.

"I NEED A lunch meeting if possible, something important to discuss. How's your schedule?" said Jake.

"Somewhat flexible, especially around lunchtime. Yours?" Belinda Brant was regarded as the sharpest young tech mind in the DC cyber division. Undergrad at Cal Tech. Master's in computer engineering at Stanford. She could make five times the money in the private sector. People wondered why she didn't.

"Let's try tomorrow," said Jake. "I'll run by your office at eleven forty-five. Try to clear two hours if you can. I've reserved a booth at a great spot."

"Jake." Belinda laughed. "I'm pesco-vegetarian."

"Not a problem. I'm tolerant of all sexual lifestyles."

She smiled.

11:56. NEXT DAY. Jake held the door at McDonald's open for Belinda. As they sauntered in, he happened to notice her sensible heels accented the shape of her legs.

Belinda was tall with a slim build, small breasts, little makeup, early thirties. And she wore stylish, smart girl glasses. Jake would take one cerebral, natural woman over twenty-five of the fabricated, cheerleader airheads that used to come his way.

"What can I get you, Belinda?"

"I've got it right here, a salad." She tapped a crumpled brown lunch bag. Her ecological sensitivities caused her to use one bag for half a year. "No, wait. A cup for water, please."

She eyed Jake's tray when he returned. "I thought you were some kind of martial arts guy, or athletic or something."

"Yeah, I work out a little," said Jake as he put extra salt on the fries and opened three ketchup packs. "I heard a long time ago the great Herschel Walker went to McDonald's for his pregame meals at Georgia. It won him the Heisman."

Jake wore a banded sleeve, black polo shirt today. It complemented his olive skin and dark hair. Big Mac or not, Belinda's eyes walked over the masculine cut of his arms.

"So, what's on your mind, mister?"

"Couple issues. One thing, cryptocurrency, the other, hacking into someone's computer. Know anything about it?"

A frown creased her face. *Come on, now.* "Only two hours for this lunch? I don't think so."

"Come on, how can I hack in?" said Jake.

She rolled her eyes. "Okay, give me some info. Who owns the computer and where is it located?"

Jake filled her in on Theo. High-level mathematics and computer degrees. Looked and acted like a geek. Had a tower computer in his office as well as two laptops. "This is a guy that has been a nerd his whole life. A guy who takes digital stuff seriously."

Belinda sparingly poured some homemade vinaigrette dressing on her salad and opened a package of wheat crackers.

"Okay. Not easy. Likely impossible. A lot of people like that are inherently paranoid about others getting into their stuff.

They know like-minded geeks that will try to commandeer their computer for the thrill of it, so they're cautious."

"Well, shoot. So, you think I'm screwed on that aspect of it?"

Belinda sighed. "Not sure. But it will be difficult." She had some lettuce on her fork, poked it toward his face as she spoke, said, "You can damn sure bet on this. That guy has encryption that even the NSA couldn't crack in a thousand years." She placed the salad in her mouth, chewed, then spoke. "So, it would do you zero good to steal the computer."

Jake had eaten 90 percent of his Big Mac. He focused on every word. He'd never thought a woman was sexy while she ate, but somehow Belinda was. Something with her lips.

He took a swig of Coke. "Any ideas?"

"Is that a real Coke? Oh, never mind. So, you've been in this guy's office more than once, right? If you can tell his laptops apart, which one is he using?"

"Yeah, I can tell them apart. One has a *Mr. Robot* sticker on it. But he's always using his tower computer when I've seen him. The laptops are always charging."

Belinda smiled. "Bingo, baby!" She did an fist pump. "Might have something." She reached across the table and grabbed two salty french fries, dipped them in ketchup, and slid them in her mouth. "Oh my God, that's so good ... Father in heaven, forgive—"

"Okay, what do we have?"

"Computers charging. You and I and most people have a work computer and a personal computer. My guess is if any shenanigans are going on, it's in the one with the *Mr. Robot* sticker. By the way, I've seen every episode of that show. Your guy obviously likes devious machinations. All of us geeks do. The plan is this."

Jake's eyelids narrowed as he listened.

"I'm going to give you a handful of USB ninja charging cables, different colors and lengths. The wall plug is implanted with an attack payload that you can physically upload into the guy's computer. In this case, I suggest something like a keystroke logger."

"How the heck do I do that?"

"That's the tricky park. If possible, and a big if, you need to get in his office and swap out the cables on both laptops. Then you need to be within forty feet of the computer when it's replugged in. Then you activate a Bluetooth trigger programmer, and whammo ... you've dumped malware in his computer."

Jake raised his eyebrows. "Interesting. Calls for a french fry." Jake ate a couple. Finished with a slug of Coke.

In a flash, Belinda grabbed the last fry.

"You know ... this is illegal without a court order," she said, smiling conspiratorially.

Jake looked at her, expressionless for a couple of beats. "I go by military standards. Don't ask, don't tell. We never had this conversation. It's just a peek, anyway. Now. Cryptocurrency for dummies. Know anything about it?"

"Yes, quite a bit. I even own some. What do you want to know?"

"Well, I don't understand any of it. I've been reading site after site about the stuff on the internet. I'm still clueless. Here's the deal. We know the extortion money went overseas. Now, our forensic accountant says funds in a Hong Kong account have been exchanged for Bitcoin. So, take it from there."

Belinda took a breath, looked at her watch. "Not a whole lot of time. Okay, Jake, I can explain it to you, but I can't understand it for you." She shot him a skeptical look.

He shook his head. "Aw, now come on. You damn Stanford chicks." He picked up his McDonalds cup. "You'll have an easier time today. This stuff is packed with sugar and caffeine for my brain." He wagged his fingers toward himself. "Give it to me."

Terminology spewed out of Belinda's mouth, leaving him even more confused. Internet exchange of digital assets. Decentralized blockchain. Bitcoin pseudo-anonymous. Digital wallets. Public keys. Private keys. Fungibility.

Jake raised a hand. "Hold it. One question. Bitcoin. Can this be traced to the owner?"

"Well, transactions occur across cryptographic addresses, and anyone can create a boatload of addresses. But it *is* possible to trace back to your IP address. All transactions are public history, and they can be analyzed for spatial and temporal correlations. If one address can be linked to a person, the related transactions could be identified. Bottom line, it's possible."

"Hold it, hold it, Belinda. It just dawned on me." Jake shook his head, befuddled. "That's why this is *your* job, not mine."

She laughed, placed her napkin over her mouth trying to suppress it, but her face lit up.

"It's not that funny." Jake grinned, too.

"No, no. It's just that you reminded me of something. You on those TV commercials with that Big Jake Grill of yours. Playing that doofus. You're hilarious." She stopped laughing. "I've even thought of buying one, you know, for fish. I just feel like I need to road test one first."

Jake processed what she said ... did he just hear an expression of interest? He didn't miss a beat. "Probably nobody more qualified to demonstrate the thing than me. Seriously, it's a Cadillac. How about I grill you a nice, thick slab of well-seasoned black grouper, whip up a superstar vegetarian salad, and open a nice Sauvignon Blanc, over at my cottage this Saturday?"

"Are you serious? You'd do that? I'm free then, too."

"Shoot, yeah, I'd love to," he said. *Heck, that was easy.*

"That sounds great, really great." Belinda's eyes sparkled.

"Glad you're excited. The weather's supposed to be perfect, low humidity, a little cool front. I've got a great fire pit. We can eat outdoors. It'll be a nice evening for us." He loved her enthusiasm. And it was kind of her idea, which meant *game on.*

"Not for me, dummy." She flashed a palm at him. "My husband is *dying* to meet you. We'll bring the salad. That man can talk football for hours."

Huh?

91

BLACK POINT, ALABAMA

LUCAS KNIGHT, CEO of Knight Force, arrived in Black Point with two hard men who would make most guys feel overmatched. One six-three, the other six-four, both a firm 240-250 pounds. Squared shoulders, blocky heads, but neat. Well-trimmed haircuts like a first-day IBM salesman could wear.

During a phone interview, Lucas told Bill he could get on the scene fast with the highest caliber, battle-hardened men available in America. Money was discussed. It was expensive but Bill said money wasn't an issue, so let's do it.

Lucas said, "Not so fast. I meet you. I check out the scene. I hear you verbalize your needs to me in person. I don't accept any jobs in which I have not personally met my client. I want to see your office and your home. And, Mr. Burnham, I want you to evaluate me and my guys. I want you to interview the men protecting you. Ask them anything about their history and capabilities."

"That works, Mr. Knight." Bill was encouraged. And impressed.

LUCAS SPENT ONLY four hours in Black Point, and that included a lunch of ham biscuits and vegetables at Lyrene's.

He noticed Bill's eyes light up when he introduced W.C. Powell and Lorenzo Johnson, and knew it was a sealed deal. Lucas first perused the law office. Then they went to Bill's mansion on the bay. Then back to the office for a meeting in the conference room. Lucas explained that both men would be with him, entering the office in the morning and the home at night. One man would always accompany him. The premises would be searched any time they came in cold. The office and home would be swept daily for electronic surveillance. And Bill would have instant access to Lucas 24/7, via personal cell.

"Let's do it," said Bill.

Bill and Knight signed the contract, cancelable at any time with two weeks' notice. Burnham wrote a check for $25,000 as a refundable deposit.

They shook hands. "Good luck, Mr. Burnham. Always remember, be vigilant. You never know when the enemy is in your own backyard."

Lucas walked out of the conference room and stopped at the reception desk. "Ms. Liz, it was so nice to meet you." She noticed Theo watching from ten feet away. "Oh, Mr. Knight, I want you to meet my nephew, Bill's stepson, Theo Fuller. He handles research for us. And let me tell you, this kid's a crackerjack on a computer."

Theo walked over and extended his hand. "Theo Fuller."

"Lucas Knight." Lucas maintained his grip as Theo attempted to let go. His eyes locked on Theo's. "It's always good to have a resourceful man who understands the digital world."

Theo knew that Lucky was 100 percent sure he just shook Zeus's hand.

Georgetown, Washington, D.C.

JAKE WALKED OFF the grassy lawn in front of Georgetown University's Copley Hall at 5:10 p.m. on a scorching Sunday. He was ruminating over something.

Diversity.

The hot new buzzword. He'd just played ultimate frisbee with a motley crew of grad students. Male and female. Black, white, Asian, African, lesbian, straight, and maybe a few transgender Australian shepherds. It was fun because nobody gave a damn.

It puzzled him. Why couldn't people just get along on this planet?

Ultimate frisbee had been a Sunday ritual for the last seven years. Followed by an hour of beer and bull-shooting with a bunch of seriously smart, interesting kids. But no politics. One wrong word and it could turn into a pop-up protest mob in five minutes.

On his languid stroll back to the Bradley estate, he decided on the margherita pizza from 90 Second Pizza. He'd order the pie, hit the shower, and the delivery guy would arrive in time for *60 Minutes.* Fifty yards from the cottage his phone vibrated in his pocket. He saw the caller and the day's joy vanished. "Hello."

"I'm ready for the sumbitches, Jake. Got me two big-ass rent a warriors," said Wild Bild.

"What are you talking about?"

"Green Berets. Ass kickers, man." Burnham was practically out of breath. "I've got my own security team. So I say, bring it, bro."

"Bill, that's what Peter John Clemmons said out in Colorado. Remember how that turned out?"

"Uh, remind me."

"Clemmons and his two guards caught .338 caliber rounds to the head and chest that may have been fired from five football fields away."

"Well, that poor bastard didn't have W.C. and Lorenzo. I'll still sleep better, anyway. Wish I'd had them when I got jumped at the office. These men could snap a neck like a matchstick."

"How'd you find these guys? Are they local?"

"They found me. A company called Knight Force. They're running security for five or six other big-dog lawyers. I vetted them with those attorneys, and they are very satisfied. Knight Force is global, Jake, bigtime boys."

"I'm coming down to Black Point soon. I'll see you then. And I'd like to meet these fellas."

In the shower, his second-best place to think, Jake rolled that info around his mind. Military. Special forces veterans. And they contacted Bill first.

Something there ... something ...

92

BLACK POINT, ALABAMA

$72.1 MILLION DOLLARS had been transferred into cold cryptocurrency wallets. Zeus thought about that beautiful number. He was sitting in a dark, dreary room in his stepfather's law office scouring LexisNexis for information on contaminants in foreign-made ibuprofen tablets. All for nineteen bucks an hour.

The financial trend was promising—Green, $14.3 mil, Clemmons, $21.6 mil, Kimbrell, $36.2 mil.

An unfortunate mishap to a certain Mr. Draper Sims might just bounce that total to the $100 million goal.

Zeus grabbed his laptops, told Liz he'd be back in a couple of hours. In twelve minutes, he had his coffee and was logged on to his *Mr. Robot* computer at Coffee Loft. Time to drill down for some intel for Lucky. He laughed at that, intel. Military lingo.

DRAPER SIMS WAS the brash, overcaffeinated, presiding partner in an eight-office litigation firm. Everything about the group looked to be a powerhouse. They even had a European headquarters in London.

Sims' home-run ball was a $400 million judgment in an antitrust lawsuit a couple of years ago against a monster software firm.

The lawyer utilized four cell phones, all Samsung Galaxy models running Android. It wasn't that he didn't like the Apple iPhone, he did like them. It all stemmed from the fact he once represented Samsung after they'd been sued by Apple over a patent infringement case. He couldn't be seen in public with an iPhone in his hand. He could change brands now but just couldn't bear the techno-hassle of it.

One phone was explicitly for family contact. One was for legal business. Two phones were for monkey business.

One was dedicated to Chelsea Stonington, a thirty-four-year-old, energetic, blond fireball who double majored in cheerleading and fraternity boys at LSU. She was now a New York-based flight attendant for Delta.

The other was for a thirty-five-year-old tall, dark-haired, clear-skinned ingenue who was the youngest daughter of one of Sims' wealthiest clients. That meant *wealthy* wealthy. She was smart, holding an MBA from the Booth School of Business at the University of Chicago, but didn't use it. She called herself a consultant. In reality, she was a smart rich girl who didn't do squat. She wintered in Aspen and summered in the Hamptons. Europe and Australia were available when boredom set in.

Draper Sims enjoyed the dichotomy of the ladies. He particularly appreciated that neither was his wife. One was a dumb blond. Stupid could be oddly sexy at times. One was a deep-thinking, intellectual brunette. The naughty antics that could come from the mind of a Mensa member. You'd never think it. Even wilder than stupid.

ZEUS HACKED THE TEXTS of all four phones. He was encouraged by the fact that an intellectual woman could send the most salacious photos he'd ever seen to a fifty-four-year-old lawyer carrying forty extra pounds and sporting a diagnosis of diabetes that required a daily insulin injection. Thought he might personally have a chance in the dating world. He liked smart girls.

It took him twelve hours to hack the office computers. This law firm wasn't playing games, IT-wise. Zeus didn't waste time chasing info in the cloud, because he was able to hit Sims' schedule via his lead assistant's computer, and that's all he really wanted.

Sims had a trial in Washington, DC, approaching. A two-week block of time was carved out for the trial.

The wandering fish would jump into a barrel.

Zeus loaded all critical data on Sims up to DataCage. Pinged Lucky.

93

PENSACOLA, FLORIDA

11:35 A.M. CENTRAL TIME. A wisp of a southerly breeze caught Jake's hair as he exited the Pensacola air terminal. He wore a pair of Wayfarers, had a canvas messenger bag over his shoulder and a carry-on in his hand.

His mother was fifty yards away, parked at the leading edge of the passenger drop-off area. She was leaning on Jake's Land Cruiser like a cabbie at LaGuardia. Jake waved and hustled toward her.

They drove I-10 West, headed to Black Point.

Washington D.C.

AT THE SAME moment Jake's Land Cruiser hit sixty, Lucky arrived at the posh Mandarin Oriental Hotel in Washington, DC. He paid the taxi driver cash.

Draper Sims' flight from Atlanta was due to arrive at Reagan in fifteen minutes.

Lucky hadn't shaved since he met Wild Bill. He wore black, thick-rimmed non-prescription glasses under a ball cap, and a Washington Nationals T-shirt emblazoned with the name "Soto." A digital Canon camera hung over his neck, tourist style.

He parked himself on an empty bench under the portico of the loading zone, leaving him with an excellent view of the new arrivals. Lucky stretched his left arm outward over the top of the bench. His right ankle cocked up, rested over his left knee. Casual. He flipped through a glossy DC travel magazine, glancing at ads for restaurants and museums.

Four high-efficiency bellmen zipped around him tossing out five-star service. Impressive quality, he thought. Lucky ran an eagle eye over the top of the shiny magazine as new arrivals unloaded.

Despite all the commotion taking place, something nagged at him. The farther this mission went, the more impressed Lucky became with Zeus's abilities. The guy wasn't just blowing smoke, he was in control.

Zeus knew all the dirt.

That made him a liability.

THIRTY-EIGHT MINUTES after Sims' plane touched down, a gleaming black Escalade arrived at the curb. The rear hatch popped open the same moment it came to a stop. A tall, Black gentleman, impeccably neat in dark suit, white shirt, black tie, exited from the driver's door, walked around the front of the vehicle, and opened the rear passenger door.

Two bellhops attacked the limo like it was on fire. The baggage was offloaded in twenty seconds.

A woman and man, both dressed in conservative business attire, stepped out from the rear seat. Lucky didn't recognize them.

Another man sat in the front passenger seat, staring through the windshield, talking intently on his cell. He rang off, slid the phone in his suitcoat pocket, opened the door, threw his legs out, and stood up into a full stretch. He slung a computer bag over his left shoulder.

Draper Sims held the corner of a folded fifty in the air with two fingers of his left hand. The driver eased the bill into his hand like a magic trick and performed a slight bow with his head. “Thank you, sir.”

King Draper had arrived.

Alpha predator eyes watched his every move.

94

BLACK POINT, ALABAMA

JAKE PARALLEL PARKED beside Black Point pharmacy, in the heart of downtown. He left the windows down, hopped out of the truck wearing a fresh oxford and sunglasses, and started the 100-foot trek to Wild Bill's office.

A white ninja USB computer charger was in each side pocket of his pants.

A pleasant scent welcomed him as he walked into the office, but he couldn't place it. Liz was speaking into her headset. She held up a finger. The call ended twenty seconds later.

"Good afternoon, Jake."

Jake sniffed the air. "The room smells nice, Liz, what is it?"

"Lemongrass and sage. It's supposed to enhance energy and invoke mental clarity."

"We could use some in DC. Right now, we have the embedded scent of bureaucracy, which invokes bloated inefficiency, laziness, and clock-watching. What's going on today at the mighty legal machine?"

Speaking with a hearty laugh, she said, "Well, for me, I'm shopping for some clothes online on Bill's dime. I'm going on a cruise out of New Orleans next week. Mexico. Honduras. Belize. Can't wait."

"Did you book me a ticket?" He leaned in, dropped his voice. "It could be our little secret."

"Don't I wish." She winked. "Otherwise, my team is working away in their cubicles. Teddy just left for his afternoon session at Coffee Loft and Bill is upstairs with one of his bodyguards, Lorenzo.

"What's that mean, afternoon session?"

"Teddy runs by there for an hour or so every morning and afternoon. Good coffee but I'd just as soon stretch my legs and walk over to Latte Da or Refuge. Heck, they all make a good brew."

A soothing symphonic sound emanated from Liz's mini switchboard. She looked at it. "All my staff are on their phones. I've got to take this." She punched a button and spoke into her headset. "Burnham Law office."

Jake mouthed the word "restroom" to her and pointed down the hall. There were two unisex restrooms directly across from Theo's office. Jake scampered down the hall, passing one door open to a room with four paralegal secretaries working from expansive cubicles. They didn't appear to notice him.

He reached the end of the hall. Restrooms on his left. Theo's office on the right. The office door was closed. It had to be locked. Jake glanced down the hall toward the front of the building. Heard Liz still talking. He placed his hand on the doorknob to Theo's sanctum, slowly turned it.

Unlocked.

He zipped in. Silently closed the door. The laptops were gone. Their chargers were plugged in the wall. He quickly bent and exchanged chargers, placed the originals in his pocket.

Opened the office door, listened. He stuck only his head out, then stepped into the restroom, flushed the toilet, and ran some water in the sink. He came out and walked toward the lobby, passed Liz, and climbed the stairs to the second floor.

A large Black man stood immediately from his seat and walked toward Jake with an unsmiling, stony look on his face. His chest and biceps were about to rip through the fabric of his polo shirt.

"Jake Montoya, FBI. Please let Bill know I'm here."

Lorenzo Johnson eyed him suspiciously. Jake saw his eyes dart toward his pants pockets. They were inflated with the tangled wires of the charger. "Yeah, I'll do that. Stay right here, please."

"I need to take a leak. Be right back," said Jake.

"Yeah."

Jake stepped into a restroom, locked the door. He pulled the jumbled cables out of each pocket and started wrapping the wires in a neat configuration. He stopped. Saw something. A tiny red dot, maybe three millimeters in diameter, drawn in Sharpie on the wall plug. He looked at the other plug. Same small red dot.

That paranoid mother ... DAMN! Theo will be back any moment. Gotta leave 'em. Need one sign-on ... only one.

Stepping out of the restroom, Jake almost walked right into the former Green Beret. "He said run on back." Lorenzo glanced at Jake's pistol. "Think I'm about to put my old Beretta nine out to pasture. Probably going Glock, like you. That a .40?"

"Nope. A .45. If I hit someone, I want them down."

"Roger that, chief."

"Come on back, Jake." Bill stood at the door of his office.

Bill sat at his desk, threw his feet up on his mini-fridge, and picked up his green plastic bottle of Mountain Dew. "My doc says I gotta get off this crap. Says it's fighting my anxiety meds."

"Are you going to donate your trailer parks?"

Wild Bill scraped both hands up and down his jowls like he was scrubbing a pot. "Well, looks like I've got a choice. Donate 'em and hope I never hear from them again, or star in a gruesome movie I won't live to see. Or maybe Lorenzo and W.C. can live with me forever."

"That's why I'm here. I want to talk to them. But tell me again. How'd they end up here? *Exactly* how."

Bill told Jake about everything, from the postcard to the meeting with Lucas Knight.

"So, Lucas Knight. What's your take on him?"

"Clean cut. Serious. A businessman. He wanted to see the office and my home. Then he left. He wasn't here for more than a few hours. I assumed he was busy, running a company operating worldwide and all. Why?"

"I want my old buddy protected by the right people. Did Knight go into his background, any details?"

"Not really. I just figured he was ex-military. Once he introduced me to W.C. and Lorenzo, a couple of Green Berets, that's all I needed. Knight looked like a Cub Scout compared to those two. I mean, damn, Jake. You just met Lorenzo."

"He's formidable, I'll give you that. By the way, the money you sent to Panama was then sent to Hong Kong."

"Ahhh, hell. You've got your eyes on it, right?"

"The financial team in DC says it went into Bitcoin from Hong Kong. They're trying to track it, but it'll be slow. Do you know anything about crypto?"

"Jake, I only understand three things—Bama football, suing people, and bourbon, you know, the bedrock of America. Theo could probably explain it to us."

Now, that's an idea, thought Jake. *Theo.*

"I'm gonna run. I want to talk to Lorenzo a moment."

"Yeah. Make sure he knows his job."

Lorenzo was sitting at a desk facing the stairwell. His eyes were studying a web page on his laptop. Fishing charters out of Orange Beach, Alabama. He saw Jake looking. "I get a week off soon. Wouldn't mind getting a day fishing offshore in the Gulf."

Jake slid a chair up next to the desk. "Lorenzo, what's your take on things?"

Lorenzo had a sweet demeanor, like a big teddy bear. Jake knew he was anything but.

"Well, I don't really have one yet. I feel like I'm sitting in Mayberry. Black Point's a mighty fine-looking town. Hard to picture any serious violence around here."

"How long have you worked for Knight Force?"

"It's my first gig. An army buddy of mine started working a similar detail on a lawyer in Michigan. Said it was a sweet deal. He passed my name on to Mr. Knight. Told him I was available. And here I am. I introduced Knight to W.C. And here he is."

"Yeah. I haven't met your boss. Is he coming to Black Point any time?"

"Not sure. But he might pop in soon to bring my relief."

"What's his background?"

"Military. That's all he said. Military."

“Special forces?”

“No clue. He plays his cards close to his vest. Very focused, eye-on-the-ball kind of guy. I picture him as a former officer of some sort. Once he told me Knight Force was paying twice what anybody else was paying, I didn’t ask questions.”

“All right, then.” Jake nodded, glanced around the room. “Lorenzo, I want you to be careful. We don’t know who’s behind this, but I know they are very calculating. They’ve demonstrated they’re cold-blooded killers. I’m pretty sure Black Point’s sedating sunsets won’t siphon any gas from their tank if they want to hurt Bill. Or you.”

“Damn right I’ll be careful.”

Jake stood, shook his hand, clapped him on the shoulder. “Thanks for your service, Lorenzo.” He pulled a card from his pocket, scribbled his number. “Call me anytime day or night if something comes up.”

95

JAKE WALKED INTO Lyrenes' five minutes after leaving Burnham's office. His mind was running wide open. Thought number one was a pick-me-up. He ordered a slice of apple pie with vanilla ice cream and an ice water from a young waitress. It was 3:25 in the afternoon.

Theo takes daily sessions at Coffee Loft. Morning and afternoon.

Jake scrolled through his phone until he landed on Andy Grissom of the Mobile, Alabama, field office. Punched "Call."

Five rings, then voicemail. "Andy Grissom. Please leave a message." Jake asked him to call at his earliest convenience.

Jake was relaxed. Contemplative. Lucas Knight. Knight Force. Handling security assignments for other lawyers. Needed to look into the company background. He was typing "Knight Force" into Google when his phone rang. Grissom.

"Andy, that was fast."

"Sorry I couldn't answer right when you called. Paying for a burrito at Chipotle. Late lunch. What's the latest?"

"I told you I'd need you sometime. Now's the time."

"What can we do for you?"

"Surveillance. Here in Black Point. I need at least two people. I'm watching a guy who goes into a coffee shop twice a day and gets cranking on his computer."

"You want us to try to get a glimpse of what he's looking at?"

"No, no, not at this time. Just trying to nail down his patterns related to going to the shop. What times of the day, how long does he stay, is he meeting people, that kind of thing."

"For how long?"

"Not sure. But probably ten days minimum. Weekdays only, for now."

"No problem. We can play it by ear. I can have somebody there by lunch tomorrow."

"Great. I'll get all the particulars, including a photo, in an email to you this evening. Remember, this is Black Point. No sport coats or ties. Wear shorts, T-shirts, that kind of thing. Make sure to bring laptops. The look of the average coffee-shop freeloader."

"How about a female part of the time and a male part of the time?"

"Perfect."

Jake had just hung up when he felt a hand on his shoulder. He turned around and saw a wiry woman who looked like dried beef jerky, wearing a cotton dress likely purchased in the 1950s. Her face had more lines than an Arkansas road map. Ninety-two-year-old Lyrene herself, a woman who had outlived four bad husbands. "How'd I do on that pie, boy?"

"Miss Lyrene, that was better than three cheerleaders on a Saturday night."

She started cackling, stomping her boots on the floor. "Damn, Jake, I love that ... three cheerleaders ... if I could have one more sorry man, I'd want it to be you. I bet you're some kind of dangerous animal in the sack."

Jake was at a loss for words at that.

After a short conversation, Lyrene cleared his table, and he went online and scoured the Knight Force website. Glanced at his watch. 4:00 p.m. Hopefully Theo was back at the office. Time to implement part two of the cyber babe's plan.

He walked to the Land Cruiser on the corner and removed two Bluetooth remotes for the charger cables. He picked up a trade paperback book from the floorboard. With the Bluetooth devices in his pockets, he strode toward the Burnham Law office with the book swinging in his right hand.

Liz watched him walk into the office. She held a red, wild berry Tootsie Pop in her left hand as she leaned back in her chair, swirled her tongue around it as she looked at him. "Well, lookie here, won't you? You do want to go on that cruise with me after all."

"More than anything, Liz. But no more vacation time until December."

"Well, unlucky you."

"Theo back? I've got something for him."

She pointed down the hallway. "He's in the den of darkness."

Jake strolled down, knocked on Theo's door.

"Yes?"

Jake walked in.

"Agent Montoya. How goes it at the Bureau?"

In a blip of a moment Jake saw both laptops on the folding table. They were plugged into their chargers.

"Every day's a struggle, Theo. But, hey, I followed your suggestion. I read *Fall of the House of Zeus and* loved it. You were right, a helluva southern Greek tragedy. Liked it so much I bought this, *Circle of Greed.* It's about William Lerach, another lawyer who went down in flames. Man, this guy's a piece of work."

Theo took the book out of Jake's hand, read some of the blurbs on the back cover. "Ha, John Grisham liked it. A crash and burn story, huh." A cagey smile creased his lips. "Love those. I'll check it out tonight. Thanks."

"Just wanted to dump that off. Pass it on. I don't need it back."

Jake closed Theo's office door as he left. He glanced down the hall, then popped into one of the bathrooms and punched the button lock. Fifteen feet maximum from the computers. He pulled both USB Bluetooth devices out of his pocket. He launched his customized payload, a malware keystroke logger.

Malware was now dumped in both of Theo's laptops.

Jake would see every word typed, every login entered, every document accessed, and every website pulled up. *Thank you, Belinda.*

AT 5:47, THEO had had enough legal research for one day. He decided to run by Guthrie's, grab some chicken fingers, then go back to Coffee Loft to recheck the latest on Draper Sims.

Theo powered down his tower computer. Then he bent under the folding table and unplugged both laptop chargers. He was hoping more than anything that the Sims murder would get them over the hump.

His thoughts went to the DataCage IPO as he placed both laptops in the computer bag. A hefty chunk of change was coming from that. He began wrapping cable around one charger and stopped. The wall plug felt slightly larger. He looked at it. Turned it over in his hand.

It was larger, barely. And there was no red dot.

Theo knew exactly what he was looking at.

96

JAKE HID BEHIND a thick hedge at the rear of the downtown Hampton Inn. He snapped seven photos of Theo as he walked to his Subaru in the city garage. Used a Nikon zoom. Crystal clear.

After Theo pulled off, Jake walked into the hotel for some air conditioning. He took a seat in the breakfast area, scrolled through the contacts on his cell. Found Jeannie Hunt. He knew he might catch some hell, but he had to call. She was a Georgia girl making a name for herself as an investigative reporter for the *Washington Post.* He took a breath, punched CALL.

Three rings. "Well, well, well ... J. Edgar Hoover resurfacing."

"Jeannie, look, girl, I've been on the road almost nonstop for the last several months. The Dragons and those hijacking murders in Silicon Valley. And these trial lawyers going down ... it's hectic. Just stretched on time. That's all it is."

"Well thank goodness, my tax money is well spent. And here I thought it was me." Jeannie's words came out in a steamy, southern accent, which drove most guys slightly wild.

"But I've got good news, Jeannie—I mean, if you're available."

"Let's hear it."

"James Taylor and Bonnie Raitt are playing a week from Saturday at Merriweather Post Pavilion. Two legends. I'm thinking we might take it in."

"Well, I'll be, J. Edgar, that is good news."

"So you can make it? Great. I've got seats up close, too, fifteenth row."

"Shoot yeah, I can make it. And I'm making it with Peter Dunleavy. He has second row seats, plus we're meeting James and Bonnie backstage after the show."

"Dunleavy? That trust-fund sissy?"

"Okay. He's a little scrawny and a lot bald, and he bounced out of Princeton, but he has nice eyes. And his phone knows how to call me."

"What about those freakin' Dumbo ears ... okay, okay. I surrender. I hope you enjoy it. But there is one other thing, Jeannie. Something tiny."

"I knew it, I dern well knew it. Montoya, I was almost feeling good about your call. Now this."

Jake's face scrunched.

He glanced at his watch. 6:25 central time, 7:25 in the east. "Let's negotiate. You're a reasonable woman, Jeannie. Plus, you've got a strong stomach, Dunleavy, and all. So, here's what I'm thinking. A long weekend in Manhattan at Christmas. Shopping, festive lights, fine restaurants."

"Okaaay ... First volley from Montoya. Now what do you need?"

"I've got something for you on the dead lawyers. I need it in tomorrow's morning edition of the *Post*. Has to be attributed to unnamed sources."

"What! Tomorrow? I'm about to start my spinning class, you jerk. And, by the way, Peter thinks my figure is beyond nice for thirty-seven."

“He’s seen it? Ahhh, man, I can’t go there.” Jake shook his head. “You know, here’s another thing. Why, with all that money, can’t he get some braces? His teeth look like ten miles of bad highway ... but never mind. I wanted to make this a scoop for you and you only. And there are lots of other reporters out there, you know. We’re chasing the trial lawyer’s extortion money overseas, and we think it’s being manipulated by Asian gangs based in Los Angeles and Macao. You could puff it up all mysterious like you do. But Asian gangs are the critical info.”

“Interesting. That’s doable. Very doable. I could skip my class, go flabby for Peter, and write something amazing for you. I could post it to our online edition tonight with a huge eye-grabbing header and get a nice placement on page three in the morning’s print edition.”

“That a girl! That’s it exactly. You’re amazing.”

“Yes, I am. But I’ll pass on New York. I’m thinking five days in Aspen at Christmas. Festive lights, fine restaurants, shopping with dusty NFL money, celebrity spotting, and high-energy skiing.”

Jeannie had him in a headlock. “Yeah, great idea,” said Jake, wincing.

“Separate beds, of course.”

What?

97

JAKE SLICED AIR with Woo Chow on the bluff for thirty-five minutes before the sun floated soft light across the bay. It was 6:05 a.m., and the water looked like blue glass. As they finished, Woo said, "Jake, I'm seventy-four and I don't know the answer."

"To what?"

"Anything … Everything … Life … The lack of daily civility on the planet."

"Nobody does, Woo. I don't care what they tell you. They don't know, either."

"So I worried for nothing?"

"Yes, absolutely."

"Good news, man. Good news. Let's race down to the Magnolia Hotel and back. Five miles total."

Jake exhaled. "Woo, you've never beaten me in thirty years. Not once, ever."

Woo squatted until his butt almost touched the ground, then shot toward the sky with both feet coming off the ground, landing with a lopsided grin on his face. "But this could be the day. Fill your life with hope, Jake. Live with optimism. I'm feeling it in my legs right now. Feelin' it, man."

"That's the Woo I know. You scared me for a moment."

Jake was mid-sentence when Woo shouted, "GO!" and blasted off at full speed.

"DID YOU GET the photos in the email?" Fifty minutes past seven in the morning. Jake was talking to Andy Grissom from the Mobile office as he pulled Bonnie's Corolla into the parking lot of an Allstate Insurance office. Across the street was the Coffee Loft. He wore a Braves cap pulled low, dark sunglasses, and had the sun visor pulled down.

"Yep, I've got them. I passed them on to Marcia Allen. She'll be arriving in Black Point around noon or so. Hopefully, she'll be in the shop when the target arrives in the afternoon."

"Great. Listen, Andy, give Marcia my number. Have her call me when she gets over the Bayway. I want to meet her someplace to go over a few things."

The insurance agency location gave Jake a great view of the coffee shop parking lot. He put the *Devil in the White City* audiobook on, a sinister tale about one of the first known serial killers. Then he lowered his profile by letting his seat back.

Settled in, he watched.

His cell vibrated at 8:35. He knew it'd be toasty in the Corolla, so he was in shorts and T-shirt. He saw the caller—John Simmons—turned off the audiobook and answered. "Bring me good news, John."

"We're screwed, Jake," said Simmons, the forensic accountant.

Jake's body slunk lower. "Ahhh, crap. What's up?"

"The Burnham money. Panama to Hong Kong. Then converted into Bitcoin. We were tracking Bitcoin, right?"

"Yeah, ledgers and stuff I don't understand. I knew that."

"Well, the architect of this scheme has now purchased Monero with the Bitcoin."

"Okay. What's that mean?"

"Monero is another cryptocurrency. And it's untraceable. Wild Bill Burnham's five million has gone dark. Poof. Sitting in a digital cold wallet only to be unlocked if you know the codes. Which gets me back to my original thought. We're screwed."

"Ahhh, man. That was our top lead. I thought we'd have something on that."

"Got one more thing. Better news. We've had two bankers that filed SAPs, suspicious activity reports, to FinCEN. They passed the info on to us. The bank customers, both lawyers, do not know of their filing and will not know we are investigating. Neither of these bankers were suspicious at first when their clients wired big money overseas. But they follow the news and are aware of the extortion, and both of their clients are very heavy hitters. So, we have two more rabbit trails to follow. A bank on the Isle of Man received $3.2 million. Another $4.9 million was wired to Lichtenstein."

"I'll be damned. Okay, John, thanks. Just do your thing, man." Jake hung up, took a sip of a half-frozen Powerade he pulled from a cooler, switched the audiobook back on.

At 9:43, Jake had to shake himself. Sitting still in the heat had him nodding off. Finally, a green Subaru zipped past with its left turn signal on.

Theo Fuller pulled up to a front-row parking space, stepped out a moment later with a laptop bag in his right hand.

THEO GLANCED AROUND the room after two swallows of coffee. He saw a few middle-aged regulars and a girl in her early twenties holding a monster textbook titled *Pharmacology for Nursing.*

Last night Theo went home knowing he could stay ahead of the malware attack because he was sure he had not logged on with those charger cables. *That damn Lucky!*

Lucky must have had Lorenzo do this, he thought. But why would he? Because Lucky thought he was getting cheated by the financial master. Had to be why.

By 7:10 last night, Theo had dismantled the USB ninja. He was able to identify the malware payload by manually uploading it into a wiped trash computer. It was the Data Moccasin, a dangerous application that could suck your computer dry. *Thank God they missed the red dot.*

Theo obliterated the hard drive in both computers with a ball-peen hammer and industrial metal snippers. He threw the pieces in a bag.

On his way to Best Buy, he stopped at a dumpster behind a nearby Cracker Barrel, opened the top, and threw all the slivers of metal away.

He bought two new computers with cash.

By midnight they were ready to go.

98

JAKE PUNCHED IN a call to Tolleson**,** his analyst in DC

"Is this the legendary Montoya?"

"Damn right it is. Ross, I have a job for you."

"Well, make it simple. I'm heading to Nags Head next week for some R and R. And I promise I won't be answering my phone when I'm surf fishing."

"Spoken like a career bureaucrat. Here's the deal. Get a pen. Need background on a guy named Lucas Knight. He's from the San Diego area, likely in his forties. Also, the company he runs, Knight Force. That's k-n-i-g-h-t-f-o-r-c-e. Two words. There's a web page but not much to it. It mentions Knight, but there's no photo and no background history. First thing I want you to run is DOD records. I think he's ex-military. I need to know doing what, where, and when."

"Got it. Back to you soon."

Jake watched Theo pull out from the coffee shop. 10:45. He'd spent about an hour in the building. Jake smiled. *Let's see what you had to say, tech boy.*

Jake fired up the Toyota, raised the windows, and placed the AC on the coldest setting. Pulled out heading north, the opposite direction than Theo. Chick-fil-A was fifteen minutes away. He'd grab an early lunch, borrow some Wi-Fi, and wait for Marcia Allen's call.

Driving down US 98 he recalled what Agent Brant had told him in Washington. The malware uploaded into Theo's computer would email a detailed system-activity report every two minutes. It would arrive at an obscure email address that would be stored in an FBI server. That would only happen when the computer was signed onto a Wi-Fi signal. Brant showed Jake an example of an actual report and explained how to look at screenshots as well as individual keystrokes.

Genius, he thought.

The cathedral of the holy chicken had more parked cars and drive-through action than any three McDonald's combined. Jake had to park next door at Target.

His grilled chicken salad was up super-fast. He found a seat, poured some ranch on his salad, and signed on to Wi-Fi. He slid the salad to the side, took a sip of tea, and input his sign-on data for the email address.

He clicked the inbox. No emails. *What!* Jake popped a call to Belinda Brant.

"Hello there."

"Belinda, hi. I'm doing something wrong here. I got the ninja cables installed yesterday. The target was on his computer for an hour this morning at a coffee shop with Wi-Fi. I'm at a restaurant utilizing Wi-Fi myself right now. I signed onto the email server. Nothing's there. No mail. You said every two minutes, right?"

"Okay, hold it, let me get on. I have the credentials right here. Oh, guess who ordered her husband a Big Jake Grill ... just take a wild guess."

Jake rolled his eyes. "Ummm ... you."

"Yep, me. The big brown truck will be at our house any day now. All I heard was 'Jake this and Jake that' for two days after you cooked for us. It was my husband's wet dream meeting you."

"That's great, we'll do it again sometime." *Never again for any reason.*

"Okay. I'm signed on. You're right. Nothing there. Did you actually see him use the computer or are you assuming he used the computer?"

"Assuming."

"Okay, he hasn't logged on yet. Just keep checking."

Jake had a call beeping on his cell. "Gotta run, I'll get back to you." He answered, "Montoya."

"Agent Montoya, this is Agent Marcia Allen. Grissom's sending me over. I just pulled off I-10."

"Great. I'm at Chick-fil-A, about five miles down on your left, next to Target. I'm sitting in the last booth near the restroom, window side. See you in a few."

Jake cut the chicken into smaller pieces, then punched the plastic fork into the lettuce. *Something's not right,* he thought. He replayed everything he'd done with those cables.

He'd gotten it right.

Eight minutes later he spotted a woman with wheat-blond hair pulled back in a short ponytail bob. Combined with her summer-tanned skin, it was an attractive combination, he thought.

She wore a navy T-shirt that said "Antidepressant" written above a golden retriever with a leash in his mouth. Agent Allen stopped at his table. "Agent Montoya?"

"Yes, call me Jake." He tried to stand, but she pushed him back with a hand on his shoulder. "No, need."

"Marcia Allen." She offered a handshake. It had the firmness from a woman with her build. Five-six, probably 160, 165. Built in the arms and legs.

Marcia sat, pulled off the ponytail holder, shook out her hair, looked him straight in the eye.

"Ready to do it, Montoya?"

He processed her for a moment. Brown eyes. Athletic. No bulky purse. No garish makeup. He thought if he grabbed her crotch like he was Trump, he'd probably feel a derringer.

But with that dog T-shirt, this could work out.

"Definitely ready. Here's the program. We'll have you lazing around a coffee shop named Coffee Loft in Black Point, diddling on your phone or computer, watching for," Jake turned his computer screen toward her. "This guy."

"Well, let's do it. I know the spot. I have the photos. Save my number in your phone. I'll call when he leaves ... or if he's a no-show."

Marcia stood and walked down the aisle displaying the tightest ass he'd ever seen.

Gym rat. Landmine squat presses by the hundreds ... had to be.

99

WASHINGTON, D.C.

LUCKY PLANNED SOMETHING theatrical for Draper Sims. He'd witnessed results of the practice in the Middle East. An Al-Qaeda punishment, pure IMAX material. Big screen and bright colors appropriate for a blockbuster film.

This was Lucky's third day of surveillance that was headed nowhere. His burner rang once at his hotel. It was 9:37 p.m. Zeus.

Lucky walked two blocks to Starbucks, signed on to Data-Cage.

Interesting Update.

Libby Grambling, the hot daughter of John Grambling, CEO of Grambling International, has booked a cottage for the week-end on the river in Cambridge, MD. Sims is banging her on the side. Here's the text:

Draper. I have booked a secluded sweetheart cottage for Friday, Saturday, Sunday. I'll fill it with steak, seafood, wine, and candles. And maybe something a little sheer and naughty. See you Friday. It's been too long. Can't wait. Lib.

Whatcha think? Opportunity?

Hell yeah, opportunity. He quickly researched Cambridge. Rural. Small town. Cottage on a river. Perfect.

Let's make a movie, Mr. Sims.

100

EASTERN SHORE, MARYLAND

THE DRIVE WAS just under two hours from DC. Cross the Chesapeake on 301/50, cut south on US 50. Cambridge was an old small town famous for its beauty, sitting hard by the Choptank River. It was easy to see why Libby Grambling had nabbed a cottage here. Quiet spot, no bustle.

Lucky rented a bicycle from a stand at the waterfront.

It took him twenty-five minutes to travel a few miles on his slow-going cruiser. The landscape was a charming collection of well-kept cottage homes, picket fences, and trim gardens. A place people were proud of.

Libby's getaway was a cedar-shake cottage with a backyard view over a small beach. A 100-foot dock walked into the Choptank River.

Excellent, he thought. *Secluded. Thick hardwoods in the front yard. No cars.*

He'd swing by tonight after dark to check the lighting in the area.

BY NINE THE following day, Lucky was headed on a scout mission to the Blackwater Refuge, a place he spotted in a tourist rag advertisement while eating dinner. It was located twelve miles outside of Cambridge.

Battleship-gray clouds whizzed by on a bleak morning. Temps would reach the high by noon, with showers expected by late afternoon. A cold front blowing in from the west.

The refuge was pristine, an unspoiled expanse of nature. Tidal waters sifting through the boggy peat in the marsh left the waters a tannin color. A mucky earth scent drifted in the air.

Secluded, woodsy, and free of people.

After surveilling the refuge, Lucky parked the van on the edge of Maple Dam Road at what he thought was an opening into the woods. He walked forty yards into the trees on a double-track fire road. Thick weeds grew uncut in the median.

Eerie. A beautiful spot to leave a body.

He had just started the van when he spotted a ranger truck approaching from the rear. Kept his eyes locked on the mirror. The ranger eased by slowly, maybe ten miles an hour. The pickup stopped twenty yards in front of the van, then backed up until side by side with Lucky. Both men rolled their windows down.

"Mornin.'"

"Good morning, ranger, glad you stopped."

"How can I help you?"

"I just finished a construction job yesterday, got a few days off, and decided to drive out from Germantown for a little kayak fishing. Brought my bike, too. But now I'm sitting here listening to the weather report on the radio. Starting to bum me out. You know how it is, get a couple days, you kind of say screw the weather, it'll work out. What's your take on the forecast?" Lucky wore an Orioles cap over dark sunglasses.

The ranger laughed. "Been there, done that, partner. Looking bleak for today and tomorrow. Sunny on Sunday. But anyway, good luck." The ranger raised two fingers in a wave goodbye, let off the brake, went forward twenty feet, hit the brake, and backed up.

"Listen, if you get a wild hair and decide to take the kayak out, call our number on the website, leave a message, and we'll keep an eye out. Believe it or not, we've had people make one really bad decision in their lives and die out here."

Lucky suppressed a smile.

Add one more to that list, ranger.

101

BLACK POINT, ALABAMA

"Y'ALL PROBABLY SEEN this," said Vernon, the barber from across the street. He was holding an article in front of Liz's face as she sat at her desk. She pulled her readers on, read the headline, "Murder Investigation Focuses on Asian Gangs."

"I printed it off Drudge," said Vernon. "They think Asians are killing these lawyers, taking their money."

It was Jeannie Hunt's piece from the *Washington Post,* landing squarely where Jake wanted it to. He had read it online the night she posted it. Worth every dime of an Aspen trip. He'd work out that separate bed misunderstanding, he hoped.

Liz took the article, did a quick read. "Well, I'll be. Thanks, Vernon, we hadn't heard that. Bill will be very interested. Finally, a lead."

"The only Chinese guy I've seen around is Woo Chow. I cut his hair every ten days on the dot. See him at his restaurant every time I go by, so I don't think he's behind it. But can you ever really know somebody?" Vernon cocked one eyebrow.

Theo walked in the building in the middle of their laugh. "Oh, good. Theo, you'll find this interesting," said Liz, maintaining eye contact a little longer than she had to.

Theo took the article from his aunt. He read it carefully, eyes slowly gazing over each word.

Very, very, very good news, he thought. "Huh. Good news." He'd bump a note about that up to the cloud for Lucky.

JAKE'S COMPUTER RESTED in his lap. It was 10:05 a.m. and he had just signed on to the Black Point public library Wi-Fi. He sat in a plush leather armchair with a huge window at his back, allowing natural light to wash over him. Two yellow legal pads rested on the lampstand, scribbled with information about cryptocurrency. Bitcoin and Monero.

First, he checked the Bureau email account linked to Theo's computers. Nothing. Not a damn thing. Yesterday at 3:42 p.m. he'd gotten a call from Marcia. "Fuller just left. He was here on the computer for seventy-six minutes."

Jake walked outside the library, dialed Marcia Allen. "Morning, Jake."

"This is a very important question, Marcia. Yesterday, did Theo's computer have a *Mr. Robot* sticker on it?"

"What?"

"A sticker that said *Mr. Robot*, like the TV show."

"No." She didn't hesitate.

"Are you sure?"

"I'm positive. I was eight feet away from him. I could clearly make out the Dell circular logo on the cover. There were no stickers at all on the computer."

"Dell? Not Apple?"

"Dell. I'm positive."

Damn! The sticker was on a Mac.

BACK IN HIS seat, Jake glanced over some notes he'd taken last night about Bitcoin while Bonnie had binge-watched three episodes of *Ozark*. Cryptocurrency was frustrating. Too mathematical. He just didn't get it.

Bonnie had been mostly quiet while he worked. Two bowls of ice cream helped, but at 10:15, she said, "Jake, have you noticed how Jason Bateman hasn't aged a day in the last twenty years? He's cute, too. But what I really like is he can be funny, sly funny. I love that." Jake closed shop on that note.

This morning was focusing on Monero. He punched "Monero cryptocurrency" into Google.

After three hours, Jake had gleaned one unfortunate, pertinent thing. It came from Wikipedia.

"Monero uses an obfuscated public ledger, meaning anybody can broadcast or send transactions, but no outside observer can tell the source, amount, or destination."

Dark. The money went dark. *That's* what Simmons was talking about.

His stomach rumbled as his cell vibrated. It was from Washington. "Hold on, Ross. I need to step outside."

A wind gust hit his face as he stepped under the covered entrance. Fat, slow raindrops from an overcast sky started splatted across the sidewalk.

"Okay, Ross, get anything?"

"Interesting assignment, Jake. It makes me wonder if I know what I'm doing."

"Lay it out for me."

"Okay, Lucas Knight. The Department of Defense has two active Lucas Knights. One is an army surgeon at Landstuhl Medical Center in Germany. He's fifty-three and is there now. He has no son with the same name. There's a Lucas Knight in naval basic training in Chicago. He's nineteen. The army had another Lucas Knight, a thirty-one-year-old who holds a civil engineering degree from Arkansas State. He's been out of the military five years. He's currently employed by Walmart and has a home address in Bentonville."

Jake put his right foot up on the arm rail of a bench as he stood there. The breeze was picking up. "Not our guys," said Jake. "But nothing is something."

"Saving this for last. I checked in with Homeland Security. They're over the Coast Guard. A Captain Lucas Knight retired eighteen months ago. He grew up in Orange Park, Florida, basically Jacksonville. Last post was San Francisco. He's forty-six years old."

Montoya put his foot back on the ground. Liked the sound of that. "Damn, Ross. Smart checking with the coasties. That could be the guy. Where does he live now?"

"Not sure. His retirement check is direct deposited into Atlantic Coast Bank in Orange Park. They have a P.O. Box listed for him. And I checked. It's paid a year at a time. Oh, I got a cell phone number."

"Ross, how'd you get people to give you this info so fast? That's private stuff."

"A phone line that says FBI when I call. And threats. Go heavy on the threats. I'll show you how to look up a number and dial sometime."

"Right, right, right." Jake snorted a chuckle. "We need a picture of the good captain, as well as height and weight."

"Working on it." Ross gave Jake the cell number for Lucas Knight, formerly of the Coast Guard. Jake had no intention of calling. He wanted deep background first.

"Now, Knight Force," said Ross. "It's a Wyoming LLC formed in early May. The registered agent is the lawyer who formed it. The likely reason it's formed in Wyoming is that you do not have to list shareholders or company officers."

Early May? Four months ago. Around the time of the first murders. Jake's antenna went up.

"The office number on the website is a real landline. I called it, asking to speak to Mr. Knight. A female said he was out of the country, and would I care to leave my name and contact number? I said I'd get back. Then I called our San Diego office, asked them if they had any guy around Oceanside, where the office is located."

"Sounding good."

"Yeah. I wanted somebody to run by the Knight Force location. Agent Stanley Kemp, they said. I called him and told him if he could do us one single thing, I could get him an autographed *Sports Illustrated* cover photo of the legendary Jake Montoya spiking the ball in the Super Bowl. Know what he said?"

"You're a prick, Ross. What?"

"Who the hell is Jake Montoya?"

Jake pulled the phone away from his ear, Ross was laughing so loud.

"Now that's funny, Jake. Stanley's a good dude. He went by yesterday. Said there's a cheap sign on the door. The office was locked. He went next door and asked the neighbors when the office was open. They had no clue. They'd never seen anyone there."

"Interesting. Priority number one. Bust your ass to get me a picture and status on Captain Lucas Knight."

"On it, man."

Has to be the coastie, Jake thought. When he got a picture, he'd show it to Liz.

Confirm it. But then what?

102

CAMBRIDGE, MARYLAND

LIBBY GRAMBLING'S POWERFUL black Mercedes zipped past Lucky, who was watching the home from fifty yards away. He was hidden in a small patch of woods with a pair of compact binoculars slung around his neck.

The 650-horsepower car had a throaty rumble and a sleek look. It should, it cost $150K. He didn't get a good look at her, but he knew that a Benz with the top down would transform a plain woman into a stunner.

He lifted the binocs to his eyes as she pulled in the drive. Libby went to the front door of the cottage, fumbled with a code, unlocked the door. She skipped back to the car, retrieved a paper grocery sack and an overnight bag.

Fifteen minutes later a cloud of white smoke began to swirl in the breeze from the bungalow's chimney. Cozying up the place.

A deepening gray filled the sky. Light mist hit him as he reached the van a half-mile away. It was approaching five p.m. Temps were dropping.

A SEXY WOMAN, years younger, fine wine, good groceries, and a crackling fire on a chilly night. Draper Sims practically trembled at the thought. He could already smell her.

His rental car was mired in a mob of Friday afternoon traffic racing out of DC as he drove across the Chesapeake. His mind was laser locked on the thought of Libby's long, smooth legs. Plus, she had a little freak in her, something his wife lost twenty-four hours after they were married.

It all had the promise of an exciting weekend.

9:35 P.M. FIFTY-EIGHT DEGREES, heavy mist. Lucky stood in a shadow outside the cottage window wearing a dark, rain-resistant parka and a black ski mask. His work boots were two sizes too large, bought at Walmart in Easton. Mud leaves footprints. He'd rather not leave his exact shoe size.

The window shades were drawn, but there were still areas of light shining through, small peek-a-boo holes.

Sims' rental was parked behind the Benz. No porch lights on. Lovers in the dark. No moonlight. Stars blocked by clouds. A truly dismal, mid-Atlantic summer night. His van was parked next door at an empty, dark home with a Vrbo sign in the yard.

Lucky skulked around to the rear of the cottage. Through a beautiful span of four French doors, he spotted Draper and Libby engaged in a romantic meal.

Draper sat at the head of a long table, Libby to his right. Two candles flanked a small bouquet of flowers. Draper poured some more wine into Libby's glass as they came into Lucky's view. Their plates were pushed to the side. Libby took a sip, smiled, said something. Draper stood, went behind her, placed his hands on her shoulders and leaned over to kiss her neck. She turned to give him a long, slow kiss on the mouth. Draper took her hand and led her slowly to the bedroom.

A quarter-inch slit in skinny venetian blinds allowed a glimpse into the bedroom from the side of the cottage. Lit candles on the dresser and nightstand. A low height, king-size bed.

The lovemaking started slowly with foreplay. Clothes came off. Draper's hands explored every inch of her body. Kisses followed his hands. Things escalated quickly after that.

Draper maneuvered Libby onto her knees and elbows and eased her to the foot of the bed. With the bed low enough, Draper stood on the floor, lined himself up, and launched into his performance. Then he started smacking her bottom. Whether it hurt or not, she squawked with every pop. Draper talked throughout the experience, likely voicing expressions of his male dominance.

Lucky knew he himself didn't understand women. Libby was smart, tall, attractive, and outlandishly wealthy. *What does she see in this aging, married lout?*

Everything ended abruptly when Draper crashed to the bed like his heart had stopped. He lifted his head, grinning like a lottery winner. *Well*, Lucky thought, he got his, *not sure about Libby*.

Was that it? Sacked out for the night? If so, Lucky would give plenty of time for them to get to sleep. The street was dead. Not a single car had passed since he'd been at the house.

He wrestled with how to handle Libby. Knew he wouldn't kill her. Decided to watch the dynamics of the scene over the next hour, make the decision.

Ten minutes later Draper got out of bed. He walked to his suitcase looking like a man losing the battle with time. Flabby chick breasts, loose fat around the midsection, legs going skinny. *What are you thinking, woman?*

The lawyer, dressed in baggy pajamas, padded barefoot into the great room, turned a table lamp on, took his wine glass from the table and refilled it. He threw another log on the fire, sat down, and propped up his tablet.

Libby walked into the room wearing a robe and a sultry look, stood in front of him, leaned down and gave him a kiss, whispered something, and smiled. She stood up, slipped off the robe, tossed it on the couch. Totally naked, she put her arms behind her head for him to take a long look. A real glamour puss. She spoke to him. Lucky imagined something like, "So how do you like Cambridge so far?" Then she walked to the bedroom displaying a very firm figure.

Lucky hurried back to the side of the house. He placed his ear to the window. It was quiet for two minutes, then he heard the shower running.

His decision was quick.

He sprinted back to the front stoop. The porch light was off. Blue nitrile gloves on his hands.

Draper sat on a couch facing the rear of the house, focused on his tablet. Lucky put his hand on the doorknob, slowly twisted.

Unlocked.

The door opened silently.

Lucky took four quick lunges to the rear of the couch and slid his right arm around Draper's neck. He pulled up hard into the rear naked choke hold. Sims could only release a low moan. Impossible to hear from the shower. With his right arm snaking tightly around both carotids, Lucky pushed the lawyer's head forward from the rear with his left hand. He then hunched backward with his shoulders, the last step.

The blood flow to Draper's brain slammed shut.

Ten seconds. Draper Sims was out.

Lucky pulled tape from the pocket of his parka and spooled a loop around the lawyer's mouth. Next, he zip-tied Draper's wrists and ankles. He picked the tablet off the floor and placed it on the table next to the wine glass.

With both hands under Draper's armpits, Lucky dragged him through the still-open front door onto the grass. He stepped back inside and listened. Still heard the shower. He locked the front door from the inside, went back to Draper and dragged him to the van.

LIBBY, SCENTED WITH a peach and white jasmine body wash, sang a Coldplay song in the steamy hot shower while the two-minute action scene took place.

She thought the evening could not be going any better.

103

THE MIST BROKE to the point that Lucky didn't need to use the wipers. He drove cautiously, five miles an hour below the speed limit. Damn sure hoped he didn't pass the ranger's pickup.

Draper Sims was now conscious, thrashing with a futile hope.

It took twenty-five minutes to reach the target spot at the refuge. The narrow firebreak road was more of a wide path, covered with wet pine straw and strewn with damp hardwood leaves.

At fifty feet in, total blackness swallowed the van headlights. What it looks like from the inside when the coffin lid closes. Lucky drove another hundred feet, stopped the van, and left the headlights on bright.

He dragged two bald dump-truck tires, bulky and unwieldy, out of the van and stacked them on top of each other. Lucky hefted a five-gallon canister filled with an oil-gasoline mixture and sloshed fuel over the tires. He hustled two more tires from the truck and staged them on the ground.

Back at the van, Lucky pulled Draper out by his ankles and let him slam to the ground. Sims bucked like a bull in a summer rodeo, moaning nonstop.

"Stop fighting so we can negotiate your ransom." Lucky bent down with the idea of throwing Sims over his shoulder. The lawyer kept thrashing.

The taser came out. "I asked nicely." Lucky blew a shot into Sims' chest. Sims rolled on his side and bellowed. After thirty seconds Lucky removed the darts, grabbed Sims under his arms, and dragged him to the tires. Lucky tossed off his parka. Sims was tall but skinny, maybe 170 pounds.

Lucky bent down, grabbed Sims, attempted to throw him over his shoulder. Sims bucked wildly until he was dropped. Lucky grabbed his nine from the parka. The barrel was three feet from Sims' left knee when the bullet was fired.

"I've got more ammo if I need it."

Sims tried to bend into the fetal position, but it was agonizing.

"Let's try it again." Lucky forced Sims into a sitting position, squatted down and pulled him onto his shoulder. He groaned as he lifted the dead weight. He placed the lawyer's tied ankles into the tires and stood him up in a standing position.

"Stay still. Let's work this out like gentlemen. Don't move if you want to live."

"My knee, you bastard. I can't take it."

Lucky ignored his plea, took his hand off the lawyer, grabbed another heavy tire and managed to get it in the air above Sims' head. He dropped it on the lawyer's shoulders and roughly pulled it down over the man's chest.

Sims hollered as the tire battered him, ripping his pajamas.

The tire came to rest on the other two tires. Lucky bent over with his hands on his knees, huffing. *Damn, truck tires are heavy.*

At this point Draper was locked in. The tires reached his waist, his wrists were handcuffed in high-tensile nylon.

Lucky glanced down at the last tire. *Let's do it.* He exhaled as he lifted the tire. The fourth tire slammed around Sims' neck. Lucky pulled it down until the rubber met.

Draper Sims now had tires encircling him up to the top of his chest. He was in his torn PJs, shaking like a paint mixer. Tears poured from his eyes. His face contorted into uncontrolled fear.

Van headlights blinded the attorney. All he saw was a black, evil silhouette in front of him.

"In case you're wondering, counselor, it's about the money. It was a simple but direct invitation to contribute. But you ignored it. Only a pittance of your massive net worth. Bet you'd like to rethink that decision."

Lucky ripped the tape off Sims' face. "Okay, just to be lawyerly fair, your turn to interrogate."

"Burn in hell, motherfucker!"

"Mighty rough language, sir. But rest assured, I'll be in the suite right next to you, counselor. Gonna give you a preview right now."

Lucky hoisted the heavy fuel container and began to pour. Gasoline and oil sloshed over Sims' head, down into his eyes and mouth, and soaked his pajamas to his feet. His eyes burned like they were scorched with acid. He started spitting, trying to get the god-awful fuel out of his mouth.

Lucky placed the Canon into position to capture what would happen next. Then he soaked a rag with the fuel.

"Draper, I think I'll get George Clooney to play you in the movie. We'll get Jennifer Lawrence to play your little squeeze in the cottage. *The Draper Sims Story* is gonna be a blockbuster."

The lawyer hollered prayers to Jesus, Allah, Buddha, Muhammed, the Holy Ghost, and to any god, in any heaven, in any universe.

Then he became a lawyer. He negotiated.

"Anything. You can have anything. I SAID ANYTHING!" His words broke up between coughs. Fuel oil seeping down his throat.

Lucky picked up a four-foot-long pine limb and skewered the fuel-soaked rag onto the end of it. He pulled a lighter from his pocket, flicked out a flame, and touched the rag. Lucky stood as far away from Sims as he could get.

"Nonnegotiable, Mr. Sims."

Sims watched the flaming rag inch toward him until...

WHOOOMPFFF!

Sounded like a muted explosion. The fire started at Draper's feet and raced north toward his head. Flames sucked the oxygen from the air.

Draper glowed like a biblical sacrifice.

The lawyer's screams did not stop until his face melted off his skull. Fire raced into his eyes. It chased the fuel in the ear canals, burning straight into Sims' brain.

Caustic gasoline seeped into his stomach and lungs. The blaze chased it all the way down into his intestines.

Draper's ribs burned and popped like fatwood kindling.

Somebody might see the light from miles away.

Lucky packed the camera and quickly backed the van back out of the fire road. He sped off seeking US 50 and the bridge across the Chesapeake.

He didn't pass another car for eight miles. No radio. Bleak night.

Nothing but the droning beat of the wipers in a light drizzle and road water whining into the wheel wells. And thinking. Hard thinking.

Rain stopped by Fredericksburg, Virginia, south of DC. Lucky picked up speed, making Emporia, Virginia, in three more hours. He pulled through a twenty-four-hour McDonalds, stopped at a speaker to order.

He ate fast in the truck. Across the highway, he spotted a Holiday Inn Express, booked a room for a night, and got the Wi-Fi sign-in.

In the room, he loaded the video into his computer, chopped himself out, and popped it up to DataCage. Pinged Zeus.

First priority was a long shower. He cranked the water as hot as he could stand ... wanting to burn off his evil.

It felt so damn good. With his eyes closed, he thought about Libby Grambling coming out of her shower, no doubt smelling spectacular, wearing who knows what, finding Draper Sims gone. What the hell could she do? Call the cops? Tell 'em she was bangin' this married guy and he ran off after he got his rocks off? Of course he did. He's done, sis. Maybe she could call his wife. Tell her if her husband shows up to send him back, because she's still got one more round in her.

Lucky laughed out loud.

It was Saturday morning, 5:42 eastern standard time. He walked out of the bathroom feeling slightly edgy, with one thought bothering him like a rock in his shoe.

If your life is on the line, leave no loose ends.

And there was one glaring loose end.

A computer wizard.

104

BLACK POINT, ALABAMA

ZEUS SAT TRANSFIXED, staring at the video on his laptop, earbuds inserted in both ears. His coffee and muffin sat untouched. The film moved slowly, just tires stacking up, Sims standing inside the tires. Everything silent. Then audio hit. Sims' crying, pleading, cursing. Zeus saw the man was completely soaked. He could almost smell the gasoline.

A stick eased into the scene with a flaming rag on the end. The rag kissed the tires.

Zeus's left hand went to his mouth.

And the screams, oh, dear God, the screams.

He glanced around the room, shaken. Zeus took twenty-eight minutes to edit the rough video down to a two-minute film that might net $50 million on opening day.

A blockbuster.

105

BLACK POINT, ALABAMA

TOLLESON'S TEXT HIT Montoya's phone at 1:20 p.m.

See if this helps.

There was a photo of a current California driver's license. Lucas Knight. He saw a headshot of a guy with a slim face and a shaved head. Looked younger than his age. Listed him as five-feet-nine, 161 pounds.

Jake printed out an eight-by-ten copy on his mother's cheap copier. He rushed down to Bill's office to see Liz Donovan.

"AFTERNOON, LIZ."

"It's a Monday, Jake. Please, just make it stop."

He grinned. "Look, I'm trying to complete some of our files. Generally, we like to have photos of the major players in our investigations."

"You got mine?"

"Nope. Hold it." He pulled out his phone, swiped to camera, pointed it at Liz. "Wait, you got a bathing suit stashed around here?" She laughed. "Aw, never mind. Moisten your lips." She did. "Close your eyes. On three, open them. One-two-three." Click. He showed her the shot.

"I can live with that."

"Knight Force is working with a number of lawyers, but Lucas Knight's photo isn't on their website, Liz. We've got his California driver's license to pull his pic from. Hate to waste your time, I just want to verify it." Jake pulled the photo from a manila envelope, handed it to her.

Immediate response. "Nope. Not the guy who came here. Our Lucas was six feet, maybe twenty-five pounds heavier, thick dark hair. This guy's five-nine and no hair."

"Well, dang. Wrong Lucas, I guess."

How can a guy be this hidden?

THE AFTERNOON SQUALL hit hard and died in twenty minutes. The sun arrived right behind it.

Jake powered up with two granola bars dipped in honey and a diet soda. He loaded his kayak onto the Cruiser and drove three hundred yards to reach the Black Point beach, next to the pier. He took off his shirt, tossed it in the truck, put on his black sunglasses, and launched the kayak.

The air carried the hangover of humidity from the squall, but also brought the sweet, delicious smell that only fresh rain could bring. He paddled around the pier, then pointed south toward the Magnolia Hotel in Point Clear, a perfect route to steal a glance at the bayfront estates.

An hour in on his paddle, a sheen of sweat highlighted the contours of his chest and arms. A late afternoon breeze kicked up, bringing a chill to his skin. He stopped paddling to watch some pelicans dive-bomb a school of fish. The moment was perfect. Silent saltwater tranquility.

Then his phone rang.

Agent Garrison. "Good evening, Randy."

"Well, it's not a good evening here. I've been sitting in a dead stop on the GW Parkway for the last thirty-five minutes.

Amanda's got my favorite spaghetti getting cold on the damn table as we speak."

"So, you're calling people because you're mad, or bored?"

"Both. But I got a call twenty minutes ago. I was going to touch base this evening. We believe another lawyer has been taken down but may not be connected to our case. This guy was up to some shit."

"I thought they were all up to some shit."

"Well, yeah, that's probably right." Garrison laughed. "But anyway, it's not totally confirmed. We suspect it's Draper Sims out of Atlanta. It's an odd story so far. He's got a trial going on here in DC but met a much younger woman in a cottage Friday night on the eastern shore of Maryland. The daughter of one of his clients."

"Is Sims married?"

"His wife thinks he is. He went missing late Friday night. His babe was taking a shower, got out, and he was gone. No sign of a tussle. Front door locked. Sims' car in the drive. She waited two days to report it. None of Sims' colleagues could reach him. His work phone was ringing at the rendezvous cottage. The woman, Libby Grambling, answered it and said they had a business meeting." Garrison laughed at that.

"Let's make this quick, Jake, traffic's starting to move. Speculation is that Draper Sims was burned to death standing in the middle of some big truck tires. This was all on federal land, a wildlife refuge. Oh, damn, the guy in front of me just tapped the car in front of him ... man, I've got to get off, got to get around this nonsense. Bottom line. I need you to get to Cambridge, Maryland, fast, to meet the detectives. Gotta go." The phone went dead.

Jake turned the kayak around, paddled north, and tried not to let this news interrupt his *qi*, as Woo called it, his life energy.

Most of his thoughts have focused on getting a picture of the CEO of Knight Force.

Now, this.

106

ZEUS TAPPED THE SEND key on an email. He leaned back, took a last sip of his fourth coffee of the day. A bomb was about to drop in Burnham's lap. Zeus grinned at the thought.

He checked his watch. Six twenty-seven in the evening. Only two other people in the coffee shop.

TWO MILES AWAY, Wild Bill sat back in his chair, boots resting on his mini-fridge, boasting about his past athletic ability on the football field to W.C. Powell, one of his bodyguards. W.C. had made the mistake of asking about the high school jersey encased in plexiglass on the wall.

"You've heard of Zeke and Izzy Washington, right?"

"Of course. Former pro running backs."

"That's right. They were on my high school team, along with Montoya. Well, it was my blocking that got those two dimwits into college. If it wasn't for me, those two would be stocking light bulbs at Home Depot right now."

Bill's computer chimed. An email. He leaned to look, maximized his email page from the task bar.

Titled: **PLEASE OPEN IMMEDIATELY.**

Sender: **panic@protonmail.com**

"Damn, W.C., come around here, boy." Bill's body tensed. "Awww, gawd."

The guard hustled behind Bill, looked over his shoulder. Two attachments. Bill popped one open. Another invitation:

The Perfect Week, Bill.
We're Looking For a Press Release
'Black Point Philanthropist Donates $30 Million To Charity'
The Crispy Critter In this Video
THOUGHT WE WERE KIDDING
Too!!
This Week, Bill. Chop Chop.

A cold sweat busted out on Bill's forehead. He clicked the second attachment, a video. He hit play. Within forty seconds, Bill and W.C. saw Draper Sims pleading maniacally, then burning to ashes.

Bill's face fell into his hands. His left hand broke away, pointed toward the bathroom. "Wet cloth."

Bill leaned back, resting his head on the chair's headrest, laid the cloth over his face, and started to hyperventilate.

"Drink. Pour me a damn drink, W.C."

107

JAKE GAVE A final tug on his tie-down straps cinching the kayak onto the truck's roof rack. The sun was settling over the bay, with violet hues surrounding the billowy, dead-still, coastal clouds. Folks arrived at the pier at sunset hour like it was daily Mass, a religious experience. People were already filling benches and lawn chairs.

Jake strolled over to a shirtless country boy strumming his guitar as he sat on the tailgate of a worn pickup. He was kicking out "Tin Cup Chalice." A Buffett tune about oysters and beer.

Jake dropped a five in the boy's cigar box and made a snap decision to walk out to the seafood shack on the pier, grab an outside table, order a dozen oysters, a cold beer, and enjoy the twilight.

His phone rang as he hit the pier. Bill. Jake's *qi* was destroyed before he heard the first word.

"What, Bill?" Exasperated.

"It's them, Jake, it's them. It ain't Shedd, it ain't nobody else. It's them. They just burned a lawyer to ashes. I just watched it." Bill's voice was weak. He sounded like a man about to pass out.

"Where are you?"

"The office."

"I'll be there in three minutes. I'm at the pier."

CRESTING THE TOP of the bluff, Jake's phone rang once more. He answered without looking at the caller, expecting the drama king.

"What?"

"Jake, it's Marcia Allen. I just left the coffee shop. Your man was there for three hours and just pulled out. He appeared very focused. Agent Benton was there this morning for two and a half hours, watching him. Theo Fuller's putting in some extra time."

"Thanks, Marcia." Jake held the phone with his left hand, shifted gears with his right, no hands on the wheel. "Need you guys on it for the rest of the week. I want daily reports including total minutes. Oh, just to keep you up to date, there's a possibility another lawyer went down in Maryland. I'm on that right as we speak. Pass that on to Grissom and tell him I'll speak with him tonight. I might leave for Maryland tomorrow."

"Will do."

BILL'S OFFICE DOOR was unlocked. Jake hustled up the stairs to the second floor.

"You Jake Montoya?" W.C. Powell blocked the door to Bill's office. His right hand fingered a holstered pistol.

"Yeah, Bill just called. I was down the street."

W.C. extended his right hand for a shake. "W.C. Powell, sir."

"Call me Jake, W.C." He pushed past the guard.

"Show me what you got, Bill." Jake saw a man who had the look of a hospital patient going south, sweating, ghostly pale. Apprehension wrapped across Bill's face.

"I can't look at it again. It's two attachments."

Jake looked at both. Some trick, he thought. Dropping somebody into four tires then blowtorching the man. He wouldn't look at it again, either.

"What's your plan on the trailer parks?"

Tears dripped out of Bill's eyes. He sniffled. "Gonna call the Mobile and Black Point newspapers tomorrow. Alert them to a coming press release."

"I'd say that's your only choice." Jake placed his hand on the computer mouse and forwarded Bill's email to his Bureau account.

"I'll be heading to Maryland tomorrow. That's where this happened. Within the last hour we got word of it."

Jake spoke to W.C. "You and Lorenzo are taking a week off, right?"

"Yeah. Could be any time. Mr. Knight said very soon."

"Oh, okay. How'd y'all get here when Mr. Knight came to town?"

"On the company plane. Mr. Knight is a pilot."

"Wow, that's cool." Jake held off on more questions. He didn't want to throw up red flags.

"Bill, I'll be in touch. W.C., you guys need to be on high alert."

Jake hustled out of the building, hopped in the Land Cruiser, and grabbed his phone. He dialed Garrison in DC.

"Didn't we just speak?" said Garrison.

"Yes. You home?"

"Just walked in. I'm staring down at a rewarmed plate of spaghetti with Italian sausage, clams, and ground beef. Make it quick."

"Your guy in Maryland is now on our plate. They just sent a video to Wild Bill Burnham. And, man, it's ugly. I'm going to forward it to you in a few minutes. I hope to be in Cambridge tomorrow or the next day."

"I thought Burnham paid up?"

"He did. Five mil. Now they want him to donate his thirty-plus-million-dollars-worth of trailer parks."

"That chubby schmo has *thirty million* in damn trailer parks?"

"I MADE LASAGNA and salad if you're hungry," said Bonnie. "I've already eaten." Jake walked into the cottage feeling exhausted. "Sounds great, Mama. Give me fifteen minutes."

He popped up his computer, went to his Bureau email, and forwarded the messages to Randy Garrison. Now he needed to make a call that he didn't want his mother to hear. She was her own social media department, a telephone call to every blabby woman in town.

He stepped outside, walked to the corner of Fels and Great Bay Road, and stood in the orangish glow of a streetlight. The last hint of pink was on the western horizon. Dialed Agent Andy Grissom in Mobile.

"Andy, it's Montoya. Things are hopping. And Allen and Benton are doing fine with the surveillance."

"Good."

"An hour ago, I received news that we have a lawyer burned to death in Maryland. I'm heading up there tomorrow."

"What can I do?"

"It's a big ask on short notice. I need two people at all times watching Burnham."

"I thought he had top-dollar protection."

"Not protection, surveillance. I've got suspicions about the man they work for. So, no interaction with the bodyguards. I don't want them to know we're watching. Your guys need to be very concealed. But here's the main thing."

"Shoot."

"I need a man with a camera and a telephoto lens watching Bill's office. I want shots of everybody coming and going. Looking for men. I think the owner of the security outfit is bringing in two new guys soon. I'm running background on him. Can't find much. His general description is white, forties, a trim six feet with thick, dark hair, neat haircut."

Andy repeated the description as he jotted it down. "Got it."

108

THEO HAD A BRAINSTORM. He just needed a little luck. And he felt Bill's desperation was the luck he needed.

"What's up, Lorenzo?" said Theo, walking toward the door to Bill's second-floor office.

"Chillin', keeping an eye on your daddy."

Theo knocked, heard Bill say come in. He entered, careful to close the door. "Hate to bother you, Bill, but I might have something of interest."

"Oh, yeah. And what's that?" Sandpaper in his tone.

That's right, Bill, bring the attitude.

"Liz told me about the squeeze on you with the trailer parks."

"She's got a big damn mouth, that woman," Bill barked.

Theo maintained a look of calm and put up a hand. "Just hang on. She wants to help. We both do. I know somebody that can offer a solution. I gave him a call and talked in generalities about the situation."

"Do tell, Theo." Burnham shook his head, sarcasm in his voice. "And who might that be? Some friend of the Russian you tried to bankrupt?"

"Nope. Jack Halloran, a tax specialist in New York. He's regarded as one of the best tax men in the country. The guy handles a lot of complex work for the big money crowd at the investment house where I consulted. And he's accepting no new clients."

Bill rolled his eyes. "No new clients. So how does that help me?"

"He owes me a favor. A big favor."

"Owes *you* a favor?" Bill snorted. "How could that be?"

Theo pulled up a chair, sat down and crossed his legs. Confident, now.

A smug grin unfolded on his face. "Seems old Jack accidentally finds himself on Tinder from time to time. Now, understand, Bill, Jack's fifty-six, married with three grown children, seven beautiful grandchildren, and is quite proud of his role as an elder in a very prominent Episcopalian church. Not to mention his top-drawer status in the rarefied New York business community. A man of the highest morals and ethics." Theo winked at the last statement.

Bill smiled, anticipating the crash and burn coming. *Tinder.* "Dipped his wick, didn't he?"

Theo grinned. "Worse. Inexplicably," Theo chuckled, "photos of Jack's weewee were sent to a *transsexual* from Jack's own cell phone. He thought it was a woman. And, somehow, every time Jack was in the Plaza Hotel with her, all their perverted antics were caught on film. And now, this *individual* wants two million dollars to keep the film and photos out of public view."

Bill laughed. "How do you fit in, genius?"

"I was the guy who got all the digital images of the photos and video removed from this person's phone, her three computers, two separate cloud sites, and disappeared them for posterity. But I won't take all the credit. Two Italian gentlemen Jack knows reasoned with this *lady* for thirty minutes before I did my thing. And out of professional courtesy, there was no charge on my part."

"Theo the humanitarian. He damn well owes you. So, what can Halloran do for me?"

"He suggests donating your mobile-home assets into a charitable trust that he would establish here in Alabama that would provide college scholarships in the disciplines of STEM—Science. Technology. Engineering. Mathematics. These are the hot careers. And listen closely. This is the part you'll like. At the end of three years, the trust can be disbanded, and funds redistributed to the founding donor or donors. It all revolves around precision fine print in establishing the trusts and whether certain tax benefits are claimed by you. But"—Theo held up a finger—"the disbanding would still be at the discretion of the trustees."

Bill ran his hand across his mouth, thinking. "That sounds good, Theo. But where could I get trustees who would vote it back? I'd need somebody I can totally trust. I mean, that's thirty mil."

The knock on the door was timed perfectly. Liz walked in.

"Bill. You're looking at the trustees. Me and Aunt Liz."

"Well, hell," Bill said, grinning. "Can't get any safer than that."

109

CAMBRIDGE, MARYLAND

MONTOYA WAS ESCORTED into a conference room at Cambridge's Public Safety Complex, where he met the chief and a detective. Both were in their fifties and had the seasoned look of experience in a town so picturesque that you wouldn't expect any crime.

It was 7:45 a.m.

According to the detective, he and the chief had been called into the station Sunday night after Libby Grambling and her lawyer filed a missing person report.

"I can tell you, Agent Montoya, the story is not new. Older married man banging a younger woman. But Libby Grambling's story was odd."

For thirty minutes, Montoya and the cops discussed what Libby had to say. Then the chief mentioned the fire at the refuge and a ranger named Mike Jeffers who spoke to somebody in a white van parked near the bonfire site on the day of the murder.

That news jolted Jake. "Chief, I need you to do something for me right now. See if you can get Mike Jeffers on the phone. I need to speak to him in person. This morning."

MIKE JEFFERS WAS eating a cold Pop Tart when Jake arrived at his office. The smell of coffee filled the room. Jake saw him minimize the ESPN website as he walked in.

The ranger stood. "Mike Jeffers, Agent Montoya. How are ya?"

"If not for this calamity, I'm doing well, thank you."

Jeffers looked puzzled. "Agent, you're a big, fit-looking guy. This might be crazy, but you're not the same Jake Montoy—"

"Yep, I am. Seems like a lifetime ago."

"I'll be damned. Well, I'm worried about the Skins my friend. I'd put money down right now that coach Gruden's out by mid-season."

"Mike, I haven't caught a Redskins game in four years, so I don't have much to offer on it. Hope they can turn things around."

Jeffers looked at him askance after that response.

"Mike, I believe you're holding some critical information. But first, let me share this. We know the victim was Draper Sims, a hot-shot attorney from Atlanta. Last week he was in DC for a trial. Here's why we know it's him. There was a video made of the murder and, brother, it's gruesome. We think he's the fourth in a string of related attorney homicides taking place around the country."

Jeffers' forehead wrinkled. "Yeah, I've seen something about that."

"So, I need to know exactly what you saw and spoke about with the guy in the van. Exactly."

"Okay, lemme think a second." Mike glanced out the window for a moment with a blank look, then back to Jake before beginning his story.

Jeffers was still talking when Jake's cell rang. Tolleson, his analyst. Jake held a finger up to Jeffers. Answered. "Can't talk right now, Ross. Call you back in an hour." Rang off. "Sorry. What made you back up to the van?"

"Well, I wondered if that old truck broke down on him. So, I back up, roll my window down. He rolls his down. I ask him if he needs anything. He said he didn't. Then he said he was over from ... let me think ... okay, yeah, Germantown, and had a couple days off, a three-day weekend. Planned to fish and bike."

Jake focused, nodding.

"But, by his voice, I could tell he was bummed. We talked about the rain and cool front socking in that evening."

"How many people were with him?"

"Only saw him. But it was a cargo-style van, no windows on the back sides. Maybe some guys were back there. I don't know."

"Did you see any fishing rods or bicycles?"

"Nope. Figured everything was in the van."

"Here's the biggie, Mike. What'd this guy look like?"

"Ah, hell, knew you'd ask. Only saw him from the shoulders up. He wore an Orioles ball cap and sunglasses. He also had a black beard, nothing well-developed. Scraggly, maybe a few weeks without shaving."

"What about any hair coming out from the hat? Long hair or short?"

"I didn't see any hair. No ponytail shooting down or anything. No hair over the ears. So, I guess a regular old haircut."

"What's your thought on age?"

"Tough one. Guessing ... hmmm ... mid-thirties to forty. He had the voice of someone that age."

"Would you recognize the voice if you heard it again?"

Jeffers clucked his tongue. "Very hard to say."

Jake told the ranger that a sketch artist would be out later today. "Mike, write down everything you remember. Verbatim if you can."

"I'll do it. Think that's the killer?"

"Have you ever seen a twenty-year-old cargo van that didn't arouse suspicion? Now, where's a good breakfast spot in Cambridge? I'm starving."

JAKE ORDERED A crab omelet, home fries, and an iced tea at Black Water in downtown Cambridge. He walked back out front and bought a *Washington Post* and a *Wall Street Journal* from the paper boxes. He didn't want liberal angst to upset his appetite, so he started in on the *Journal* first.

He ate fast, left a generous tip, grabbed his newspapers, and went out to sit on a bench on a pleasant morning. He speed-dialed Tolleson.

"Make my day, Ross."

"Jake, I hate it, man. We've got nothing matching after running the accommodations in Charleston, Orlando, and the Telluride area. Well, I say nothing. We had multiple hits with the Smiths, Johnsons, Williams, Browns, and Jones that matched with the first names James, John, Robert, Michael, David, Charles ... you get it, we had a triple match on one name, David Jones, and double matches on three other names. None from the same state and address. So that's nine people. I had field guys pay them all a visit at home. Average American families. All of them are employed. Six were on vacation. Three were on work trips. So, there we are on that."

Jake had an ankle crossed over a knee and one arm extended over the top of the bench. He let out a sigh. "I was hoping, Ross. Damn. Thanks for the effort, I know it was a hassle. But you know what I need you to do now, right?"

"Oh, no. Please don't say lodging on the eastern shore."

“Sure, okay. This time let’s try accommodations on the eastern shore of Maryland.”

110

BLACK POINT, ALABAMA

ZEUS'S EYES FIXATED on the detailed algorithmic sheet on his computer screen. It was a complex mélange of monetary amounts, foreign banks, bank account numbers, and crypto-currency exchange accounts.

Three days ago, late in the afternoon, Zeus had fired all his demands out to forty-three lawyers. He was confident that four dead colleagues would let these clowns know one thing. *We ain't kiddin' around, folks.*

It was 11:23 a.m. at Coffee Loft, and a soft rain was falling outside under a gray morning sky.

Zeus was oblivious to Agent Mark Benton sitting on a nearby couch. The agent wore canvas shorts and a turquoise T-shirt advertising Sailmaker's Supply in nearby Biloxi, Mississippi. An accounting and statistics textbook rested next to him on the couch. A spiral notebook was open in his hands.

Zeus had twenty-two foreign bank accounts opened digitally and minimized on his screen. The algorithm sheet helped him maintain the integrity of the scheme he'd concocted.

He was systematically shifting money from one bank to another bank. And then another. Then into Bitcoin. Then from Bitcoin to Monero.

Zeus drove a Ferrari wide-open while the cops chased him on a skateboard.

Adrenaline roared through his veins as he thought about the scheme. He'd crafted the perfect plan. Felt like he wanted to scream and dance. Lucky would receive a missive later about the amounts. After Draper Sims, Lucky's take would hit the target of $80 million, if not more.

But what if it was more than $100 million? Zeus thought about that. And smiled. *Hell yeah, I'll keep it.*

WASHINGTON, D.C.

JAKE AND AGENT Brant grabbed lunch at Au Bon Pain, near the FBI headquarters.

"The smell of the bread alone draws me into this place at least twice a week," said Belinda. "Never get tired of it." She ordered a salad with green goddess avocado dressing on the side. "Any keystrokes coming in on the email site?"

"Nothing." Jake leaned forward, took a sip of hot soup. "Man, this is good. Here's what I'm thinking. Theo Fuller has a third computer somewhere. Maybe five computers, ten, I don't know."

"You said you believe the two laptops left his office every day, right?"

"I think so. They were gone the day I slipped in the ninja chargers. He was at the coffee shop. They had to be with him. The secretary told me he does computer work there every day."

"Has surveillance seen him on the laptop with the *Mr. Robot* sticker?"

"Nope."

"Okay." She wiped her lips with a napkin. "You've been had. Fuller is smart. I think he caught something different on the cables, just don't know what. Why do I think that? Because you don't have one single keystroke coming in from either computer." She took a sip of water, thinking. "If he is the bad guy, I'm sure he destroyed those computers."

"Gotta be a way to get in his system."

Belinda squished her lips together in a dejected smile, shook her head. "That guy's way too smart to touch a phishing email."

"I wonder if we could put any cameras in the wall of the coffee joint?" Jake raised his eyebrows as he said it and looked Belinda dead in the eyes.

"Interesting." She rocked her head left to right. "That's an idea. Get some photos of the place, and information on where Fuller sits. Email 'em and I'll discuss this with our surveillance folks."

"Sounds good. Give me a day or so."

"Here's what I don't get, Jake. Why all the focus on this one tech guy working for his stepdad? Who's to say he's involved in any of this? He's from MIT, for crying out loud."

"Number one. They blew the stepdad's car apart ... *after* he'd already paid. Number two. There's a clear boner from Theo Fuller against trial lawyers. Number three. There's no love lost between Fuller and his stepfather. I get that from Burnham's point of view. Number four. Fuller could probably have twenty high-compensation job offers in two weeks if he wanted. He's working for nineteen bucks an hour. Number five. Fuller knows global finance. He knows crypto. He was involved in it in London. His CV says so."

"Nineteen bucks?" Belinda smirked. "With dual degrees from MIT? I agree. Something's off."

"Yep, crazy. Number six. We have nothing coming in from anywhere else. These lawyers are skittish. Look what happened to Clemmons out in Colorado after he opened his mouth."

"Something will break." Belinda drew her legs around, about to stand, but remained seated. "Let me tell you something critical about Fuller and his computer. When I say critical, I mean probably life or death for this case. If there's a takedown, *you have to grab him when he's signed on.* Have to. A guy with his talent will have encryption that no team of humans on the planet could break through. That laptop must be open, and you must witness him typing something, anything, beforehand. Then BANG! Nab it. *DO NOT LET THAT TOP CLOSE.*"

Jake's face creased in frustration. "Awww, man."

111

FEELING FULL AFTER lunch, Jake leaned back in his office chair, placed his feet on his desk, scrolled his contacts, found Marcia Allen, texted: ***Can you talk?***

I sure can.

Jake dialed her. "Good afternoon, Marcia." Talking with his eyes closed, relaxed.

"Hey, you in town?"

"Nope, DC. I'm assuming Fuller's not in the shop."

"That's right. I'm getting paid by the federal government to shop for running shoes on Zappos. Yesterday, I watched three episodes of *Ray Donovan*. Gotta say, old Ray can lay some wood on your ass with his baseball bat."

"Enjoy it while you can. Listen, I need something right now. I need precision photos of the coffee shop relating to where Fuller sits. These are going to our surveillance guys. We want to explore the possibility of getting cameras implanted to scan our man's computer screen."

"Smart. I've only seen him in two seats. I'll fire some shots to you in ten minutes."

"Thanks. Talk later."

He kept his eyes closed for a short power nap and was just about to doze off when his phone rang. Black Point area code. Didn't recognize the number.

"Montoya."

"Sir, this is Agent Stan Wills in Black Point. Andy Grissom passed your number. Think I have your man."

A wave of electricity raced through him. He threw his feet down, stood up, started walking around his office, wide awake. "Fill me in."

"We're in an old painter's van converted for surveillance. Three video cameras are hidden in our ladder racks filming the office straight-on, as well as both east and west on Black Point Avenue. Three men walked into the office twenty minutes ago. I've got solid facials of all three coming down the sidewalk. Two guys have the look of a security team. But one man fits your profile."

"Man, that's good news."

"I've pulled some stills out of the video and blew them up for you. But don't worry, they're crisp. Right now, I'm just waiting for them to leave the office. I'm sitting directly across the street. Pretty sure these next shots will be even better than what we've got so far."

"Outstanding, Stan, great work. Any way you can email those to me quick?"

"Check your email. I'll blast them out. And I'll have the others to you fifteen minutes after they walk out of Burnham's office."

Jake didn't wait for Agent Wills' email. Marcia Allen's text hit while he was talking to Wills. Seven clear shots of the coffee shop. He walked down a floor to Belinda's office. Door was open.

"Hey, it was quick. I've got pics of the coffee joint," said Jake. They looked at them together.

"Interesting. Quite an eclectic décor. Is that a fish carved out of driftwood on the wall? I know we can work with that.

Forward them to me. I'll get back to you. But, hey, we'll need a judge down there to approve."

Jake shot her a side-eye. *Judge … right.*

Back at his desk, Jake tapped up his email. There they were. The photos from Wills in Black Point. And they were much sharper than he expected. He leaned back in his chair, put his hands behind his head. *Who the hell are you, Lucas Knight?*

Jake closed his eyes, wondering.

Three minutes later he flew out of his chair, pulled up his contacts on the phone and walked over to the window as he tapped "Call."

"Ben Staggers, old buddy. I'm buying you lunch tomorrow, because I have a critical favor to ask."

"Sure."

"Let's make it Luke's Lobsters in Georgetown. Elevenish."

112

NEW YORK CITY

TOMMY XEROX shuddered as he read the fourth victim's name, Draper Sims. He sat at the same spot at least four mornings a week, enjoying the briny scent of the East River while soaking in the spectacular views of the Brooklyn Bridge and lower Manhattan. It was the Pier 1 area of Brooklyn Bridge Park.

The day was a pleasant sixty-four degrees with a breeze spilling off the river, and Wesley Gunterson—Tommy's real name—was digging through headlines, checking in on his usual morning fare. *The Guardian* from the United Kingdom, the *Wall Street Journal,* the *New York Times,* and the *Washington Post.* Thirty years in the CIA had left him feeling unarmed if he wasn't current with events around the world. The early fall day couldn't be much finer.

Then he read the Draper Sims report. A large iPad Pro was in his hands, pulled up to the national section of the *New York Times.* Wesley was looking back at some archived articles.

Dateline Cambridge, Maryland.
GRUESOME MURDER
Lawyer Burned Alive

The article concluded with a brief recap of the names of the three prior attorney murders and the heinous circumstances of the killings. An FBI spokesman reluctantly speculated all the murders were connected.

Wesley unscrewed the cup from the top of his thermos, poured hot, black coffee into it. He took two sips, stared absentmindedly at the skyscrapers in the distance.

Gunterson's mind was still razor sharp. He'd seen those names together before.

And he thought he knew where.

PUBLIC TRANSPORTATION TOOK forty minutes to deliver him to his document lab in Ozone Park, Queens. He powered up his work computer, logged on, and unlocked his encrypted files. The specific file was easy to find, because it was the single largest piece of work he'd ever performed, over one hundred exquisitely perfect bogus IDs. He popped up his tablet and looked at the dead men's names again. Green. Clemmons. Kimbrell. Sims.

Every one of them was on his list.

He went into a small break room and pulled a Pepsi and strawberry jelly out of the refrigerator. White bread and a jar of peanut butter were on the counter. He made a PB&J sandwich, busted open a snack-size bag of Cheetos, and sat down.

He thought about the career he had given his country. He thought about the fear he'd felt when in the field around the world. He thought about men and women who were his friends, a few deadly agency assassins. All working for the good of America. He had wanted to supplement his retirement, because the United States hadn't made him a wealthy man, especially after paying the enormous medical bills for his wife.

But he damn sure didn't sign on for murder.

It took thirty-five minutes for Tommy Xerox to arrive on one of the dizzying, colorful commercial streets of Chinatown. The scene was busy enough to swallow a man whole. He walked into a small store crushed between two identical acupuncture centers. Sign said "Electronics." It took less than ten minutes to walk out of a shop no bigger than a three-couch opium den with a prepaid burner phone.

At a subway stop he hopped on the 7 Train. He popped out at Grand Central Station, a massive building that 750,000 people passed through every day, and went into the main concourse, an area swarming with people on a mission, a good 30 percent walking with a phone to their ear.

He pulled out his burner, punched in 1-800-CALLFBI. He spoke slowly and deliberately to a woman with a midwestern accent.

"Listen very closely as I tell you two things. This is regarding the attorneys murdered in Charleston, Colorado, Florida, and Maryland."

"Number one, look for someone who goes by berkeleyblue2 on TorBox. That is a darknet exclusive email. That's one word, all lowercase, the number two. b-e-r-k-e-l-e-y b-l-u-e-2. TorBox is t-o-r-b-o-x.

"Number two, this individual has no fingerprint file on any known database." He hung up.

After leaving the terminal and walking down East 42nd Street, he crushed the phone with his foot and kicked the pieces into a sewer grate.

113

WASHINGTON, D.C.

JAKE AND BEN STAGGERS sat on square-topped metal stools scrunched against a two-person-wide mounted counter, just over two feet away from a wall of white-washed, rough-hewn wooden planks. Space was tight and the restaurant was making the most of it.

It was 11:20 a.m. and a steady mob was flowing into Luke's Lobsters on Potomac in Georgetown.

Jake rested his left elbow on a manila envelope on the counter and faced right to look at Ben. "Big favor, Ben. *Big* big. And delicate."

Ben took a swig of iced tea. "You're really serious about this. Okay, shoot."

"First, do you have any idea how many guys are in special forces across the branches? I mean Delta, SEALS, Green Berets."

Staggers squinched an eye. "Hmmm ... Somewhat. Delta has a little more than a thousand, SEALs, I think, are maybe between twenty-four and twenty-five hundred, and Green Berets, I'm pretty sure, are seven thousand or so."

Jake nodded. "Okay. This has to do with the case I mentioned a while back when I asked you about a spec ops soldier going bad. You know, the combat tomahawk and the long-distance sniper kills."

"I remember."

"We had another lawyer go down not too far from here, out on the Maryland eastern shore. Burned to death. The guy was stuck down into a tube of stacked tires that were soaked in fuel. It was touched off by a burning rag."

Ben sat upright. "I didn't hear that part on the news. The tire prison, that's what it's called."

"What? Tire prison? Why would you know that?"

"It's a crude Taliban thing, for traitors." Ben chuckled. "And guess who would be well acquainted with the concept?"

"Spec ops soldiers."

Ben Staggers nodded. "As well as other soldiers."

Their conversation was interrupted by a waitress dropping identical lobster rolls and poppy seed slaw on the counter. "Enjoy."

Ben took a big bite out of his sandwich, chewed. "Aww, man, awesome, I never have lobster. Great idea, coming here."

Jake ignored his food. He pulled an eight by ten color photo out of the manila envelope, a crystal-clear facial image of Lucas Knight exiting Bill's office. "Ever seen this guy?"

Ben was about to fork some slaw in his mouth, stopped, took the photo out of Jake's hand, and studied it. "Nope. Don't know him." Pushed the slaw into his mouth.

"Here's what I'm wondering. Any way you could show this photo to your contacts in Delta and SEALs and see if anybody knows him? I mean *very* quietly. Can't let this guy know we're looking."

Ben laughed. "You guys were photo-blocked in DOD files, weren't you?"

"Yep."

"We maintain a lot of secrecy for the special operators. But, yeah, for a lobster lunch I can do that. Delta will be easy. They know me. SEALs, they'll be cautious. I know three retired guys around here and a couple in Virginia Beach who were based at Little Creek. Team Six is housed at Dam Neck, close by. Problem is, I don't know a soul in Coronado. First thing I've got to do is come up with a story, why I want to know."

"I've got your story, bubba. The man in the photo has a company called Knight Force. Elite security outfit. He goes by the name Lucas Knight. You're looking for high-end security work, but you don't want to work for some half-baked yokel."

Ben ate the last bite of sandwich, followed it with a slug of tea. "That'll work, cowboy."

JAKE PULLED THE Tahoe off Potomac onto M Street, had his fingers on the radio dial when his phone rang. "Jake Montoya."

"Agent Montoya, this is Laura Shillings from the tip line. An anonymous caller phoned in a tip an hour ago on one of your cases. I just wanted to verify you saw the email."

"I hadn't yet. Do you mind reading it to me, I'm driving right now?"

She read it to him.

Interesting. Darknet. But ... why would somebody know about the fingerprints?

114

WASHINGTON, D.C.

"GOT HIM." The office door was open four inches and Jake walked in without a knock. "We got him, Belinda."

It was 8:20 in the morning. Belinda had her face in a laptop and her hand on a Dunkin Donuts cup. "Uh, what ... got who?"

Jake narrowed his eyes, cocked his head looking at her. "Are you okay?"

"Yeah, eighth wedding anniversary. Spent the weekend at a wonderful bed and breakfast on the South River in Annapolis. Thank God I only have another fifty years of that crap."

Even her smile looked tired. He laughed.

"Tried to find you Friday afternoon," Jake said.

"Friday afternoon my husband was turning me into a pretzel in a bedroom full of dainty Queen Anne furniture."

Jake put his fingers in his ears. "Can't listen. My mind is easily prone to erotic visualization. And, besides, it's Monday morning."

"But good news," he continued, "an anonymous tip came in about our dead barristers. Somebody says we should look at an individual that goes by berkeleyblue2 on TorBox." He spelled the ID out for her. "Let's see if you can backtrack the owner of that."

"Sorry. No chance. TorBox is darknet-based. The Tor browser system. We can't crack it."

"Well, dang."

"Let me think on it, Jake. I need to make a call to a guy. Get back to you later."

RANDY GARRISON WALKED into Jake's office at 9:30 after a long breakfast meeting. "You know the Redskins suck, right? Guarantee they lose to the Bears this week. Oh, I forgot. You don't even remember that you won a Super Bowl with them." Garrison rolled his eyes. "Anything interesting yet?"

Jake handed the tip transcript to Garrison, who put his readers on. "Came in on the tip line Friday." Garrison read it quickly. Then read it again. Slipped off his glasses, raised his eyebrows. "Now that is interesting. Any idea who could have sent this?"

"No clue." Jake informed him about the meeting with Belinda Brant. "I've been thinking about this all weekend, the fingerprint thing. I want to hear what first pops into your mind."

"Hmmmph. No fingerprints on file ..." Garrison rubbed his hand across his mouth and chin, crossed his legs, glanced over to the wall, not really focusing. "Okay. First thing that hits me is, how in the hell does someone really know another person hasn't been printed ... ever?"

"Exactly." Jake nodded. "That's what I thought, too."

"Alright," Garrison said, "so if we know that someone *does not* have prints on file that could exclude him from what?"

"Background check for certain jobs, military applications, arrests ..."

"Yeah, and how about professional licenses, like medical? People who work with kids. Teachers, day-care staff, probably adoption and foster parenting. Do you need fingerprints for life insurance applications?"

"Not sure." Jake shrugged. "How about banking, Randy? That's a biggie here. Have to be printed when you work around money, right?"

"You'd think. *How* could an individual know that someone else has no prints on file? I mean, really know."

"You just ask them. Or this, they just tell you," Jake said.

"Yeah, yeah, maybe." Garrison was nodding, lower lip poking out. "Or, you have their print on something and you run 'em."

Jake shot a pointer finger at Garrison. "Okay, latent prints. Starts to get interesting on that point. And, who has the ability to do forensics on that?" Jake knew the answer.

"Cops."

Their eyes met.

115

3:00 P.M. MONTOYA TAPPED twice on the closed office door.

"Come in." Seeing Jake, Belinda said, "I was just about to ring you."

"Better be good news."

"It's not. The colleague I mentioned this morning was a fellow grad student with me at Stanford, a man whose brain stands way above. He's at the NSA. Anything black, anything clandestine, he has his fingers on. Microscopic chance to uncloak berkeleyblue2. And they have no time to spend on this."

Jake sat in a chair, crossed his legs. "Not surprised. I want to run something by you. And, afterwards, if you want to think my brain also stands way above, that's okay."

Belinda smiled, cupped her hands behind her head and leaned back in the chair far enough to tighten her sleeveless blouse across her chest. It briefly made Jake think of Dr. King David Brillstein, an erudite Jewish guy with a doctorate in nursing that he knew. He had also been the third-string center for the Redskins and odds-on the least athletic guy in the NFL. The King used to say with unabashed authority that small breasted women possessed greater intellect than large breasted women. Said he knew what he was talking about because, he emphasized, he was not only a nurse, but he was also a *doctor* nurse. Jake always figured that was anecdotal nonsense. Until now. And Brant *was* in Mensa.

"I did some Ph.D.-level research, Belinda. I punched berkeleyblue2 into Google. Guess what popped up?"

"Surprise me."

"I think I will. Berkeley Blue was Steve Wozniak's hacker name back in the seventies. Before Apple, Wozniak and Steve Jobs built blue boxes to do some of that phone-phreaking crap, where the boxes allowed you to hijack an analog phone to make free long-distance calls."

"Interesting." She pulled her arms down, placed her elbows on the desk, and leaned into Jake's conversation. "Good work."

He held up a hand. "Keep listening. Then I searched free email sites to see if berkeleyblue2 was available as a username. Gmail, Yahoo, AOL, Outlook, Mail.com, Yoho, and a few more. The name was *not* available on Yandex, Gmail, and Proton mail."

"Niiice. What else?"

"I'm wrestling with something, though. For our investigation, is berkeleyblue2 a techie, a killer, a finance guy ... or all three?"

"Good question. Another thing. Blue is one of the school colors for Berkeley University, so high probability of an alumnus."

"That's right. So, there could be a boatload of Berkeley alumni with some form of that username."

"Back to your question, Jake. I'd X-out the killer. I'm thinking more of a techie, or a finance person who might have gone to school there."

"Right. So, Belinda, I need a website, fast. Just a home page. And a corresponding email associated with the site."

"If you're asking, Jake, yes, I can get you one, and you're welcome. I could have one by nine tomorrow morning. But why?"

"Bait. I'm running on the theory that berkeleyblue2 is a techie. I want to solicit those three email sites or a coder. Troll the waters." He pulled a sheet of paper from a manilla folder and handed it to her. "This is the legend of a fictional company."

Company: 4th Down Analytics
Mission: We provide intricate detail of every stat you know as a coach and many more that we will teach you. Using mathematical and statistical methods, we access, manage, and analyze critical data that helps you win big ball games. We are dedicated solely to High School Football and bring pro quality data at a price even small schools or booster clubs can afford.

CODERS NEEDED
Full Time or Part Time—Work From Anywhere
Highest Pay in the Industry
Stock Options and Full-Time Employment Opportunities
We are an extremely well-funded company with thousands of potential customers.
Please email your interest and resume to: CTO@4thdownanalytics.com

She looked up with a cute, crooked smile. "You sly bastard. I love it."

"One thing I haven't mentioned about Theo Fuller in Black Point, the MIT grad. First day I go in his office, I notice some old clunker computer encased in plexiglass on a desk. It was under the *Mr. Robot* poster. I asked him if he'd bought it at a yard sale, kidding around, but a little serious. He started huffing around at that. Said it was an iconic piece of history, the Apple 1 computer."

"Oh, wow. He's right."

"Fuller says it was created in 1976, and was one of maybe sixty in existence, and he'd been offered $500,000 for it."

"Whoa." Belinda's eyebrows popped.

"I know. Now pay close attention here, Belinda. I step over and take a closer look at it, right?"

"Okay."

"There's an engraved brass plaque attached to the plexiglass. It says, "Apple 1. Designed and built by Steve Wozniak." I asked Fuller, where's Steve Jobs' name? He came out of his chair, almost apoplectic, telling me Jobs was nothing more than an appliance salesman, that he really knew nothing of the intricacies of technology, and that Wozniak was the genius of the company."

Jake stopped talking, let his face go stone still, waiting to see if she made the connection.

The punch line didn't immediately come to her. She returned his stare. Then her brain processed their conversation, a smile creased her mouth, and she turned her head, looking askance at him.

"Yes, I dug up info that Wozniak's handle was Berkeley Blue."

"Jake Montoya, you big-brained SOB ... Berkeley Blue2."

He grinned, pointed to his head, then placed his open palms out to each side, as if he were holding a beach ball on his shoulders.

116

FORT WORTH, TEXAS

"LET'S MEET," Cecil William said into the phone. "I have something interesting."

Cecil was a CPA with a law degree from UT Austin who ran his own forensic accounting business. He was also Broyle William's brother, and Broyle knew him as a clever man with a sharp pencil, with a broad knowledge of accounting and tax law.

Broyle had Cecil working on a very private task for him. "It looks odd, but don't ask questions." Broyle told Cecil that attorney William Burnham owed his company a substantial amount of overdue money for painting services on commercial buildings. Broyle said he needed to untangle some of Burnham's financial dealings, starting with the bus crash legal case.

Cecil was unaware the banking documents he had examined were obtained under the duress of a break-in, but he was suspicious. But then he was suspicious of most work that came his way.

Broyle flicked up his sleeve, caught the time. "Let me think for a second. It's eleven twenty. I've got another meeting at one. Can you make the In-N-Out on South Hulen around twelve? I gotta see somebody located about ten minutes from there."

"Sure. See you then."

CECIL WAS WAITING just inside the door. "I've got lunch, Broyle. What do you want?"

"Number one with a sweet tea. Thanks."

They found an empty booth in the back. Both dug in on their hamburgers. "Let's hear it. What's interesting?" said Broyle, chewing.

Cecil held up a finger while he chewed, nodded. Took a swig of drink. "Okay, yeah."

He laid down his burger.

"I found nothing in the way of a multi-million-dollar check being paid out to anyone after the bus case. But apparently, Burnham has established an organization named the Codger Traumatic Brain Injury Research Foundation. It's a nonprofit that was set up eleven months ago, in September, not long after the huge judgment in the bus crash trial. The foundation has a website. It delves into the background of the crash. Quite a bit focuses on the child who lived for a while, Abigail. Oddly, there's no mention of Bobby Carl Codger, Dude, as you call him. Doesn't mention he's dead or missing or anything. The site does mention there are no surviving members of that nuclear family."

"Did we get you financials on the foundation?" said Broyle.

"Yes. I have what I believe is clear documentation on the movement of funds after Burnham prevailed against both the bus company and trucking firm. Seventy-seven million went into Burnham's trust account."

"Damn!" Broyle said.

"Yeah, really. Then Burnham sliced what appears to be a third out of that amount for his firm's fees, $25.4 million. Next, he paid what I assume to be all outstanding medical bills for Abigail. A total of $1.9 million went out. They had no medical insurance."

"Don't tell me. Burnham stole the rest."

Cecil ate a couple french fries, then shrugged as he took a swallow of tea. He pointed his cup at Broyle as he spoke. “Here’s where it gets interesting. Burnham had $48.5 million to establish the foundation.” Cecil’s forehead furrowed.

“Right.” Broyle leaned forward, listening carefully.

“Burnham sets up five separate investment accounts with the $47 million. He placed $1.5 million in an account at a Black Point bank. He will probably dole out research funds from there. From what I can tell, the $47 mil is in conservative investments, which is smart. He probably hopes to pull in six to nine percent a year off those investments. Most people will use the return on investments as capital donation funds. Rule of thumb—don’t touch the principal.”

“So, he might be looking to have a couple million to donate yearly, right?”

“Exactly. And Burnham’s already in business with the foundation, managing it. Let me digress here for a moment. I did my own research on this so-called Wild Bill Burnham. Very slippery guy. Seems like the type to try to stiff you on painting bills.”

Broyle laughed. “Hit the nail on the head. He’s got like ten thousand billboards. The man’s an outrageous spectacle.”

Cecil coughed a laugh. “Okay, back to the business part. Burnham’s doling out money. He sent $11,500 to a privately funded study on cognitive decline in college soccer players related to heading the ball. That was in association with the Albert Einstein School of Medicine, in New York.”

“Then he’s got $6,000 going to the National Institute of Health, which is doing a study in conjunction with Massachusetts General Hospital in Boston.”

“To study what?”

"Traumatic photalgia. The phenomenon in which even moderate light can bring on pain in people with a brain injury." Cecil threw his hands in the air. "I had to look that up."

"Sounds somewhat legit, don't you think?"

Cecil nodded. "Yeah, I do ... to a point. Now, here's why I wanted to meet. A donation of $55,000 went to Positex Pharmaceuticals. Positex has an office in Los Angeles, but it's a corporation formed and based out of Wyoming, which is a key state for sham business shell corporations. The Secretary of State's office has a registered agent only, a lawyer who does this for thousands of corporations. No other ownership listed. And Positex has a website, one of the cheap-ass template jobs. States the primary research objective is to create a next-gen seizure med for those with TBI."

Broyle stopped eating, cocked his head, focusing.

"So I called the Los Angeles number and got a pleasant secretary on the line. I asked to speak to their R&D office. She said she would pass the message on. I left her the message that I represented a wealthy family trust that was interested in donations related to research on seizure medications."

"What happened? Did they jump at the money?"

"Nope. I got a call the next day, same female voice, who informed me they were not taking outside funding at this time."

Broyle rubbed his chin with his right hand, thought about that.

Cecil tossed a fry in his mouth, talked while he chewed. "And there's another outfit. Bristol Research. Burnham sent them $95,000. Bristol also has a cheap limited-info website. Office address is in Atlanta on Peachtree Street, a half mile from the Shepherd Center, a leading center on neurologic rehab, which they happen to reference on their website. Bristol is incorporated in Nevada. Just like Positex, it's anonymous.

Their research is on brain-mapping technologies using artificial intelligence. So, guess what I did?"

"What?"

"I had a light day and thought what the hell, and I grabbed a cheap flight to Atlanta. Thought I'd pay these tech wizards a visit. Took a taxi from the airport straight to the office of Bristol Research." Cecil smiled.

"Oh hell, what?"

"It was a single damn desk in an executive-suite operation. A guy at the reception desk said he'd never personally seen anyone from Bristol."

"Well, hot damn." Broyle shook the ice in his cup, popped off the top, dumped some into his mouth, chewed a moment. "Okay, so back to my question. Is Burnham stealing the money?"

"Damn right he is. That sly bastard's sucking it dry and not paying you one red cent."

Broyle's jaw tensed. One red-hot thought seared his brain.

Dude Codger's up to his eyeballs in this scam.

117

WASHINGTON, DC

JAKE AND ROWDYfinished their three-mile run by 6:40. The morning was a brisk fifty-four degrees, fall rushing in like a heavy tide.

Jake showered, fixed breakfast, and was out the door in a sport coat, button-down, and gray wool slacks. Adjusted his shades. The breeze tousled his dark hair as he zipped down M Street in his top-down 280SL.

A guy who looked like *somebody*, even if you didn't know who.

HE ANSWERED HIS office phone after the first ring. It was 8:24.

"Okay Jake, you're live, complete with the email CTO@4thdownanalytics.com to use as the initiating email. Your password is grillmaster, all lower case."

"Thanks, Belinda. I'll keep you updated."

For the rest of the day, he launched his emails. His focus was on the responses, if any, from berkeleyblue2. But he hedged his bets. He and two assistants sent out 900 emails in total. Berkeleyblue followed by digits 1 through 100 to nine free email sites.

And waited.

JAKE ARRIVED AT his cottage at 5:45. He changed, ate a snack, fed and walked Rowdy. Just before leaving, he turned on Animal Planet. "Here you go, boy, *Lone Star Law.* Pretend you're on patrol in Texas."

Leaving the estate, Jake plodded along in a slow three-quarter mile jog to M Street, walked through the white door to the left of Lululemon, and hustled up the stairs to Kinesis. It was 6:50 p.m., a pleasant evening. The Georgetown sidewalks were crowded with walkers, dogs, and strollers. Seeing the stylish women, he wished he'd invested in athleisure wear.

Ben Staggers was in the back of the room, punishing a speed bag at warp speed, with sweat splashing off his face. He stopped as Jake walked up.

Breathing hard, he said, "Sorry, man, nothing yet. I showed the photo to two guys here in DC, but they didn't know him. But these guys are in their early sixties, so before your boy's time. But a couple hours ago I emailed the photo to another former SEAL down in Virginia Beach. He's in his late forties and was in Team Four, mostly South American missions."

"Sounds good. I appreciate the effort. If you can't dig up his name, I might have to go on post at Little Creek and Coronado. But like I said, I'm trying to backdoor this."

Both men went into a series of stretches for about five minutes, chatting about nothing important.

"Think I'm good. Let's do it."

They started in easy, warming up, light jabs loosening the arms, slow sidekicks stretching out the legs. Both dancing with light, balanced movement, feet in constant motion, like they were on hot coals.

Staggers phone rang. He held up a glove, garbled out, "Might be our guy." Three hops and he dumped his gloves, grabbed his cell off a shelf, looked at the caller. He glanced at Jake, nodded.

"Freddie, anything on our guy?" He listened, looked at Jake, and gave the thumbs-up sign. Then he mimed writing.

Jake went to the counter, leaned over it, spotted a pen and pad, and ran them over to Staggers.

Staggers sat, placed the pad on the floor, and started writing.

"And so, you know the guy personally?" He listened as Freddie spoke. "Okay, that's cool, man. Look, here's the deal, I want to get out and get some work, make a little extra money. Going stir crazy at home, you know. But I haven't spoken to my wife about any of this, so it's all preliminary." He listened. "Yeah, yeah, I know you know the deal." He listened. "That sounds great. I'll be in Virginia Beach in a couple of weeks. I owe you a steak, buddy. You take care."

Staggers looked up at Jake. "Freddie says that guy's name is Luke Hendrickson. He was in SEAL Team Six, a rock star. Freddy met him but doesn't really know him. Said Hendrickson was a commander, one of the Naval Academy guys who wasn't a pussy."

Jake's brain started sparking. *That name. That name ... where?*

"Freddy says the guy has a good rep. Super smart. Confident, not a big guy. And he actually heard something about Hendrickson starting an outfit of contractors but didn't have details."

Jake moved in a blur. He threw his gear in his backpack, headed for the door. "Sorry, Ben, gotta run. And thanks."

He ran down the stairs like a fireman, burst out the door, and broke into a run.

It's in one of those cases. Somewhere.

ROWDY JUMPED OFF the sofa into a red alert stance when Jake burst through the cottage door. *Lone Star Law* was over. Rowdy was watching Steve Irwin relocate a ten-foot crocodile in Australia. The Mali tended toward anxiety without *Animal Planet.*

"Easy, boy, the croc's okay." Jake powered up his laptop, flipped a treat to Rowdy, and Googled "Luke Hendrickson."

Fernandina Beach High School. Salutatorian. A few sports-related mentions in the local paper. All-Region in baseball. United States Naval Academy. *Impressive.* Four smiling faces in a happy photo in the *Fernandina News Leader.* Luke Hendrickson in a crisp, white uniform on graduation day in Annapolis, Maryland, accompanied by his father, Crede, his mother, Wanda, and brother Deke.

Not a mention of special forces. He checked Facebook. Nothing. Twitter. Nothing. No social media. *Those guys live off the radar.*

He bounced out of the newspaper site and popped into the cloud site that Theo Fuller had created. Burnham's lawsuit cases. The bus crash file was stand-alone. He clicked the file open. It slapped him in the face.

Codger vs. Hendrickson Trucking. Home office, Yulee, Florida. Basically, Fernandina Beach.

Lightning shot through every nerve in Jake's body.

He Googled "Hendrickson Trucking." The earliest articles from years back were about rapid growth, bright prospects, the goal of the founder, Crede Hendrickson, to pass the company on to his sons. The most recent articles, slightly over a year old, were about misfortune. The company's bankruptcy. And worse.

The most in-depth article was posted by the *Jacksonville Business Journal.* It detailed the lawsuit after the bus crash, as well as Crede's inability to refinance after the verdict, which forced the company into bankruptcy. The reporter had churned out a poignant piece about Crede, a well-liked man without a college education, forming a family business that was capitalized with the financial backing of his father-in-law. The company was prosperous for over forty years, then disappeared faster than smoke in a breeze.

Jake's jaw tensed after he read the final sentence.

"Crede Hendrickson's life ended in Macon, Georgia, when he drove his pickup at high speed into the very same I-75 bridge abutment that killed his mother in 1964."

Bus crash. Wild Bill Burnham. Lawsuit. Bankruptcy. Suicide.

Now Luke Hendrickson shows up.

A government-trained killer.

118

FBI HEADQUARTERS

CHECK THE EMAILS. That was the first thing on Jake's agenda. A slammed-full inbox. He bounced page to page to page taking inventory. Best count, 846 bounced emails ... no actual email address. He deleted them all.

He now had a single page with seventeen replies. By his reckoning, he had thirty-seven emails that went to an actual address, but there had been no replies.

His focus was on berkeleyblue2.

A Gmail response: A guy named Walton James in Asheville, North Carolina. "I'm in. Sounds exciting!! How do we proceed?" His resume had some splashy-sounding techie-speak. Ruby on Rails. WordPress. Full-stack development. And this: Crypto-currency Expert.

No way! It can't be this easy.

The head shot showed a kid only a few years out of high school, twenty-one, maybe. Jake became skeptical. The education portion of his resume was thin. One year in Immersion Bootcamp, whatever that was. Theo Fuller's LinkedIn resume looked like Alfred Einstein's compared to Walton James.

Jake also knew a gaunt resume didn't mean squat related to digital technology. Some people are born with the knowledge embedded in their genes. Edward Snowden didn't have an undergraduate degree. Gates dropped out of Harvard, no damn degree. Zuckerburg quit Harvard, no degree. Jobs, no degree. Michael Dell shucked Texas.

Yes. He'd check in on Mr. Walton James.

Berkeleyblue2@protonmail. Nothing. *What's protonmail?* Jake Googled them. Based in Geneva. Developed by CERN and MIT engineers. *Brains.* Data centers located in a former military bunker under hundreds of meters of granite in the Swiss Alps.

The same email outfit the killers had used to contact Wild Bill.

Jake opened a response from berkeleyblue2@yandex.com. Yandex was a Moscow-based company. He found Mala Dumitru. Mala had included an impressive background. Lived in San Francisco. Four years in the Romanian Army, with two tours in Afghanistan. Bachelors in applied science and computer science, Academie de Studii, Bucharest. London School of Economics, Bachelor of Science, banking and finance. Full stack web development, University of California, Berkeley.

Mala reported, "I am qualified for virtually any coding scenario conceivable. I possess a mind capable of deep critical thinking that can be applied to any life or commercial application. I've seen and done things in my life that most can't conceive. Don't make the mistake of not speaking to me."

Jake's eyes looked blankly into space.

I definitely WON'T make that mistake, Mala.

His hand reached to his cell phone on the desk. He punched the phone icon on Randy Garrison's number.

"Mr. Montoya, how's your wet Wednesday going?"

"Exciting, that's how. Damn exciting. You're flying out of town tonight and you'll be back Friday night?"

"Something good?"

"Yes. I need another set of eyes and ears on a couple of people I want to interview. This could be critical."

"I'll make it work. The noise is getting very loud after Draper Sims got turned into a wiener roast."

Jake hung up, then emailed a short note to Walton James. "Lots of interest in the job. Can you meet tomorrow in Asheville?"

Next, Mala. "Excellent credentials. You bet I want to meet you! Need to meet quickly. How about San Francisco on Friday?"

Both responded within thirty minutes. It was a go.

THE RAIN HAD STOPPED. Jake grabbed his fleece and a recent issue of *Garden and Gun* magazine, marched out of the building at 12:55 onto the still-damp street and headed to Oyamel Cocina, two blocks away on 7th. The rain left a cooling breeze, but the reluctant sun was struggling to break through some fast-moving clouds.

He was two tacos down with a third one left. Half of his guacamole dip remained. He was about to start reading his favorite section of the magazine *Good Dog* when his phone vibrated. A text from Tolleson: ***Where the hell are you?!!!***

Jake dialed him immediately. "Where's the fire, Ross?"

"In your office. Get back here!"

"Got something?"

"Hooo, yeah."

"See you in fifteen, maybe twenty." He wasn't about to let the last taco go to waste. He started reading. *Hold it, what's this?* An article by Sonny Brewer from Black Point, Alabama, writing about his dog, Bobby. *My hometown. That's cool.* One paragraph in and Jake was hooked. *Sonny Brewer can by-God write, and Bobby? Helluva good dog.*

Walking back to headquarters, he thought about Bobby ... and Sonny. Next trip to Black Point, Jake wanted to drive a Big Jake Grill by their house and cook 'em both a fat sirloin.

He needed to meet that dog, Bobby.

119

JAKE WALKED THROUGH his office door and found Tolleson pacing like a man about to be executed.

"Ross, what's up? Can't be that bad, can it?"

Tolleson turned toward Jake, cocked his head, opened his palms out by his side like, *Huh, HUH?* "Oh, no, not bad at all."

Jake sat at his desk. Ross pulled a chair up close, sat on the edge.

"First of all, not all that many hotels and accommodations out near Cambridge. We got some responses from places without having to get a subpoena. They just shot the guest list to us in an email."

Jake sat up, felt something good coming.

"We got a hit. Eastern Shore of Maryland and Charleston."

Jake slapped the desk, stood up. "Hell yeah!"

"The man's name is John Thomas Turner, address Germantown, Maryland."

"Wait, wait, wait." Jake snapped his fingers. "Same town the wildlife officer gave for the guy he saw in the van. Aw, man, that's good!" On Jake's desk was the sketch-artist drawing from the refuge ranger. He picked it up and flashed it at Ross. "This guy. Keep going."

"Turner was at a hotel in Easton, Maryland, for two days prior to Sims' murder. He also had a room at the Doubletree in

Charleston booked for two weeks prior to Green's murder. And get this. He checked out four days early ... *the very morning of the day of the Green murders."*

Montoya did a double fist pump. "We got this guy! Ross, get a sketch artist into the Doubletree. Speak to anyone who saw him." Jake clucked his tongue. "But, man, that's five months ago, and that place is filling and emptying daily. So, we might not get much. Or maybe nobody's story matches. Let's see what comes out on the sketch and see how it compares with the pictures of Lucas Knight. We'll see the sketch first, then show the picture of Knight."

"Already on it. I spoke to the hotel general manager two hours ago. Get this. Surprisingly, he has some memory of the guy."

"No way! Any reason why?"

"Yes. First, Turner went by Dr. Turner, but was not a medical doctor. He said he was an agricultural plant guy, a Ph.D. meeting at the medical school there for drug research. What made the manager remember was that Turner didn't want the house staff cleaning his room if he wasn't there. Turner said something about valuable company data."

"Get a Charleston agent into MUSC, the medical school, with a picture of Lucas Knight and the story of meeting there in April. Speak to everybody, research, pharmacology ... whoever. Let's see if that story holds up. And screw that sketch bullshit for now at the hotel. Photograph first. If it's not Lucas Knight, *then* get the artist to create what *they* remember."

"On it."

Jake pinched his lips with his fingers, thinking. "You know, that's quite a story he was spreading at the hotel. Think about this. Why would John Thomas Turner take a chance on making what could be a blatantly memorable impression of himself? He needs to be a ghost."

"Don't know, but he bought the farm right there."

"Well, anyway, awesome work, Ross. Keep it up."

"Sit down, there's more."

"You got more!"

Ross indicated with his palm to take a seat. "This right here is three pay grades above you, so, easy boy. Do you know the Son of Sam case?"

"Serial killer, everybody knows that. Something about the takedown was interesting, but I've forgotten the details."

"You're gonna love this. The Son of Sam, David Berkowitz, is killing away in New York, right, and nobody has a trace on him. So, an NYPD detective brainstorms the idea of looking into any auto citations that may have been written in the areas of the murders around the time of the killings. His colleagues thought that was ridiculous."

Jake leaned back in his chair, curious, focused. "Alright."

"The detectives found a parking ticket issued the night of a killing for parking too close to a fire hydrant. It was that damn Berkowitz, parked within two blocks of where the body was found. They thought, what the hell, let's knock on this guy's door. Berkowitz opens the door, sees the cops, and gives himself up ... *right on the damn spot.*"

"That's crazy. But so? Wait ... no, no, don't tell me you've been running citations?"

Tolleson nodded in slow motion while a smug smile creased his face.

"No. No way. Tell me. A hit? You got a friggin' hit?"

"Yep. But it's not Turner. It's Jerry Trask from Austin, Texas. Trask was issued a warning ticket for speeding just north of Durango, Colorado, two days before Peter John Clemmons and his bodyguards started collecting .338 ammo in their heads. Trask was heading in the direction of Clemmons' ranch. And the other half of the Trask story is that he was registered in a room near Disney World in the three days leading up to Kimbrell's swimming adventure in Kissimmee."

"Damn, Ross, outstanding! Help me think for a second here ... let's put this together."

Tolleson watched Jake think. "Hell, I did my thinking, I'm ready for a beer. What's next?"

"This. Get a team in Texas to run by the Trask address."

Tolleson extended his right palm in the air, facing Jake. "Hold it. Germantown and Austin. Bogus addresses. No such places. I've had the local cops verify that."

"Okay, no surprise there, I guess, right? Get a sketch artist on the deputy in Durango. Let's see what we get. We can compare it to the Maryland sketch."

Tolleson stood. "On it."

"One more thing. I want you to get a photo of the refuge ranger and the Colorado cop in their uniforms, as well as a civilian shot in some casual clothes. Need to be a clear facial shots, chest up."

"Why?"

Jake smiled, pointed to the door.

"Um, hold it, Ross. That's some fantastic work. Call Sally right now and tell her she's going with you to Joe's Saturday night for stone crab and steak, just because you love her. Maybe she'll give you some. Tell her it's on me."

"Tell her it's on you and she'll give *you* some."

"Then let's go with that. Definitely tell her it's on me."

120

ASHEVILLE, NORTH CAROLINA

MONTOYA AND GARRISON arrived at the McDonald's on Fairview Road, just off 40 in Asheville, at 8:20, ten minutes ahead of schedule. Walton James told Jake he was "between offices" and said the restaurant was convenient.

They bought two OJs, grabbed a booth in the back next to a large plate-glass window. Jake kept checking the time on his phone while he watched the parking lot. "Fifteen minutes late."

"Might have made us. Or maybe he heard what you did to those Dragons in Virginia Beach. That'd spook anybody."

Jake coughed out a laugh.

Five minutes later a silver, early nineties Corolla pulled into the parking lot. A skinny blond-haired kid got out, blew a vape cloud in the sky, and started walking toward the restaurant holding the pipe like a pacifier.

They watched Walton glance around inside the restaurant. Jake threw up his hand, waved him down.

"You're kidding me. This guy's in the eleventh grade, and that's only maybe," said Garrison.

Walton wore skinny jeans and a black tee that said *Fortnight.* A pair of metal-framed glasses rested on his face. He introduced himself and offered each of them a handshake that felt like a flimsy noodle connected to his wrist.

"Sorry I'm late. I got wrapped up in *Resident Evil 2*. I haven't slept in twenty-three hours."

Garrison cut his eyes over to Jake.

"Let's get to it, shall we? Tell us why we should hire you, Walton. Start with your background," said Jake. *Total waste of time.*

Walton had never been out of the country. He'd never traveled farther than Atlanta. He'd never worked at a bank. He didn't graduate college. He'd never been in the military. He lived with his parents. And he drove his brother's car.

"This is a company about football statistics," said Garrison. "Did you play?"

"No."

"Do you participate in online fantasy football?"

"No."

"Are you a football fan?"

"No. But I can code the snot out of stuff. I thought that's what you needed." Walton alternated looks between Garrison and Montoya.

"Crypto's interesting," said Jake. "We're entertaining taking Bitcoin for payment of services. Believe you said you're an expert."

"Dude. You whacked? You think high schools are gonna pay you in Bitcoin?"

"Walton, that's why we're talking to you about crypto. We don't understand it."

"Damn right I have experience. I own eighteen hundred bucks of Bitcoin. I bought it early on for $150. Sat on that coin. Now I'm looking pretty damn good." Walton spoke with the swagger of a guy who just said he owned the New York Yankees.

Garrison stood. "Gotta hit the men's room." He looked at his watch. "Jake, let's don't be late for the next interview." He looked at Walton. "Busy day here, partner. We've got twelve people lined up."

THEY DROVE STRAIGHT back to the airport in Charlotte, turned the car into Hertz, and had plenty of time to grab lunch.

Thirty minutes before boarding, Jake called Hope in Black Point. Last night he'd had a rather provocative memory of the evening they went to the Anchor. He let her know that he'd briefly spoken to Sarah Bradley about her dreams for the Refuge of Hope.

"Hope, Ms. Sarah's not a tire kicker, she's a trigger puller. She wants to fly down to Black Point in a few weeks and look at land. She told me, and I quote, 'Jake, at my age I'm looking for a "statement investment."' So, keep your eyes peeled for anything interesting."

"Land! Are you serious?" Hope gushed on, happiness hugging Jake through his phone. He liked the sound of it, thinking about it maybe a little more than he should.

At 3:05, Garrison and Montoya lifted off on a nonstop flight to San Francisco.

They knew they were about to meet the mastermind of the scheme.

121

SAN FRANCISCO

THE MEETING WAS set for 8:30 at the WeWork office in the Central Market district. At their hotel, Jake and Randy ate toaster waffles with juice and discussed interview questions. They checked out at 8:05. 1161 Mission Street was two blocks away.

Cold air slapped them in the face as they walked out of the hotel, Jake, with a duffel slung over his shoulder, and Randy rolling a small carry-on case.

"Thank God for a peep of sun. How the hell does it get so cold in this place?" said Garrison.

WeWork's building was a 1920s-era former industrial structure tuned up with a hip millennial-purposed interior. "Wow," said Jake, as they walked in. "Great-looking space."

They both scanned the setup. Wood floors, exposed ductwork, tasteful plants, and architecturally appropriate furniture. Jake spotted a boxer, a golden retriever, and two Bernese mountain dogs. *Dog friendly, not bad.*

At the community bar they hopped on stools, grabbed herbal teas, and glanced at the clientele, mostly wearing jeans, T-shirts, hoodies, and headsets.

"Maybe we should stash our sport coats in the trash can," Garrison said.

Jake saw creative self-starters who had the possibility of landing on the cover of *Inc.* magazine in the next five years.

A tall, imposing figure approached them. “Mr. Montoya? 4th Down Analytics?” The rich baritone voice that didn’t mesh with the person Jake was looking at. “I’m Mala Dimitru.” She pronounced it “mall-ah.”

Mala was every bit of six feet one in a conservative, navy-colored dress and flats. She wore chic librarian glasses. Her dark hair dropped to her shoulders, straight as broom straw. A computer bag hung over her shoulder, and in her right hand she held a heavy leather leash snugged up tight on a heavily muscled Rottweiler. The dog wore a muzzle below fierce eyes. Mala nodded toward the dog. “This is Cocoa.”

After introductions, she said, “Follow me.” Jake and Randy lagged a solid seven feet back from Cocoa. They went into a stairwell, walked up two flights.

Jake and Randy’s eyes met.

WTF!

Mala walked with the stride of an athlete. Seeing her calves flex, Jake knew he had played ball with boys at Bama who didn’t have muscles that imposing.

She took them to a small, private conference room with solid frosted-glass walls facing the hallway. A massive window flooded the room with natural light, exposing a cityscape view of San Francisco.

Mala sat across the table from Jake and Randy, pulled out a sleek laptop, powered it on, and typed something. The men watched, digesting the shape of the morning so far.

“I’m a major fan of American football. I mean major.” The accent was European morphing into American English. “I purchased season tickets to the 49ers. The prospect of 4th Down Analytics appeals to me.”

No one mentioned that Jake was a former all-pro with the Redskins.

“So, gentlemen. You say you’re well capitalized. How much have you raised in your early round financing?” Mala was no wallflower. She charged out of the gate, forcing the meeting into the direction she desired.

"We're starting with $5.5 million and believe that will last thirty-six months," said Randy. "We're not looking for a lot of hires, just exceptional people."

Mala nodded. "Let me be candid up front. If I can't negotiate an equity stake for participation, I likely would have no interest. I've been fortunate to have made some nice money lately, especially over the last six months. I'd like to hear your qualifications for me to obtain company equity, as well as your expectations of my programming skills."

"We'll get to all of that," said Jake. "But first I'd like you to go through your background with us. Your CV is quite impressive but ..." Jake paused, looking for words.

"But my physicality is not what you expected."

Jake wobbled his head. "Yeah ... I guess that's right."

"I'll be glad to run through it."

Randy jumped in. "Hey, I'm always fascinated by success stories. What'd you get into to land you that big recent payday?"

Mala maintained a poker face, glancing at each man. "Some things a lady keeps to herself. Why don't we move on?"

Jake thought, *Pushback, private.* He interpreted her look to say, *Why do you want to know?* Suspicions rose at that point.

For thirty-five minutes, Mala described her past *prior* to the last six months. She told them she was an officer in the Romanian military, focusing on cyber intelligence when she could no longer masquerade as a man. She detailed her transition through hormones and surgery. She moved to San Francisco to live a judgment-free life in an area flooded with tech firms and opportunities. Mala had equity in two start-ups that were very promising, although she wouldn't name them. She preferred freelance coding opportunities rather than the tedium of a full-time job at a single enterprise.

"Mala, I've got a question," said Randy. "What is berkeley-blue2?"

"I went to Berkeley and am extremely proud of my degree. It's hard to get into that school and even harder to graduate. So, yeah, I'm quite proud."

"Are you familiar with Steve Wozniak?" said Jake.

"Are you serious?" Mala smirked. "Of course. He's a Berkeley grad and an icon. That's like asking Elon Musk if he's heard of Henry Ford. In fact, I'm signed up for a tech conference in Scottsdale in a couple of weeks and Woz is a keynote speaker. Really looking forward to it."

"What's the conference focus? Maybe we should go," said Randy, glancing at Jake.

"Blockchain. Cryptocurrency. Cybersecurity. Things I'm very interested in."

Both men froze.

122

MONTOYA AND GARRISON arrived at SFO at 11:35. They quickly ate a sandwich and chips, took a pee break, and lifted off on United an hour later, headed to McCarran International. Las Vegas. On the ninety-minute flight, they discussed getting a team on Mala and doing a deep dig on her past, particularly the last half of the year.

"We need to get into her banking, try to find the origin of her good fortune," said Jake. "Not to mention crypto accounts."

"Gotta say, all weirdness aside, she was impressive. Takes major balls ... excuse the pun ... to do the transition thing. But I could see her for this," said Randy. "Let's dig into the military end, see if she has any sniper experience. Maybe she just decided to omit that from the conversation, thinking we might not need a sniper in 4th Down Analytics." Both men laughed.

In the Vegas terminal, Jake put down his duffel and pulled up the number for Philly Boy Richardson, punched CALL.

"Phil, this is Jake Montoya, I'm at the terminal."

"Great, Mr. Montoya. I'm at the Casino Royale, in the middle of the strip. You can get here in twenty minutes. Meet me in White Castle, I need about ten of those burgers."

"Will do."

"Oh, I'm wearing a black tee, jeans, and a Raiders cap."

"Got it. My partner and I will be the two guys in sport coats that look like accountants from Wisconsin."

THEY SPOTTED PHILLY immediately. He was sitting at a table that had ten hamburger boxes on it. Philly waved as they approached. "Sorry, can't shake your hands." Philly held up his right palm. "Burger grease."

Randy looked at those tiny square burgers. "Man, those look delicious. I'm getting a few. Want any, Jake?"

"Shoot, yeah. I'll start with four. Plus a Diet Coke."

Tolleson had called Jake with something interesting yesterday. Theo Fuller had been a poker player while at MIT. Tolleson found an old picture in *The Tech,* MIT's school newspaper. It was of Fuller and three other guys, one being Phil Richardson. Tolleson tried to track down a couple of the guys, and Phil was the one he found first. He had a master's in electrical engineering and an undergrad degree in computer science. Ultra-sharp guy, but no real job.

He was a professional poker player.

Jake had set up the meeting by phone yesterday. Said he was FBI, wanted to discuss someone Phil knew. But he wouldn't give up a name.

Jake ate his first burger in three quick bites, took a sip of Diet Coke. "Awesome. Hadn't had one in a long while." He wiped his lips with a napkin. "Phil, I'm curious, this is interesting as hell. I've never met a pro gambler. How does a guy with your engineering background end up here?"

"Welp." Phil was chewing and held up a finger. "Okay. I found out quickly I don't like what people would consider a regular job. I get bored easy. For the first five years out of MIT, I worked for two different companies, Google and Qualcomm. Just wasn't my thing. I came out to Vegas on weekends in college and liked it. Now I do what I want when I want."

"That's cool," Garrison said. "No boss harassing you every minute."

"Most of my gambling is online. I can do a lot of traveling, both for tournaments and, also, for the joy of the road."

Garrison waved a french fry as he spoke. "So, you really can make a living at this?"

"Well, most people can't. Poker is a very hard way to make an easy living. Here's the deal. I'm good with numbers. People who are good with numbers are generally better poker players. Fact of the matter is, I'm probably in the top fifty of the most successful poker players, at least in America. I've made $8 million gross in the last five years. But I do treat it like a J-O-B. I play eight to ten hours a day, six days a week. I eat right." He laughed. "Well, except for these ten burgers. I exercise seventy-five minutes daily. I'm a professional in a sedentary, neon world."

Jake saw Phil take a quick glance at his watch. He didn't want to take a man from his livelihood. "Man, that's fascinating, it really is. Phil, I'll get to the point. I want to see what you can tell us about a guy from your past. Berkeleyblue2. As a username, does that ring a bell?"

Phil finished his bite, leaned back, looked at both Jake and Randy, expressionless.

Jake felt a contrived response coming. A fat lie.

Phil stuck a tongue in his cheek, looked away, then looked back at them.

"Berkeleyblue2." He nodded several times. "Oh yeah, does more than ring a bell. Bottom line. He's unethical, he's a liar, he's a thief. He's a criminal. We flew to Vegas to play poker for at least seventy-five weekends. We were tight. He was my best friend on this earth for a couple of years. We gravitated to each other in Boston. In year three, I finally figured out what I was dealing with. And that was it. Saw him once, about two years after we graduated. Why? What'd that bastard do?"

Jake neutralized his voice. "Well, he might be orchestrating murders."

Phil huffed out an exasperated exhale, glanced over their heads. "Can't say I'm shocked. Hell, if you told me he was doing the killing himself it wouldn't shock me."

"Did you ever hear Theo talk about his stepfather, Bill Burnham?" said Jake.

"Theo Fuller. Bill Burnham, the lawyer," said Randy.

Phil's face squeezed into a puzzled look. "Theo wasn't berkeleyblue2, his roommate was."

Jake and Randy looked at each other. Then leaned forward, elbows on the table.

Their question was spoken in unison.

"Who was Theo's roommate?"

123

"MIKHAIL KUZNETSOV." That's what Philly Boy told them.

"So, you guys don't know who that is?" Phil raised his eyebrows. "You sure you guys are FBI?"

"Tell us about Kuznetsov," said Jake.

"He's from Little Odessa ..."

"You're talking about Brighton Beach, right?" said Randy.

"Yep. In Brooklyn, New York. I've been there several times with Mike. At MIT, he went by Mike. His comrades in New York called him Mikhail. And there's definitely some shit coming out of Brighton Beach. Russian mafia. Mike tried to impress us at college about his uncle being a badass in the Russian mob. At first, I thought it was malarkey. But then I met his uncle and some of his cronies in a restaurant called Skovorodka, years back. If there's a Russian mob look, these guys had it. Scary mothers."

THE SOUTHWEST FLIGHT was clocking 550 miles per hour at 36,000 feet, headed to Washington National. Smooth air, no turbulence. Muffled roar of jet engines lulling passengers to sleep.

"I think it's a three-man deal at a minimum," said Jake. "Theo and Mikhail hatched the plan, and they've got a former SEAL doing the rough stuff. But still ... it's hard to believe a

Team Six guy would do this. A Naval Academy grad … I mean, damn, that's out there."

"Before we hit Vegas, I thought we had our guy … girl, you know, in San Francisco. Mala looks like she could stir up a serious calamity," Randy said.

"No kidding."

"I've got a contact in the organized crime unit in New York. I'll call him tomorrow. See what he can tell us about Kuznetsov," Randy said. "And can you believe that? Phil's pulled in $8 million playing poker. Damn."

Philly Boy had filled them in on what he currently knew about Mikhail, which wasn't much. Kuznetsov was a leading suspect in the ransomware attacks on hospitals and businesses around the world, as well as in sophisticated European and American hacks into bank accounts. They were walking away with millions.

"Do I think he's smart enough to do it?" Philly had asked, rhetorically, earlier in the day. "Definitely. Do I think he'd want to do it? Absolutely, beyond any doubt. He's been enamored with criminal enterprise since he was a boy."

The mention of ransomware resonated with Jake. *Ransomware payments were in Bitcoin …*

JAKE TURNED ON his phone at the Reagan terminal. A single text popped up:

Got Something! Call me. Agent Loomis Fagan.

Loomis, an FBI special agent based in Charleston, South Carolina, answered on the third ring. "Fagan."

Jake could hardly hear over a band playing in the background that reminded him of his Friday night lights years. "Hey, hold on a minute, can't hear." The sounds faded away.

"Okay, let's try it now."

"Loomis, this is Agent Jake Montoya. I just landed in Washington. I was on a plane when your text hit. Whatcha got?"

"Sorry for the racket, Jake. My boy plays football at a high school in Mt. Pleasant. They just got ransacked."

"Hate to hear that."

"Well, you know, it's a character builder. Oh, hey, I hear you're the football Montoya. Mind saying a quick word to my boy, Clayton? Here he is." Jake heard Loomis tell his boy it was Jake Montoya, played at Bama and all-pro for the Redskins.

Ahhh, gawd. "Clayton, how's it going, man? Your dad said it was a rough game."

"It was, Mr. Montoya. We lost 56-6. Missed the extra point."

Jake squeezed his eyes shut. *Youch.*

"Clayton, look. Nobody's ever played the game who hasn't lost a couple. And I've lost way more than a couple. But listen, despite the negatives, every game has a positive. Give me one positive from tonight."

"I scored the touchdown."

"That's it, that's the focus. Focus on the TD. Take that positive into next week's practices and bust your tail. To be a winner you have to think like a winner. Be positive. Look out the windshield. Forget the rearview mirror."

"Yeah, but I only ran for twenty-one yards on fifteen carries and had two fumbles."

"The touchdown, Clayton. That's all you think on, man, the score. Good luck next week." *Go back to the oboe, kid.*

"Thanks, great advice, here's my dad."

"Appreciate that, Jake. But, yeah, we got something. First, we scoured the medical school, talking to basic science folks, then the clinical departments. Nobody's heard a thing about any joint testing with an agricultural company. After we asked, we showed everybody the picture of Lucas Knight. We told them the man's name is Dr. John Thomas Turner. Nobody had heard the name or recognized Knight."

"Great work, Loomis."

"But the Doubletree was a slam dunk. We spoke to the general manager first. He remembered the name, Dr. John Turner. We walked in with two six-person photo lineups we created. Really mixed it up. Ten seconds and he nailed Hendrickson out of twelve people. He suggested showing the lineups to two desk clerks. One was out of town. We'll talk to her next week. The other was at home. We ran by her place. She was a sharp, young Jamaican woman. Bang. Another ID in ten seconds. She checked Dr. Turner out of the hotel, and they had a conversation about Asia. Turner, er, Hendrickson, told her he was heading there soon."

"Damn good work, Loomis. Let me know what the other clerk says next week. Next time I'm in Charleston, I'd like to meet you and your son and buy dinner. Steaks, seafood or whatever."

"Man, we'd love that, Jake."

Commander Lucky Hendrickson in Charleston. Kuznetsov. Theo Fuller. Yep.

124

WASHINGTON, DC.

IT WAS 9:42 on a Monday morning in September, the third best month of the year. Jake flipped through pages on a yellow legal pad reviewing notes on the White Dragon's robbery in Silicon Valley. Tough questions were coming his way at an 11:00 a.m. conference call with agents in California, which was to include the CEO of IntelliSurg.

Three Matisse surgical robots had been seized four days ago coming off a ship in Lagos, Nigeria. Seven still missing.

Jake had already spoken to Randy earlier about Kuznetsov. According to the OC division in New York, Kuznetsov was definitely a bad actor. And he was in the wind. No sign of him for three years.

Jake's computer chimed with an incoming email.

From John Lozano. La Plata County Sheriff's Department. Durango, Colorado. The message was sent to Tolleson first. He forwarded it to Jake. An attachment named "Trask Sketch-Lozano" was included with the mail. Jake opened it, stared. He pulled the Maryland wildlife officer's sketch out of his desk drawer to compare. *Same sunglasses.* Both sketches showed a bearded man in a cap and shades. Jake lazily nodded to himself.

John Thomas Turner. Ford Van. Cambridge, MD. Jerry Trask. Jeep. Durango, CO.

Twin drivers.

Jake picked up his phone, dialed the cell number for Lozano listed in the email.

"Deputy Lozano."

"John, this is Jake Montoya, FBI. I'm calling from Washington. I just got my hands on your sketch. And thanks. You guys have a fine artist. If you have a moment, could you give me a rundown on your encounter with Trask?"

Good fortune, just like the Doubletree clerk. Lozano remembered because of an extraneous conversation about kayaks and Lozano's wife. The deputy remembered everything. *Jeep speeding. Kayak on roof. Fitness. Lozano and his wife should kayak together. Texas driver's license, Austin residence.*

"Agent Montoya, I was a hair away from not writing the ticket. I wrote it, then we had such a nice conversation that I became benevolent. I crumbled it up, put it in my pocket. Trask left and I got to thinking. I needed to look like I was doing something besides staring at the blue sky. I uncrumpled it, listed it as a warning, and filed it."

"So as far as Trask knows, there is no record of a ticket?"

"That's right."

"This is important, John. Did Trask ever take off the shades?" *Please say yes.*

"No, I'm sure of that. And I was standing right at the driver's door, chatting. This dude was cool, not an inkling of a guy driving down the highway headed to kill somebody."

"I'm about to email two photos. Are you near a computer?"

"I'm logged on right now. Fire away."

"Hang tight." Jake attached two photos of Lucas Knight taken in Black Point. Glasses off. Glasses on. Hit SEND.

"Got it." It only took a moment. "Well, this guy is clean shaven, no cap. But the shades are dead-on. So, a chance it's the guy, but I couldn't swear to it."

"How about a southern accent?"

Lozano didn't remember one. Jake ended the call, then punched in Ross Tolleson's number.

"Same guy in the sketch, don't you think?" said Ross.

"I do. Listen, you said the vehicle was rented in Albuquerque, right?"

"Yep."

"Okay. Check out flights coming in and out, as well as hotels for seven days before and after the murder. See if they have anything on Lucas Knight, Lucas Hendrickson, John Thomas Turner, and Jerry Trask."

"On it."

"Two more things, Ross."

"Come on, Jake, it's Monday. I have to ease into the week."

"Check all the smaller airports taking in traffic from business and personal aircraft. Luke Hendrickson's a pilot. And do the same thing for airports in the Orlando area. And grab any video footage from the hotel Trask stayed at in Orlando."

"Do you want to give me your lunch order, too?"

Jake laughed as he hung up.

125

AGENT BELINDA BRANT arrived at Jake's office carrying a legal pad and a pen. It was five minutes after 3:00 p.m. She took a seat and crossed her legs, leaving a single black high heel in the air. "Tell me something positive."

A pleasant scent followed her into the office. Very light. Fresh. Citrus? A tinge of vanilla? Unusually alluring for a Monday afternoon.

Jake told her Walton James in Asheville was a washout. Then he went into detail about Mala Dimitru in San Francisco, including the minutia about the transition surgery and a big pup named Cocoa.

"We're digging into Mala's background now," said Jake. "*They* said they'd made out big on money in the last six months, which opened our eyes. For participation as a coder, *they* want equity in our fictional company. *They* even proposed investing in 4th Down Analytics if *they* liked what *they* saw."

Belinda eased a quirky smile onto her face. "Okay, okay, what is this *they* stuff?"

"Learned it in a transgender PC seminar. Some kind of woke pronoun crap. Not really sure what it means."

Belinda rolled her eyes. "Keep going."

He told her about Philly Boy Richardson and Mikhail Kuznetsov.

"Kuznetsov was Theo Fuller's roommate at MIT. He used berkeleyblue2 in his personal emails back then. Now he's hiding overseas. Prime suspect for ransomware threats and bank account hacks."

Hearing this, Belinda waggled her right foot subconsciously to the point her heel slipped loose. Jake's eyes gravitated toward it. She watched him watch her. Her foot kept waggling.

"So Tolleson found Philly Boy for you? That's good work. I'm definitely liking Mikhail." She pronounced it "mick-hah-EEL."

"Here's what I need from you, Belinda. I need you ready to go to Black Point on very short notice."

"What? Why?"

"I'm seeing a plan come together, but it's not quite there yet. Step one, though, is to take down Theo in the coffee shop with his computer running. I don't trust a soul to touch the computer but you. I mean *nobody*."

Belinda looked earnest, began nodding, stared into Jake's eyes. "I definitely want a peek into that box, too ...I do. Good plan."

126

BLACK POINT, ALABAMA

WADDELL SKIPWORTH, wearing white painter's pants and four days of ragged beard, leaned his head over the table and bit into the most authentic Mexican taco to be had in Black Point. Remnants of meat, cheese, and tortilla shell splattered back into the paper boat the delicacy was served in. He scooped up the morsels with a plastic fork and shoveled them in his mouth.

It was the last bite of his third taco. Which also meant he had two final sips remaining in his third Dos Equis. One Taco. One beer. According to Waddell, proportionality kept the earth on its axis.

The restaurant was a low ambiance taco joint nudged into a busy convenience store. People didn't come expecting mariachi bands, just food like they'd find in Oaxaca.

Waddell's eyes shot through the large plate-glass window past a scenic vista of nine gas pumps. He didn't notice the pumps. His mind was in a daze, thinking deep thoughts. 'Cause that's what house painters do.

Was Gomer Pyle really gay? Or was it a publicity stunt?

Three beers had Waddell's engine primed. It was 6:25 p.m. He was about to shove off, drive two miles south, and get his drunk on at the Rusty Anchor bar. He'd ask Alonzo what he thought.

Gomer was a Marine. So he couldn't be gay, right?

A black streak sliced into the convenience store parking lot, disrupting his musings. A distant brain cell sparked. A black Ford F-250 gleaming like a new Ferrari. Lone Star Paint Works logo on the door.

A tall, pale man hopped out of the driver's seat wearing buffed cowboy boots and a green range-wear shirt with pearl buttons. A Hispanic man stepped out of the passenger seat, likely early fifties, balding, heavy through the gut. Two doors opened in the extra cab. A couple emerged, both Hispanic, couldn't be more than thirty.

Waddell tried to crank open a memory. *Where, where, where?*

He decided to leave, drive down to the Anchor. See if Mr. Daniels might provide some liquid grease to his neuronal connections.

127

GEORGETOWN, WASHINGTON, DC.

JAKE MONTOYA'S FISTS slammed the heavy bag. He was shirtless and barefoot, sweat draining down his face. A moist sheen highlighted his chest.

"Come on now. Crush it. Bust the son of a bitch open." Ben Staggers stabilized the bag as Jake threw deep, hard punches. "Switch. Speed bag." Jake took two long strides to his right. In an instant his fists connected with the teardrop-shaped bag swiveling on a screw eye. Both fists were a blur. His arms were lithe, defined, powerful. They would have been a gift for da Vinci's sketch pad.

"Legs, let's go, Jake, don't let up, start popping." Back to the heavy bag. Jake's right shin guard crashed into the bag, rocking Staggers backward. A low kick. *Thwack ... thwack ... thwack.* "Harder. Crush his thigh ... come on ... he's drawing a weapon ... chest ... slam the chest." Jake turned his pelvis, jumped forward, thrusting a right heel into the center of the bag. *Thwack.* Staggers recoiled, struggling to hold the bag. "Cracked his sternum. Come on, F him up ... both wings now, bring him to the ground." Jake slammed the bag, alternating right and left legs. Like a switch hitter in baseball, he delivered power from both wings. Staggers counted kicks. "Eighteen ... nineteen ... twenty. Stop."

Montoya bent over, hands on his knees. “I can barely stand up.” He wobbled, picked up a towel from the floor, wiped his chest, grabbed a bottle of water, emptied it over his face, toweled the water off. He walked slowly around the room, breathing hard.

Staggers had trained Jake in Muay Thai for eighteen months. Elbows, knees, shins, fists, feet. Body weapons that leave an opponent bloody and often with broken bones. Sparring with Montoya was like walking into an airplane propeller.

Jake’s phone rang. It was 8:10 on a clear, dark Tuesday night in Washington, temperatures dropping until they hit a low in the high forties.

Wild Bill Burnham. Montoya answered. “Evening, Bill.”

“Jake, I’m hundred-and-seven-percent drunk.” The words were slurred. “Bad fuggin’ news.”

“What happened?” Jake toweled his chest as he spoke.

“The Asians is what happened. They want my mansion. My beautiful home. My dock and boat. They want it. Got an email forty-minutes ago ... and now I’m drinking as fast as I can.”

“What’d it say?”

“It said panic at freakin’ Proton mail, them bastards. Absolute auction to the highest bidder. My hot-damn house. Donate the proceeds to the foundation that owns the trailer parks.” Jake heard ice tinkling as Bill slurped down his alcohol.

Next, he heard what he thought was crying. But it wasn’t. Bill was laughing.

“What’s so funny?”

Bill was howling, now, slapping his palm on his desk. “’Cause ... ’cause ...” Bill fought to stop laughing. “’Cause those dumb yoyos don’t know that Liz and Theo control my foundation and ...” Bill sounded like a laughing bag. “Jake ... Jake ... I’m getting all my property back in three years. Theo set it up that way. My stepson’s a hot-damn genius. That boy’s watching out for my ass." Another drunken belly laugh. "All of it. Every single square inch of land. Even the house if I give it to them. Those China bastards got nothin' on old Wild Bill."

Jake's upper eyelids lowered slightly. *Theo set it up.*

JAKE RAN HOME in seven minutes. He threw his small backpack on the couch, grabbed a cold water from the refrigerator, booted up his laptop, entered his Bureau credentials on the sign-in page. Opened daily reports. Benton and Allen from Black Point.

Theo Fuller was averaging three hours and nineteen minutes a day on his laptop for the last six weekdays at the Coffee Loft. Allen's impression: *Highly focused. Thoughtful. The face of someone taking an important test.*

Jake walked to the kitchen, glopped some peanut butter on a few saltines, leaned back on the counter, started eating. And thinking. After five crackers he grabbed a hot shower. The second-best place to think. Steam heat expanded his mind.

Twenty minutes later he was sitting on his leather couch wearing flannel pajama pants and a gray Alabama football sweatshirt. An old Crosby, Stills & Nash album played on low in the background. Rowdy was next to him, entranced at people on television peeking at gorillas in the dark, wearing night vision goggles.

Jake picked up his phone, scrolled contacts, punched CALL. A female answered after three rings.

"Montoya. It's time."

128

WASHINGTON, DC

BEN STAGGERS WALKED through a block and a half of light rain to reach the Hoover building. By 8:57 he was hanging up his wet parka in Jake's office. A mug of coffee and a Morning Glory muffin sat on the outer edge of Jake's desk.

"Bought both from Dog Tag Bakery in your honor, Ben. Pull up a chair."

Jake introduced Ben to Belinda Brant, who'd been in the office batting around the pluses and minuses of a plan.

"Here's the deal, Ben," said Jake. "I've been thinking hard since our workout last night about how to draw Lucas Knight, you know, Hendrickson, back into Black Point. I'm about to try to reach him by phone. This is where I throw out your name as a possible hire. In effect, bring reality to the ruse you told Freddie. Your interest in contractor work with Knight Force."

"Absolutely."

"Could you go to Black Point for an interview if he asks? Or if he outright says he wants to hire you.?"

"Hell yeah. Otherwise, I'm gonna do what? Grab a three-hour lunch at Subway and try to put together a game of pickleball?"

"But I'd prefer you not to go to Alabama, not in the next few days, anyway. The last thing I'd ever want to happen is you get hurt … or worse. Remember, this is not you, a fine citizen free-lancing out to the Bureau. This is you interviewing for an actual contractor position in the private sector. You're on your own."

Staggers rolled his eyes, shook his head. "Montoya, I believe my resume speaks for itself." He laughed. "I'm in, guys, I'm in. Call him."

"Okay. Gotta take a leak first. Collect my thoughts." While he was splashing pee into a urinal, Jake's mind rapidly went through the phone narrative he had devised last night.

Back at his desk, he said, "Okay, quiet." He glanced at his watch. "It's six twenty in California, if that's where he is."

Jake exhaled and punched the number Wild Bill had given him into his office phone touchpad. He was recording the call but would not alert Lucas to that fact.

"Knight Force. This is Lucas Knight." Knight's voice was clear and awake but sounded breathy.

"Mr. Knight, I'm Special Agent Jake Montoya with the FBI, calling from Washington."

"Yes, sir, Agent Montoya. Whoa, let me slow down." Jake heard Lucas huffing. "I'm running interval training. You got me at the end of a two-hundred-yard sprint … Bill Burnham mentioned your name to me. I believe he said he's known you since kindergarten."

"That's right. Played ball together in high school. We're close. I'm worried about him. That's why I'm calling."

"Something come up I didn't hear about?"

"I'm not sure. You know he paid out a significant sum of money in May. Then his Rolls blew up in June."

"Yeah, yeah. That was months ago. I've got four top-notch men rotating in with him. We're watching him closely."

"Well, I'm more concerned after the last two demands came in. Bill donated $30 million in real estate to a trust for scholarships for college students. That was last week."

"Well, good for him. Bill's a generous fellow."

Did Jake hear a note of surprise in Knight's voice? "It wasn't his idea, Mr. Knight. It was a donation under threat of harm."

"Oh? But, please, call me Lucas."

"Sure, thanks, Lucas. Oh, by the way, I met Johnson and Powell when I was in Black Point. Sharp guys, appear extremely capable."

"They are. Absolutely."

"But Bill has asked me if I know of anybody else to add to the detail. I do, but I don't want to step on your toes. I'd like a man I know to email his resume to you. He's a guy I train with in martial arts, retired from Delta Force. I think he'd be a great addition if you're hiring. And he's available today."

"Delta Force? Yes, definitely. Get his CV to me and I'll contact him right away. My company's growing faster than I can staff it."

"Well, Bill's told me he's very pleased with your team so far. But let me get to my most immediate point. We're about 90 percent sure of one or two factions behind this. And, frankly, I'm worried. They've definitely got a boner on for Bill Burnham."

"Okay. Who are your suspects?" Jake tried to detect concern in Lucky's voice but couldn't find any. He sounded as casual as if ordering a beer at a ball game.

"The main suspects are a crew of Russians involved in ransomware. Most of that is done out of Eastern Europe, with payment in Bitcoin. We're also getting some hits on a Chinese cyber gang based out of Macao, with a strong faction in Los Angeles. Right now, the Russians are our focus. Our New York organized crime division fielded a call yesterday from an informant. The guy's name is Utkin, says he has information on these four dead lawyers. He knows who planted the car bomb, too. That's what he says, anyway."

"Well, that sounds like good news. An inside man talking to you."

"It's great news. But the bad news is Utkin heard some rumbling about something going down in New Orleans. And that's two hours from Burnham. We think Utkin is in New York, and we're looking for him under every rock."

"I'm glad you called me about that. I've got to let my guys know we're operating under an imminent threat."

"And that's exactly why I'm calling, Lucas. I want to share the info we have on these guys with your team. I've got photos on active Russian street soldiers. What I'd like is for you to be in Black Point to review this with your men and me. Is that possible?"

"I've got teams on five other lawyers. I definitely need to be in the loop on this. I can be there tomorrow. That work?"

When Jake smiled, Ben and Belinda did too.

"Yes, Lucas, tomorrow sounds perfect."

"And, hey, watch for an email coming in on Ben Staggers. He's a good man if you need him. I'll text you my cell number when I hang up. You shoot me an email address. And thanks for your help on this." Jake hung up.

"Academy Award, Jake." said Ben.

129

LUCKY CHANGED INTO long track pants and a fleece after a shower and shave. A Channel Islands Surfboards cap on his head and a pair of dark sunglasses over his eyes. He drove his Jeep back down to the boardwalk for breakfast at Woody's.

It was ten minutes after seven, sixty-one degrees, sunny. Early birds walking the beach.

He sat at the counter facing the ocean, sun at his back, a couple of people on either side of him. He spooned some oatmeal with sweet fruit into his mouth. Thinking.

Russians? He raked everything that had happened in the last ten months into a small pile in his brain. He could picture everything. Theoretically, nothing farfetched about the Russians. Montoya had even mentioned the Chinese. Lucky Googled the news daily for any breaking information about the murders. He'd read about the Asian suspicions.

But he couldn't contain his smile. *The Russians.*

Lucky gazed down the beach, seeing nothing, thinking about Montoya. Burnham said he was badass. He had Googled him after his first meeting with Wild Bill. Exceptional athlete. Pro baller. Big guy. Won a slew of mixed-martial-arts bouts. Killed three men in Virginia Beach in the last ten months. Two other violent work incidents. Took four men down at a white supremacist compound in Idaho using a full-auto M4. Also a

Chechen man in Florida who was being questioned about the Boston Marathon bombing. He'd attacked Jake with a knife. The knife ended up going into the man's heart. Repeatedly.

Rumblings out there about excessive use of force. *Woke sissies.*

Lucky glanced at the time on his phone. Thirty-five minutes past nine in Black Point, Alabama. He scrolled his contacts. Found it. Ed Wall Grass Airstrip. Tapped CALL.

Three rings. "Hello."

"Ed, this is Lucas Knight. I met you a few weeks ago in Black Point when I had that great biscuit at your mother's restaurant."

"Oh, yeah, sure. You have the Cessna Caravan, right?"

"That's right. Good memory. Listen, I wonder if the offer still stands to fly into your grass strip. I'm heading to Wyoming to fly fish in ten days with some buddies and I'll be flying in on dirt."

"Absolutely."

"I'm arriving in Alabama the next day or so and would like to practice some touch-and-goes on natural terrain if possible."

"Ahhh, sure. Use it all you want. But listen, I'm out of town for a week. I'm in Port Canaveral with my wife right now. We're taking an anniversary cruise down to Belize and Nicaragua."

"How many years, Ed?"

"Thirty."

"That's impressive. Congratulations, Ed. And thanks for your generosity."

Out of town. *Perfect.*

130

BLACK POINT, ALABAMA

CHIEF TATUM ARRIVED in his office at 7:00 a.m., his weekday ritual. His cell phone rang five minutes later. "Good morning, Jake." Montoya filled him in on the generalities of the play in motion.

"Pike, you probably know the guys working at the airport, right? Taking fees for the planes coming in and fuel and whatever else they do."

"Of course. Why?"

"We're expecting Lucas Knight to fly in today. I need to know when he arrives. Very quiet-like. Just a call that he's in town. Could you speak to them and give 'em my number?"

"You bet. I've gotta run by Lyrene's, grab breakfast, and I'll drive out there myself and give them a heads-up."

EVERYBODY ARRIVED EARLY. Some by thirty minutes. 8:15 a.m. A degree of controlled tension sifted through the small conference room in the four-story hotel overlooking I-10 in Daphne, Alabama. Coffee, danish, and juice were available on a side table. With drink cups in hand, introductions were being made.

TEN MILES SOUTH of the meeting room, Theo Fuller booted up his computer at the coffee shop. He'd calculated he had ten more business days to transfer the rest of the Bitcoin into Monero Cryptocurrency.

And create the final chapter for Wild Bill Burnham.

EIGHT FBI SWAT team members from Birmingham joined four men from the FBI's Hostage Rescue Team, an elite tactical squad. They had been called in to Black Point to oversee the possible apprehension of one of America's most dangerous killers.

The dress was casual. Slacks and collared button-front shirts. No ties. Benton wore a long-sleeve tee over Adidas track pants. Marcia Allen looked like a high school basketball coach, muscular legs barely covered by her shorts.

Belinda Brant wore the stylish Black Point mommy-wear a young woman fresh from morning yoga would be seen in. A fitted blue hoodie. Sleek, black, three-quarter leggings covering her trim legs.

Brant, Allen, and Benton would all be in Coffee Loft at some point during the day.

Marcia was showing eight-by-ten photos of Theo Fuller to Belinda. "It's a small place, you can't miss him. Always with his back to the wall wherever he sits. Slim. Usually wearing black. Nice hair, curly and dark. Works on a Dell. I'll be down around eleven."

Belinda left the hotel in a Chevy rental before the official presentation began and headed to the coffee shop. An ultrathin laptop rested on the seat next to her in a chic laptop case. She also brought a book along as a prop. *Light On Yoga,* by B.K.S. Iyengar.

It was a morning of surveillance for her.

After some mingling, Jake went to the front of the room.

"Everybody, please have a seat, let's get started. I'm Jake Montoya out of the Washington office, coordinating this operation."

Jake introduced Garrison, Grissom, Allen, and Benton. He mentioned that Brant came down from Washington, one of the sharpest agents in DC's Cyber Division, then began his presentation.

"Our goal is to take down two suspects here. One is dangerous with a computer. The other is dangerous in every other way conceivable to man. I'll start with the least dangerous first."

Jake read through Theo Fuller's CV. He described the relationship to Bill Burnham and the odd nature of a man with his talents working for nineteen bucks an hour. "People, from everything we know, he hates his stepfather, Bill Burnham. And he's planted himself right under Bill's nose."

Jake ran through slides of Bill's office, Bill's mansion—both from the highway and up close on the front and bayside of the home—and the Coffee Loft. He displayed five photos of Theo Fuller.

"We believe there is significant money—millions, I'm talking about—leaving the country because of extortion demands. Fuller's resume revealed he has worked for a Russian oligarch's hedge fund in London. He knows high-level corporate finance. We believe Theo Fuller is controlling global movements of millions of dollars from his laptop in a podunk coffee shop in a sleepy Alabama town."

Jake saw smiles of disbelief. "I know, it sounds absolutely crazy. But here's the plan. Tomorrow morning we're taking him down at the coffee shop while he's working on his laptop. There's a third suspect, also, an American-born Russian named Mikhail Kuznetsov, a former college roommate of Theo Fuller's at MIT. The Bureau has been looking for this guy for three years related to ransomware attacks. He's deep underground. At this time, we're focused on two men in Black Point."

Jake popped up a Power Point photo.

"Now, let's look at someone you don't want to turn your back on. His name is Lucas Hendrickson. He went by Luke until high school. And somewhere in that time frame, people started calling him Lucky. That's what he went by in SEAL Team Six. Everybody knows Six and their reputation. Top dogs. Now listen to me. This guy's not strolling around on luck. He is a well-seasoned, highly skillful killer. It's not verified, but he was reportedly in on the raid at Bin Laden's compound."

"That's cool," said an HRT guy.

"Yeah, no kidding. He's here under the name Lucas Knight. Knight was his mother's maiden name and is his middle name. He's created a security outfit called Knight Force, which we believe he's running as a legitimate outfit. Let's look at what we think is the handiwork of Lucky Hendrickson."

Jake ran through a twenty-photo deck of the murder scenes of the four lawyers. The room became silent as they witnessed the carnage. He showed them a picture of Burnham's white Rolls. Then the street scene after the blast.

"Serious business, that guy." One of the SWAT agents.

"Very serious." Jake laid out the deep background and Lucky's motivation. Hendrickson Trucking. The bus crash. The lawsuit. The company bankruptcy. The suicide.

"And, yet, somehow, Lucky Hendrickson ends up guarding the life of the man who was responsible for his father's death. Anybody think this is a coincidence?"

Heads shook.

Jake's phone rang. Tolleson, in Washington. Jake raised a finger to the crowd. "One moment, please."

"What's up? I'm in a meeting."

"Pause the meeting. We need to talk."

"Folks," Jake spoke to the crowd, "Take fifteen, please." People stood, stretched, started milling around for the restroom or more coffee or fresh air. Jake grabbed a legal pad, a pen, and took a seat at the table.

"Okay, Ross. Whatcha got?"

"So, you know we combed through the names we got from One Strike Tactics, right?"

"Yeah. Regarding the tomahawk used in Charleston."

"Right. And the guy running that outfit is a good dude, a former Green Beret named Sexton, who wanted to help, but said we'd have to get a court order for the names. He has a lot of special ops customers who don't ever want to be identified. Guys that follow the rules, keep their mouths shut, move in the shadows, and all that sneaky-ass crap."

"Right." Jake felt a tinge of optimism.

"Okay. We got the hits on names, right. Jerry Trask. John Thomas Turner. And Lucas Hendrickson, after you showed his photo to Staggers."

"No way! Somebody's on the list?"

"Hold on, follow me, now. But no. Those names are not *specifically* on the list."

"What's that supposed to mean?"

"Shut up and listen, Jake. You're hearing research from the mind of a genius."

Jake snorted a quick laugh, stopped talking.

"Eight hundred and twenty-three One Strike Battle Hawks have been sold. They're handmade and they ain't cheap. Seven-hundred-seventy-nine bucks a copy. Nothing on those names, unfortunately. So, I grabbed four interns in the building. Sat them in cubicles with phones, a list of purchasers and their phone numbers One Strike provided through subpoena."

Jake's foot began to tap, excitement creeping in.

"I told them to call every name on the list. If they weren't in, we left a message, and called back. The interns identified themselves as running a satisfaction survey for One Strike, the company. How do they like their tomahawk? Did they buy it as a gift? If so, for who? And so on."

Jake's heart pounded. *Give me something, Ross!*

"So, we get this fellow on the line in Perry, Georgia, a small town. He's a high school football coach there. Name's Arrington. Said he bought one as a present for one of his most favorite players, ever. Now, here's the beauty part. It wasn't a kid from Georgia. It was a kid he coached in Fernandina Beach, Florida, years ago when he was an assistant there. Coach said the kid was a terrific ballplayer, ultra-hard worker, a natural leader, and developed into one of the finest men he ever knew. Drum roll, please. For one million dollars, do you know this football player's name?"

"Lucky Hendrickson."

"Bingo. Have a nice morning, Jake." Ross hung up.

Jake reconvened the meeting. "Great news, folks. I just received news that Lucky Hendrickson owned a battle tomahawk just like the one used in the Green murders in Charleston. The one I showed you in the slide. Okay, so here's where we are. Take your vehicles and familiarize yourself with Black Point. I have maps for you marking Burnham's office, his home, and the Coffee Loft. The weather's beautiful. It should be an easy day. Grab a lazy lunch but don't bunch up. Everyone's phone numbers are also written on the map. The basic plan is this. We'll take Fuller down on his computer in the morning. Then we'll deal with Lucky Hendrickson. We believe he'll stay at the Hampton Inn in downtown Black Point. It's also on the map. Photos of Hendrickson and Fuller are with the maps, too. If you spot either guy today, keep cruising. Don't stare. No alarms."

People stood, ready to clear.

“Oh, one more thing. Hendrickson’s a pilot. Take a ride to the airport, familiarize yourself with how to get there. Take Highway 98 five miles south of Black Point. Turn left at the light at 32. Airport is right there on the right. He’s supposed to fly in today.”

Montoya felt a tinge of adrenaline.

And it felt damn good.

131

CONCERN GNAWED AT Jake's gut. It was 3:57 p.m. and no word from Lucas Knight.

Jake called the Black Point airport twice after lunch. Nothing. He called the Hampton Inn asking to be connected to Knight's room. Knight *did* have a room reserved, they told him, but he hadn't arrived. Montoya drove to Barnes and Noble, four miles away. He hoped browsing the magazines would give his mind a break.

Jake's cell went off at 4:38. Saw the name, tossed *Hemmings Motor News* back on the rack. Lucas Knight.

"Montoya."

"Agent Montoya, I deeply apologize. Something came up. I've been running hard to nail a big security contract in London. On overseas calls all day. I apologize. I'm still in California but I will be in Black Point tomorrow, guaranteed."

"Yeah, I understand, Lucas. Tomorrow will be fine. Check in with me when you hit town." Jake fought the urge to press … *Call me with flight times, airlines. What about your plane? Where are you staying?* Left that stuff alone.

"Oh, I spoke to Ben Staggers. He sounds like a superstar. I'm covering his ticket and he's flying in two days from now. And if that guy wants a job with Knight Force, he's got one."

"Sounds good, Lucas. We can all grab dinner. I know a great spot."

"See you tomorrow, Jake. I'll call you when I arrive."

LUCKY HENDRICKSON WASN'T in California. He wasn't setting up a contract in London. He wasn't going to call for commercial flight times.

He was sitting on a bench under a clock tower at the main intersection in downtown Black Point. Ninety minutes ago he had landed his rugged plane on Ed Wall's bumpy grass airstrip, three miles east of downtown, tucked in behind a conglomeration of self-storage units.

He walked 550 yards to an urgent care medical clinic in front of Walmart. Hertz employees waited there with his rental, just as promised. He tipped the two guys a twenty each, drove into downtown Black Point to his Airbnb rental on Church Street, a hundred yards from the back door of the Hampton Inn. It was a simple studio above a detached two-car garage on the property of a half-million-dollar home.

After stowing his gear, Lucky changed, then strolled downtown for thirty minutes, staying close to other walkers when he could, seeking a vibe. SEALS were trained to feel the unseen. Detecting nothing, he sat on the bench by the clock tower, admired the flowers on all four corners of the intersection, and dialed Jake Montoya.

The eyes of six separate FBI SWAT members glanced over Lucky as he meandered through the commercial district of the charming village. They noticed nothing. He was a guy in stonewashed jeans, a crimson Alabama jersey with number thirteen in white letters. Quarterback Tua Tagovailoa. A Bama cap was snuggled down to his eyebrows, and a new pair of sunglasses covered his eyes.

Lucky Hendrickson was dressed like fifty thousand other football zealots in the state of Alabama.

132

BLACK POINT, FIRST FRIDAY IN OCTOBER

4:15 A.M. MARCIA ALLEN DROVE southbound along a car-free Colony Street, fifteen miles an hour above the speed limit. Reaching the shop, she braked hard, cut right, and stopped dead against the curb of the Coffee Loft. Soft orange light from two sodium-vapor lamps glowed across the empty asphalt parking lot.

The morning still. Quiet. Shop closed.

She drove a 1991 Honda Accord, 326,000 miles on the clock. An impound vehicle purchased for $300 bucks from the Mobile Police Department.

Mark Benton pulled his dark government Ford in right on her tail. He stopped. Allen jumped in. Benton pointed the black sedan north on Colony, laid on the gas. The drop took seventeen seconds.

8:50 A.M. THEO FULLER parked his Subaru in the empty parking lot of the closed barbecue restaurant across the street from the coffee shop.

The eastern sun was sharp. No humidity in the air. A perfect Gulf Coast morning in the best month of the year.

He crossed Colony Street, walking to the coffee shop strutting right by the driver's door of the Honda Accord, then stepped up on the wide concrete sidewalk running across the front of the shop.

Two men sat at an outside table that held two coffees, one open computer, and several colorful flyers. Theo spotted the real estate listings. He did not spot the Sig .40 caliber semi-automatics or bullet-resistant vests hidden by their untucked, oversize shirts.

Inside the shop, the line moved fast, commuter traffic dying. Theo repeated his routine. Large coffee. Two muffins. Took his seat with his back against the wall. Booting up his computer, he spotted the poor sap working on his accounting degree.

Benton, his nose buried in his textbook, coffee cup in hand, saw Theo, too, in his peripheral vision.

Theo took a moment. Thought about it, his plan. Sure, it sounded crazy in the beginning, preposterous, actually. Now it was 95 percent complete. The hard part was over. One hundred and sixteen million dollars as a total haul. Just needed to seed it into Monero.

He thought about Montoya, snorted out a laugh. Bumbling around. Pretty boy football jock. Not a clue.

Theo found himself with an ethical dilemma. Sixteen million dollars came in on top of the $100 million goal. *Eighty percent of the total to Lucky?* He made his decision right there. *No way!* He'd slice the $16 mil off the top, apply it to his stash.

Belinda Brant walked into the shop at 9:10 wearing abstract-patterned blue tights under a form-fitting hoodie top. She purchased a banana smoothie, took a seat near the front window.

Theo's eyes drifted over her feminine ankles as she walked by.

Agent Brant sat on the opposite side of the building from the Accord parked out front. She took a sip of her drink before flipping open her yoga book.

Marcia Allen breezed into the shop at 9:55. She wore a heavy gray sweatshirt that said Black Point Volleyball with blue jeans and running shoes. A small Glock 42 was holstered at her mid-back. With her athletic swagger, she approached the counter. "I'll take an iced dark mocha espresso, please. Small." Placed a five on the counter. Dropped the change in a tip jar.

She took four steps away from the counter, stopped, took a sip. Her eyes glanced toward the front door. She caught Belinda's eye. Belinda dipped her chin. Benton peered over the top of his textbook. He watched Belinda nod. His eyes cut toward Marcia. He flicked a nod.

Theo had his laptop open, eyes focused on the keyboard, typing.

Agent Allen's cell had a one-word prewritten text on the screen. She tapped SEND.

GO!

JAKE SAT IN in the driver's seat of the rugged diesel tow truck the Bureau had rented from a local towing company. He was parked on a side street, 150 feet away. The truck rumbled with heavy vibration while it idled.

His cell vibrated with Marcia's text: **GO!**

Montoya keyed his handheld police radio, spoke an order. "Block the road."

"Copy north." A beat later. "Copy south." Black Point police.

Jake eased the heavy steel monster into gear and drove up to the stop sign at Colony Street. He looked right and left. Perfect. Blue lights flashed from Black Point PD SUVs blocking the street, seventy yards down in both directions.

He pulled onto Colony, clutched the twelve-ton bruiser into second, drove ninety feet, lightly braked, steered a hard left into the coffee shop parking lot. The truck was lined up directly behind the Honda Accord.

Jake bumped the gas.

The back half of the Accord obliterated in a loud crash of steel and glass against the truck's heavy steel push bumper.

Agent Brant jumped, screamed as loud as she could. Two caffeinated college girls did the same.

Theo Fuller jerked, pushed his open laptop onto the couch, blasted to his feet to see the commotion.

It was lightning quick. Benton and Allen crashed into Theo like linebackers. He hit the floor hard, landing on his chest and hands. He twisted his head down and backward, spotting his computer. It was seven feet away.

Wide open.

Belinda raced to the computer, spotted Theo looking her in the eye, pain on his face. She grabbed it and speed-walked to the back of the shop. She removed a Dell charger and three thumb drives from her hoodie pocket. Plugged the charger into the wall and computer. Couldn't let the battery die.

"FBI! DON'T MOVE! PUT YOUR PHONES DOWN!"

FBI SWAT in the building. They jerked Theo's hands behind him, cranked steel cuffs around his wrists. Two agents each grabbed an arm, lifted him, walked him out of the building to a vehicle idling at the street.

Fuller was pushed into the backseat of the blacked-out Tahoe. A bulky SWAT agent crushed into each side of him. The doors slammed.

Agent Grissom was at the wheel. Agent Garrison sat shotgun, looked over the seat at Theo, said, "Good morning, berkeleyblue2." He said to Grissom. "Hit it. Let's fingerprint this guy."

The whole grab took less than three minutes.

Jake met eyes with Theo as he was pulled from the building. He said nothing, walked into the shop, glanced around, saw nothing but dazed looks. "It's okay, folks. It's over." He knew that one or more of these patrons had likely zipped out a short video shot on their phone, ready to go viral.

He walked deeper into the shop, spotted Belinda with her fingers on the computer keys, eyes fixed on the screen, typing. A thumb drive was stuffed into a port.

"Anything?"

She gave him the side-eye. Then smiled. "I count over twenty-four accounts open and minimized, plus DataCage."

"What's DataCage?"

"A cloud storage site. Known for the tightest encryption on the planet. And it's logged on. Thank God." She winked.

"So, are we good?"

Belinda, radiating suburban sunshine in her happy athleisure outfit, pointed to Theo's computer with her hand in the shape of a pistol.

"We've got this fucker nailed to the wall."

133

WADELL SKIPWORTH SAT on a closed five-gallon paint bucket slapping a glossy coat of white paint onto Florence Harrison's Chippendale paneled fence fronting her estate. Her deceased husband had made a boatload of dough in the commercial heating and air business, which afforded her a $2.4 million waterfront home next door to Wild Bill Burnham.

Waddell was lost in thought as Rush Limbaugh played on low on a battery-powered AM-FM radio. *Who killed Kennedy? Somebody knows.* Even thought about dialing Rush himself, see what he'd heard on the downlow.

Then he heard a rattle.

Lawn equipment clanging around on a trailer as the truck slowed to pull into Wild Bill's driveway. He glanced back at the same time his left hand shot up for a wave. That's how they did it in Alabama. Didn't have to know the folks to be cordial.

It was a clean white van with a colorful logo on the side that said Wild Green Yonder. The trailer was loaded. Mowers, weed whackers, industrial plant shears, shovels, gas cans, and whatnot.

And if anybody was vigilant, they might notice a Texas license plate.

Waddell tensed when he saw the face fifteen feet from where he sat. The tall, pale white man wearing a Wild Green Yonder cap in the passenger seat, looking straight through the windshield. Waddell jerked his head down immediately and kept painting.

The Jack and Coke flushed his mind a couple nights ago at the Rusty Anchor, after seeing the black F-250 at the taco stand. His brain retraced backward two and a half years.

Paleface drove Dude Codger's Camry off the lot of the Rusty Anchor bar at 1:30 in the morning.

And ain't nobody seen Dude since then.

134

THE VAN STOPPED on the circular rock drive at the front door of Bill Burnham's estate. Clyde Boland hopped down from the driver's seat wearing the company uniform, dark green twill pants with a vivid green T-shirt sporting the company logo. He wore a cap and shades. Javy Quintano and Luis Aquilla emerged from the van dressed similarly. They joined Clyde at the front of the van.

Broyle William hopped out, went to the trailer, and started unloading equipment. Maribel Quintano hopped on a zero-turn mower, fired it up, and rode it, standing, to the backyard.

Broyle pulled three yanks on a weed whacker, and it finally hit. Smoke spewed out, filling the air with the smell of gas and oil. He gassed it a few times, making a lot of racket, then found some weeds to rip apart.

Clyde, Luis, and Javy went to the front door. They'd been watching Wild Bill's every move for the last four days. They saw the two big men with him. Clyde pinged the doorbell. Waited half a minute, blipped it again. They expected the landscaping equipment alone to wake up the sleeping guard. After another minute, Clyde began banging on the door in a three-knock sequence.

They heard somebody yell, "Coming."

"Get ready, here he is." Clyde heard footfalls inside. He faced the door with his left shoulder. His right hand held a taser that was hidden behind his right thigh.

W.C. Powell opened the door. A big dude. Six-four, 240 pounds. Barefoot, white T-shirt bulging with muscle.

"I'm sleeping, guys. What do you need?"

Pffft. Fifty thousand volts of electricity rode the dart into his right chest. Powell shouted, took one step backward, and fell to the rug.

The three men jumped him. Clyde and Luis rolled him onto his belly. Javy sat across his calves, locking down the legs. Flex cuffs zipped tight around wrists and ankles. Duct tape wrapped in circles around his head, covering his mouth.

They grabbed the guard's legs and dragged him into a bedroom. Walked out and closed the door.

Not one word uttered during the takedown.

"Now, put on your gloves." Nine years in a Texas penitentiary had made Clyde an honorary professor of criminality.

11:50. THE LANDSCAPING VAN pulled out of Wild Bill's driveway, turned north toward Black Point. One occupant, the driver. Maribel was headed to a sub shop to pick up lunch.

The driver's side faced Waddell. He twisted his head. Barely a glance. All he needed. A young Mexican woman.

He recognized her.

135

FRIDAY AFTERNOON

4:45 P.M. JAKE SAT in Chief Tatum's office. He'd been on edge since 3:00 p.m., an arbitrary time. He thought he would have heard from Lucas Knight by then.

It would be dark in ninety minutes.

"Something hinky about this, Pike. But one piece of good news. Theo Fuller has never been printed. Found out an hour ago. I think we've got the right berkeleyblue2." Jake had been discussing the anonymous tip that came in about the email username and the info that the individual had no prints on file.

"Every little bit helps." Pike thought about that. "I'd like to know who called that in. A very interesting twist." His cell phone rang, and he hit the button for speaker. "Yeah, Frank, how's it looking? You're on speaker."

"Chief, I think it's going to be one of our busiest First Fridays. The streets are filling up fast. Great temperature, perfect night. We're keeping our eyes peeled, too."

"Thanks. Stay vigilant." Pike slid his phone onto the desk. "Maybe the best thing, Jake, him not showing. These art walk deals are growing every month. We could have 45,000 folks rambling the streets in a little while. I mean free wine and hor d'oerves, live music, so why not? Tonight's gonna look like a small-town Hallmark movie."

136

5:30 P.M. LUCKY HENDRICKSON WALKED from his Airbnb rental seventy yards south down Church Street until he came to the entrance of the town's two-story parking garage. He played it smart. He inserted himself into a scrum of three couples walking to the event.

Lucky walked right past two SWAT officers on Magnolia Avenue. They were as disguised as he was. Neither noticed the other.

He cut off from the couples, passed through the parking garage, entered a short pedestrian alley, and emerged onto Black Point Avenue. A bank and a children's clothing boutique flanked him.

He scanned the streets. It was crowded and he was dressed like a native. Gray shorts, running shoes, Auburn cap, and a loose Tommy Bahama shirt over a black tee.

A twenty-something couple was next to him playing an acoustic version of "Norwegian Wood" with a guitar and violin. Guy sounded just like Lennon. Damn good. About ten others were standing close, enjoying the groove.

Bill Burnham's office was directly across the street. The front door was open. He spotted lit candles on an outside table stocked with wine and refreshments. A knot of people milled around, enjoying the offerings. The scene was repeated up and down the street. Very mellow vibe. Melodies drifted in from bands on other streets.

He spotted Liz. She was standing at the restaurant next door to Bill's office, speaking to a couple dining alfresco.

Lucas assumed Burnham was not in the office. He was supposed to be in his mansion with two armed bodyguards, per his orders. Lucas had talked to him via phone last night and informed him that he was arriving in town soon with information about additional security. A Delta Force man. Also told Bill he didn't want him downtown in the crowds of First Friday. Too dangerous.

Lucky knew all about the First Friday Art Walk and crafted that into the meet with Montoya. It was time. He scrolled his contacts, found Montoya, tapped CALL.

"Jake, I deeply apologize. I got the earliest available flight I could get out of San Diego today. Booking was tight."

"Not a problem. Glad you made it."

"I rented a car and drove straight here but had to park three blocks away. I haven't even checked into the Hampton yet. Right now, I'm sitting down here at Bill's office in the conference room sipping a nice merlot. The streets are packed, what's going on?"

"First Friday Art Walk. It's a busy night. What's the chance of you meeting me at the police station, out of the hubbub?"

"Not tonight, agent, I'm too whipped. I could hang here a few minutes if you want to stop in."

JAKE HAD LOOKED at Pike, pointed at the phone, and mouthed, "It's him." His mind raced to devise a plan. He had to react to Lucky's actions. Were they n purpose or by chance? He knew the answer. "Uh, yeah, sure I can. I'll be there in twenty-five minutes."

Jake hung up and called Grissom.

"Yeah, Jake."

"Knight's downtown in Burnham's office. He just called me. Where are you?"

"Randy and I are eating at Arby's. Maybe a mile out. What's the plan?"

"I'm gonna meet him, lay out some facts, and gauge his reaction. Like we talked about, I'll let him know Theo Fuller has been grabbed. I need you to alert SWAT, make sure they're in position. When I spot you and Randy at Black Point and Colony, by the clock, I'll assume we're good, then I'll walk to the office. And then ... we'll see."

Jake thought that, honest to God, there was no way Lucas Knight could really know what was happening, could he? If he did, why the hell would he show up? But ... if he had an inkling, he'd love the crowds running cover for him.

SWAT HAD SPENT the last ninety minutes with twelve men in position. They had set up with two men at each end of the block that contained Bill's office. They also maintained the same positions on the two streets running parallel, Magnolia and De La Mare.

They were dressed casually, with loose shirts over slacks and versatile hiking shoes. They wore Kevlar vests strapped under their shirts. Handguns hidden on their waists. No helmets, no dark fatigues, no MP5 submachine guns, no oversized FBI lettering on navy windbreakers.

Grissom spoke to the SWAT commander. "Need you in position. Target is inside the law office. Montoya is going in to talk to him in a few minutes. All we're doing is watching. No takedown planned. We could get twenty people killed instantly."

"Copy." The SWAT team heard it all through earpieces. "Take your positions, people," said the commander. "Switek, see if you can get a table at the bistro next to the law office. If you can't, just mill around. Cooper, need you covering the back door of the law office." They were pulled from the two most distant intersection locations.

"Switek, copy."

"Cooper, copy."

BUT LUCKY WASN'T in Bill's office. He was cocooned at the very front of a six-deep, growing crowd listening to the acoustic combo. He had momentarily stepped away from the music to make the call.

Twenty minutes later, he spotted Montoya walking down the sidewalk headed to Burnham's. Lucky scanned both ends of the street for several minutes before making his way away from the band. He didn't detect anyone on Jake's tail or watching him. The band was in the middle of "Me and Bobby McGee" as he peeled away from the crowd.

Three forty-somethings hipster women were chatting giddily at the refreshment table in front of Burnham's. Lucky said, "Excuse me." Leaned in to pick up two plastic cups of red wine. He was positive he detected the aroma of ganja on them.

Lucky entered the office's empty waiting room like he worked there. He eased down the hall to the conference room. The door was open. He popped in.

Jake Montoya was seated at the table, face cold as stone.

137

"AGENT MONTOYA, I stepped out to grab us both a glass of wine from the fine citizens of Black Point." Lucky placed both cups on the table. Jake stood and they shared a sturdy handshake. "This is a helluva town, agent. A real comfortable place."

"Yeah, it's nice," said Jake. "It's really come into its own in the last ten years."

Bullshit on the wine. You're watching every step I take.

Jake was fit. He knew that. At this moment he was reserved, contained. He'd studied the art of calmness through the martial arts for thirty years. He was in a room alone with a man three inches shorter and forty pounds lighter than him. Trim with a health club tone. Clean shaven, close-cropped, neat hair. Nothing like the menacing, hyper-ripped hulks he had faced in pro football.

Yet, Jake's skin began to crawl. Lucky looked like a State Farm agent, but he wasn't. He was a highly skilled predator, an assassin. No telling how many people he'd killed in battle.

Jake had seen video handiwork of Lucky's work in the States.

Hendrickson was brutally deadly without a second thought.

Lucky immediately outmaneuvered Jake. He sat in a chair at the table closest to the door. Jake didn't want to sit right next to him, so he walked around the table and took a seat directly across from Lucky. There were no windows. Only a single door. And it was on the other side of the table from Jake, behind Lucky.

Music floated into the office from the building's open entrance door. "Let's close this so I can focus on your recent developments." Lucky closed the conference room door. "Looking forward to meeting Ben Staggers tomorrow. Thanks for bringing him to my attention. I just hope he'll want to come on board."

"He's interested, I can tell you that," said Jake. "Listen, I appreciate you coming. We're making headway, but I think danger's coming. I don't want your men caught off guard. And I don't want anything to happen to Bill."

"Roger that. Intel keeps people alive."

"Mikhail Kuznetsov." Jake blurted out the name and stared at Lucky's face as he said it. Watched for any reaction. Any twitch. There was no response, nothing.

Lucky flared out his palms, face neutral. "Okay. Who's that?"

"He's the Russian we think is behind everything." Jake pulled a photo from a manila envelope, slid it to Lucky. "This is from about twelve years ago. Ever see this guy?"

Lucky studied the photo. "Not the best shot. Kind of grainy. But, no, I don't recognize him."

"Yeah, the photo is crap. An enlargement pulled from an old group photo." Jake pulled the original group shot out, slid it to Lucky. He watched Lucky's eyes closely as he glanced across the six college boys. Theo Fuller stood two people over from Mikhail. A goofy smile crossed his face. Theo was rail thin with shorter hair in the picture. Lucky slid the photos back. Didn't mention Theo. Jake didn't bring it up. "Interesting. Don't recognize the guy."

"That's a poker crew from MIT that flew out to Vegas on weekends. One of the guys in the picture introduced our suspicion of Kuznetsov, who's reportedly hiding in Europe. The guy's deep into crypto ransomware attacks and bank hacks. Reportedly a true computer genius."

"No shit. And you think he's coming after Bill Burnham?"

"He's already hit Burnham pretty hard. Five million to start."

"Wow. Bill didn't share a number with me." Lucky swiped the back of his hand across his mouth. "That's strong."

"Last week Burnham donated $30 million in trailer parks to a charitable trust. He was under pressure to do so. Now they want his mansion. But we can't figure out one thing. Why Burnham? At this point it seems very personal. I want to show you what Kuznetsov is doing to these lawyers."

Jake pulled out a stack of color photos from the envelope. Slid three to Lucky. "The Green family in Charleston. A slaughterhouse." Jake leaned over the table, pointed at the tomahawk next to Green's wife's head. "Look at that freaking hatchet. Kuznetsov's boys sliced Hallett Green's head off with that thing. That's some kind of military weapon, we're told. You ever use anything like that?"

"No, but I could have sure used one in the Middle East."

Bingo. Denied the weapon.

"You aren't going to believe this deal." Jake slid over two pics from Colorado. "Some guy shot the life out of Peter John Clemmons and his two bodyguards. Headshots from hundreds of yards out. A .338 caliber. A sniper. Had to be military training."

Lucky focused on the photos, nodded. "Fine shooting, right there, without a doubt."

It was subtle but Jake felt it. Lucky avoided his eyes.

After tossing out a single pic of Draper Sims burning alive, then one of Jack Kimbrell drowned underground in Orlando, Jake leaned back in his chair, put his hands behind his head. "What're your thoughts, Lucas? Russian ex-military?"

"I'd definitely lean in that direction. Those guys can be hired for anything if the money's right. A good dozen of those men have responded to my website. And it sounds like Kuznetsov would have the money to pay top dollar."

"But we've hit on some better news. Much better." Jake leaned forward on the table, slid two more photos out of the envelope. Two men in casual attire. He slid them to Lucky. "Ever seen these guys?"

"Nope. Are they in on it?"

"Well, yeah, they are in on it in a certain manner of speaking." Jake placed his finger on Mike Jeffers. "This guy's a wildlife officer at Blackwater National Wildlife Refuge in Cambridge, Maryland." Tapped his pointer finger on the other picture. "John Lozano's a deputy sheriff in Durango, Colorado."

Jake watched Lucky's eyes. *Stoic. Nothing.*

Lucky nodded. "Okay. But so what?" He flashed open palms again.

"We think they saw the killer. In Maryland, the guy went by the name John Thomas Turner. In Colorado, he went by Jerry Trask. Here, let me show you something."

If Lucas Knight was concerned, Jake couldn't feel it. Was he wrong about his first tinge of hope?

Jake pushed a couple of sketches across the table. Some parts were color-tinted. In both pictures a man with shades, a cap, and a beard. One pic from farther back. A white van. The other a deep-green Jeep with a kayak on top.

"Looks like the same guy. Who is it?" said Lucky.

"Not a hundred percent sure. Not yet."

Jake arrived at a crossroads. He thought about it. Wanted to say, *It's you, Dude.* Wondered if he should push it right here in the conference room? Or should he stop right now, watch what Lucas Knight did overnight?

He thought about the SWAT placement. Two guys on the corners. Grissom was going to bring a man to the restaurant next door and another to the back door of the legal office.

He figured between himself and the SWAT men they could handle it now.

So, screw it. *MOVE!*

"Lucas, I haven't gotten to the best part yet." Jake fought the smugness he felt.

"Oh, yeah?"

"Yeah."

138

JAKES HEART POUNDED. Sweat tickled under his arms. Heels lifted until only the balls of his feet touched the floor. Nerves hummed with electricity.

He thought of Woo Chow. *Be like water.*

Jake was totally convinced of one thing. Within the next few minutes, Lucky Hendrickson was going to bolt out of the door behind him. Jake planned to jump the table and drop him before he made it to the street.

"This morning we arrested Theo Fuller in a local coffee shop."

"Who?"

"Bill's stepson. He worked in this office, in the room next to us. He hates Bill. We think he's moving money into cryptocurrency along with Kuznetsov. Kuznetsov was Theo's roommate at MIT. They're both in the group photo I showed you."

"No way. But, yeah, I met that guy. Seems like a pasty video gamer."

Lucky's performance was masterful. Surprised, but not alarmed.

"Theo's computer is headed to Washington right as we speak. The Bureau will have every secret out of it by lunch tomorrow."

There was no tomorrow. Belinda Brant was inside the computer right now at the hotel in Daphne, talking to the financial boys in Washington. So far, they had identified $91 million that had gone dark into Monero Cryptocurrency. She was about to scour DataCage.

Jake pulled out a couple more photos. Both young women under thirty. One black. One white.

"I mentioned John Thomas Turner in Cambridge, Maryland. He was also in Charleston staying in the Doubletree during the time of the Green murders. These young ladies work at the hotel, said they remember Turner to a T. Said he was Dr. John Turner." Jake arched his eyebrows. "They're putting together sketches right now. I'm telling you, Lucas, we're close."

Jake wanted to tell Lucky they had already identified him from photos. He'd wait just a moment. One more question to test his reaction.

"Got a question for you, Lucas. Remember a fellow named Marvin Arrington? He was a football coach in Fernandina Beach, Florida."

"Shoot, yeah. I loved that man. Anything happen to him? I heard he moved to take a head coaching job in Georgia, what, maybe twelve years ago?"

"Well, you're right. He's a head football coach in middle Georgia. We spoke to him there. He told us that he bought a Battle Hawk Tactical Tomahawk from One Strike Tactics and gave it to you as a present some years back." Jake tensed his muscles, leaned into the table.

"*Exactly* like the one used in Charleston."

What happened next seemed slow at first, so very damn slow. But it wasn't. It happened in a blip lasting little more than a second. Ultra-smooth. Nothing awkward or jerky about it. The draw had been practiced thousands of times.

A government-trained killer pointed a semiautomatic pistol at Jake's face.

139

6:30 P.M. BILL BURNHAM was strapped face-down to a king-size bed. He was stripped naked.

Broyle, Luis, and Clyde sat on kitchen chairs they had brought into the room to watch the spectacle.

Javy tried to reason with Bill at first. "The hard way or the easy way. Your choice."

Maribel nudged her husband out of the way, took over. "Tough guy, right?" she said. "Where is Dude, you fat prick?"

"He's dead. Nobody's seen him for two years. His whole family's dead." Sweat beaded on Burnham's brow.

Maribel sniffed, hearing the answer. She spread her lips in a snarl. "Keep lying, fat ass." She grabbed a ponytail band from her pocket, pulled her hair back with both hands, slid the band on to keep the hair out of her face.

She was going to work.

Her left hand fingered the coarse leather of the cat o' nine tails. A wooden handle in her right hand. No instructions needed. Maribel gripped it like a hammer, nodded, and snorted. "Dead. Really?"

The whip struck like lightning. A whistling sound as the leather sped through the air. Rough-edged knots ripped into Bill's flank. She scraped the whip toward her as Javy had taught her. Three eight-inch gashes opened on his skin.

"Ahhh ... nooo ... nooo." Bill's arms and legs jerked against the ties.

The tails went back over Maribel's right shoulder, then shot forward in a blaze of speed across Bill's middle back. Skin ripped. Blood flowed.

"Ahhhh! ... noooo ... please nooo." The bed rocked.

"Great technique, baby, arm back, drop the hammer, contact, drag the leather," said Javy, as if he was giving his wife a tennis lesson.

Javy was setting up the *picano,* a high-voltage, low-current torture device, similar to a cattle prod. It had two bronze tips and an insulated handle. Maribel's father had it from his days as a young soldier in a drug cartel. "Almost finished here, baby. Give him a few more shots for a warm-up."

Maribel was petite but carried some young muscle. Her mind drifted back to her humiliation two years ago at the Rusty Anchor. Dude had drugged her. He pushed her bra up, grabbed her breasts. She told him no. NO. He carried her to the back room. NO, she told him. Over and over and over. NO. NO. NO.

The leather roared down and ripped skin from Bill's ass.

"Where's Dude?" She whispered in his ear.

Bill shook his head. "He's dead. I told you, he's dead." The rank smell of sweat trickled off him.

Maribel raged. "You liar!" Huffing from the intensity of her anger, underarms sweating.

Bill cried, moaned. Blood soaked onto the sheets. His skin was shredded from his shoulders to his thighs.

"Here, baby," said Javy, "take it by the handle. *Picano* time. Let's have some fun."

Bill watched Javy plug the orange industrial cord into the wall receptacle, place the wooden handle in Maribel's hand. "I saw this on YouTube, baby. Works better when wet."

Javy opened three plastic containers of rubbing alcohol. He flushed the wounds with the liquid. The alcohol would scorch the shredded flesh like a blow torch.

"NO NO NO NO ... nooo ... AHHH ... I can pay you ..." Burnham's voice was deepening, guttural.

"Ready here, baby."

"Showtime, you fat white bastard," she said.

"Maribel Electric Company at your service."

140

"DON'T EVEN TWITCH, Montoya," said Lucky. "I'll blow three holes in your face for your mother to see. And you know I will."

Jake believed him. Lucky's voice was as calm as a mother cooing to her newborn.

He'd never been closer to a more dangerous man. His eyes focused on the gun. He recognized it. A Sig P365. A nine with a ten-round magazine and one in the pipe. The Holy Grail of concealed pieces.

Jake eyed the barrel opening. It looked the size of a cannon.

Lucky's cantilevered arm was stone still. Not a hint of tremor at the muzzle end. His finger caressed the trigger. A light squeeze and Jake's head would explode.

And you know I will. Those words reverberated through Jake's mind.

Lucky stood. Twisted the lock on the door. "Stand up."

Jake stood, eyes on the gun.

"Take off the jacket. Slowly." Jake's gun was exposed on his left hip.

"Two fingers only on the bottom of the grip. Place it on the table." Lucky brought his left hand up to stabilize his right.

"Now the cuffs."

"No cuffs. Got nothing else on me."

Lucky took a step back from the table. "Go to the end of the table. Push it down to the wall. Then I want you to lie on your belly on the floor."

The table was moved. Jake went to his knees.

"Here, take this." Lucky pulled a double-loop flex cuff from his pocket, tossed it in front of Jake. "With your hands behind you, slide them in the loop. You know the drill."

The loop was loose on Jake's wrists. "Lie down. Totally flat." Lucky stepped toward Jake and placed the gun barrel against his back, right behind the heart. "A single twitch and you'll catch two rounds. I'm not a single-shot guy."

Lucas snugged the tail of the loop tight. Heavy teeth dug into the high-tensile nylon.

"Let's get the feet and I'm gone. Everybody still breathing. Don't move. Lift your left foot off the floor."

Jake raised it six inches. Lucky bent at his waist. Tried to lasso the foot. Took three tries to get it around Jake's ankle. "Raise your right foot, put your ankles together." Jake did. "Ah, hell," said Lucky.

The loop wasn't big enough to lasso. He'd have to force the right foot through. Lucky kneeled. He placed the gun on the floor.

Jake sensed Lucky kneeling at his left side. He twisted his head, lowered his chin toward his left shoulder. Looking. He spotted the gun on the carpet.

"Turn around," said Lucky. Jake straightened his head. He'd seen what he needed.

Speed and balance, that's what Woo preached. Speed and balance.

Jake rolled left for leverage. His muscular right leg flashed back in a donkey kick. His heel slammed into the center of Lucky's face, launching him onto his back. Jake swept the pistol across the floor to the wall with his left leg. He rolled on his back, hands flush against the floor, knees flexed, both feet pulled to his ass. One groaning thrust.

Montoya was up.

Lucky was at the door tasting blood, hand on the doorknob, when Jake's right leg slammed into his right thigh. The kick brought Lucky to his knees. He saw the next blow. Jake's left knee racing for his head. He ducked it. Lucky stood up roaring, rammed into Jake's midsection, spitting blood in Jake's eyes at the same time. Both arms cinched around Jake's waist. Lucky pumped his legs, thrusting Jake backward.

Both men growling, huffing. Blood pounded in their ears. Off balance, they flipped backward over a chair, crashing to the floor. Lucky forced Jake onto his belly, hands still cuffed at his back.

Lucky's brain analyzed. He faced death row. No other choice.

Time to kill.

He pulled his Karambit knife from a belt sheath. It was deadly evil. Cold steel curved like a raptor claw. Rip it fast. Rip it deep. Shred everything in Montoya's neck. Dead in minutes.

But he couldn't do it. Montoya was one of the good guys.

Lucky decided to buy time.

Riding Jake's back, Lucky slid his right arm around his neck. Snugged it. Jake bucked, moaned. He forced a twist with everything he had. Rolled onto his back with Lucky under him.

It worsened his situation.

Lucky wrapped his legs around Jake's waist. He locked on like a jungle ape. Then he squeezed. And squeezed.

Lucky's arm pressure tightened down Jake's carotids, both sides.

Jake was done. Caught in a deadly martial art move. Hands cuffed. No chance to break free.

Thought of his mother, Bonnie. Ed. Rowdy. Ms. Sarah. Kimbo. Hope.

Then his world went black.

Lucky bounced up as Jake went unconscious. The precision choke-out. Not dead. Lucky had bought himself a few minutes head start.

But he wasn't finished. He rolled Jake on his side. Grabbed his knife. Clawed an "L" in Jake's right cheek, an "H" in his left. *You'll remember who won.*

Lucky holstered his pistol at his back. Needed to wash his face, scrub the knife.

Get back to the plane. Quick.

Lucky walked into the hall. Froze. A big man stood seven feet away.

Special Agent Switek.

141

7:10 P.M. JAVY HELD the rheostat. Maribel, the *picana.* "Get after it, baby."

She pushed the bronze electrodes into Bill's blubbery flank. "Hit it, babe." The juice jumped through the electrodes. Bill shrieked. His body lurched, fat shaking like gelatin.

Maribel zapped him in the neck. Then his buttocks. Then his face.

"Open your mouth. Suck this, you fat scum." Bill's head jerked backward from the voltage as she put the electrodes on his lips.

Maribel laughed. "Where's Dude? WHERE IS HE?"

Bill blubbered. Drenched in blood and sweat. "He's alive ... Dude's alive." Voice weak. "But I don't know where he is. Swear to God I don't."

"WHERE!" Maribel screamed.

Bill said nothing.

She pushed the prod into Bill's bottom, spreading his cheeks, incising the rectal tissue. No juice yet. She forced it in three inches. She looked at her husband, nodded.

"No. Nooo!" said Burnham.

Javy jacked it.

The lawyer lit up. Bucking. Screaming. Bleeding.

Vomit spewed. Acid seeped into his lungs. He coughed. And coughed. And coughed.

Then two mumbled words.

"Central America."

142

SANTO DOMINGO, DOMINICAN REPUBLIC

9:10 P.M., ATLANTIC STANDARD TIME. Daviel Rodriguez was covered with a sheen of sweat as he held the young woman's arms over her head. He thrust his pelvis into her like he was deliriously possessed.

Her name was Agostina, which meant "worshiped." She was twenty-one, dark-eyed, and tall. An erotically beautiful Dominican woman.

An hour earlier, the couple had enjoyed an intimate dinner of steaks and cocktails at the lavish Pearl Urban Lounge on Avenue George Washington before returning to Daviel's luxury condominium, a three-bedroom penthouse unit.

The double French exterior doors of the master bedroom were open, with a soft sea breeze filtering in. The lights of the boats in the Caribbean night provided a romantic backdrop for this intimate moment.

Over the last year, Daviel's olive skin had baked into a darker brown from his extensive time in the sun. His soft, dark hair melded with the native population. A strenuous exercise regimen had added fifteen pounds of muscle on his lithe frame.

Daviel grabbed Agostina's hips, flipped her from her back to her tummy. He slid two pillows under her, bumping her bottom in the air. He kissed up her back until he reached her neck.

In Spanish, he whispered into her ear. "I've got what you want, baby. Make you a real woman."

Agostina felt something wet drip between her cheeks. Daviel's fingers swirled the slippery sex lube around his target.

Something pushed at the entrance of her bottom. "No."

Daviel didn't stop. He held her tight. Then came the force.

Agostino's scream pierced the night.

Dude Codger smiled. And plowed on.

143

DOWNTOWN BLACK POINT, ALABAMA

7:13 P.M. "SWITEK, REPORT." The SWAT commander on the radio. He was at the end of the street by the clock. Grissom and Garrison were with him. Anxious. Watching. Waiting.

Switek had dressed for the art party by wearing a long-sleeve, aquamarine-colored fishing shirt, one of the ventilated jobs. Frat-boy khakis covered his legs.

He brought his left wrist mic to his mouth. "Montoya went into the office. Hendrickson went in right after him, carrying two cups of wine. Neither have come out. That was thirty minutes ago."

"It's been too long. I need you to take a look. Grab a glass of wine, anything. You look like a local, now act like a partier. If anybody asks, tell 'em you need to take a piss."

"Roger."

"Got a bad feeling," said the commander to his colleagues. "Let's ease that way." Burnham's office was forty yards down the street.

Switek stood from his table, eyed the crowd. He hadn't expected this many people on the street. Instinctively, he ran his hand over his right waist. Felt the weapon under his shirt. He was eighteen feet from the front door of Burnham's office.

Cups of red and white wine rested on the table by the door. He grabbed a cup of red with his left hand. Stepped into the waiting room. Didn't see anyone. Didn't hear anyone. Stairs to the left. The hallway to the right led deep into the building. He chose the hall.

Passed a pod of candles. Lavender and vanilla. Calming. He needed it. His muscles had tightened. He walked through the waiting room. Inched forward, listening. The hallway was unlit.

But he spotted a ruler-straight line of light coming from under a door, fifteen feet away.

He stopped, let his eyes dilate. Hell with the wine. He placed the cup on the floor next to the wall. He was six feet into the hall. The words to "Fire and Rain" drifted in the front door from across the street, following him.

He took one more step. Slow. Very slow. Listening. No voices in the building. No vibration in the floor. No movement. *Were they here? Place felt empty. Upstairs. Had to be.*

He lifted his shirt. Placed his right hand on the grip. Ready.

A bright light flashed across the hall. The conference room door opened.

Switek froze.

Lucas stepped out, heading straight across the hall to the restroom. His eyes cut left, landed on the figure in the hall.

Years of close quarters training had prepared Lucky.

ANALYZE. ACT.

Lucky saw a big man. Maybe six-five. Built. Crouched in a defensive posture. Right hand high at his hip. *GUN!* A wire swirled upward from under his collar to an earpiece.

Lucky's brain screamed *HOSTILE.*

Switek had no chance.

Lucky's thumb was still locked in the steel loop at the handle end of the Karambit claw. Four fingers tightened around the grip. Blade back, parallel to his wrist. Military style.

Lucky was aggressive. Decisive. It was immediate. Two quick steps. Lucky's knife took a ferocious slice deep into Switek's neck, swiped right to left. The claw ripped through the carotids, jugulars, and windpipe. Lucky's arm reversed course across the neck. Deeper.

Switek's hands went to his throat.

Lucky bent. The Karambit blade at the level of Switek's knees. He savagely ripped the blade upward through Switek's left inner thigh. The mighty femoral was sliced in two.

Blood pumped from the body.

Switek went to the floor. Gurgling.

Done.

TANGO DOWN.

144

LUCKY BOLTED TO the front door. Stopped. Ripped off his Panama shirt, wiped blood from His nose as best as he could, threw it to the ground.

Stepped outside. Nonchalant. Looked to his right. Thirty feet away he spotted three men. Stony look on their faces. Their eyes were locked on the entrance to the law office.

Lucky sprinted left, knocking over an outdoor table at the restaurant, and broke into a full run. Bumping people, dodging people. Moving fast.

Grissom and Garrison broke into a run. The commander spoke into his mic. "Target's running west on Black Point toward Church Street."

The juice hit Lucky hard. Man's warrior response. Adrenaline. His heart pounded. Blood pressure spiked. Pupils blew open, sucking in ambient light.

STAY ALIVE!

He spotted two men running toward him from the intersection. One straight on, dodging people. Another slicing at an angle across the street.

Three men chasing from behind.

Twenty-five feet away, he spotted the sign. Alley Bistro. A California mission-style structure that had a by-god pedestrian alleyway cutting through to the adjacent street.

Lucky ran wide open at the approaching man, ripped a left into the alley. He picked up steam, running hard past candle-lit tables and happy diners.

Reached De La Mare Avenue. A large throng of people were listening to Latin music in front of an ice cream shop.

Lucas didn't stop, didn't slow. He shot across the street. Didn't look. Didn't listen. Blazed to his right, deep into the one-car-width Bernhardt Lane.

Speed. Speed. Speed. All that mattered.

Lucas heard his breath. Powerful huffing. Felt his heart jolting. Feet tapping the pavement like a racehorse.

He knew he'd gotten the jump on the feds. Wearing shorts. Running shoes. Ran forty miles a week. Swam eight in the open Pacific. Superior stamina.

The agents plodded along in long pants, chunky Kevlar strapped across their chests. No chance.

Lucky ran through a car-jammed city parking lot. Past the Black Point kiddie park. Blitzed past the old elementary school.

He reached the jungle, the dark, quiet neighborhoods.

There was only one way out of town.

The long way.

145

LUCKY RAN HARD for two and a half miles, mostly south and west, hitting shadows, avoiding streetlamps. He cut through backyards. Jumped fences.

Racing to Mobile Bay.

He stopped in the shadows at Orange Street and Great Bay Road. Stood behind a thick live oak. The bay was across the street. Spotted the skyline lights of Mobile, Alabama, toward the northwest, fifteen miles away.

In the shadows, Lucky caught his breath. Watched. Listened. A lone SUV was headed south on Great Bay Road, moving slowly in his direction. Black Point police.

They drove by.

No traffic. No strolling couples on the sidewalk. No dog walkers. Lucky sprinted across the road to the waterfront park. He scrambled down a six-foot tangle of brush to reach the beach sand.

Saltwater brine filled the air. Mobile Bay. It felt comfortable. He was a SEAL.

He waded in. Ducked under.

Gone.

146

MOBILE, ALABAMA

8:15 P.M. JAVY QUINTANO HAD his foot hard on the gas as he sliced off I-10 onto I-65 north. Five more miles and Broyles' F-250, and the landscaping truck following them, would exit at Airport Boulevard and turn right into P.F. Chang's.

Maribel was next to him in the front passenger seat. "I'm starving, baby."

"Me, too," said her dad, Luis, from the back seat.

Broyle William's eyes had been glued to his tablet since they left Black Point thirty minutes ago. First, he looked at street views and satellite views of an eight-story condominium building situated directly on the Caribbean, in Santo Domingo.

"That prick has good taste. Burnham gave us number 811. It's a penthouse apartment looking out over the sea. The building's gorgeous," said Broyle.

"Screw him," said Luis.

"Yeah, screw him," said Javy.

As they parked the truck at the restaurant, Broyle studied flights and hotels on Kayak. "I see some good rates on flights leaving Monday from DFW. And there's a Hilton within a block of the condo. That's perfect."

Maribel listened to the men.

"Just remember," she said. "I throw the *bastardo* off the balcony."

"No parachute, baby," said her husband.

They all snorted out a laugh.

147

DR. KEITH WEST MOVED close to Jake, focusing on the lacerations from several angles.

Jake had met West, a kid from Long Island, New York, in an English 101 class, first semester in Tuscaloosa. They had also taken a badminton class together. Laughed at the absurdity of it.

"Remind me again, Keith. How long have you been doing this?"

"Finished plastics at Emory fourteen years ago. General surgery at Yale before that. Smile for me."

Jake did. Keith touched his face lightly on both cheeks. "Feel that?"

"Yes."

"Good muscle response. Sensitive to light touch. No nerve damage."

"As far as I'm concerned, this is the most important surgery of your life, you know that, right?"

"Right, right. Hold on a sec."

Keith stepped away, pulled a large-screen cell phone from a scrub pocket. With a few taps, he brought up a video on YouTube. He watched it a moment, then stepped toward Jake while it continued to play. "Might need you to hold this for me while I try this. The only time I stitched up initials it was on some frat-boy's ass, down for spring break. He didn't say, do a good job. He said, don't tell my mother."

Jake looked at the screen and howled. It was a farmer stitching up a donkey's muzzle.

An hour and fifteen minutes later, Dr. West said, "Forty-nine sutures, Jake. I think it'll look pretty good, might need a revision later." West gave Jake a shoulder squeeze. "It'll give you a little character. Lets people know you mean business. Now, what kind of guy would do this to you?"

"Watch the news. I'll call you in a couple of days. Thanks, man, but I gotta run."

GARRISON AND GRISSOM escorted Jake out of the hospital. They walked into a clear, black night freckled with stars. Temps dropping. Three hours ago, Lucky had run out of Bill Burnham's office.

"I screwed up, guys." Jake was humiliated, embarrassed. But mostly pissed. "Damn, I screwed up."

"I don't think so," Garrison said. "Unexpected circumstances. Hendrickson wouldn't have been around tomorrow. I'm sure of that. But I wonder. Was it pure dumb luck or was it planned? Hendrickson got us over a barrel with this friggin' art walk."

"They call him Lucky. But he planned every inch of this." Jake shook his head.

148

MOBILE BAY

9:45 P.M. LUCKY SWAM NORTH two miles to reach the red clay cliffs in Montrose, a high-end residential area located just north of Black Point. He spotted a pier with a lone, dim bulb. Reaching the end, he climbed onto the walkway from a wooden swim ladder. Weathered switchback stairs led forty feet to the top of the bluff.

At the bluff summit, he took a moment to rest. He had a general feel for where he was and where he needed to go. Inhaling a lungful of air, he broke into a jog off the property onto the dark neighborhood street.

For five miles, Lucky avoided streetlights, hid from automobiles, and covered himself in the night shadows. Stayed off the main drag.

Reaching the grass airstrip, he surveilled the area around his plane. Quiet. A splash of light from an old barn lamp illuminated one side of the plane.

Lucky ran to the Caravan, slung the cargo door open, and hopped in. He pulled dry clothes from a duffel, changed into them.

He placed his hand under one of the passenger seats, found the plastic bag containing a smartphone. He powered up the device and situated himself in the pilot's seat. Tapped open the Foreflight app.

Lucky digitally filed and opened a flight plan originating from the tiny Perdido Winds Airpark in Elberta, Alabama, located at the edge of the Alabama-Florida border.

The flight path was over the open Gulf of Mexico. Destination: Tampa, Florida.

He ran his checklist, then fired up the turboprop. He eased the plane to the end of the dark grass airstrip. He saw the lights of a convenience store in the distance. County Road 48 ran perpendicular to the end of the strip. Vehicle headlights have him perspective for the takeoff.

The strip was short. Concerningly short. Had to get up and over the road. And miss the power lines.

Lucky braked the plane. Ran the engine's RPMs up. Way up. The plane vibrated. He dropped the brakes. The Caravan raced down the dark runway toward a used car lot directly across County 48. At seventy knots, he pulled back on the stick.

The plane cleared the power lines by twenty-six feet. Crop-duster close.

Coming off the grass, the plane was headed south. Lucky banked the plane westward, continued a loop, and began a northwest heading. The lights of downtown Black Point came into view ahead of him.

He dropped altitude, flew low, real low. Two-hundred feet off the deck. He maintained his heading, straight over downtown Black Point.

MONTOYA, GARRISON, AND GRISSOM reached the Tahoe in the hospital parking lot. Each man had a door open when they heard the engine overhead. It was coming fast and loud and low. A beefy turboprop airplane engine raging through the night.

Barely over the treetops, Lucky buzzed the hospital parking lot at 220 miles an hour.

"Call it in, Grissom! That plane's going down," Garrison shouted.

Three seconds later, the plane buzzed downtown, straight over the police department. The Cessna was over Mobile Bay in three more seconds. Lucky pulled back on the stick, gaining altitude. A smug grin crossed his face.

Jake didn't twinge when the plane flew close. "That plane's not going down. That's Lucas Hendrickson screwin' with us."

149

FLYING NORTH, LUCKY skirted the eastern edge of Mobile. Forty miles later, he rolled the plane into a lazy banking turn to the east, and then south.

The Caravan was now on a heading that would take it directly over Perdido Winds Airpark, the originating location of his flight plan.

Lucky locked in the coordinates into his autopilot. The plane was headed toward 380 miles of open sea, straight toward Tampa.

He unbelted, stepped to the rear of the plane, strapped on a military-style parachute, and placed goggles over his eyes. With his feet, he slid a medium-size canvas duffel to the front of the sliding cargo door, then strapped it to his chest. He unlatched the door, slung it open. Cold air rushed over him.

Directly over the airpark, Lucky launched into a black, fifty-three-degree night. Free-fall 10,000 feet. Runway lights were his guide. He spotted the large metal hangar. Small planes tethered to the ground came into view. He deployed the chute at 2,000 feet.

Lucky steered the nylon canopy into a soft landing on grass.

He bundled his chute, situated the duffel across his shoulder, and began a slow jog toward the silent parking lot. A twelve-year-old Suburban waited unlocked, keys under the passenger seat.

Lucky fired up the truck, zipped out of the lot, and headed north through the night for I-10.

He had $250,000 in cash in his duffel. His cold cryptocurrency wallets held $93.2 million. Zeus had provided passwords for the wallets. Lucky had changed those passwords within fifteen minutes of receiving them.

Now, only he had access to the fortune.

Two hours later, the Cessna Caravan sheared apart as it crashed into rising six-foot seas in the Gulf of Mexico.

Exactly where Lucky programmed it to disintegrate.

150

FOUR DAYS LATER

THE SIGNATURE ON William Burnham's will, dated six-and-a-half years ago, was almost perfect. It should be. Wild Bill had started having his most trusted ally, Liz Donovan, sign his name a decade ago on all legal documents in an effort to increase efficiency.

It had taken Liz approximately ninety minutes the night before to create this counterfeited masterpiece. The major beneficiary was Colleen Burnham, the former Mrs. William Burnham, and Liz's only sister. Wild Bill generously left her his major real estate holdings, $33 million in trailer parks, and a stunning bayfront home in Point Clear valued at $3.4 million.

Liz was particularly pleased with what the court would read at the bottom of page three.

"To my dear friend, a colleague who helped make all of this success possible, I bequeath my Vanguard FAANG Portfolio to Elizabeth Donovan."

FAANG. Wall Street term. Facebook. Apple. Amazon. Netflix. Google.

With the stroke of a pen, Liz owned a technology portfolio worth $22.7 million.

She felt nothing but air under her feet as she locked the office front door and headed to probate court.

151

TWENTY-ONE DAYS LATER

WADDELL SKIPWORTH, A man who never allowed house painting to get in the way of drinking, stood beside US Highway 98 in front of the convenience store next to the Sherwin Williams store.

It was 7:10 on a crisp morning. A hard eastern sun shone on his back. Waddell had a half-full Budweiser balanced on the ground between his boots, a payphone headset to his left ear, and a scrap of paper with the direct-line phone number to the Black Point Police Department in his right hand. He tapped in a number.

Kaitlyn Sheffield fielded his call.

“I need to speak to the chief. About to solve a murder for y’all.”

Kaitlyn walked to the chief’s office, smiled. “You need to pick this one up. Line one.”

Pike Tatum picked up the handset, punched the lighted button. “Chief Tatum.”

“I seen the killers, chief. I know who done it. I know who got Dude and Wild Bill, both of ’em. What’re we talking on the REE-ward?”

“That you, Waddell? You drunk at seven in the morning?”

Waddell hung up without answering. He chugged down the rest of the beer and walked toward Sherwin Williams to grab his paint. Rung the outside trash receptacle with his empty can.

“Boom. Three-pointer.” He danced a little jig.

“About to be rich. Yesiree, ’bout to be rich.”

152

TWENTY-NINE DAYS LATER

JAKE MONTOYA'S FEET were resting on his desk at the Hoover building when he heard a double knock on his door. Normally he operated with his office door wide open. The door had remained closed since he'd gotten back from Black Point. His mindset vacillated between sullen and angry. Anger was winning.

"Come in."

An efficient administrative assistant entered the office with a single sheet of paper in her hand. "For you, sir. It just came in on the fax."

Jake's eyes sped across the paper. It took only a moment to read it.

United States Coast Guard

155 Columbia Dr., Tampa, Florida

Re: Lucas Knight Hendrickson D.O.B. 07/19/1976

ACTIVE SEARCH SUSPENDED: PENDING FURTHER DEVELOPMENTS

He crumpled the sheet, threw it across the room.

His muscles tensed. One thought raged through his mind.

The earth is not big enough for you to hide, Hendrickson.

I'm coming!

ABOUT THE AUTHOR

Sam Cade lives on the Gulf coast in Fairhope, Alabama with his wife and their golden retriever, Rowdy. He works full time in medicine, plays tennis three or four times a week, and squeezes in time to daydream and write.

Share any thoughts, ideas or questions via email at samcadebooks@gmail.com

WEBSITE: samcade.net

If you have a sec, please leave a review on Amazon! Thanks!

Made in the USA
Monee, IL
29 July 2023